MacA
Macalister, V. A.
The mosquito war

$ 25.95

1st ed.

THE MOSQUITO WAR

A Tom Doherty Associates Book
New York

THE MOSQUITO WAR

V. A. MacAlister

THE MOSQUITO WAR

Copyright © 2001 by V. A. MacAlister

Design by Jane Adele Regina

A Forge Book
Published by Tom Doherty Associates, LLC
175 Fifth Avenue
New York, NY 10010

www.tor.com

Forge® is a registered trademark of Tom Doherty Associates, LLC.

Library of Congress Cataloging-in-Publication Data

MacAlister, V. A.
    The mosquito war / V. A. MacAlister.—1st ed.
      p. cm
    "A Tom Doherty Associates book."
    ISBN 0-312-87870-2 (alk. paper)
    1. Terrorism—Prevention—Fiction.   2. Pharmaceutical industry—Fiction.
  3. Biological warfare—Fiction.   4. Malaria—Fiction.   I. Title.

PS3613.A32 M67 2001

                                                                2001033522

Printed in the United States of America

0   9   8   7   6   5   4   3   2

Acknowledgments

This book is dedicated to all those who work so tirelessly in the field of tropical medicine and "forgotten" diseases.

So many people have given generously of their time and expertise. I particularly want to thank the researchers at Walter Reed Army Medical Center, the Columbus Center for Marine Biology, Martek Biosciences Corporation, Dr. Marc S. Micozzi, Dr. Aileen M. Marty, and Robert S. Desowitz.

For valued readings of several early drafts, thanks to Frances Jalet Miller. And thanks to my agent, Nancy Yost, for infectious enthusiasm and unending support.

Any technical errors or literary awkwardness remain my own.

THE MOSQUITO WAR

Prologue

irport security was tight. The luggage had been examined, carry-on bags x-rayed, passports scrutinized, metal detectors tuned so acutely that belt buckles and earrings were setting them off with annoying frequency. The experts had spun a hundred terrorist scenarios and fortified against each of them. But on January 10, thirty thousand feet over the Pacific, three hours out of Bangkok, an hour after the flight attendants had cleared away the wrapper scraps of lunch, and just about ten minutes into the movie, the terrorists attacked.

And no one noticed.

These terrorists arrived in a specialized transport vessel, undetectable on radar, barely visible to the eye. Their ship was equipped with finely-tuned sensors that guided it to the target with unfailing accuracy. Heat receptors sought out the warmth of flesh. Carbon dioxide filters caught the tang of human breath.

The terrorists rode crowded together, thousands strong, in the hold. They were leaderless, but guided by the singular goal and fierce dedication of the fanatic. Of course to them the cause was not fanatical at all. It was pure and righteous and very simple. *Our race must survive.*

When the sensors locked onto the target, an alarm was sounded and the troops positioned for landing. A transport tunnel was lowered and the commandos slid down. The assault was precise and deadly, though not swift. It would in fact be more than a week before the victim knew what had happened. In the intervening days there would be nothing more perilous than a slight itch, a little red bump.

Apparently, just another mosquito bite.

One solitary mosquito. Tucked into a fold of clothing, hitchhiking on a suitcase or blown by an opportunistic breeze, no one would ever know how this one mosquito got aboard the plane. Ordinarily, no one would care. But this one accidental mosquito carried a battalion in its belly.

Parasites: the world's original terrorists. Microscopic in size, devastating in power. Parasites are individual living creatures seeking nothing more than the routine elements of life: food, shelter, and a chance to reproduce. Only these creatures satisfy their needs by invading another animal and destroying it slowly from within. In exaggerated size they have been a staple of horror movies from *Invasion of the Body Snatchers* to *Aliens*. In reality, they are far smaller, vastly more common, and infinitely more deadly.

By the time Randall Asher felt the sting, the mosquito had already feasted on his blood, delivering its load of parasites in the process. When he slapped his wrist, the swollen insect burst, leaving a smear of blood on the cuff of his freshly laundered shirt.

"Damn!" he muttered, as he plucked back a paper napkin from the lunch tray and wiped away the gore. He asked a flight attendant for some soda water and daubed it on the bloodstain. He scratched the itch, went back to his magazine, and thought no more about it.

Delivered so cunningly into Asher's body, the parasites began their assault with stealthy precision. Over the next few days, as he made reports to the company and love to his wife, they invaded his red blood cells and began to feed. As he read bedtime stories to his daughter, they began an orgiastic frenzy of breeding. While he was reluctantly passing up the spaghetti carbonara for the healthier *primavera* at his favorite Italian restaurant, they were gorging on the iron-rich hemoglobin in his blood. They blew his wasted cells apart, piling the shards into blockades like so much construction rubble, stemming the flow of blood, starving the tissues.

There was no malice. He was in fact a random target. Except to family and friends, Asher was a man of no importance, an advertising executive trying to boost soft-drink sales in Asia. He was chosen from hundreds of passengers simply because he offered the most available square of flesh when the little mosquito grew hungry. A few days after he arrived back home in New York, Asher began to feel ill. At first he thought it was jet lag. Then maybe a touch of the flu. Five days after his return from Bangkok, he woke with a crushing headache, fever, and chills. That afternoon, he went to a doctor.

The doctor, experienced with suburban maladies, sent blood samples off for more exotic scrutiny. By the time the test results came back the next morning, Randall Asher was in a coma. Now at last, the terrorists were discovered. Now they had a name. *Malaria.* It was one of the oldest diseases known to man, but still one of the deadliest. Experts identified an unusually virulent strain called *P. falciparum.* One after another, every known antimalarial treatment was tried. One after another, every one failed. The doctors were puzzled. It was, after all, only *malaria.* Surely *something* in the modern arsenal would kill it. But nothing did.

The liver was conquered first, then the kidneys. Tissues broke down and lungs labored under the swill of leaky body fluids. The swollen blood vessels of Asher's brain began to burst, like balloon animals drifting into the barbecue. Leaking blood was trapped under the skull where it pooled and clotted, crushing the soft lump of life in the center. Two days after the malaria was diagnosed, Asher's brain exploded.

1

Malaria was an awful disease. The press hated it. Although the first reports were intriguing, NEW YORK MAN DIES OF DRUG-RESISTANT MALARIA, it turned out there wasn't much chance of even a small outbreak, let alone a good epidemic. For one thing, it was January and there was snow on the ground; hard to get excited about mosquitos. The tabloids did manage to whip up panic the first couple of days, with headlines full of killer mosquitos (they had plenty of practice by now with the West Nile virus) but health officials quickly reassured the public that they were safe. Outside of the mosquito angle, malaria was nothing like West Nile. Malaria was a parasite, not a virus, much more complicated. The parasite had all these different stages and incubation periods, partly in the human body, partly in the mosquito. And the *Anopheles* mosquito, the only one that could transmit malaria, wasn't as common as the *Culex pipiens*, which carried West Nile.

Hard Copy did send some blond reporter out to a Meadowlands swamp in a pair of waders (revealing, incidentally, a shockingly high prevalence of sexual fantasies involving this attire among male viewers) to scoop up a jar of mosquito larvae, but even this couldn't fan the fire for long. The right kind of mosquito would have to have bitten Asher at just the right time, then waited a week or so and bitten someone else at just the right time. The chance that Randall Asher had infected anyone else was virtually nonexistent. So where was the excitement in that?

48 Hours got one show out of it by milking the germs-on-airplanes angle. They showed a computer simulation of an airplane cabin swarming with disease: each pathogen a suffocating swirl of different-colored fog enveloping the helpless passengers. It was pretty dramatic, but people were still going to fly, weren't they. A couple of public radio shows tried to go for the bigger picture: *emerging diseases in the wake of global warming.* . . . But nothing really took off.

The biggest problem was that Asher wasn't bitten *here* but *over there*. Everyone knew *over there* was full of weird diseases; that's why smart people went to Disney World, not Bangkok. West Nile used to be from *over there*, but now it was *here*, so it mattered. Aunt Millie could be out pruning the roses in her Brooklyn yard and get West Nile, but malaria wasn't going to be *here* with just one lousy victim. One victim wasn't enough to start an epidemic. For a real epidemic, you needed a larger pool of infection. For a real epidemic . . . oh well, who cared.

Ebola, now there was a good disease. Ebola was death in a box: quick and simple. Breathe it in and you're shopping for a cloud. Flesh-eating bacteria the same. It's a bacteria. It eats your flesh. What more could you want? Hell, you could get more excitement out of a plain old salmonella outbreak. But malaria was a lousy story. The papers ran a couple of small articles, but for most Americans, the story quickly slipped into oblivion.

In the labs of SeaGenesis Biotech in Gaithersburg, Maryland, however, Su Thom Nguyn was not about to forget malaria any more than he could forget to breathe. It was the first thing he thought about in the morning, the last thing at night, and a frequent specter in his dreams.

Whenever he lifted his eyes from the microscope he saw the newspaper clippings tacked to the wall at the back of his laboratory bench. They were already yellowed and brittle. RARE STRAIN OF KILLER MALARIA . . . DRUG RESISTANT MALARIA CONTRACTED ON BUSINESS TRIP. . . . NO THREAT TO PUBLIC, SAY NEW YORK HEALTH OFFICIALS . . . That one dug at him the most. *No threat.* Malaria might not be a threat to Americans, but to the rest of the world, where two million people died of it every year, malaria was more than a back page story. To the little boy who had watched the disease burn through his village, it remained the greatest threat of all. Those memories were forever im-

printed on him, the sounds of weeping, the smell of blood, the un-
earthly quiet that last morning when there was no one left to bury the
dead. Su Thom wrenched his thoughts back, angry with himself to be
wasting time on such feelings. There was only one way to banish the
memories forever.

Su Thom picked up one of the little vials. The serum was a clear,
pale green, and sparkled like melted emeralds in the cold neon light.
Capjen88 was the technical name, but it was derived from a coral reef
sponge that looked like a clump of spinach, so someone at the research
station in the Bahamas had nicknamed it "popeye." The name didn't
matter to him; all that mattered was seeing it work.

Su Thom put the vial in the rack and turned his attention back to
the microscope. He tweaked the focus and stared with growing excitement at the magnified carnage spread before him. His heart pounded and
prickles of sweat bloomed on the back of his neck. Yesterday this blood
sample had been swarming with malaria parasites. Today they were dead.
One hundred percent mortality. He sat up and blinked his eyes. Of course
they wouldn't know how well it really worked until they tested it on
monkeys, but it was still dramatic, especially since this particular sample
of malaria had been cultivated from the tissue of Randall Asher. Labs
all over the world were examining the strain, but nothing had ever killed
it. Nothing that is, until popeye.

Until *some* samples of popeye anyway. The drug was still madden-
ingly inconsistent. That wasn't unusual with compounds derived from
natural products, but it was frustrating.

"Su Thom?" He was startled by Ulla Raki's voice. His supervisor
was a tiny woman with a shy voice, who, despite her position as head
of the marine pharmacology division, tended to creep around the lab like
a midnight cleaning lady. Ulla was Indian, Brahman-born, youngest child
and only daughter from a family of brilliant scientists from Bombay. She
was thirty-five, but looked younger, with a plaintive beauty that she was
completely oblivious to. Everything about her, the soft step, the tiny
hands, and deferential manner, disguised her as meek, but there was keen
intelligence in her dark eyes. Raki tucked a notebook into the pocket of
her lab coat and came over to the bench.

"What are you doing still here? It's nearly six."

"Waiting for you to get out of the meeting." Su Thom leapt to his feet. "Well?" he pressed. "What did they say? Do we get our monkeys?"

Ulla looked down. "I'm afraid the protocol has been passed over for now," she said quietly.

Su Thom's face darkened. "Why?"

"Dr. Fairchild is concerned that this might be changing our focus too much."

"Our focus? Did you show him the latest test results? Did you tell him that popeye is killing the Asher culture?

"Fairchild was impressed." She looked at him directly now, and he saw the sadness in her own eyes. "It's just not something SeaGenesis is ready to pursue at the moment."

Su Thom smacked his hand on the lab book. "What the hell is he waiting for?"

"You know it's complicated, Su Thom," Ulla explained. Her voice was still quiet, her manner controlled, but she was angry as well. She was just as excited over popeye as Su Thom was. It was her discovery, after all. But she was reluctant to speak ill of Dr. Fairchild to an intern. Despite her largely American upbringing, her cultural roots were deeply imbedded in respect for men, elders, and superiors.

"Dr. Fairchild wants us to concentrate on getting something to the market right now. SeaGenesis only has three drugs in phase two testing and only one in phase three."

"Fairchild wants a *profit*," Su Thom said bitterly. "That's all he cares about. Fairchild wants a cure for baldness, the miracle fat-burning pill."

"That's not true and you know it."

Su Thom shut the lab book with a disgusted finality.

"Of course it's true. Who gets malaria? People who can't afford a bowl of rice, let alone medicine. What's two or three million less of them a year? Probably a relief."

"Su Thom, stop."

He turned away, quashing his anger, horrified that he had even raised his voice to her, a mentor he both respected and adored.

"Popeye might not be top priority right now, but I'm sure we'll get approval soon," Ulla said reassuringly. "Yes, SeaGenesis is trying to develop drugs that will eventually bring in profit. That isn't evil." She turned away in frustration, for she could easily remember when she was a young scientist on fire to cure the world, back before she had to deal with the financial realities of pharmaceutical research. SeaGenesis was a progressive company, but research was costly. People would pay for a new diet pill.

"It's just been a bad year financially," she groped. "Fairchild is trying to secure new investors, and they want to see profit potential. I'll work on the proposal and resubmit next quarter."

"Well, how come we haven't been getting any more popeye in?" Su Thom pressed. "We barely have enough to finish this next test series."

"I know." Ulla sighed. "Maybe they just aren't finding much of the sponge. And there were all those storms this spring. I'll see if I can get a radio call through to Shadow Island tomorrow and ask Zee."

Su Thom just nodded tersely.

"You know this is important to me, Su Thom," Ulla said. "I won't just let it go."

"Sure. I know." He switched off the microscope light and began to gather his papers. Ulla frowned. Su Thom looked pale, the slack pale of too many hours under laboratory lights. He needed a haircut. He could use some care and feeding in general, Ulla thought. She had been so wrapped up in this latest round of grant applications and protocol reviews. She definitely needed to concentrate on the more holistic aspects of mentoring. Su Thom was a valuable lab assistant. He was serious, dedicated, and smart. At twenty-nine, he was older than most of the other interns, but she knew the circumstances of his life had given him a slower start. He came to the United States at the age of ten, a Vietnamese orphan with no formal schooling and little English.

"We'll get our monkeys," Ulla said. "I promise. I won't let this fall through the cracks. I believe in this. You know I do." Ulla looked at the rack of vials, those precious few ounces of hope. "Go home now, Su Thom, get some rest. I'll put these away."

"I'll do it," he said, taking the samples from her.

"OK." She smiled. Su Thom felt ashamed.

"Ulla . . . I'm sorry . . ."

"I know." She cut him off gently.

Ulla went to her office, a little cubicle just off the lab floor. Su Thom watched her through the window, her face bathed unromantically in the glow from the computer screen. His anger was sharp and heavy, like a chunk of obsidian lodged beside his heart, but he was even more angry with himself for showing it, especially to Ulla. It wasn't her fault. It was Fairchild. It was all the greedy investors and all the complacent Americans.

No Americans cared about malaria. Why should they? How many Americans knew or cared about West Nile virus before it showed up here? And West Nile was a relatively benign disease. But after a handful of fatalities in New York, the president had declared a state of emergency and tossed them five million dollars. "Woefully inadequate," declared Mayor Giuliani, noting the city had already spent fifteen million on West Nile.

He stared at the newspaper clippings so intently that he felt he might ignite them with his gaze. The paper was old now, turning yellow and brittle, like pages from an ancient text. Malaria had been killing millions before AIDS even appeared, but no Hollywood stars wore ribbons for malaria. There was no quilt for malaria. Most of the victims would be grateful for a scrap of cloth for a burial shroud.

He snatched the clippings off the wall and crumpled the brittle paper. Su Thom stared at the little vials of popeye. Suddenly, they seemed to be glowing with a bright phosphorescence. *No threat to the public . . .* The lights in the lab seemed to be getting fantastically bright, and the room was empty of sound, except for a strange, steady buzz in his head.

There was a thick airless feeling in the room. Tan, the pharmacist, didn't speak. His hands rested on the counter, his stubby fingers making no move toward the pile of coins Su Thom had spilled there.

"I need the pills," the boy's voice quavered. "For the fever. I have sixty-four American cents and these other coins. My brother will bring you more." Tan sadly shook his head and gently pushed the coins back toward Su Thom.

"It's too late, little boy," he said sadly. "Take your coins to the temple."

Su Thom's fingers shook so he could hardly pick up the

money. He turned and ran home. His little brother Lo was sitting outside their hut, making circles in the dirt with his finger. Su Thom lifted the curtain. A shaft of sunlight cast his shadow across his mother's body. There was a queer, heavy stench, metallic and musty all at once. Death had not come quietly. The fever had racked her with convulsions, burst bloodily out her nose and ears, stained her eyes red as a demon's then finally exploded her brain. Her eyes were closed and sunken into the waxy skin. A neighbor woman had come already, to clean and tend the body, but there were still bloodstains on the mat and the dirt floor.

Su Thom walked quietly to her side. The useless coins were a heavy bulge in his pocket. Right now there was no sadness, only anger. Only a sharp black rage. He walked back outside. The village was terribly still. Fifteen had died already; so many others were sick. He crouched down beside Lo and the little boy looked up at him. Su Thom felt a new stab of fear. The boy's face was flushed, his eyes dark with fever. Su Thom pulled his little brother close to him and felt the burning skin. It was too much. There had to be some medicine to stop this! He would pay anything! He would get enough money somehow.

Three days later his brother died.

Now they were so close to a cure. And no one cared. Why should they? Americans would not care about malaria until their own children woke screaming with the fever, until they started burying small caskets in their own country. He picked up a flask with the malaria *Plasmodium*. This was only a tiny sample, but it wouldn't be hard to culture more. It wouldn't be hard at all. In fact, someone with the right knowledge, time, and patience, could quite easily put together his own malaria factory. The equipment was little more than what would be found in a high school biology lab: a microscope, petri dishes, test tubes, incubators . . .

The idea was so simple. So horrible. So perfect. Americans did not care about anything until it was a threat to their own people. Well, then, that could be arranged.

2

June 20

Connor Gale stood in the marble foyer of Meridian House sipping a glass of sparkling water, waiting for his quarry to arrive. The glimpses he caught in an antique mirror across the hall convinced him that his appearance betrayed none of the upheaval he felt. The queasiness in his stomach and the sour knot in the back of his throat didn't play on his face. He had subjected himself to a suburban hair salon that afternoon, where they had trimmed and pouffed his hair into a salesman's blow-dried perfection. He wore lightly tinted aviator-style glasses, purchased at the Salvation Army that afternoon. There was no need for outright disguise, just enough changeable little factors that he would be remembered wrongly, if at all. Connor had dark curly hair and slate-blue eyes. He had strong, angular features which could be mistaken as aristocratic at first glance, until the scars on cheek and chin, the slight tilt of a twice broken nose, and a certain wary poise betrayed him as a commoner. Still, it was an attractive enough combination of features that women tended not to recoil. The homely glasses, the dated hairstyle, an affected slouch and an occasional vigorous probe of his ear with his little finger had been enough so far to dissuade any potential flirtation.

The reception was already crowded. The National Pharmaceutical Association was sparing no expense. The waiters were passing shrimp and the bars were stocked with good liquor. Connor glanced at his watch. It was quarter after seven. Adam Fairchild should be here any minute.

Fairchild was to be given an award tonight. His company, SeaGenesis, was being honored for pioneering work in the study of marine pharmaceuticals. There was a picture of a coral reef on the cover of the program, and there seemed to be an underwater theme in the table decor.

His hands were dry and did not shake. This, in a way, was the most disturbing. It shouldn't be this easy, and it disgusted him that it was. Why had Mickey asked him to do this? And why couldn't he have just said no?

Finally Adam Fairchild pulled up in his black Jaguar. Connor's muscles began to burn softly, like a great cat's, when sighting its prey. Here was that sweet familiar thrill: the delicious anticipation of the game. But this feeling now collided headlong with disgust. He thought he was prepared for this job, but he had failed to anticipate the war of emotion now raging within him. He felt soiled and depressed just at the thought of his task.

Fairchild got out of the car with an unhurried case and turned the Jaguar over to the valet, unclipping the bulk of his keys from the ignition key and slipping them into his briefcase. Right so far, Connor thought. He knew Fairchild wore expensive suits that should not be spoiled by keys in the pocket.

Fairchild paused at the curb, smoothing the sides of his hair and glancing toward the elegant old building like a lord surveying his estate. The founder of SeaGenesis was in his early fifties. His light brown hair was beginning to turn an elegant gray. His features were even, his skin tanned and strangely blemishless, a smooth, even tone. There were few lines, not the slightest nick or mole or even variation of tone. It was an eerie sort of handsome.

He stood out in the group, which, aside from a few overgroomed young salesmen, was mostly older and saggier. Most were pharmaceutical company reps, government lobbyists, and PR guys. There was a sprinkling of actual scientists, obvious for their awkward social presence and undisguised pleasure in the shrimp. Fairchild stopped to shake several hands as he walked up the stairs.

He stepped up to the registration table. Connor noted the hostess's shift in posture and expression. Her smile brightened, her touch lingered as she handed over his name tag and directed him to the coat check room. Fairchild looked her up and down like a man comfortable with such attentions and used to better. The woman flushed with embarrassment. Connor felt sorry for her. She was neither pretty nor plain, an average girl of average shape, counting on perms and magazine advice and the brief bloom of youth to secure a husband and its attendant life happiness. She was all hair and nails and frozen daiquiris; not Connor's type, but undeserving of scorn. Fairchild's small cruelty made Connor's job a little easier, but also reminded him to be careful. Off the top of his head he could think of at least one arrest and three broken bones that had resulted from championing the downtrodden. And he wasn't even that big a fan of the damn downtrodden.

Fairchild checked his briefcase and raincoat, slipped the ticket into his suit pocket, casually smoothed the already perfect lapels, then went to the bar and ordered an Absolut on the rocks with a twist. Connor followed. Two men with the blue tags of conference organizers immediately converged on Fairchild. A waiter was circulating with a tray of hors d'oeuvres. That made it almost too easy. Connor hadn't expected to move this soon but he saw the opportunity. He eased over to the bar.

No one saw it happen, but all of a sudden there was a spilled drink, and crabmeat-stuffed mushroom caps skidded across the floor. There was blotting with napkins and an apologetic waiter, and during the distractions the coat check ticket and magnetic entry card to SeaGenesis labs were deftly transferred from Fairchild's pocket to Connor's. Connor turned and slipped into the crowd. Even after all this time, it was so damn easy.

He went to the coat check and presented Fairchild's claim ticket. He retrieved the briefcase and got the keys. There was a key shop only a few blocks away. He would have these copied and the originals returned to Fairchild's briefcase before the salad was served. The magnetic card couldn't be copied so easily, but he had a facsimile that would pass visually, and Fairchild wouldn't know it was not real until he tried to use it tomorrow morning. In about twenty minutes Connor would have complete access to the SeaGenesis labs, and Fairchild would have no clue.

It was a smooth operation. As Connor headed toward the front door, however, things suddenly got profoundly less smooth. A man stormed up the steps toward him. There was a crazed look in his eye and the purple flush of fury on his jowly face. He was a huge man. An oak bookcase of a man. Connor caught a bow wave of alcohol and tensed as the man rushed toward him.

"Fairchild! Fairchild, you son of a bitch!" The man roared past Connor.

"Goddamn you—you're not gonna get away with this, you bastard!" The man fumbled with his jacket pocket and pulled out a gun. The blue tag men, who seconds before were fawning over their guest of honor, scuttled away like mice, leaving only a startled Adam Fairchild and an eighteenth-century porcelain vase for targets.

"You screwed me, Fairchild! You're not getting an award for screwing me!" The man was choked with rage. His plump executive hand looked absurd wrapped around the little pistol, but he seemed ready to use it. Connor swore under his breath. He knew the closest thing to security guards were a couple of docents, both on the frail side of eighty, one with a cane and a dowager's hump. They were there to guard the antiques from clumsy caterers, not the guests from crazed gunmen. No one else seemed ready to jump in and save their honored guest.

"A goddamn award!" the man ranted on, waving the pistol unsteadily. "Well, you can take your goddamn award and shove it up your . . ."

"Aw shit," Connor muttered to himself. With more force than finesse, he sprang. He leapt at the man from behind, and grabbed the gun hand. The man staggered but did not fall. He swung around with a blocky fist that caught Connor in the eye. Connor kept both hands gripped around the gun hand and tried to twist it down. Connor was six-two with an athletic build, but the man outweighed him by at least sixty pounds, and booze and rage gave him strength.

People screamed and ran for cover. The man tried to swing again, but lost his balance. Connor took advantage of the stumble and drove his knee into the back of the man's leg. The big man fell heavily, letting out a deep whoosh of breath. Connor winced as his own knee crashed against the marble floor. He kept hold of the attacker's huge paw, but the man was sweating so heavily it was like trying to grasp a canned ham. The attacker still did not yield. He kicked and struggled, punching at Connor with his free hand. Connor had no martial arts fanciness, but barroom brawls and parking lot fisticuffs were not without some use, nor was the simple training he had learned at his father's knee.

What are you gonna do, a wee little boy like you if you're caught up by a big strong copper? You gonna punch him? You gonna flip him over your shoulder like that Kung Foo fella? No, boy, use you wits! The childhood trick came back automatically. Connor got hold of the man's middle finger and jerked it backward. The man howled in pain as his knuckle crunched out of joint. Connor pried the gun out of the injured hand and spun it away across the shiny floor. With the gun gone and the attacker dazed, the pharmaceutical crowd got bold. Five men now ran over and grabbed hold of the man.

Connor got up and staggered back against the wall. People were drifting back, talking animatedly and looking at him. That was no good. He heard police sirens outside. One of the blue tag men took his arm and Connor shook it off.

"Sorry," he mumbled, holding his hand to his mouth as if it were bleeding, which maybe it was. "I'm fine, let me just clean up a minute." Chaos was a reliable, but short-lived ally. He needed to slip away quickly. He straightened his jacket and ducked into the crowd. *Just walk away calm, boy, never run.* Connor could almost feel his father's tight grip on his shoulder steadying him. He resisted the urge to look back and continued past the rest rooms. Out in the garden, a string quartet, oblivious to the drama inside, was just setting up.

Connor slipped over to a corner. He heard voices spilling out into the garden and the cackle of police radios as squad cars arrived out front. Time to vanish. He slipped through the trees and let himself over the wall, dropping down ten feet to the sidewalk below. He brushed himself off and started walking away.

Su Thom's heart was racing. He was late, and he seemed to be on the wrong side of an endless brick wall. He had never gone to a big affair like this and never would have if Ulla Raki had not asked him. He was certainly not there to watch Adam Fairchild get a stupid award. It was only for the chance to be with Ulla. He knew there was nothing in her invitation besides wanting a buffer for her shyness at an event she was obligated to attend, but he didn't mind. His love for her was pure and therefore distant. He had no intention of sullying it with common lust. He wished he could tell her his secret. For that was the real reason his heart was hammering so hard at the moment. His lateness was not due to traffic or parking problems, but to success. The mosquitos were beginning to hatch.

Two weeks ago, in the simplest of mail-order efforts, he had obtained five hundred *Anopheles* mosquito eggs. As he dealt with the mundane daily tasks of hatching the eggs then tending the larvae, it had become in a way, just another set of lab tasks. But today, as he walked into the basement and heard the faint sweet buzzing of his first hatchling, the magnitude of his plan had become real again. Soon they would be ready. While the mosquitos were developing, he had been culturing the malaria *Plasmodium*. The process was exacting but not technically difficult. In a couple of days he would feed the *Plasmodium* to the mosquitos and let the next stage of development begin. In about two weeks he would have hundreds of mosquitos ready to transmit malaria; hundreds of little silver dragons ready to carry his message to America. What would he do then? The plan had been born of anger and frustration. He had had time now to consider it more carefully. When it came time, when the mosquitos were ready, what would he do?

As he turned a corner, he almost crashed into a man coming from the opposite direction. Connor and Su Thom startled each other. They both stepped to one side, then the other, in an awkward pas de deux. Had his own body not been so flooded with adrenaline, his own senses not so tuned to the signs of anxiety, Su Thom might not have noticed the similar energy in Connor. There was an instant, if fleeting, connection between them, an odd sort of recognition, though they had never met. But it quickly passed as both men feigned calm.

Connor ended the accidental parrying by stepping fully against the wall.

"Is the entrance this way?" Su Thom asked.

"Right around the corner there," Connor said with only a hint of breathlessness. Su Thom thanked him and hurried past, noticing only fleetingly that there was dirt on the front of the man's suit jacket and what might have been a welt above one eye. But Su Thom was too distracted to give it any more thought. He combed his fingers through his hair and felt his tie as he turned the final corner. He stopped. There were police cars all over the street. He turned away and ducked back around the corner, his heart slamming in his chest. *It can't be!* he told himself. *There is no way they know anything! They aren't here for you. Calm down.*

He took a deep breath and pressed his back against the hot brick wall, waiting for his nerves to settle. He looked back down the street and just at that moment Connor also turned. Their eyes met for just a second. Su Thom turned away. Connor hurried on. *No problem there,* he assured himself. *Just some guy late for the dinner. Nothing to worry about.*

Connor drove with all the windows down and the radio blasting. Damn! He was thirty-two years old; why did the thought of this confrontation with Mickey make him feel like he was fourteen? *And this isn't even a screwup!* he reminded himself. The rush of adrenaline was fading quickly. By the time Connor got to the office he felt depleted and slightly unsteady, as if he had run too far too fast.

The office was located in one of the small, featureless office buildings that ringed the capital beltway, locations just outside the ring of power, modest accommodations for those who couldn't afford or didn't need a prestigious address. Connor walked down the silent hallway to a plain wood door with a frosted glass panel that bore, in simple lettering, the name CHAPMANS. The name stood for nothing. It was merely a simple, solid name with a vaguely British ring to it. A name designed to sound dependable and reassuring in an innocuous way.

Connor opened this door and entered a narrow, vaultlike vestibule with a much sturdier steel door. He waved a magnetic card over the scanner and looked up to the camera lens, waiting to be recognized for admission. Connor wasn't convinced they needed this level of security, but Mickey loved gadgetry.

Mickey Sullivan was in his office, waiting. His desk was a massive construction of dark wood which rose, footless and blocky, like the Rock of Gibraltar in the middle of a gray carpeted sea. Except for a few file cabinets against one wall, all of the other furniture in the room—a small table, two armchairs, floor lamp, bookcase, and an oddly pretentious dictionary stand—were clustered around the desk as if drawn in and held there by the man's own gravitational field. Dozens of family photographs smiled at him from the top of the bookcase like a devoted choir.

Mickey was not happy. His broad face had the rosy flush of tension, and despite the chill of the air-conditioning, his thick white hair was damp at the crown from perspiration. But he looked up and smiled as Connor came in.

"Well, if it isn't the Lone Ranger to the rescue!" he said with unexpected levity. "Good lord, have you ruined your one and only suit? And what have you done to your head?" The welt above Connor's eye had puffed up and reddened like a small plum.

"It's nothing," Connor said. Mickey's good humor threw him off. He was expecting a blustering tirade, or at least a terse disappointment, not this welcoming joviality.

"Put some ice on it."

"I will." Connor placed Fairchild's keys on the desk. Mickey looked at them and his frown deepened.

"Well, get yourself a drink then. If you don't care for the ice at least take the whiskey."

Connor walked over to the file cabinet where he knew Mickey kept a bottle of Jameson's and pulled it out.

"You want one?"

Mickey shook his head. Connor poured himself a generous shot and drank half of it down. Various sore places were starting to clamor throughout his body and the whiskey flowed right to them. He walked back over to the desk and sat in one of the facing armchairs.

"So," Mickey pressed his fingers together expectantly. "Tell me the details."

"There's not much more to tell," Connor said. He had called from the cell phone shortly after he left Meridian House to explain the basics. Now he fleshed out the story, recounting without embellishment how he had successfully picked Fairchild's pocket and struggled with the gunman. When he was finished, they regarded one another for a few long seconds across the acre of polished mahogany, then Mickey leaned forward and picked up the bundle of keys. He held it as if it were a block of uranium. He slowly leaned back again. The huge chair squeaked beneath his weight. At six-foot-four, Mickey had only a couple of inches of height over him, but almost twice the mass, and Connor always regarded him as a giant. This was also because when they had first met, Connor had been a very skinny ten-year-old, dangling by his belt from Mickey's hand, having been caught in the process of burglarizing his home.

Mickey slowly tumbled the keys from one hand to the other.

"You didn't like my little scheme, did you?" The question caught Connor off guard.

"No," he said.

"Why not?"

Connor hesitated, unable to fasten words to the emotions he had felt, or maybe just unwilling to confess them. *Because that's not who I am anymore. Because it disgusts me. But how can it disgust me?* He tossed back the rest of the whiskey.

"It was too complicated," he said simply. A half-truth was still truth.

"But it would have worked."

"Well, it *did* work," Connor pointed out drily. "Up until the part where I had to jump in and save the mark from a rampaging gunman."

"Yes, I suppose it did." Mickey pressed his big fingers together and gave him a long disapproving look. It was a look Connor knew too well. "But please remember, son. In *this* side of the business they are called *clients*, not *marks*. You need to have a little respect for those who pay your salary."

Connor knew Mickey was teasing, but he felt a surge of anger anyway. How the hell could Mickey pressure him into the deed then chafe at the language?

"Well, it seems to me that respect for our *clients* ought to include not picking their pockets," he said sharply. "We shouldn't be doing stunts like this. It's stupid. It's risky. This is, after all, the largest, most respected private security firm in the tri-state area," he chided, using the advertising copy from Chapmans's own brochure.

Mickey looked genuinely surprised by his reaction.

"Connor, it was just a game. A joke. I explained all that to you. I wanted to make a point to Fairchild. We installed a very extensive, state-of-the-art security system for SeaGenesis, but Fairchild puts it all at risk by carrying his keys and entry card around with him all the time. I wanted to show him how vulnerable that makes him."

"Did you ever consider just *telling* him this?"

"I have told him. He doesn't take it seriously. He carries a card with the alarm codes around in his wallet! I thought this would have more impact. If you didn't want to do it, you should just have said something."

"Oh what, so you could ask one of the *other* pickpockets on the staff to pull it off?" Mickey looked at him with an inscrutable gaze. Finally he got up and went to the file cabinet and got the bottle of whiskey. He poured Connor another shot and splashed a little in a glass for himself. Connor just held the drink. His hand was trembling, and he felt hot and sick to his stomach.

"Connor, I'm sorry," Mickey said with surprising gentleness. "It really bothered you, didn't it?"

"It was just too risky," Connor said evasively. It did bother him, though, far more than he would ever have expected. Why? Was it his own secret pride in being able to pull off a good scam? Or shame that Mickey still thought of him that way?

"If I had been caught, it would have been a mess."

"Get caught?" Mickey's smile was broad but tight. "You who could pick a piece of lint out of Janet Reno's bra?"

"It was too complicated," Connor repeated.

And why put it hard on yourself, boy? Connor could almost hear his father's smoky voice, spouting this simple advice years ago as he watched his young son practice picking locks on the door of their motel room. *Why put it hard on yourself? Choose the right mark and keep it simple.* Back then they never did anything complicated. Open windows, unlocked garage doors, keys pinched from purses at the beauty shop, or from coats at a restaurant. By the time he was eight years old Connor had been stuffed through doggie doors from one end of the country to the other.

Mickey Sullivan did not have a doggie door on his house but he did have a slightly open upstairs window that day, twenty-two years ago. A window that could easily be reached by a nimble child boosted up to the roof of the porch by his larcenous father. The house was a large, imposing old brick colonial with generous grounds and old trees in a moneyed neighborhood of Chevy Chase, Maryland, a close suburb of D.C.

They had been strolling the neighborhood for a few weeks, observing comings and goings, and had already liberated some family silver from two other houses. Just the tableware, nothing bulky, nothing that would be missed right away. That's how you work a neighborhood like this, Connor's father had explained. The trick was to milk it slowly. They would take the silver at first and maybe a few bits of jewelry if the marks were elderly and not likely to notice. You could clean out one house for a nice haul, but these folks had clout with the police. One real burglary and they would all be on the lookout for weeks with extra cruisers up and down the pretty, tree-lined streets all day. *Houses like these, son, is what's called old money. Families rich for generations. Fortunes, as y'know, build on the backs of the poor working man like m'self and my own poor dad.*

A neighborhood like this, you hit in summer. No one used the sterling in summer. And you just took half the cash from the top dresser drawer, not all of it, so husband thinks wife just went on a shopping spree, or wife thinks husband played an extra round of golf. And most important, you watch. Comings and goings and who has dogs or stay-at-home nosy neighbors. They had watched the Sullivan house and knew the family went out for ice cream every Friday night. They stayed away about an hour and came home with a half-gallon in a thick white paper bag, and the younger son, who looked about nine, always had a balloon.

There'll be nice heavy silver and buckets of diamonds inside, his father had said as they stood in the shadows watching the family leave. Connor would never forget that night, standing across the street with his father in a light drizzle, watching as Mickey and Lois and Sean and Daniel piled into the family car. There were, of course, no buckets of diamonds, and as Connor was later to find out, no old money in this particular house. Mickey had come from a tumbledown poor Baltimore family and made his own fortune, rising from a dockworker at the age of fifteen to chief of security for an international shipping company. The house was comfortable, but the drawers held little of value.

At first, everything went as planned. As soon as the family left, Connor was boosted up to the porch roof where he climbed to the window, crawled inside and hurried downstairs to let his father in the front door. They began a methodical search, with his father, as was his method, beginning with a good shot from the liquor cupboard. But while Connor was searching for treasure in Lois's jewelry box, Sean and Daniel had started fighting in the car. Lois told them to stop or they wouldn't get any ice cream. They didn't stop. Mickey counted to ten. Daniel said a swear word. Sean punched him. Daniel hit back. Mickey flung an arm over the seatback and swatted at both of them. He turned the car around, the ice cream expedition abruptly canceled.

The drizzle had become a steady rain, muffling sound. The first thing Connor heard was the front door opening, followed by crying and somebody running up the stairs. *Escape—always think how you escape.* He hadn't thought. He had screwed up. He felt his stomach turn and tried not to throw up. *Think!* He was in the master bedroom, in the front of the house, no porch here, out the window was a straight two-story drop. Where was dad? Connor heard the front door slam, then Mickey's angry footsteps coming up the stairs. Connor tugged on a window but it stuck with barely room to squeeze through.

"Daniel! You get out here right now! Don't you dare leave when I'm talking to you!"

Connor was shaking with fear. It never occurred to him to hide, only to escape. But even if he could squeeze through the window and manage to get down somehow he couldn't just run away and leave his father in the house! Connor ducked back against the wall, out of the path of doorway light. He saw Mickey's shadow coming up the steps. He held his breath, but his heart pounded so loudly he was sure the man could hear it. The shadow dipped and folded across the landing. Then the man himself, big as god, stood not ten feet away, his back to Connor.

"Daniel, you open that door right this minute!"

Connor pressed himself as flat as he could. What if he just ran past the man now? He could probably make it down the stairs and out the front door. He looked back out the window to the dark yard. Through the hedge, maybe. But what about dad? All of a sudden he heard a woman's scream from downstairs. Then he heard the front door open and saw a spill of yellow light across the wet lawn. Then Connor saw his father running away from the house. He ran across the broad lawn and through the hedge. He did not look back. A cry escaped the boy's throat. Mickey turned, peering into the dark bedroom. Connor lunged for the window, squeezing and wiggling to pull himself through, desperate enough to chance the long fall.

The oddest thing, Connor remembered, was how he could feel the vibrations of Mickey's stride in the window frame against his back. Mickey's walk shook the walls. The next thing Connor felt was a powerful hand on his back. The rest was history.

Mickey looked at his watch. "The dinner should be winding up in another hour or so. I'll take the keys down there and meet Fairchild when he gets out. He might not be in the best mood to take my joke, but I suppose it shouldn't wait until morning now."

"I still don't get it," Connor said. "Even if Fairchild does compromise his security by carrying everything around with him, your average criminal isn't going to go to all the trouble of pickpocketing keys and entry codes."

"Your *average* criminal isn't going to be breaking into a biotech lab at all," Mickey said. "Anyone with the brains to know what they would want to steal from SeaGenesis would also be able to figure how to get it with some ease. The weak points are all human. I've been trying to get that through to Fairchild. He's a little bit too trusting."

Although he had only observed the man a few times, "trusting" was not the first word Connor would have used to describe Fairchild.

"So what about the gunman?" Connor asked. "Seems we should be a little more concerned with someone trying to shoot one of our best clients than with hypothetical pickpockets."

"Yes. Well, it wasn't a real gun for one thing. It was a starter's pistol." Connor squelched a smart remark, something about checking to be sure next time, before he put his life on the line for a *client*. Mickey noticed his effort and almost laughed. The tension eased.

"The man who attacked Fairchild is Charles Lofton, CEO of another biotech firm called Genelink. Genelink is in financial trouble and Lofton is an alcoholic. Genelink recently lost out to SeaGenesis on a big government contract. Fairchild receiving this award was the last straw. Lofton just blew."

Connor was not surprised at the extent of Mickey's knowledge so soon after the event. Mickey came from a three-generation cop family, and had founded Chapmans originally as a retirement occupation for the relatives. With dozens of ex-cops on the payroll and dozens of current cops looking forward to a job, information was never a problem.

"Fairchild told the cops he didn't want to press charges," Mickey went on. "Lofton will probably be released to his doctor's care and put on the next plane to the Betty Ford Clinic. Needless to say, I'm requesting discretion on your part as well."

"Needless to say."

Mickey looked at Connor. "You did good here, son. Really," he said. "Maybe it was a stupid idea. But you did good." Connor was annoyed at how inordinately happy the man's approval made him feel. Mickey scooped Fairchild's keys into his briefcase.

"Talk to Billy in the morning about your next assignment. He's working on some burglaries, similar MO, no forced entry. I'm sure he could use your professional expertise." There was a slight but perceptible tinge of sarcasm. The moment of warmth, the hint of connection, if there really had been one, was gone. This was how it had always been between them: struggles and challenges, sometimes camaraderie and respect, and maybe, Connor sometimes dared to think, maybe something more.

"You go on." Mickey nodded toward the door. "I'm going to make a couple more phone calls, then head downtown." Connor put the glass down on the desk and got up to leave. Mickey was already picking up the phone. "I'll see you tomorrow night." Connor looked puzzled.

"The party?" Mickey said. "Don't tell me you forgot about Lois's birthday?"

"No. Of course not." Damn. It was on his calendar, wasn't it? Of course he would have remembered. But Mickey had this way of always catching him up.

The night cleaning crew had just arrived and were blitzing through the outer office with military precision, talking and laughing as they worked. They were all members of an extended family from El Salvador: Rosa Jiminez, her sisters Carmen and Marie, assorted husbands, cousins, and children. Connor knew enough Spanish to understand they were poking fun at one young man who had just gotten engaged that day, but couldn't pick up all the rapid slang or the unspoken family subtext. Rosa waved at him over a cubicle partition. Rosa and her daughter also cleaned Mickey's house twice a month, and sometimes Connor translated for her. Once she begged him to convince Lois not to clean up before they got there.

He paused and watched them work. They seemed almost choreo-graphed, working quickly, each person somehow knowing exactly where the other would be with the cart or trash bin or vacuum cord. Their conversation rose and fell over the cubicle partitions, and swirled over the noise of the vacuum. They were all happy with the news, talking about the wedding, about other weddings, and bands and feasts and how many flower girls there would be this time; four, no, five. Maybe seven, because there might be enough money now to bring Ricardo's family north.

Connor listened to the talk and wondered if he would ever under-stand this mysterious thing called family; the dynamic of attachment, the burdens and connections, the things you didn't have to say, the way everyone fit somehow. He had no illusions about it, wasn't looking for any rosy Norman Rockwell life, had, in fact, seen plenty of friction and disharmony in the extended Sullivan family, but still, there was some-thing about it that kept drawing him in. He had gone away for years at a time, but something always lured him back. And if he always felt himself floating around the edges, it was not for their lack of welcome, but his own hesitancy. Sometimes he felt destined always to be on the fringes, only watching, like an anthropologist or a spy.

3

Zee Aspen swam slowly, the glittering school of tiny fish parting around her like a shimmering curtain. The late afternoon sun slanted in beams through the clear water, setting off the colorful reef like fireworks. There was no sound except for the slight hiss of her scuba regulator as she breathed. She was glad she let herself get talked into making a dive today. This was one of the best reefs in the Caribbean, yet she rarely found the time to enjoy it. Running the Shadow Island research station took up so much time that it had been two weeks since she had put on a tank. It was ironic, really, that the more a marine biologist advanced in her career, the less time she actually got to spend underwater.

Zee hovered a moment to watch a giant blue parrotfish cruising over the coral below. The fish looked like something from a child's fantasy drawing, gaudily colored with turquoise, yellow, lavender, and green. Zee swam closer and watched it scrape bites out of the coral with its birdlike beak, then lazily swim off, pooping out a plume of sand behind it.

A pair of bright yellow butterfly fish darted through the coral, circling each other in a dainty minuet. A green moray eel poked a toothy face out of his hole, but ducked away as her shadow sliced over him. A timid fellow, despite his fearsome appearance.

She looked up and saw Arthur Padgette swimming on the surface, towing their Zodiac, a small, inflatable boat with an outboard motor. Zee laughed at the sight of him, sending a burst of bubbles rushing toward the surface. Padgette was not a graceful swimmer. All squares and planes, his body seemed more geometry than anatomy, loosely hung and hammered together.

Padgette's personality had almost as many rough edges as his physique, and there had been some friction between them during the first few months on the island. They both ran different aspects of the operation, but technically Zee was the chief of the station. This designation of authority had been a surprise to both of them. At thirty-three, she had accumulated good credentials, but she didn't have the seniority Padgette did. In her heart, Zee knew she was competent, but she also knew that SeaGenesis was as media savvy as it was truly progressive. Adam Fairchild and the SeaGenesis PR department knew Zee Aspen made good copy. The work they were doing here was new, very experimental, and extremely expensive. It didn't hurt to have good media buzz.

During the first few months on Shadow Island, a couple of magazines had done features about her, and a TV news show had come down to interview her. "She's smart, she's sexy, under the sea or behind the microscope. In the race to cure cancer, Zee Aspen hunts for new drugs in the sea. . . ." Roddy Taylor, their resident engineer, had gotten a lot of mileage out of that one, dubbing her the "Pelagic Princess." A photographer had caught her coming out of the water, backlit against the setting sun, a pure cheesecake shot. Roddy sent a copy to *The Journal of Microbiology*, suggesting they publish an annual swimsuit edition.

Whatever dubious advantage all that had given her in the hiring decisions, it was still up to her to prove herself able, and now, after two years, Zee felt she had done that. The station was running well, outside of the inevitable glitches that occurred operating in this sort of environment. By working twice as hard and being twice as sensitive to Arthur Padgette's ego, they had settled into a reasonably good working relationship.

Getting along with Roddy was much easier. He was Australian for one thing, where uptight seemed to have been bred out of the gene pool. He was a tall, strapping blond of twenty-five with a boisterous manner that belied a gentle nature. Roddy didn't much like Padgette, but had no professional issues with him. As engineer and divemaster, his domain was clear and more separate. He kept all the equipment running, supervised the diving, and oversaw the experimental nurseries where they were trying to grow various invertebrates. Zee and Roddy had come to be good friends. And would be nothing more, she realized early on, when she discovered that his rebuffs of pretty young female grad students were not entirely due to professional ethics.

"Just your luck, babe," he teased. "Stuck on a desert island with Crocodile *Fairee*."

It had been, in that department, a long two years. It was kind of depressing when your sex life was less active than a sponge's. But it was hard to keep up any kind of relationship when you could only visit every two or three months. Especially, as in Zee's case, if you were trying to date a paleontologist who was off on his own expeditions half the time, digging up bones on the other side of the earth. They had finally given up about a year ago. A bit of fame had gone to his head anyway. The last she heard he was engaged to a producer for the Discovery Channel who had edited his documentary.

So here she was, in the company of fish. Not bad company, really. A grouper nested in a barrel sponge like a fat man on a saggy sofa. He rolled one eye up at her as she swam over him, but did not move from his comfortable spot. Under water the rhythms of life seemed simple. Up above, it had been a completely rotten week. First a whole shipment of supplies from SeaGenesis had been lost somewhere in Nassau, then the generator had bugged up, just when she had a sensitive production run going. To top it off, Roddy had discovered a fallen bee's nest in the compressor shed and incurred several very nasty, very allergic stings. They had shot him up with epinephrine in time, but he remained very cranky. With a new group of grad students arriving tomorrow (hopefully with a duplicate list of the lost supplies), she knew it would probably be weeks before she had another chance for a pleasure dive.

She looked up again and saw Padgette motioning for her to catch up, his underwater slate bobbing up and down in one hand as he pointed toward the reef ahead of her. They were actually doing some work on this dive, surveying a new section of reef. By snorkeling on the surface, while she dove beneath him, Padgette could take bearings and record surface landmarks in case she found anything interesting. She swam over to see what had caught his interest and found they were over a broad, deep crevice. Some ancient rhythm of current and tides had split the reef, hollowing out a deep chasm. There were honeycombs and caves, lacy overhangs and narrow passages overgrown with bright feathery Christmas tree worms in a riot of colors.

Zee checked her gauges again and began to swim down to investigate. Just inside the top of the crevice, a gray reef shark appeared, gliding effortlessly through the water, scrutinizing her with its cold eye. Zee wasn't afraid; the shark was calm and probably only curious. It wasn't unusual for any large animal to check out another large animal such as herself. Then two more sharks appeared. These were black tips, smallish, but territorial. Underwater, Zee was in practically no danger from the sharks, but a snorkeler on the surface, especially one who flapped around as much as Arthur Padgette, might be. Zee looked up and saw that Padgette had already sighted the sharks. He was motioning for her to surface and swimming toward the little Zodiac.

Roddy was strict about always diving with a buddy. Diving alone with a snorkeler was already stretching the rules, and technically she should surface, but it was so interesting here. The sharks weren't displaying any aggressive behavior. It was a little unnerving to have them circling her, but there was so much variety and life here, she had to explore a little more. It could be a good collection site. Zee looked up but saw only the bottom of the little boat; Padgette had already climbed in.

She would just look around the immediate area. Five minutes more. Zee let herself drift down to sixty feet, adding a short burst of air to her buoyancy compensator. The buoyancy compensator, or BC, was an inflatable jacket that helped a diver swim comfortably at any depth. Since water pressure increases the deeper one goes, a diver "weighs" more and sinks faster at greater depth. The BC was connected to the scuba tank and a diver could push one button to add air and float, push another button to release air and sink. Underwater, small regulations in the amount of air in the BC allowed Zee to adjust to the water pressure at varying depths, remaining neutrally buoyant.

The crevice was a strangely beautiful place. The sunlight dappled faintly on the distant bottom. Zee swam close to the reef wall to see what invertebrates might be growing here. There were some tunicates, dark brown blobs, which she knew were actually bright red and showed promise for a new cancer drug. In the protected niches, she saw some Bryozoans and red algae they were also testing.

Then, just inside a small crevice, almost hidden by some thick patches of fire coral, was a veritable wall of popeye. This was a small green sponge, which looked for all the world like a clump of spinach, leading of course to the nickname, for the cartoon sailor who gained strength from his spinach. It was a great find. SeaGenesis had been re-questing lots of it lately and she had been scrambling to supply enough. They were trying to grow the sponge in the nurseries, but so far had had little success. The sponges were difficult to grow, and whatever the bioac-tive compounds were, they didn't always appear in their farmed samples. Now here was a fantastic crop just waiting to be gathered. Zee swam back from the reef, scanning the wall for distinguishing features that would help her find the place again.

Suddenly she felt as if she had just tumbled into a river. The reef wall was flashing by in a blur. A strong current was sweeping her away. It was alarming, and momentarily disorienting, but Zee didn't panic. She had been diving for fifteen years, and had dealt with currents before. It was probably just a tidal surge, she thought, where water was forced between a narrow cut in the reef during the changing tide. She hadn't bothered to check the tide tables. It was just going to be a little pleasure dive.

Suddenly her dive computer began to beep and her ears hurt. She knew she was sinking, but the sandy bottom was also falling away rapidly as if she were floating up. Zee felt dizzy. Visually, it appeared she was drifting up, but the pressure in her ears told her she was going down. Her depth gauge read a hundred and ten feet! She pushed the inflator button and pumped more air into the BC. Her head whirled with vertigo. She spun around, trying to get a fix on the reef, but couldn't see it anywhere. She re-alized she had already been swept away from the reef, out to the open ocean. She looked at her gauge again and discovered, to her horror, that she had been dragged, in about five seconds, down another fifty feet.

Zee was on a freight train to the bottom of the sea. Damn popeye! If she hadn't been so distracted looking for it! It damn well better save the whole world for all this! She reached for the buckle of her weight belt, prepared but still reluctant to ditch it. It would help her escape the pull of the current, but without the weight belt, she wouldn't be able to control her ascent. No current this strong should last very long. It would end soon and she would have a long way up to the surface. An uncontrolled ascent could be just as deadly as drowning, putting her at risk for the bends.

Breathe, she told herself. Slow, deep breaths. Panic didn't have her yet, but it was brushing up close. Zee steadied her nerve, closed her eyes, summoned every ounce of strength, and kicked as hard as she could. The depth gauge yielded a grudging ten feet. There was nothing to see but the endless blue of open ocean. Her thoughts were slow and hazy now and she felt oddly peaceful, almost removed from herself. At this depth, the compressed air in her scuba tank had an intoxicating effect—nitrogen narcosis, it was called, the rapture of the deep. It was like laughing gas at the dentist, or that second margarita on a hot afternoon. She had seen people get "narked" and try to swim to the bottom of the sea, take their regulators out, thinking they were one with the fishes. It was little comfort knowing what was going on. She knew how easily one little mistake at this depth could set off a chain of disaster.

There were so many ways to die down here, Zee thought with detached interest. Sharks, drowning, the bends; she had an absurd picture of each possible fate arranged before her like cereal boxes on a supermarket shelf. Would anyone find her body before the sharks got to it? Who would tell her family? She pictured her mother in an old blue skirt, milking goats on the commune where Zee had spent her early childhood. She remembered her first look at the sea, how wonderful and scary it was. She saw the movie of her life spin by on a fast reel: mud fights with her brothers, the taste of garden peas, a yellow dress, blue bicycle, red wine, kisses. Was this it then? No more snowstorms, no Fourth of Julys, no babies? She pushed the thoughts away and concentrated on what she had to do. Kick, swim, breathe, focus.

It seemed like hours, tumbling along in the cold blue void, but finally the fierce current loosened its grip. She felt herself actually drifting up. Her dive computer was going crazy, flashing her danger. She stared at the gauges and tried to concentrate. As she rose, the warm narcotic fog drifted away and her brain became clear again. It hadn't been so long really, barely five minutes. But five minutes at that depth was a long time. She was now just about a hundred feet down and her air was only 200 psi. Very low. It was enough to get to the surface, but not enough for decompression stops along the way.

The danger now was from decompression sickness, the dreaded bends. If she went up too fast, nitrogen bubbles would form in her bloodstream, expanding as she ascended, wedging in her joints and spine, blocking off blood vessels throughout her body. She could wind up crippled or dead. To come out of this safely now, she had to ascend very gradually and give her body time to decompress at progressively shallower depths. There was an extra tank of air in the Zodiac, but had Padgette seen her being swept away? Even if he had, would he have been able to follow the trail of her bubbles this far? It was hard to find bubbles in the open sea.

The water was lighter and warmer as she rose. The endless blue gave her a lonely feeling. At forty feet, Zee stopped, adjusted the air in her BC and hung there. The greatest danger was the last thirty feet to the surface. She scanned the surface and listened for the Zodiac. The current was still pulling her, though not so fast. She could be a mile or more off the island by now. She took a slow, shuddering breath and felt the tug of resistance in her regulator. The air was almost gone. Might as well go up. The bends weren't *always* fatal.

Suddenly she heard the faint sound of the Zodiac motor approaching. Padgette had seen her! But then the boat turned and zipped off the other way. So he hadn't actually seen her, just saw the rip current and knew she was out here somewhere. He was steering a zigzag course, still look-ing for her. Zee felt a tug in the regulator as she tried to breathe. One more breath, two, then with a dreadful finality, her tank ran dry. There was no choice now but an emergency swimming ascent. She looked up and began to kick, steadily, not too fast, forcing herself, against every normal desire, to breathe *out* the whole way. Holding her breath would be about as sure a death as drowning, since the compressed air would expand as she ascended, basically exploding her lungs.

She reached the surface on the verge of blacking out and took a great gulp of air. The sun felt intensely hot and the air thick. She saw Padgette some twenty yards off, standing up in the Zodiac, scanning the water.

"Padgette!" she screamed. "Over here!" He didn't hear her at first, then he did. He gunned the outboard and zipped over.

"I need the tank." Zee gasped as she caught hold of the hot rubber pontoon. "I have to decompress."

"Any pain now?" Padgette grabbed the extra tank.

"No."

"You sure?"

"I'm sure." No time for more discussion. Every second on the surface increased her danger. Padgette hoisted the fresh tank, with regulator already attached, over the side. Zee did not bother to shed her own gear, just swam back down to the safety of depth, holding the fresh tank by the valve. She could sort things out from down there.

Roddy was waiting on the dock when they finally arrived, oxygen tank and backboard ready.

"You all right, babe?" He helped a shivering Zee out of the Zodiac onto the dock. He cast a dagger glare at Padgette, obviously furious.

"I'm fine."

"Sit," he commanded as he pushed her down on the bench and plopped an oxygen mask over her face. "Any pain? Joints? Shoulders? Neck?"

"Nothing." She fought to control a burst of giggles. Her whole body was shaking. She concentrated on calm. "I did a complete decompression."

He picked up her dive computer. "You hit one-eighty."

"That was a bounce, Roddy. Five, ten seconds max. Mostly I was above one-forty."

"You're still grounded for forty-eight hours," Roddy insisted. "And you know the rest of the drill, no hot shower, and lots of fluids." Zee nodded. "And no alcohol," Roddy added. "Which is fine with me 'cause there's only two beers left anyway." Zee grinned, glad to see him relax. She hadn't been in all *that* much trouble. Had she? Sharks, a downdraft, and a seaward current. Zee shivered. Well, maybe just a little trouble.

"Here, take these just in case." He gave her two aspirin. Aspirin had a slight blood-thinning effect that was thought to be helpful in preventing the bends. "You sure you're OK?"

"I'm fine," Zee insisted. "Really, I'm sure I'm OK. But Roddy, we have to go back to this place—it was just crawling with popeye!"

"Popeye?" Padgette looked up eagerly.

"A whole wall of it. We've got to go back."

"Go back! You could've been sucked out to Cuba!" Roddy interrupted. "Now shut up and breathe."

"SeaGenesis has been requesting a lot of it." Zee's voice was muffled through the mask. "We'll just have to plan it better."

"Yeah, right. We'll have to plan a lot of things better." He took away her wet towel and wrapped a dry one around her shoulders. "Do another ten minutes on the oxygen. We'll break down the gear." Once they were out of earshot, Roddy turned on Padgette.

"What the fuck did you think you were doing out there? You should have radioed right away! She could have died!"

"I chased her as soon as I realized what was happening!" Padgette said indignantly. "I didn't want to lose sight of her bubbles. I could hardly call you, steer the Zodiac, and look for Zee, now could I?"

"You didn't even tell me you were going out! And why go that far in the Zodiac? That's a toy boat, for zipping around the nurseries, not for trips to the end of the reef!"

"The sea was calm and I knew you wanted to work on the whaler," Padgette said defensively. The whaler was their main boat, a large, sturdy craft that could carry a dozen divers and gear. It was equipped, as always, with dive gear, oxygen, and other emergency equipment.

"I wouldn't have taken apart the goddamn engine if I knew you were going out. What were you thinking! No one on this station ever goes diving without me knowing it!"

"I'm sorry. You weren't around. It was just going to be a little survey dive. I'll fill out an incident report if it will make you happy."

"I don't want an incident report. I want to keep your sorry asses alive."

"Look, I'm truly sorry Dr. Aspen had a scare." He said it as if she had been frightened by a spider in her shoe, not dragged to the bottom of the sea. "I handled it. OK?" He dropped his snorkeling gear into the rinse tank and slipped his sandals on. "It was just an accident. Accidents do happen."

4

SeaGenesis was surprisingly accident prone, Connor thought as he looked through the file. There had been a series of incidents over the past year, most involving the research station on Shadow Island. There was a generator explosion, electrical fires, diving equipment malfunction, a boat sunk at the dock, shipments of supplies mysteriously vanished, and recently, a staff member almost fatally stung by bees. All of it could be normal misfortune, but when taken together, it seemed just a little too much.

He examined the rest of the file. There were copies of proposals, description of services, invoices for the alarm systems Chapmans had installed, all the usual stuff. There were also copies of two magazine articles. Connor pulled these out. "She's smart, she's sexy, under the sea or behind the microscope. In the race to cure cancer, Zee Aspen hunts for new drugs in the sea. . . ." The photo looked like an advertisement for *Baywatch*. *Maybe I should have paid more attention in science class*, he thought.

Next was a list of facilities and equipment on Shadow Island and a summary of operational costs. Clipped to the back of this was a single sheet of paper with a handwritten list. Generator fire. Gas line. Roof. Samples. Hornet nest. Supplies. Current. It looked to Connor like an abbreviated list of the "accidents."

"What are you doing?" Mickey suddenly appeared at the cubicle. He saw the SeaGenesis file in Connor's hand. "Where did you get that?"

"From the file cabinet."

"What for?" Mickey frowned.

"Doing my job?" Connor suggested.

"You were supposed to be working on that series of burglaries."

"I was just interested."

"Why?"

"One of our clients was attacked right under my nose last night. I thought there might be something to it."

"I told you, Lofton is just an unstable drunk. He snapped."

"What about Cronzene twenty?" Connor pressed.

"What about it?"

"The EPA contract, the one Lofton was so upset about, actually is kind of suspicious."

Mickey frowned. He took the SeaGenesis file from Connor and tucked it under his arm. "Come to my office."

Mickey took his chair with a weary sigh as if Connor were a troublesome child pestering for a favor. "Okay, what have you found out that makes you so suspicious of this contract, besides the fact that a drunken old fool thinks he was cheated?" Connor ignored the patronizing tone.

"The EPA contract went to SeaGenesis for field testing of a pollution-eating bacteria called Cronzene twenty. Now Lofton's company, Genelink, also has a pollution-eating bacteria, called Biosol. According to all the reports, Biosol appeared to be more effective than Cronzene twenty and it was much farther along in the approval process. It looked like Genelink was guaranteed the contract.

"Then along came this group, the Coalition for Responsible Science, CRS, a watchdog organization. CRS objected to Biosol being tested in the Chesapeake Bay since it's an open marine system. They raised the idea of killer bacteria run amuck, that sort of thing, claiming that since Biosol was an engineered bacteria it was too risky. Cronzene twenty is a naturally occurring marine organism, from mangrove swamps. The CRS lobbied for Cronzene twenty, claiming it was safer. The EPA pulled support from Genelink and awarded a valuable contract to SeaGenesis."

"Wait a minute, where did you get all this?" Mickey interrupted. "This isn't in our files."

"You've got half a million dollars of computers and on-line services here." Connor laughed. "What's it supposed to be for?"

"Since when do you know how to use the databases?" Mickey peered at him suspiciously.

"Billy's been showing me. It isn't all that hard once you get a sense of it."

"You found all this out just today?"

"Like I said, it wasn't hard. It was mostly on the Internet."

For a rare moment Mickey did actually seem surprised beyond words.

"Well, I am pleased with all this initiative," he said finally. "Unfortunately, this isn't exactly news."

"So you've considered that Lofton might be pissed off about losing the grant?" Connor pressed.

"Well, he pretty well demonstrated that last night, don't you think? But I'm sure SeaGenesis has a dozen competitors pissed off about something or other. It's the nature of the business world."

"What about all the accidents on Shadow Island?"

"I think they're accidents," Mickey said simply. "SeaGenesis is a young company. Shadow Island is a new operation in a difficult environment. Things are bound to go wrong."

Mickey closed the file and put it on the corner of his desk with a dismissive gesture. "I'm afraid you've wasted a lot of time and energy. If Adam Fairchild were suspicious of Genelink, he would have told us about it in the beginning."

"Even if he was doing something illegal?" Connor suggested. Mickey's frown deepened.

"Why would you think that?"

"Before this whole duel of bacteria, there *was* no CRS." Connor almost bounded out of the chair. "I searched environmental groups, political action committees, radical fringe. No mention of them anywhere. No such group registered as a nonprofit, or any other kind of association or corporation. Then, just when the EPA was about to award the contract to Genelink, surprise, here's a well organized, politically savvy, and extremely effective protest group sprung full blown out of nowhere."

"These groups splinter and re-form all the time, Connor, especially the greenies."

"Sure, but they don't usually quit after one issue, do they? Especially if they have a huge victory their first time out of the gate? The CRS hasn't done squat since the grant went to SeaGenesis. No spotted owls, no redwoods, no bald eagles, nothing. I called their headquarters. The phone has been disconnected."

"And so you think . . . ?" Mickey waved one hand through the air in a "go on, prove it" gesture.

"If SeaGenesis had anything to do with rigging the deal for the EPA contract, Fairchild wouldn't likely admit it, would he?" Connor pressed. Mickey leaned back in his chair to a soft chorus of leathery creaks.

"Any information we receive from, or discover about, a client is completely confidential," he said carefully. "But I do believe that if Fairchild had reason to suspect Genelink, or anyone else, he would have mentioned it."

"Suspect them of what?" Connor said quickly. "All these little accidents on Shadow Island?"

"I didn't say that." Mickey looped his huge hands behind his head, looking at Connor with new seriousness. "Where is all this interest coming from, anyway?"

The question caught him off guard.

"What do you mean?"

"Connor, you've never been exactly zealous about working here before. I mean, you drifted around the country for ten years, stopping back through town now and then when you were worn out or broke, or in some kind of trouble, then all of a sudden you decide to move back and work for Chapmans and now you're hot on the trail of, I don't know, some conspiracy theory or something. What are you trying to prove?"

"To prove? Nothing. It just seemed interesting," he offered vaguely. "And I never gave it a real try here before."

"You've never given anything a real try."

"Now you sound like one of the shrinks in juvy." Connor laughed. Mickey just fixed him with an inscrutable gaze. Connor looked around the office, stalling for time, groping for explanation, avoiding the man's probing glare. He had been back a little over a year now, but they had never really talked about it. He wasn't sure he could explain it to himself yet, let alone to Mickey. All of the easy answers sounded flip, all of the real ones ridiculous.

His eyes skipped across the rows of family photos. There were birthday snapshots and wedding photos with baby pictures stuck in the edges of the frames, graduations and canoe trips. There was one of Sean and Daniel in high school football uniforms, Daniel trying to look tough, Sean just grinning. There was a candid shot of Kerry, Daniel's wife, with their four children snuggled around her for a bedtime story. Connor appeared in only one picture and that an accidental inclusion in the background of a picnic. It was not the family's rejection of him, but his of them that had erased him from the gallery. Connor had simply ducked out of all photo opportunities. He pulled his gaze away, but not before Mickey saw him studying the photos.

Why had he come back? He couldn't pick out a reason exactly. He had been living in Montana, working construction, guiding raft trips, hustling a little pool now and then. Life was fine. He had friends, a working truck, a casual lover, and a good dog. Then one night he was driving home from somewhere. It was a clear winter night, all sharp air and shadows and a million stars in the sky. He stopped and got out of the truck and stood there by the side of the road. In the quiet night, under all that sky, he suddenly he felt like he was standing on a globe of air.

"Maybe I'm just getting too old to be a fuck-up much longer," Connor went on with a lightness that didn't quite mask the truth of it. "Looks and charm can't hold up forever."

Mickey's expression was impossible to read.

"Well, mine did," he finally said with a laugh. "Look, Connor, I'd like to see you get your life together and settle down. I know it hasn't been easy. And I haven't agreed with all of your choices. Hell, with most of them. But Lois always said we had to let you go do what you had to do. We did what we could, we had to trust that. If you're really serious about working for Chapmans now, I'm glad to see it. But you still can't go rummaging around in the files looking for thrills. We have plenty of work for you."

"I'm just tired of home security. I've been working in burglary one way or another since I was four years old. I want to see what else I can do," Connor said. "This stuff," he nodded toward the SeaGenesis file, "is more interesting."

"What stuff?" Mickey said pointedly. "There's nothing going on at SeaGenesis. I've known Adam Fairchild for ten years."

"Then you'll want to be sure his company isn't threatened by too many accidents."

Mickey leaned forward and rested one hand on the file. "OK. Just be careful," he said as he slid the papers back toward Connor. "Fairchild is a good client and he's referred us to about a half-million dollars in other business. If you find anything out of place, come to me first, don't go jumping to conclusions, and don't go bothering Adam Fairchild."

5

As Ulla Raki drove home from SeaGenesis she thought about monkeys: big monkeys, little monkeys, circus monkeys. There had to be some way to get them. She pictured herself sneaking into the zoo one night and making off with a sack full of monkeys. Maybe one of those cat carriers would be better. She laughed at the thought. As if she would ever have the courage to do something like that. A horn blared. The light had changed.

A thousand chattering monkeys filled her brain. Her malaria research was completely stalled if they couldn't go on to primate testing. Although she hid her dismay from Su Thom, she was devastated that Fairchild had rejected the project. Popeye showed astonishing results in vitro. If she could simply get a half a dozen monkeys, she would at least know for certain if this was a drug worth pursuing. That was the worst of it, to be so close and not know for sure. Now the supply of popeye might be drying up as well.

Steal some monkeys. Right. Or steal the serum. Ulla shivered at the thought, for it was much closer to being possible. If she couldn't get monkeys to her lab, maybe she could get the serum to the monkeys. What if she sent it to India? Monkeys were easy to get in India. Anything was easy to get in India if you knew the right people and paid the right baksheesh. What was she thinking of? It was crazy! Even if she could get some popeye tested in India, no one would trust the results. But it would answer her own questions. How could she even be thinking of such a thing? This would be a serious breach of ethics at best, outright theft at worst. But no one had to find out. She ran the lab, she kept the inventory. No one else at SeaGenesis knew or cared about popeye. It demonstrated no antibacterial or antiviral properties and even failed as an antiparasitic in everything but malaria. Ulla wrestled with the idea as she turned into the quiet streets of her neighborhood. God, she couldn't even let Su Thom guess at what she was thinking! He was getting obsessive about popeye.

It would be an answer. It could ruin her career. But what did that matter, her career against the lives of millions of people? It was a career born of hard work, yes, but also of wealth and privilege. She had been a young child when her family left India, but she still remembered enough. The world inside their home was clean and quiet and fragrant with incense and perfume. Outside the walls were the cripples and the beggars, people living in cardboard shelters under the freeway, children naked and dirty, and disease everywhere.

Inside there were servants, maids, houseboys, a cook, a driver, and her beloved nanny. The old woman had cared for Ulla since she was a baby and loved her like a grandmother. Then one night her old Ayah got sick. She was carried out in the night, her body shaking, her eyes clouded with fever. Ulla remembered the scary smell of her empty bed, the hot, damp sheets crinkled in reflection of the poor woman's agony. The next day her mother had taken the children out to the garden and explained that their Ayah would not be coming home. She had died of a mosquito fever called malaria.

Ulla had been frightened. Would they all die, too? Would they get the mosquito fever? No, their mother reassured, they were safe. There wasn't any mosquito fever here. Ayah had gone to her niece's wedding in the south and many people there had the fever. *But not here*, her mother soothed. *Here we are safe.*

Ulla pulled into her driveway, still in turmoil. She unlocked the door, dropped her keys in the bowl on the hall table, and picked up the mail, delighted to find a big, fat letter from Zee Aspen. Usually they corresponded through SeaGenesis deliveries, but sometimes Zee got a letter to the Bahamian mail boat. It could take a month or more that way, but she knew Ulla enjoyed the surprise. Even when they were in grade school together, and living only two blocks apart, they sometimes wrote letters, or left each other notes in secret places.

Ulla changed her clothes, poured a tall glass of iced mint tea, and took the letter out to the porch. The first few paragraphs were full of stories about island life and diving. Zee wrote about seeing two groupers performing a mating dance and about finding the neck from an old bottle.

It was the deepest dark blue and smooth from bouncing around the sand for a hundred years or more. I imagined all the things it might have held and the circumstances of its winding up here. Maybe it carried a secret tonic, a brew full of magic charms made by a sailor's lady.

Ulla smiled. Zee had a rich imagination. The second page was full of small gossip, a silly story about Roddy trying to climb a coconut tree native-style and some mild mocking of Padgette's fussiness.

He doesn't like nicknames for anything. Wants us always to use proper terminology, as if we were professors presenting to the Royal Academy and not this scruffy band sorting out sea squirts on this godforsaken island. Roddy will tell me the "yellow meanies" are flourishing and Padgette, hearing this, will ask right away for a status report on the "Sabellid polychaetes" which are yellow and have a nasty sting and so are, of course, yellow meanies and he KNOWS this, but is so snide, correcting us in this way, as if we were naughty children. And when we speak of popeye, he gets this look on his face like he had tasted something bad.

But speaking of popeye, what are you doing with it all? We've been sending you buckets and buckets and you haven't told me anything about it in ages. I suppose it's just routine to you, but on this end, where it feels sometimes like we are nothing more than invertebrate nursemaids, it is nice to hear news. So do write and tell me what fantastic cure you are brewing.

Ulla read over this part several times. "We've been sending you buckets and buckets . . ." Shadow Island was sending large quantities of popeye to SeaGenesis. Ulla had been receiving almost nothing. Where was the rest of it going?

Su Thom watched with fascination as another delicate mosquito pulled itself free of the flimsy pupal shell. Its tiny legs trembled and its wings were like wrinkled tissue but there was strength in the little body, and a fine sharp stinger. Nine had hatched so far and there were hundreds more on the way. He felt a thrill as the first one finally buzzed off in tentative flight. It landed on the screen near his face, a little silver dragon, born with an instinct for prey and a taste for blood.

The lamplight shone on the larvae still in the water, each one a bright little gem of possibility. He sat down on the rickety folding chair, the only furniture in the house. He dropped his head in his hands. Was it possible? Was there a chance that after so many years he was truly about to conquer his greatest enemy? *Conquer his enemy?* But which enemy? Malaria had killed his family, but it was a disease, with no intent, no will or culpability. He had dedicated his life to destroying it, but had never felt this sort of rage. Where had it come from—this urgent hatred? This drastic panic? It frightened him. He felt splintered; excited and terrified, bold but cowering. What was he doing? He was a healer, not a killer. He would not really let them loose. He did not want people to die, only to care. He wouldn't release the mosquitos. But he could. His little silver dragons. Was that it? Was it as simple as that, the power? He looked again at the shimmering trays of water with their precious hatchlings. The way the light sparkled on the water, twinkling over the empty shells. Bright silver sparkles . . .

Bright silver sparkles danced in the water, spinning and twinkling all around him like falling stars. Some of the boys tried to snatch at the coins as they fell, but Su Thom knew the good ones were heavier and would sink faster. He dove straight to the bottom, through a thrash of elbows and feet and wiry limbs. A solid piece plunked into his hand. A quarter? No, just a nickel, but better than a penny. He picked up pennies, too, of course, his nimble fingers curling them into his palm and then into his pocket in a flash. But today especially, he needed better than pennies.

For five dollars, he could buy ten pills. Su Thom felt another boy's hand scratch at his as he closed his fist around another coin. A real quarter! His lungs burning, he finally swam to the surface. As he burst into the air, he could see the tourists on the dock, laughing and pointing. All around him, other small faces bobbed and smiled and called for more coins. He was seven years old, small for his age but strong.

He caught the eye of a pretty woman, beamed his brightest smile and waved at her. Just a few more nickels. Ten pills. The woman laughed and touched her husband's arm. The man fished in his pocket, then his hand stretched back. Su Thom saw the sparkling arc against the blue sky and felt the splashes, like raindrops all around him. Little sparks of metal flicked against his skin. His heart sank. Even before he caught one, Su Thom knew the sparkles were not coins. They were too light, they fluttered down through the water. He caught one in his hand. Paper clips! The man had thrown paper clips!

Su Thom swam to the surface, a crazed black fury in his heart. The American man and woman were laughing and walking away. If he were stronger, he would leap right out of the water like a dolphin. He would leap onto the dock and kill the man! Two policemen were on the dock and the boys began to scatter. Su Thom took a deep breath and dove again. He swam under the dock and as far away as he could before surfacing again. Usually the police just shouted at them, but sometimes they would hit with their sticks and sometimes they would take a boy's money. Su Thom could not afford to take any chances today.

Mother was sick again. She was burning with fever. This morning her nose was bleeding and her body shook all over. Her eyes, where they should be white, were red. Su Thom was scared. The fever had been in his village for weeks and many people had already died. Even those who had money for the pills were dying. The mosquito fever had always been with them, but never like this.

Never before was there so much blood, so much screaming. The victims did not waste away in the usual slow fever. It was like their bodies were being torn apart by demons. Sixty-four cents. He saw the pills, like golden droplets burning in his mind as he ran barefooted along the dirt road, the coins beating time against his skinny leg.

Su Thom jumped over the drainage ditch, dashed past the market stalls, yanked open the screen door, and strode up to the counter of the little store. He scooped the change out of his pocket and laid it out on the worn boards.

Tan, the pharmacist, didn't speak. His hands rested on the counter, his stubby fingers making no move toward the pile of coins. His wife appeared behind him. His hands rubbed nervously together. There was a thick airless feeling in the room. Su Thom knew something had happened, but he wouldn't let it be true.

"I need the pills," his voice quavered. "For the fever. I have sixty-four American cents and these other coins. My brother will bring you more." Tan sadly shook his head and gently pushed the coins back toward Su Thom.

"It's too late," he said sadly. "Take your coins to the temple."

The young Su Thom had not taken his coins to the temple. He had run back to the dock and flung them into the sea. The big American man was still there, sitting at a café table with his pretty wife and his pockets full of paper clips. Eighteen years later, Su Thom closed his eyes and saw the big man's hand go back against the sky, throwing the sparkling shower of paper clips. It was a small thing, an insignificant tease. The American man was probably not cruel, just typically thoughtless and vastly unaware.

That day was long ago, that country left behind. That little boy was now grown, adopted, Americanized. His frail body had been nourished, his eager mind educated, but although his adoptive parents had tried, his wounded soul had never been fully repaired. He had made a vow that day, when he was that small and desperate orphan. He had labored long on what he thought was the right path. He had studied and worked long hours in the lab in a search for the cure for this killer. But SeaGenesis had more important things, more *profitable* things, to develop. And because of that, today, in the more distant world, in the world *out there*, a thousand little boys would die. He watched another mosquito flex its tiny new wings. He felt the splintered rage fade, his spirit growing calm. It wasn't his decision to make. He had been chosen.

6

June 21

U ncle Connor! Uncle Connor, do my ear! Do mine! No, do me!" Connor was assaulted with small sticky hands as soon as he walked through the hedge into the Sullivans' expansive back yard.

"Me first! No, me!" The children scuttled around him, jostling each other for the best place. Connor pulled out a quarter and the children squealed. He made the quarter disappear, then plucked it from behind Annie's ear. Annie giggled. Next the quarter appeared magically from between Mary's bare toes. Sleight-of-hand tricks were the only use for his light-fingered talents that he still enjoyed.

"Where have you been?" Kerry Sullivan's hand fell lightly on his shoulder. "I was beginning to think you weren't going to show."

"And live to tell about it? I don't think so." Connor laughed as he kissed her on the cheek. It was Lois Sullivan's sixtieth birthday, and Mickey had made it clear throughout the extended family that no excuse short of hospitalization, preferably in intensive care, would be accepted.

"Come on and get something to eat," Kerry said. "The aunts are getting restless. You know how they look forward to a chance to fatten you up. We're about to have dueling potato salad at fifty paces." The children squawked at the interruption but Kerry shooed them away with directions to go round everybody up for the birthday cake. Kerry led him across the broad lawn to the tables. She had been married to Daniel,

Mickey's oldest son, for ten years now. Even after four children and the first streaks of gray in her bouncing brown hair, she still looked every bit the rosy-cheeked girl next door. Which she pretty much was. She was also Connor's first real friend, confidant, and more. More that was best left in the past. Probably the noblest damn thing he had ever done was to skip town and leave her to marry Daniel.

Kerry led him into the thick of the party. A plate of food was handed to him, only to be snatched back several times, and returned with a new heap of some quivering delicacy. Sullivan potlucks were heavy on Jell-O and macaroni salad. There were coolers full of cheap beer and store-brand sodas. The family had never lost touch with its peasant roots. Connor plowed through the crowd, wincing under bosomy hugs and laughing at old-guy jokes.

Uncle Billy was manning the grill, wielding his tongs like a scepter, charring what might have once been chicken, and glowering in the direction of the giant oak tree that dominated the yard where a young couple leaned, holding hands, ignoring the party with the rapture of lovers.

"Is that Susan?" Connor asked with surprise, barely recognizing Billy's youngest daughter.

"Poor girl." Kerry laughed. "Her first serious boyfriend and Billy's been doing the full third degree on the guy."

"Can't say I blame him." The last time he had seen Susan she was a skinny, awkward teenager with acne and frizzy hair. Everything had sorted itself out quite nicely since then. "She's in college now?"

"Just finished her freshman year at GW. The boyfriend is Peter, pre-med at GW, Jesuit high school, altar boy even. Athlete, good student, no drugs, barely drinks." Kerry smiled at Connor. "Susan enlisted me for his PR campaign," she explained.

Billy was watching the young couple so intently he kept dropping hamburgers. There was a very grateful circle of dogs waiting intently around the grill.

"They're so in love." Kerry sighed. "And he really is a good kid. Only he shares a house with a wild bunch."

"I'm surprised Billy and Mickey don't have the place on twenty-four-hour surveillance."

"What makes you think they don't?" Kerry laughed.

Families, Connor thought, as he was swallowed up again, what a sweet, rotten, glorious mess. What would have become of him if he hadn't got all tangled up in this one?

The evening blue was fading and fireflies began to sparkle against the thick pines that edged the lawn. A flock of little girls tore across the yard, watermelon-stained sundresses flapping around dirty knees.

"Mom, Mom! You said I could help you with the cake!" Annie flung herself at Kerry with all the sweaty urgency of a six-year-old. "Chrissie said her and Mary are gonna do it!"

"You can all help," Kerry said as she smoothed the little girl's hair.

"I don't *want* them to help! I don't *want* them to!" She was on the verge of tears, her hot little face creased with fury.

"It's a great big enormous cake," Kerry soothed.

"Kerry, it's late," Daniel said wearily as he followed his frantic daughters helplessly. "Hadn't you better go do this cake business before these children go completely to pieces?" His voice was oversteadied. He tended to drink too much at family events. Being Mickey's real son hadn't exactly been easy either. Connor saw sadness flicker across Kerry's face, then she turned to the children.

"C'mon kitties." Kerry swept the little girls into a clutch. "There are lots and lots of candles to light." Connor watched them disappear into the dusk under the trees, then emerge again, silhouetted in the buttery light of the open kitchen door. Kerry moved among people as if she knew all the secrets and cures.

Daniel took up Kerry's place beside him. "Dad says you were quite the hero yesterday. Flinging yourself on some crazed gunman."

"It was just some poor old sot with a fake pistol."

"Still, I'd ask for a bonus if I were you. That sort of thing seems way beyond your usual duties."

Connor ignored the barb. There had always been friction between them. It was partly the lingering effects of ancient adolescent jealousy, partly because Daniel just had an obnoxious side. Becoming a bigshot corporate lawyer didn't help. Connor had been closer to Sean. But then everyone had loved Sean. He was the golden boy, smart, athletic, funny, and kind. A charmed and charming young man. Dead in a car crash at seventeen.

Kerry and the girls reappeared with the cake and a loud, off-key plunge into "Happy Birthday." The candles cast a glow on Lois's face. Connor felt a pang of guilt. He really should come visit her more often, take her out to lunch or something. His relationship with Mickey had always been difficult, but Lois had always been simply the good, sweet mother. It was she who had campaigned for him from the start. Well, not exactly from the start. When he was caught in her house with his pockets full of her jewelry, Lois had been just as happy as Mickey to see him hauled off by the police. But she had a soft heart. Sean and Daniel, her own sons, were almost the same age as this hardened little burglar. Two weeks after Connor arrived at reform school she sent him a box of cookies, a letter full of encouragement, and a copy of *White Fang*. Connor, still filled with rage, threw the cookies away and tore up the letter. But he could not resist a book.

Over the next few months, Lois sent him packages regularly, with books and encouraging notes, but she never imagined her connection to the boy would be anything more than this slightly guilty largesse.

But after four months Connor had escaped. With his father in jail he had nowhere to go. He made his way to Baltimore, where he lived on the street for several weeks, trying to survive on petty crime. Burglary, he discovered, was tough without a good fence. His father had always taken care of that and now Connor found himself at the mercy of pawnbrokers. Half of them couldn't tell good jewelry from crap and the other half wouldn't pay a fair price anyway. He mostly stuck to picking pockets.

The long and short of it was that one day he picked the wrong marks; a couple of Eastern Shore rednecks up to the big city on a landscaping job. Sore muscles and mean tempers, pick and shovel money was too hard-earned to be lost to a kid. Connor wound up in intensive care with a fractured skull.

He was a junior John Doe until a savvy nurse noticed a name written in his sneakers, the sneakers he had stolen from Sean Sullivan's closet six months before, the sneakers Sean had taken to gym class and Lois had dutifully inscribed with indelible marker.

The incident occurred on a Friday night when Sean and Daniel were on a Boy Scout camping trip. When the call came from the hospital, Lois and Mickey did not stop to wonder why the Scout leader hadn't called, or how their son had come to be in a Baltimore hospital when he was camping in the Shenandoah mountains. They simply hurried to what they thought was their son's bedside.

Mickey had not even recognized Connor as the urchin he had caught burglarizing his house months before, but Lois was inconsolable. First the relief that it wasn't actually Sean, then the guilt and pity for the boy it was. What better home for a wayward boy, she decided, than a family full of cops?

Lois blew out the candles and everyone cheered. Mickey presented her with a jewelry box tied with elaborate gold ribbon. She opened it up, and the women around her *ooh*ed. It was a dazzling emerald neck-lace. Lois smiled, but she looked shocked, almost frightened of such an extravagant thing. Connor had never seen Lois in anything besides a string of pearls and an antique brooch. Mickey stood behind her and fastened it around her neck. Everyone applauded.

The children swarmed around the cake, their giggling chatter punc-tuated by a chorus of crickets. Connor stepped back into the shadow of the old oak tree and watched. Kerry handed out pieces of cake on little paper plates, carefully parceling out sugar roses for every child. Susan and her new boyfriend sat on the porch steps, shoulders and knees and ankles touching, faces bent close, alone on the moon for all they noticed the world. A game of flashlight tag started up on the broad lawn. Lois began dispensing family off to their cars, accepting final hugs and bend-ing to kiss sleeping baby heads as they were carried away. Was this what he came back for? Macaroni salad, old-guy jokes, a backyard madonna with her pockets full of angels? He had resisted them so long and so hard; this family, the very idea of family, a stew of loyalties and conflicts, of obligation and hurt; uniquely acute for who else could hurt you so badly as those you loved? Yet maybe it was what he wanted, the sweet, rotten, glorious mess of them.

Lois saw him under the tree and beamed him in with a scolding smile. "What are you doing hiding over there?"

"Just waiting my turn at you." He kissed her on the cheek.

Lois took his hand and would not let him go. As people continued to drift home, she kept him by her side, letting go of his hand only for farewell embraces, then returning again, like a shy child seeking security. Her hand seemed small and made of paper. The emerald necklace looked silly with her casual summer dress, and she kept touching it nervously, pulling it away from her skin as if it burned.

Annie ran over to Connor.

"I made you the best piece," she declared triumphantly as she thrust the soggy paper plate at Connor. The cake was indeed a six-year-old's idea of perfection. A corner piece with gobs of swirled icing around a dice-size bit of cake, half an H written in blue gel, thick green icing leaves, and a great gob-sticker sugar rose: a sweet, sticky, glorious mess of cake.

It was just what he wanted.

June 25

Six vials. Six precious vials left. Ulla imagined how the small, cool tubes would feel in the pocket of her lab coat. The idea that had seemed so absurd and extreme last night, now seemed perfectly logical. Steal the remaining samples of popeye and send them to India. At least then she would know if it really worked.

"Could you please check again?" she asked the inventory clerk. "There has to be a mistake, maybe the samples have been going to the wrong lab."

"No Capjen88 has come in since April," the clerk replied with mounting irritation. "You can look at the log yourself."

Ulla searched the log. *I've been sending you buckets and buckets . . .* What was going on? She was distracted as she went to her office. She opened the door and saw Su Thom sitting at her desk. He looked up with obvious surprise. It took a few seconds for the scene to register. There on the desk in a test-tube rack was one vial of popeye with the stopper out. And there was Su Thom, a needle in his arm, pushing in the plunger of the syringe.

"What are you doing!"

Su Thom's face registered shock, but quickly hardened with deter-
mination.

"I'm testing popeye," he said calmly as he slid the needle out.

"You can't! What are you thinking!"

"I guess I'm thinking I'm as good as any monkey."

"You can't do this. We don't know what this stuff will do to you!"

"There's been no toxicity so far."

"In rats! In birds! We don't know what side effects it might have in
humans."

"None."

"You don't know that."

"None so far then," he amended. He checked his watch and wrote
the time in a small notebook.

"You didn't infect yourself with malaria, did you?"

"I know the testing protocol," he said softly. "Phase one is only for
toxicity. Phase *two* is efficacy."

"Well, there isn't going to be any phase two." Ulla pulled open her
desk drawer and grabbed her car keys. "You're coming with me right
now to the hospital. You might not feel any negative symptoms but god
knows what's going on with your liver, your kidneys, your electrolytes—
Dammit!" Ulla sat down. "Why did you do this!"

Su Thom carefully put the syringe down on the desk, furious with
himself for being so careless.

"I'm sorry. But I had to. We have to find out if popeye works," he
said simply.

"Not like this."

"How then?"

She considered telling him her own plan, but he would probably
want to help her. He could not even know about it. She would risk her
own career but not his.

"I've been monitoring my blood and urine," Su Thom went on, trying to reassure her. "Everything is perfectly normal."

"You don't know that, Su Thom. You know the sort of monitoring
required for a clinical trial! Listen, I know how much popeye means to

you. But you have to trust me. I am not going to let this drug go over-looked. Fairchild is still interested. Just come with me now to the hos-pital."

"No!" Su Thom pulled sharply away. "No hospital. You can't tell anyone, Ulla."

"I have to!"

"No." There was steely menace in his voice. "I can't let you do that."

Connor spun the Frisbee and Lucy took off after it in a streak of fur. It was nine o'clock, nearly dark, but with the heat wave, it was the only decent time to go running. The towpath along the C&O canal was a perfect place. Connor liked to run and think, the rhythm of his stride pacing the thoughts, keeping them in order, the physical exertion a nec-essary drug. The woods were starting to chitter with night sounds. Lucy sprinted on ahead, ears up, alert to a chase. Connor saw dark duck shapes in the canal.

"Lucy, no!" She stopped immediately but looked at him desperately, her body quivering with predatory urge. "No ducks! Heel!" She trotted, sulking, to his side. He didn't mind her chasing squirrels. They were canny and quick and held no hope of capture, but he thought of the ducks as slow and slightly befuddled tourists, that if not actually caught, would still be traumatized by the chase. Or maybe it was just that they were such easy marks. Sitting ducks, just waiting to be taken.

Don't mind it boy, his father explained. *They're silly old ducks. If they had something they really wanted to keep, they'd put it so we couldn't get at it. If they keep it somewhere easy to pinch, well then, they mean for it to be ours. We're just obliging them. It ain't like we're hittin' 'em over the head, is it? It's wits, lad. Wits is no crime.*

The courts saw it differently. While Connor went to the juvenile home, Mickey saw to it that his father went to prison with a twelve-year sentence. He had been released in four by a fatal heart attack.

Connor had never really questioned their life. How could he? With a child's intuition he knew his father was wrong, but with a child's ad-oration felt he could *do* no wrong. This was the same man whose first

criminal deed in every new town was to steal a utility bill out of someone's mailbox so he could get his son a library card. Every night in
whatever cheap hotel or shabby flophouse they were living, Connor's
bed was a slippery sea of children's books. Dad would get out the
hundred-watt bulb he always carried around (and hid each day from the
maids), and suddenly the dingy rooms would be a bright paradise of
adventure. They would read together until they both fell asleep.

You play your father's game and you play to win his love. Crime
was his father's game and Connor learned to play it well. With Mickey
the game was still going on, only he had never quite figured out all the
rules. Maybe this time would be different.

He crossed the little wooden bridge, cut up a small path through the
woods, and walked the last few blocks home to cool off. Once home,
Connor drank a big glass of water, showered, then flipped on the ten
o'clock news and began to look through his mail. He was only half
listening and didn't pay much attention, until he saw flashing police
lights on the screen. It was a live broadcast, from the scene of a fatal
carjacking. The reporter stood in front of yellow tape as police in the
background continued to search for evidence.

Carjackings were no longer so sensational in the D.C. area, but they
still got coverage on a slow day, especially when someone was killed.
A picture of the victim appeared on the screen. Long, black hair framed
a small bronze face with delicate features, huge eyes, and a shy smile.

"The victim has been identified as Dr. Ulla Raki, a resident of Tacoma Park. Dr. Raki was thirty-five years old, a scientist with a Maryland
biotechnology firm, SeaGenesis Corporation, where she specialized in
cancer research . . ."

SeaGenesis. The name stopped him cold.

7

June 26

H ow is it not suspicious?" Connor said incredulously.

"Of course it should make us think," Mickey replied. "I only said it doesn't necessarily mean anything." He sat stiffly in his chair, a fresh cup of coffee untouched on the desk. His face was drawn, his eyes puffy.

"Come on, Mickey. Of all the possible random victims in the area last night, what are the chances that this woman would work for a company that has been suffering a string of accidents, including an attempt, bogus or not, on the life of its president?"

"Exactly the same as they are for anyone else, except we wouldn't give it a second thought because we weren't directly involved with their company."

"Yeah yeah . . ." Connor interrupted. "I'm just not a big fan of co-incidence."

"The police report is pretty clear," Mickey reminded him. Ulla Raki's car had been found around three A.M., abandoned a few miles from the scene, littered with empty malt liquor bottles and hamburger wrappers. Two men in a car matching the description of Raki's had robbed a man at an ATM about an hour after the shooting. The police had dug a bullet out of the machine. It was a match to the one that killed Raki. There were no fingerprints and no leads on the two suspects.

"Where was Dr. Raki going?"

Mickey shook his head. "The police are interviewing friends and neighbors today."

"It just seems wrong. It's too neat."

"Well, that's just it," Mickey agreed. "If it was foul play, you would have to be awfully good, or fantastically lucky. What are the chances of a setup with no screwup? And the more elaborate the con, the greater chance of blowing it. You should know that. Besides, Ulla Raki worked in cancer research. She had nothing to do with this whole pollution-eating bacteria thing. If the police come up with anything, we'll be the first to hear. Until then, what more can we do?"

Zee sat on the dock, dropping bread crumbs in for the little fish that swarmed between the pilings. There was certainly enough work she could be doing, including calibrating the spectrometer that had arrived with the new group of graduate students, but she was still in shock over the news. She wouldn't believe it at first. How could Ulla be dead? Why would they kill her? Why not just take the car? Ulla was tiny, she wouldn't have resisted. What went wrong?

Her childhood friend, guide, and mentor. Gone. Suddenly, cruelly, senselessly. Zee watched the sun sparkling on the water. She remembered sitting on Ulla's pink satin bedspread, braiding Ulla's hair, the long, silky, black ropes heavy across her palms. Ulla had been two years ahead of her in school, and the rules of girlhood prevented them from having lunch or playing together there, but outside of school they were inseparable. Ulla's family was quiet and conservative, Zee's was loud and wild. Zee wanted that long, straight hair, Ulla craved her curls and freckles. Ulla helped her with math and Zee taught Ulla how to dance.

She blinked back tears and looked out toward the reef where Roddy and the new group of grad students were anchored in the whaler near the nursery cages. This was their first dive, a chance for Roddy to check out their skills and show them how the nursery was set up. Except for a Jamaican man in his thirties, the students were all young and pink. They would stay on the island for four weeks, collecting samples and helping with the aquaculture experiments. Zee thought about the dive last week, the strange chasm at the end of the reef. All the popeye there. Damn, just what Ulla needed, too!

Zee closed her eyes and let the warm sun soothe her. She must have dozed off, for suddenly she was pulled back to reality by a faint noise. The divers were back on the surface, climbing hurriedly into the boat. She glanced at her watch. They hadn't been down even twenty minutes. She shaded her eyes and tried to see what was going on, but the only figure she could distinguish from here was the tall Jamaican. He had climbed into the boat and was pulling someone else in. Someone was clearly in trouble. Shit! This couldn't be happening. Two years and they had never had a diving accident. She jumped up and ran to the hut at the end of the dock where they kept the emergency gear. She grabbed the air horn and gave three long blasts to summon Padgette. She pulled out the portable oxygen unit.

The whaler sped toward them, the Jamaican at the helm. Roddy must be tending to the injured student. The bow was tilted up so far that they could not see their victim until they neared the dock. "Oh god!" Zee gasped. It was Roddy who lay in the bottom of the boat, his body rigid with pain, his face ashen. Padgette came running. He caught the line and whipped it around a piling.

Roddy's left arm was discolored and swollen and a ghastly purple swelling covered most of his thigh.

"Scorpion fish," the Jamaican said solemnly. "Place crawl'n wi' dem."

"Oh shit. Hang on, Roddy," Zee implored. "You're gonna be OK." She put the oxygen mask over his face. His breathing was fast and shallow. A scorpion fish had poisonous spines on its back and inflicted an extremely painful injury. Roddy had taken two big hits.

"Come on, Roddy, take some deep breaths." Roddy was combative and his hands were trembling uncontrollably.

"Hold him, boys," the Jamaican directed. "He going off a little wild wit de poison." Zee was grateful for the Jamaican's strong hands as she tightened the straps that held Roddy to the backboard.

"Let's go!" Zee directed one of the new students to run on ahead. "This venom is heat labile. We should get him in some hot water." The Jamaican shook his head.

"Dis too much poison. You need antivenom dis much a hit."

"I'll radio the hospital in Nassau." Padgette ran toward the lab.

"He was showing us how to open one of the nursery cages," one of the women explained. "They were all over the place! There must have been four or five in that one spot!"

"Four or five?" Zee had never seen a single scorpion fish, nor had Roddy or Padgette ever mentioned seeing one anywhere near the nursery. They carried Roddy up to the lab and Zee sent a couple of the students for hot water and towels for compresses. Padgette came in, his face ashen.

"Nassau doesn't have any antivenom," he reported. "They're calling Miami."

"Christ—we need to get him to the hospital. Let's get a plane here."

"Wouldn't it be better to wait for the antivenom? I don't know if it's smart to move him."

"We can't do anything else for him here! His blood pressure is dropping, he's shocky." She was unwrapping an IV kit and reading the directions. "It will take the same amount of time for us to get to Miami as it will for the antivenom to be sent here. So go! Get me a plane. Then get me a doctor on the radio."

Roddy began to retch and his body convulsed. Zee and the Jamaican turned him on his side as he vomited.

"There's a file," Zee instructed one of the students. "A medevac procedure. It has all the numbers and contacts. In the gray file cabinet in the lab." They were three hours from a hospital at best. While a scorpion fish sting shouldn't usually be fatal to someone of his size and build, Roddy had taken two huge hits. And if he was allergic to a bee sting, what the hell was this going to do to him? Zee gave the IV instructions to one of the students for a double check. She had taken a pretty thorough emergency medicine course before coming to Shadow Island, but had never inserted an IV before. Fortunately, Roddy had good veins.

How did this happen? Scorpion fish were bottom dwellers, so well camouflaged that it was often impossible to see them amidst rocks and coral. But Roddy was a careful diver with an acute eye. And the fish just weren't that common. Four or five in the same place? That was

weird. She didn't know that much about scorpion fish, but was pretty
sure they were solitary. Was something attracting the scorpion fish to the
nursery cages? Her mind raced in a dozen different directions as she
waited for a doctor to come on the radio with more direction. Were they
upsetting the food chain, the balance of nature? Could it be a seasonal
episode? Some shift in water temperature or current that drove the fish
out of their usual crags to the sand flats? Or was it just more bad luck?
This was an awful lot of bad luck for one little island.

8

June 28

U lla Raki's memorial service was held at a small interfaith chapel a few miles from SeaGenesis in Rockville. The building was a sad example from the early seventies, when churches, eschewing the baroque and the gilt of the ages, embraced a soulless architecture of blank walls and abstract slabs of stained glass. Connor hung back and observed the mourners as they filed into the chapel. Most, he guessed, were colleagues from work.

The service was an awkward task, areligious and somewhat sterile. There were about twenty mourners, maybe half from SeaGenesis; the rest, Connor gathered from the quiet conversations, were neighbors. Ulla's father had flown out from California as soon as he was notified, but her mother was recovering from surgery and couldn't travel. He had returned yesterday with his daughter's ashes, so there was no family present. A small man sat at a small organ. He began to play an emotionless dirge. Just then the door opened and Connor glanced back to see a woman come in. She looked tired, embarrassed at her disruption, and generally frazzled. She carried a small duffle bag, which she set down behind the last row.

She was slender and tanned and had short, curly hair, sun-streaked a dozen shades of blondish brown. Some of the curls were sticking to her sweaty forehead. Connor slid over and made room for her in the pew. She had brown eyes, unplucked brows, a little scar at the outside corner of one, the sort children get from crashing into table edges. He found her vaguely familiar but couldn't place her exactly.

A minister welcomed the mourners and launched into a carefully ecumenical prayer. His sincerity seemed genuine but ultimately futile as he followed with a brief musing on the tragedy, trying to wrest some sense out of a time to be born, a time to die, when it didn't seem the time to die at all.

Then he invited friends to stand up and give their memories of Ulla. For a few long seconds, no one moved. There were a few glances and nervous coughs, but no one, it seemed, had memories of the quiet, shy scientist. Finally an elderly man creaked to his feet and told, in a leisurely drawl, how Ulla always came over and fed his parakeets when he was in the hospital, and bought him groceries if he couldn't get out, and one time when another neighbor's cat was always over scaring the birds away from his bird feeder she brought him something, he thought it was something she invented in the lab because she was a scientist, that you could put down on the grass and keep the cat away . . .

Zee began to feel light-headed as the man droned on. It felt as if she wasn't really there on the hard pew, but floating above the dreary room watching a bad dream. It should be a dream. Ulla shouldn't be dead. She was supposed to come visit the island next month and go snorkeling.

Finally the man ran out of pets and praise and sat down. There was a palpable relief. But then another neighbor got up, and with a hard glare at the old man, started telling how Ulla always came over and fed her *cats* when she was away . . .

Zee felt like she was suffocating. Finally Dr. Fairchild got up with a proprietary air, walked to the front and turned slowly. He thanked everyone and began to speak about Ulla the scientist, what good she had done, what a loss it was to the world.

Zee was sweating but also felt cold. Fairchild's voice got farther and farther away and there was a roaring in her ears. She took a deep breath, but there didn't seem to be enough air. Her skin felt clammy and damp. Her heart pounded. She grabbed the back of the pew with a shaky hand. Suddenly she felt a hand on her elbow, a light but firm grip, gently lifting and guiding her out. She let herself be steered outside into the air.

"Sit here." The hands turned her a little. She felt bricks against the back of her legs and sat down on the low wall.

"Put your head down and just take some deep breaths." The voice was calm and, thankfully, not overly solicitous. The voice and the hands let her alone for a few minutes, the body they belonged to stepped back. When her heart stopped racing and her head cleared, Zee sat up slowly.

"I'm sorry." She took another deep breath. "It was just so close and stuffy in there." She looked up, then quickly down again, struggling to quell a sudden eruption of giggles. The whole scene was so weird to begin with, and now here she was nearly fainting and being carried out by a tall, dark, and handsome stranger, like the cover of some cheesy romance novel. She kept her head down, willing her nerves to settle.

There was a spigot on the side of the building and Connor wet his handkerchief.

"Here, put this on the back of your neck." The cool cloth felt good and the world began to focus again.

"Thanks," she said, embarrassed but recovering her composure. "I'm not usually the fainting type. I hate funerals. And my plane was late. I rushed to get here." She looked up at him now, the giggles successfully suppressed. He was still handsome, though, in that tall, dark, and dangerous way. She sat up, feeling clearer now, and handed him back the handkerchief.

"Thanks again. I'm fine now." There was an awkward pause. "I don't think I've ever been offered a man's handkerchief before," Zee said.

"I'm kind of surprised I had it. I think it came with the suit." Connor smiled. Zee felt something go hot against the back of her ribs. Great smile. Nice voice. Wait a minute—this was too weird—she could *not* be getting turned on at her best friend's funeral!

Connor wrung the handkerchief out and stuffed it back in his pocket. "Where did you come in from?"

"Miami. Well, the Bahamas. I'm sorry. I'm Zee Aspen." Connor recognized her now from the magazine article in the SeaGenesis file. She offered her hand and Connor found the palm still clammy. "I work on the research station for SeaGenesis. One of our staff was injured, and we had to fly to Miami for treatment. I went along to take care of things, then I just decided since I was already in the States and Roddy was stabilized, I would fly up here. For the funeral." She ran her fingers nervously through her hair. "God, I can't believe she's dead."

"You were good friends?"

"Yes." Zee paused and looked toward the closed doors of the little chapel. "She was my best friend. We moved to San Diego when I was six. Ulla lived just a block away. We were like sisters. We both only had brothers. Her mother sometimes wore a sari and all these bracelets, and cooked Indian food. I always wanted to eat over there. And of course Ulla always wanted to come to my house for hamburgers and Shake 'n' Bake." She brushed away fresh tears and stood up.

"I thought her parents would be here. That's really why I came. I should have called, but things were so hectic in Miami. Then this morning they finally said Roddy was going to be OK. I called the office up here. They told me the service was this afternoon. I just jumped on the next plane." She shook her head as if she could shake off the pressures of the past three days. "How do you know Ulla?" She winced at the automatic present tense, but couldn't bear to correct it.

"I'm a neighbor."

"Oh god, don't tell me she fed your pets, too."

Connor laughed. "No. I barely knew her. Just to say hi, really."

They were interrupted by a clatter and rustle from the church as the doors opened and people began to file outside.

"Dr. Aspen!" Fairchild came toward them. Zee cringed a little. "I didn't know you were coming. So good to see you." He took her hand in both of his, a gesture of condolence with a hint of control. "I'm sorry it's such a sad occasion, but I am glad to see you. I'm looking forward to hearing all about our island. The fellow is all right, the one who was injured?"

"Roddy's out of danger," Zee replied. "But still in the hospital."

This injury piqued Connor's curiosity. Was it just coincidence that two SeaGenesis employees had suffered accidents within days?

"We'll make arrangements for his care. Of course. Now you just came in, what can we do for you? Where are you staying?"

Zee had no idea where she was staying. All she wanted to do right now was escape and be alone somewhere cool and quiet.

"I've offered Dr. Aspen a ride to her hotel," Connor said quickly. "It's near where I live."

Zee looked relieved.

"Have we met?" Fairchild asked Connor.

"No," Connor answered easily. "I'm Connor Gale." Fairchild's hand was dry and cool.

"You do look familiar," he pressed. Connor didn't really want to place himself as the man who had picked Fairchild's pocket at the awards dinner.

"I've given Ulla a ride to SeaGenesis a few times when her car was in the shop. Perhaps you saw me then."

"Perhaps." Fairchild's attention was diverted by others, and Connor relaxed.

"So, do you actually have a hotel?" Connor asked as they got to his car.

"No. I'm sorry, I just couldn't deal with being sociable. I haven't really slept in a couple of days."

"Have you eaten?" Connor laughed at her blank look. "If you have to think about it, you probably haven't. Look, why don't we stop by my house, I'll fix us some lunch and we can call around and get you a room someplace." Zee hesitated a little. There was no reason not to trust him; he was a friend of Ulla's and it was broad daylight.

"Okay. Thanks."

They talked little on the way. Zee looked out the window. It was strange to see cars and houses and so many people. Connor pulled into the driveway and Lucy raced up to the fence to greet them. Zee got out of the car and looked up and down the street. The houses were mostly small bungalows with neat front yards and big old trees.

"Are the azaleas gone already?" she asked.

"Azaleas?"

Zee frowned and looked around some more. Ulla had written vivid descriptions of her Tacoma Park neighborhood, about the colorful Victorian houses and azaleas blooming in every yard. Zee wasn't up on architecture, but none of these houses looked the slightest bit Victorian. She backed away.

"What's the matter?" Connor asked.

"This isn't Tacoma Park."

"No. It's called Cabin John. What's wrong?"

"You said you were Ulla's neighbor." He realized then what she was thinking. He was both sorry to have frightened her and impressed with her perceptivity.

"No. I'm sorry. I . . . that wasn't true."

"Who are you?" Zee stepped warily back toward the street.

"It's a little bit complicated."

"Who you *are* is complicated?"

"No. Sorry. I'm . . . an investigator."

"For the police?"

"No. For a private security firm. A company called Chapmans." He took out his wallet and held out his ID.

"Put it on the car," Zee directed. Connor put the card on the trunk of his car then walked back toward his house, leaving plenty of distance between them. Zee picked up the card and examined it.

"How do I know this is real? It could be something you just printed up yourself."

"I would have used a better photo, for one thing." Connor smiled. She wasn't melting beneath the force of his charm. "It's easy enough to check. We're registered with the police. We do corporate security. SeaGenesis is a long-time client."

"Why did you lie about being Ulla's neighbor?"

"It was the easiest explanation. I didn't want to get into details at the service."

"Details of what? What's going on?" Connor hesitated, not wanting to dump his suspicions right out on top of her. She still looked pale and shaken.

"Look, I really am sorry. I didn't intend to deceive you or anything, it just seemed easier under the circumstances. But it is kind of awkward to explain it all shouting across my front yard. Why don't we sit on the porch. I'll get you something to drink and we can talk."

Zee glanced toward the nearby houses and scanned the street.

"We have a chaperon." Connor nodded toward the house next door, where a woman's face was visible through slightly parted curtains. "That's Mrs. Wickham. She'll vouch for me if you like. I cut her grass. She watches my dog."

As if on cue, which she pretty much was since she spent most of the day sitting by the front window, Mrs. Wickham stepped out on her front porch. She pretended to check her mailbox and definitely checked Zee out. She gave a friendly wave and disappeared back inside.

"And my dog likes me," Connor went on innocently. "So I can't be all that bad, can I?" He grinned and Zee felt herself yielding.

"Do you have a portable phone?" Zee asked.

Connor nodded. "I'll bring it outside." He went in to get the phone. He also opened the back door to let Lucy in. The dog immediately bounded through the house and out to the front porch and sat at Zee's feet, gazing up adoringly with caramel-colored eyes. It wasn't the first time Connor had used her charms on a woman, either.

He returned a few minutes later with two glasses of orange juice and the portable phone, which he put on the table next to Zee.

"There, you can call a cab anytime you want. Or 911. Is Zee short for something, or a nickname?" Connor tried to break the ice.

"Zephyr," she replied, not melting much. "Like the wind. Why were you at the funeral?"

Connor sat down on the porch rail across from her.

"You've had a few accidents on Shadow Island in the past year. We have a file of incident reports."

Shit, so that was it. A damn insurance investigator!

"It's a difficult environment," she said cautiously. "And a pioneer project. No one's ever set up a research program like this—collecting, breeding stations, and labs all on the island. It's taken a while to figure some things out, work out the bugs."

"Tell me about the man who was just injured." *They're pissed off about the medevac. The cost of the charter . . .*

"Roddy Taylor. He's our engineer and aquaculturist. He got stung by a couple of scorpion fish. They have poisonous spines on their back."

"Are they common?"

"They're not rare. They're bottom dwellers, and really well camouflaged. Roddy apparently just didn't see them. There were several around the nursery cages."

"But you hadn't seen them there before?"

"No. It did seem unusual, but we don't know enough about them. Episodic congregations might be the norm, I don't know."

"Anything ever happen to you?"

"No. Nothing." *He had the incident reports, best to just be honest.*

"Well, I got caught in a bit of a current last week. I guess Padgette did file an incident report, but it wasn't really a big deal." She told him briefly about being swept away.

"When exactly did this happen?"

"Last week, Wednesday."

Connor remembered the handwritten page in the back of the Sea-Genesis file. Wednesday was the morning after the attack on Fairchild, the same morning when he found the list of accidents. But wasn't there already something about a current on that list?

"What exactly do you do out there?" He shifted tack a little. "I mean, I've read the files, but I'd like to know more."

"Basically we collect specimens and test them for bioactive substances. We're also trying to farm any invertebrates that do prove useful."

"Useful for new drugs?"

"Yes."

"Why farm them? Why not just collect them?"

"The levels of bioactive substances can vary a lot in the wild. And we want to be able to insure a reliable supply if something does turn out to be useful. Ideally, we would work on developing a synthetic version of the drug, but sometimes that isn't possible. Farmed samples would insure production. But it's still a long way off, and may not ever be practical. It's all very experimental."

"What kind of drugs are you looking at?"

"Well, we're studying an enzyme from a starfish right now that might have nerve regeneration properties. Also some anticancer agents, a blood thinner, all sorts of things."

"What was Ulla working on?"

"Cancer mostly, and an analgesic from a sponge. Malaria, too, she was really excited about that. And a couple of AIDS drugs. But we haven't had much luck there so far."

Cancer, heart disease, AIDS, any one of them would be lucrative, Connor thought. But enough to kill for?

"Are you familiar with Cronzene twenty?"

"A little. It's a pollution-eating bacteria."

Connor nodded. "Did you know that SeaGenesis just won a government grant to test Cronzene twenty in the Chesapeake Bay?"

"I heard something about it. But like I said, I deal with marine invertebrates. Bacteria and algae are a whole different world."

"Is it something Ulla would be working on?"

"No. I wouldn't think so. What does this have to do with insurance?"

"Insurance?"

"Isn't that what you're after, worried about all these accidents? Look, Roddy needed to go to the hospital. I know it was expensive . . ."

"I'm not concerned with insurance."

"Then what?"

"Hopefully nothing. Really. It's just the accidents. It's just our job to look into things like that."

Zee sat very still. "And the service for Ulla? You were there . . . why?"

"Just routine. A couple of days ago Dr. Fairchild was threatened at a party. It wasn't serious, the guy was drunk and upset. We're just keeping an eye on things, trying to investigate all possibilities. Look at all the accidents, make sure that's just what they are."

Zee's gaze was piercing and the glass of orange juice trembled in her hand. She put it down.

"And the carjacking?" she said quietly.

"All the evidence points to a random tragic accident. Look, Zee, I'm sorry. I'm just asking questions." Connor got up. "You must be worn out. Let me get the phone book, we'll find you a hotel. There's a Holiday Inn in Bethesda, close to the Metro." He briefly considered offering his guest room but he knew he was already on shaky ground in the trust department. Besides, it was lacking both furniture and drywall. That basically left the couch, or his bed. *Don't even go there . . .* he thought.

Zee glanced at her watch. It was almost one o'clock, ten in California. "Do you mind if I call my mother? I have a calling card."

"Sure, of course."

"I haven't been able to reach her yet since I got to the States. She's a librarian and leaves for work around noon, so if I call now, she'll probably be home."

Connor went inside and found some busy work to give her privacy. He overheard the cheerful tones and imagined a plump, motherly voice at the other end. Then Zee's voice fell silent. He heard the screen door open, and Zee came into the house. She held up a hand, motioning him to wait.

". . . I don't know, Mom. Hang on." She put her hand over the mouthpiece and looked at Connor. "Ulla sent a Federal Express envelope to my mother. She wanted Mom to send it to me on the island with her next care package."

"When?"

"Mom got it two days ago."

"Did she send it yet?"

Zee shook her head and turned back to the phone. "Did you mail the package yet, Mom?"

Connor waited through a long explanation that Zee summed up much more concisely. "No. She was going to pick up some soap I like and make cookies . . ."

"Ask her to overnight it to you."

"Where?"

"The Bethesda FedEx office. You can pick it up."

Zee gave her mother the information. Connor saw the worry in her eyes, heard the forced lightness in her tone.

"Do you have any idea what Ulla might have sent you?" Connor asked once she hung up.

Zee shook her head. "I can't imagine."

"How did you usually correspond?"

Zee tried not to think about his use of the past tense. "SeaGenesis sends us supplies twice a month. They fly everything to Nassau, then a charter service brings them to us. We have a small landing strip."

"No e-mail?"

"Not on the island, no."

"Was there ever any indication that your personal mail was tampered with?"

"Tampered?" She looked skeptical.

"Ulla thought, for some reason, that this package might not get to you through the usual means."

"No. I mean, it might just be for a surprise. Sometimes I send letters on the mail boat. You know, something unexpected. We always used to write, even in grade school when we saw each other every day. Silly things, postcards. It was fun to get mail."

Zee paced the room. She felt restless. Long flights, long hospital waits with Roddy, then the funeral, now this. Now this *what*? What was he saying?

"Your mother got the package two days ago," Connor said slowly. "You know what that means?"

Zee nodded. It meant Ulla mailed it the day she was killed.

Two hours later, after pulling some strings through Chapmans, Connor stood in the hot sun on the police impoundment lot looking at Ulla Raki's car. There were still traces of fingerprint dust around the door handles and a film of dust and pollen now coated the entire car. According to the police report, Ulla had been dragged out of the car and shot on the street. There had been no traces of blood in the car. Connor opened the door and a wave of heat punched at him. He slid into the hot seat. It had been moved all the way back. He sat still and looked around. His hands were sweating inside the latex gloves. Connor sat there quietly. Colors, textures, and odors all told a story like the theme in a symphony. Odor. There was no smell in Ulla's car. It had been closed up for days in the hot sun.

What odors should there be? Perfume? Lab smells? *Hamburgers.* According to the police report, the carjackers had partied in the car, leaving burger wrappers and bottles. Burger King or McDonald's? What brand of malt liquor? It was unlikely they picked up refreshments *before* they snatched the car, so the police should have traced the snacks to nearby stores where someone might remember them. Why wasn't that in the report? And why didn't the car smell of burgers or beer?

The car was clean. The car was *too* clean, he realized. The criminals were sloppy enough to leave their bottles and wrappers in the backseat, but had wiped away all their fingerprints? Or worn gloves the entire time? In a heat wave?

Connor put the key in the ignition and turned the radio on. An orchestral swirl filled the hot car. The next two buttons gave him WAMU and WETA, the two local public radio stations. The final button yielded an all-news station. So these two thugs joyride around for a couple of hours drinking beer and eating burgers and listening to Mozart?

Connor shivered. This might not be a routine little investigation after all. He felt a flicker of chagrin to be getting so charged up. Someone had actually been killed. Ulla Raki, a shy, dedicated scientist, working on what? What could it be? A cure for AIDS or cancer? Ulla had sent something to Zee's mother that night. Was that what the carjackers were after? But she had already dropped the package in the FedEx box before they got to her.

This was getting interesting, a game in a way. He wanted to put the pieces together. And, though he didn't want to admit it, he might impress the hell out of Mickey.

"Where the hell is Connor?" Mickey leaned out of his office, pitching the inquiry in his brother's general direction. Billy was on the phone, busily writing notes. Mickey came over to the cluttered desk and peered over his shoulder.

"He left about an hour ago. He went to look at Ulla Raki's car. I haven't heard from him since then."

"He went where?"

"To look at Ulla Raki's car."

"At her car?" There was a sudden edge in his voice. "What the hell for?"

"Clues." Billy shrugged.

"Clues?"

"Is there an echo in here all of a sudden?" Billy dropped the pencil, swiveled around, and faced Mickey. "Connor wanted to look over the car. He came to me, asked me to make a call and set it up."

"You should have cleared it with me first!" Mickey frowned.

"He's taking initiative. That's what you've always bugged him about, isn't it? SeaGenesis is a big account. He's being thorough."

"SeaGenesis is a delicate account. He's being a pain in the ass." Mickey checked his watch, glanced around the office.

"Oh come on, cut him some slack, Mickey. You know he can't ride a desk. You're too hard on him. Always have been."

"He always needed it."

"Maybe. Anyway, he's been doing good work lately. As a matter of fact, I'd say he's been downright diligent." Billy tapped a pencil on the fan of papers on the desk. "You know, I bet there's probably some kind of syndrome or something for this."

"What this?"

"When you bust your balls for so long trying to fix something and then suddenly one day it's fixed and you don't want to admit it. Connor's been doing good work, Mickey. Why don't you give him a chance?"

"You been watching talk shows, Billy? If Connor Gale ever got his ass on the straight and narrow I'd be the first one to cheer."

Su Thom sat up and rubbed his eyes. His hands were shaking. His whole body was trembling. He had done it. It was still hard to believe, even with the evidence visible right there under the microscope. There they were, in the gut of the fourth mosquito he dissected: tiny threads like strands of gossamer. These were the sporozoites, the microscopic darts of the malaria parasite that would carry the infection. He had done it. Hundreds of mosquitos, plumped full of malaria, ready to deliver.

He got up and paced the room. Now he would really have to decide what to do. The plan, born from anger and frustration, should have burned itself out by now. The original idea had been . . . had been what? Some feeble scheme. To breed the mosquitos and infect them, to have a whole cage of them ready, then show them to Fairchild. Just show him what could be. Show the world. Mail a few to the president.

But now they were actually *ready*. Now he had the power. He was a rational man. He was a scientist, dedicated to curing, not killing. But now all that had changed. Ulla was dead. Why did she have to die? Why hadn't he been more careful? How could he have let her find him injecting himself with popeye? It didn't have to happen this way. She wouldn't have taken the serum if he hadn't been so stupid.

Since Ulla's murder, the world had stalled for Su Thom. The sun shone and people laughed in cafés and cursed in traffic and watered their lawns and ironed summer dresses as if nothing had changed. Day passed day and breath followed breath with obscene indifference. There was nothing left for him now but this one task. He walked over to the cage and touched the screen. He toyed with the latch. He looked at the window. His silver dragons were ready. Inside each tiny gut, the pearly oocysts had incubated intense nuclear-cytoplasmic reorganizations of matter and now each tiny *Anopheles* held thousands of infectious sporozoites. More simply put, each mosquito was a disease-bearing bomb.

He unlatched the window and pushed it open. The hot night air drifted in, heavy with the smell of raw dirt and freshly dug clay. He caught his reflection in the darkened basement window and realized he no longer knew who he was, or what his intent had been. It was as if he had split in two, the one self still calm and rational, going to work every day, and the other self screaming, always on the brink of rage.

Helpless fury simmering beneath outward obedience. That was the way of his life. Since he was a small child he had stood by helplessly for one abuse after another. When the war ended they were enemies of the people, an American soldier's whore and her bastard son. They were sent to a camp where the women worked all the time in the fields, then sat for hours on the packed dirt in the hot sun while soldiers yelled at them. Su Thom was only a toddler, too young to know what was happening at first. His mother, Lei, was probably no more than twenty. Su Thom knew she was very beautiful, but he did not know why the captain of the camp looked at her the way he did, or why she was summoned from their hut in the middle of the night. Sometimes she came back with little bits of meat for him to eat.

They spent two years in that camp; then this captain was transferred out. His lust had kept Lei fairly healthy, and he had even grown somewhat fond of her. The other officers already had women and he knew that if Lei were left alone now, she faced a difficult time, so as a token of his affection, he got her out of the camp. He sold her to a brothel in Bangkok.

In some ways, it was a happy time. There was plenty of food for once and the other women were nice to him. He knew what was going on now, he knew what a whore was, but he learned to close it away in the secret place of his mind and go on with his work. Serve the tea, scrub the floors, and pick up all the towels, towels wet and dank with the ashy smell of sperm and sweat. But then his mother got pregnant, and when she began to show, they were thrown out.

It was another accidental fortune, though, as the conscience of the United States was starting to prick over the war babies littered throughout Vietnam. She registered Su Thom as the son of an American soldier. One of the other prostitutes had family in a village near Phuket, and she sent Lei and Su Thom to live with them while they waited. It was there that the malaria came, burning through the overcrowded village, wringing its bloody hands over so many souls. Stealing his mother. Stealing his brother. A few months later, the young Su Thom had a new life, a new country, a new family.

His adoptive family had been good to him. They had taught him to speak English and play Twister and decorate a Christmas tree. They loved him like a real son and though he could never accept them as real parents, he pretended well. He hoped his deed would not cause them any pain. But he was not an American. He was a bastard child of a bitter war who had lost his real family to a disease Americans cared nothing about. The old bitterness had lingered, sleeping for all these years beneath the new life, rocked into quietude by his easy American life, awakened finally by the promise of popeye, and now fanned into madness over Ulla's death.

He listened to the quiet buzz of his mosquitos. The night was warm with a gentle breeze that would carry them far. It was just dusk; people would still be outside, lingering around backyard barbecues, or walking out of a movie, pleasantly surprised to find it balmy, stopping for a drink at an outdoor café. The very thought of it gave him a warm satisfaction. But no. That wasn't the way. He resisted the urge and pulled the window shut. Not yet.

He would give Adam Fairchild one last chance. He would show him what he had. Send him one of these silver dragons and let him see how easy it could be. Let him feel the horror. Fairchild would authorize primate studies on popeye and Ulla's death would not be in vain. Sea-Genesis would be lavish with funding and he could carry on her work. Then no other little boys would ever have to dive for coins and come home to a corpse, or hold their little brothers in their arms as their bodies burned with fever.

9

After the spartan conditions on Shadow Island, the Holiday Inn was like a sultan's palace. A bed wide as an aircraft carrier, huge fluffy towels, and all the hot water she wanted. Shadow Island had been intended as a luxury resort, but the developer went bankrupt before he got to the luxury part. Zee opened one of the little bottles of wine from the minibar and filled the tub to within an inch of overflow. But the indulgence failed to soothe her. She was exhausted but also restless. She dried off and wrapped herself in the towels. She hadn't brought much with her in the way of clothes. She lay on the bed and stared at the telephone. She wanted to call Ulla's parents but couldn't bear to right now. Especially right now. What could she say? The whole world felt tilted and confused. Who was this Connor person? *I'm just asking questions . . .* Yeah right.

Sleep came quickly, but brought no peace. Her dreams were chaotic and intense; an underwater garden became a forest of spiny, monstrous fish. She was walking through the hallways of SeaGenesis looking for Ulla, but it was an endless maze, the walls and floor were slippery and blindingly bright. She and Ulla were girls sitting on Ulla's bed with its pink satin spread, reading teen magazines, then the bed began to float away. The magazine pages flew away and littered the water, and sharks leaped up to eat them. Caught in a current, they were spinning out to sea, the pink fabric floating around them like a water lily. Then Ulla's body was wrapped in the pink satin and burning on a funeral pyre. The flames roared but Ulla's body wouldn't burn. The heat was intense, and Zee backed away, into the arms of a man standing behind her. His body was muscular and strong. Zee felt her own body stirring with pure lust, craving sex, hard, relentless, bruising sex. She turned into the arms, hungry for the heat of his body even as the funeral flames singed the back of her neck.

She half woke throughout the dreams, panicked, aroused, confused. When Connor picked her up at ten the next morning, she felt groggy and hyper at the same time. And slightly embarrassed, as if somehow he would know by looking at her what she had done with him in her dreams.

He drove to the Federal Express office and waited in the car while Zee picked up the package, a flat, cushioned envelope. He watched her open it, look inside, and pull out a letter. She sat on a chair and read it. She read it twice, then folded it up and put it in the back pocket of her jeans. She came out and got in the car, holding the package as if it weighed twenty pounds.

"Where to now?" Connor said.

"I'm not sure."

"You can use my computer if you like. To look at the disks."

"What makes you think there are disks in here?"

"What else would it be?" He smiled, trying to put her at ease. "It's too flat for soap, doesn't smell like cookies. What else? A necklace? Some little thing? Anything else you would have pulled it out. I'm guessing computer disks."

"I have to think."

"OK." Connor started the car. "But you know I have to inform the police about any evidence I come across in a possible homicide case."

Zee glared at him, her face tight with anger, then she turned away. Her eyes filled with tears and her hands began to shake.

"Zee," he said gently. "I searched Ulla's car yesterday. I found things that make me doubt the official story. I don't think the carjacking was a random accident."

"You think someone killed her."

"Yes." They sat silently for several minutes. "If what she sent you gives us any clue, it's important," Connor finally said. "If she was in some kind of trouble, I can help."

"What is your obligation to SeaGenesis?" she asked. "What would you have to do if you found something out?"

"It would depend on what it was."

"Did you tell your boss or anyone I was going to get this package from Ulla today?"

"No."

"Why not?"

Connor looked out the window and shook his head. "I guess partly because I'm not all that good with the whole chain of command thing. But I guess mostly because if this is a big case I want the credit. If it's really nothing, I don't want to look like an ass."

"What if I decide just to keep these disks and not tell anyone what's on them?"

"Would I rat on you?"

"Yeah."

"Look at the disks. Then we'll talk."

They drove to his house and Connor left Zee alone with the computer while he played Frisbee with Lucy in the back yard. When Zee came out, twenty minutes later, all the effort of maintaining composure was evident on her face, in the set of her jaw, the tilt of her chin.

"She sent me a copy of some data, that's all. From a study she was doing on one of our organisms. She knew I would be interested."

"Can I see it?"

"It's just numbers and formulas. Stuff like that. It wouldn't mean anything to you."

"You're not really a very good liar, Zee."

"Well, maybe you're not really much of an investigator. If it wasn't really a carjacking, the police will find out. I mean, this is the twenty-first century, there's evidence. There's DNA and crime scene analysis and . . . and fingerprints."

"There are also cover-ups," Connor said. She pushed past him toward the door.

"Thanks for the ride. I'll get a cab back to the hotel."

"Wait a minute. Can't go without this." She turned. Her hotel key card appeared between his fingers like an ace from up his sleeve.

"Where did you get that?" She snatched it away.

"It was in your *other* back pocket," Connor said. "Not the one you put the letter in." Zee paled and felt for the letter. "It's still there. I didn't take it," Connor went on. "I wanted to show you could trust me."

"By *picking my pocket?*"

"By *not*. By showing you I could have easily taken the letter and didn't. By—I'm sorry, it was the best I could think of at the moment. But you have to trust someone, Zee. Would you rather go to the police? I don't know what's in that letter, but I'm guessing Ulla is telling you some things that you might not want the world to know. But if you'd rather go to the police, or to someone at SeaGenesis, I'll take you right now."

Zee knew he was calling her bluff. She felt confused and frightened and more confused. She couldn't show the letter to the police, or to anyone else. But she couldn't keep it to herself, either.

"What has Dr. Fairchild said about Ulla being . . . about . . . what you think?" She tested a new direction.

"I haven't told him yet."

"Why not?"

"Right now I only have suspicions."

"Wouldn't he be someone you would question? If you thought her death was related to her work at SeaGenesis?"

"You would think so." In his tone there was invitation; he knew what she was really probing for, and he was offering. They were circling around trust now, like wary dancers.

"The letter . . . it would hurt Ulla's reputation," Zee said, spilling it out before she changed her mind. "And mine, if I don't go to Fairchild with it, and I *can't* go to him, because of what's here. Oh shit, just read it."

Connor took the letter and leaned against the deck railing. Zee went inside. He heard her splashing water in the bathroom.

Dear Zee,

　　Enclosed find copies of all my research on popeye and malaria. I apologize for the jumble of this letter, but I want to get this sent tonight. As you will see in these reports, the drug has had quite amazing results so far. But something strange is going on. I received your letter yesterday and learned that you have been sending us regular shipments of popeye, yet none of it has been coming to my lab.

This morning I checked with inventory, and they found nothing logged in since April. Then this afternoon, Dr. Fairchild asked me to turn over my lab books and files on popeye. I have known for some time that SeaGenesis was not eager to pursue this but I never expected to have my work confiscated. Sorry, I am terribly upset right now, hard to explain.

I was sure I had enough to convince Fairchild to go ahead with primate testing, but he refuses. He claims there are other drugs that are more important.

Now here is what I have done. I have an uncle in India. I think he would be able to arrange primate testing over there. I have held onto a small sample of popeye, which I will send him. I hesitate even to tell you my plan as it puts you in an ethical dilemma. But if popeye proves effective in primate testing, I want to know that we will have all your data available, where to collect the sponge, how to process it, etc. So far we haven't had any success in synthesizing it.

I am probably overreacting and upset, but I don't know what to think anymore. My lab assistant has become even more obsessive about this, and I want to keep him out of it. Why would Fairchild be so against this? I know there are financial considerations, but since the research is so preliminary right now that shouldn't be a concern. I just don't know what to think.

I can't wait to see you in person next month. I'm sure it will all have settled down by then, but I am eager for your perspective, advice, whatever insight you might have on how to proceed with this. Right now I am sending you copies of all the data for safekeeping. Sending it to your mother seemed the best way. Anyway, during the time it has taken to write this I have settled down somewhat and am almost embarrassed at my overreaction. But I will go put this in the box before I lose my nerve. Good-bye for now. We can talk more when I come to visit.

Love, Ulla

Connor read it through twice. He wasn't sure what to think. Ulla discovered supplies of a drug were being waylaid, had her research halted, stole some samples, and wound up dead. But malaria? Zee came back outside, looked at him warily.

"Well?"

"I thought there already was a cure for malaria."

"There are various drugs, but a lot of them aren't working anymore and most of them never worked a hundred percent anyway. It's a tough disease to deal with."

"Why?"

"Well, what do you know about malaria?"

"It's a tropical disease, you get it from mosquitos."

"It isn't really tropical, although that's where it remains a big prob-lem. We used to have it all over the United States. It was pretty common until fairly recently, the forties maybe. The disease itself is caused by a parasite carried by the mosquito. I don't know a whole lot more about it myself, except that the parasite has a complicated life cycle. It develops partly in the mosquito, partly in a host animal, or human."

"So why hasn't it been cured by now? Why no vaccine?"

"The problem in developing a cure for something like malaria is that a drug might be effective against one stage but not another. And then, of course, like anything, the organism is always changing and evolving. It grows more and more resistant to any drug you throw at it. What Ulla thinks she has here is a treatment that works at every stage of the dis-ease."

"How?"

"She isn't sure. Wasn't sure," Zee corrected sadly. "Ulla suspected that popeye interferes with an essential protein that the parasite needs to metabolize hemoglobin. Starves it, basically."

"Why would SeaGenesis want to suppress this?"

"I don't know." Zee leaned back in the chair, frowning. "Malaria, diseases like that, are not exactly high in the ranks for any commercial lab."

"Why not?"

"Money, basically. Ulla is right about the profit aspect. I hate to sound cynical, but the fact is, drug development is guided more by the inconveniences of the privileged than the needs of the world. I mean, it's not like there's some overt conspiracy," she went on evenly. "Just some cold practical realities. Basic capitalism. Pharmacology is a business. It costs several million dollars and can take ten years to bring a new drug to market. For every profitable success, there are hundreds of costly failures. Then when you do actually market a successful drug, you have a limited time to hold exclusive patent rights. After that, anyone who can figure out your formula can market a generic version and you're out of luck." Her tone was regretful, but matter-of-fact.

"So this popeye could wind up costing more to develop than it would be worth?"

"Infinitely more." Zee nodded. "Let's say SeaGenesis puts in the time and money, and we're talking maybe half a billion dollars, to actually bring popeye to market, only then it costs a hundred bucks a dose. Your market is predominantly Third World, where a hundred dollars might be half of someone's yearly income. You sell it at that price and the whole world accuses you of gouging. You don't market it at all and you're practically accused of murder."

"So, either way SeaGenesis loses." It was still a pretty lame motive for murder. Connor couldn't help feeling disappointed.

Zee rocked back in the chair. "Yes, but on the other hand, if popeye really works as well as Ulla thinks it does, there should be all sorts of support behind it. I mean, it's not like there's this worldwide conspiracy to encourage the spread of malaria, it's more just general neglect. If we had a promising cure, the World Health Organization would be behind it, the United Nations, the U.S. military. They would love a good malaria cure. SeaGenesis would be rolling in glory, even if we didn't make a huge profit."

"And there's no possibility of a huge profit?"

"Realistically? No. Not unless malaria suddenly becomes a problem here."

"Could it?"

"I don't know. I don't think so, because we probably would have seen it come back by now. Or at least show up now and then. I don't know enough about it."

"Who else would have known Ulla was working on this?"

"Almost anybody in the company could have, in a casual way," Zee said. "As far as access to her actual data, just her lab assistant. And of course Fairchild and anyone else on the board who read her requests for further study."

"You guys on Shadow Island were the only ones providing the popeye?"

Zee nodded.

"Who actually handled the shipments?"

"Arthur Padgette, my colleague." Zee frowned.

"What is it?"

"Nothing, really."

"Tell me anyway. Even if it doesn't seem important."

"Well, a couple of weeks ago, Padgette was busy with something and the supply plane had come in early and wanted to leave to avoid a storm. I started loading the samples myself, and when he came in he jumped all over me. Said it was his job. I didn't think much of it at the time. Padgette is a little testy about turf."

"That shipment contained popeye?"

"Almost two liters."

"Tell me about Padgette."

"What about him? He's a *scientist*."

"So was Dr. Frankenstein."

"Padgette and I have our differences," she said carefully. "He's a decent scientist, but not aggressive and not terribly creative. His own career, I think, is stagnating. Shadow Island is a bit of a banishment for him."

"But not for you?"

"God no. I'm thirty-four and supposed to be doing stuff like this. I'm a marine biologist. Shadow Island is as good as it gets for me at this stage of my career. Padgette is forty-seven. He's a cellular biologist with no real interest in marine organisms until SeaGenesis hired him." Connor paced the deck, trying to make sense of it all.

"Would you send biological samples by Federal Express?" Connor asked.

"If they were packaged correctly, sure."

"But you wouldn't drop them in a night pickup box, would you?"

"No. What are you thinking?"

"Ulla acted quickly. For some reason, she made a spur of the moment decision to steal the samples and send you the disks. Let's say someone knew, or suspected what she was doing and wanted to prevent it. If they followed her to the FedEx box but then saw her with a flat envelope, they would know the serum wasn't in it. Maybe they wanted to intercept the envelope, too, but couldn't. Maybe there were other people around or something. But they figure she still might have the vials of popeye with her in the car."

"So someone carjacked her to get the popeye?"

Connor nodded.

"But why? She only had a small amount. And according to her letter, someone has been intercepting much larger amounts for months."

"I don't know. Maybe whoever's been hoarding it just didn't want any of it to get out, maybe there was something special about this batch." Connor slid back the screen door. "Come on."

"Where are we going?"

"Ulla's house. Either she had the serum with her that night and they got it, or she didn't have it with her, and we might be able to find it."

"Find it how?"

"Go inside and look around."

"Isn't that sort of illegal?"

"You're her friend, aren't you?"

"I don't usually go around breaking into my friends' houses!"

"Look, Zee, Ulla's dead. I'm sorry, but there's nothing we can do about that now except try and find out who killed her. She believed she had an important new drug. Maybe she did. Maybe it was important enough to have got her killed."

Connor parked on the street a few houses down from Ulla's. They waited a few minutes, observing the street. It was a hot afternoon and anybody who was home would be inside with the air-conditioning on.

"Are you sure we should be doing this?" Zee asked doubtfully. "What if we do find something? Wouldn't this mess up any kind of evidence for the police?"

"The police have already checked the house and cleared it. Her father was allowed in to pick up some of her things."

"So wouldn't they have found the serum? The police or her father?"

"No one has reported it. And she smuggled it out of SeaGenesis, remember. She probably wouldn't have left it just lying around. Her father only took her personal papers." He gave her a puzzled look. "I thought you were close to the family. Haven't you talked to them?"

"I did call from Miami when I first got there, but her father was already on his way here. We just missed each other."

"He told the police he wanted to return to San Diego so the family could hold a funeral there," Connor explained. "Someone will come back to sort out the house later."

"Lele probably," Zee said sadly. "Her oldest brother."

"It looks quiet." Connor opened the car door. "You ready?" Zee nodded. Ulla's house looked like a fairy tale cottage, with its bright garden and arched doorway draped in wisteria vines. Ulla had sent her pictures, when she bought the house, but there were so many more flowers now.

"How are we going to get in?"

Connor paused, thinking not how to do it so much as how not to let on that he was so good at doing it.

"Maybe she's hidden a spare key someplace," he suggested. As he searched all the logical places for a spare key, Connor considered his other options. There was a good deadbolt lock, attached, as was common, to a flimsy door frame that would take one good kick to break, but the idea here was a gentle entry. He led Zee around the back, his practiced eye quickly assessing a number of possibilities.

"There we go." He saw to his great relief that the bathroom window was not only louvered, but sheltered by the large bushes that snuggled all around the house. A burglar's dream. He reached up and easily wiggled the panes open, then deftly removed each one from its brackets. The window was narrow and high off the ground. Connor looked for a foothold, but Zee just stepped up and lifted her knee as if he were a groom about to help her mount a horse.

"Come on," she whispered. "You can't fit through there."

She had a point, so he cupped his hands under the bent knee and boosted her up. Zee wiggled easily through the small window then went around and opened the back door for Connor.

The bungalow was small, with a narrow hallway leading to the living room, and two small bedrooms and bath in the rear. The kitchen was in the middle of the house. Across from that was a door to the basement. The shades were all pulled and the low sun gave the room a dark burnish. Zee stood in the living room looking around her friend's home. A few Indian carvings were posed on a little table and an elaborately embroidered Kashmir shawl was casually draped over the arm of a chair, as if Ulla had just been sitting there with it wrapped around her a moment ago. Zee felt immensely sad.

Connor went right to the kitchen and opened the refrigerator. There wasn't much inside, a few cartons of yogurt, some oranges, half a bag of pita bread, bottles of salad dressing, jars of chutney and jam and mustard inside the door. It didn't take long to look through all the shelves, the vegetable crisper, and the butter compartment.

"Would it have to be refrigerated?" he asked.

"It should be. Consistent cool temperature at least."

"Well, there's nothing here." He tried the cupboards, then looked under the sink. Still no vials. They went into the living room.

"Why don't you go through her room," Connor suggested. "Check the drawers, think quick hiding place." Zee nodded and went back down the hall. Connor walked slowly around the living room, surveying it from every angle. *The thing about most people is, they don't have a whole lot of imagination as far as where they hide things*, his father would say as he walked through the rooms of a strange house, sweeping a hand beneath the mattress, ticking off a dozen usual hiding places within the first minute. But Ulla was extremely intelligent and certainly creative. According to Zee, she had pursued a rather elegant course of study for this new malaria drug.

But something was wrong. Something about the room. He had never met Ulla, and didn't know where things were supposed to be, but he had a clear sense that everything was just a little askew. Why the shawl on the chair? It had been above ninety for a week, certainly she wouldn't have been using it. Connor looked over the book titles. They were mostly scientific books, volumes on biochemistry, physics, medicine.

"There's nothing in her room or office," Zee said as she returned. "No lab book. Nothing of use."

"Someone has already searched this house."

"Her father."

"No. Someone looking for something specific."

"How do you know?"

Connor went back to the bookcase and ran a finger along the spines of the books. The volumes were arranged by subject, but also alphabetically by author. On each shelf, however, the book that should have been first in the row, was at the end. Someone had pulled a book out, checked each subsequent one by moving it along the shelf, and replaced the first book at the end.

Someone had searched the house. So someone knew, or suspected, that Ulla had stolen the serum. If she had taken it with her the night she was killed, it would have been found in the car and no one would have searched the house. So the searchers either found it here or they didn't. If they had, how would he know? If they hadn't, where would it be?

It should have been in the refrigerator. He closed his eyes and pictured the colors and shapes inside. More patterns assembled themselves. The house was clean and orderly. The kitchen was very clean. *But something about the refrigerator* . . . Suddenly he knew. There was a dribble of salad dressing dried on the side of the bottle and a crusty smudge around the lid of the mustard.

Connor grabbed a startled Zee by the arm and led her back to the refrigerator. He opened the door and took out the mustard. He found a colander, turned the water on and gently emptied the mustard into it.

The water rinsed away the yellow paste and he plucked out a small vial carefully encased in plastic wrap. He rolled the tube in a dish towel to dry it, then unwrapped the plastic.

"This is it," Zee said, picking up the vial. It was labeled Capjen88, followed by reference numbers. Zee looked at Connor with suspicion. "How did you know to look there?"

"We looked everywhere else." He shrugged. Zee flung the door open again and began to hand him bottles of salad dressing and jars of relish.

"Get the yogurt, too," Connor suggested as he emptied the jam in the colander. The jam was empty but the salad dressing yielded another vial. The colors ran together in the sink and the smells mingled in the stuffy air.

Suddenly they heard the crash of glass breaking. Connor turned toward Zee, thinking a bottle had fallen, but nothing had broken in the kitchen. Then the house blew up.

The explosion rocked the foundation. Connor and Zee were lifted on a wave of pressure and hurled against the counter. The ceiling fan crashed to the floor, two of its blades breaking across Connor's back with a brittle crack. The basement door was blown apart and smoke began to boil up from below. Zee was dazed for a few seconds, then the terror hit. The house was on fire. The basement stairs glowed a deep orange with flame shadows.

"Stay down!" Connor shouted. The noise of the fire was more intense than the heat. It was a sharp, awful sound, snarling and crackling like monsters in the forest. Connor crawled up beside her. The kitchen had no door and the narrow hallway was already filling with smoke. He peeked out in the scant layer below the thickening smoke and saw tongues of flame already shooting up along the wall in the front of the house.

"Back door!" he shouted and grabbed for Zee's hand.

"Wait! The serum!" She pulled away. "Popeye . . ." Her throat closed over the one word.

"Shit!" Connor felt for the smooth surface of the refrigerator door, then slid his hand up and pulled on the handle. A beam of yellow light spilled out into the smokey room. The cold air tumbled down and pooled around their feet like a witchy waterfall. Zee scrambled toward the bright square of light. Amidst the thickening smoke, the interior of the refrigerator looked insanely beautiful. She grabbed the hem of her T-shirt and swept the remaining jars and bottles into it. Connor took a deep breath, stood up and grabbed the other three vials from the colander in the sink and stuffed them in his pockets.

"Let's go!"

The smoke was beginning to fill the kitchen. The hallway was already dense with it. Suddenly they felt the floor rumbling and another explosion shook the foundation. A river of fire roared up from the basement, blocking their escape. Connor ducked back into the kitchen. The old house seemed to scream, and Zee felt the hairs on her neck singe.

A chunk of ceiling crashed in the living room and the cabinets along one wall cracked halfway off. Chunks of debris fell all around. So far the enclosed kitchen had protected them, but the smoke was getting too thick.

"Out the window," Connor gasped. "Over the sink." They filled their lungs in the dwindling layer of clear air, then climbed up on the counter. Connor yanked on the window. It creaked up a few inches, but the old wooden frame was warped. Connor pounded at the frame but could not break it out with his hand. Standing on the narrow counter top there was no room to kick at it.

"Stay there!" he shouted to Zee. He jumped back down to the floor and grabbed the fallen ceiling fan. The flames were licking down the walls on either side of the kitchen entrance. The heat was intense. He kicked the blades off and picked up the heavy fan motor.

"Watch out!" That was the last of his breath, and he fought against drawing in a lungful of deadly smoke. Zee hunched away, crouching against a cabinet. Her foot hit a toaster oven, sending it off the counter with a tinny clang. How long did they have now? Three seconds? Ten? Faintly, through the roar of the fire, Zee heard the beeping smoke alarms go dead.

Connor hurled the heavy motor at the kitchen window. The motor broke the glass and cracked the wooden frame. Connor climbed up and smacked it again. The window frame broke apart.

"Come on!" Zee uncurled from her protective crouch, still clutching the jars to her chest. Her foot slipped into the sink. She lost her balance. Connor caught her. There were a few endless seconds when she felt suspended in midair, then suddenly she felt Connor pushing her toward the window. She also felt him falling back into the burning kitchen. Zee fell blindly toward the ground. The jars tumbled unbroken around her. She gulped a breath of the fresh, clean air. She could hear sirens. She tried to get up but her legs had gone to jelly. She willed her body to move, rolled over and looked for Connor. Flames were now shooting out the kitchen window!

"Connor!" she screamed. A shower of sparks erupted from the house. Zee threw up her arms and turned away. Then he landed beside her. Connor coughed and gasped for breath. The sleeve of his shirt was on fire. Zee smacked at it. She pushed him over, smothering the flames in the grass. Burning chunks of house were falling all around them.

"Are you alive? Are you all right?" Zee cried. Connor jumped up, adrenaline still pumping.

"Come on," he gasped, pulling at her arm. He picked up the scattered jars and began stuffing them in the pockets of his jeans, coughing and spitting. "Can you walk?"

Zee nodded. A tub of yogurt had cracked open and Zee saw another vial of popeye in the creamy mess. She snatched it up. Connor saw a woman in a yellow housedress running to the fence of the adjoining yard. Fire engines were screaming down the street. Police would be here soon. He didn't want to have to explain why they had been inside when a fire erupted and were now escaping with pockets full of condiments.

They climbed over a low hedge into the next yard, then walked, nonchalantly, he hoped, toward the street. The neighbors were all distracted with the drama at hand. Certainly, some had seen them in the backyard, at least the woman in the yellow dress had, but by the time questions were asked, they would be long gone. His car was almost blocked in by the fire engines, but Connor managed to back it out, turn around, and drive away.

10

C onnor stood dumbly inside the front door to his own house. How was it that in the movies the hero was always getting slammed into walls, bounced off cars, beaten over the head, dropped from heights, punched and karated, and could still bounce right back up for more? Here he was, caught in a simple explosion and fire, crunched by a few falling walls, rescuing only one damsel in distress, who didn't even weigh all that much, and he was just drained. Various pains were beginning to sting and throb all over.

"Are you okay?" Zee asked. Connor nodded, but now he felt that he could just collapse any second. He saw that she was trembling. Her face, probably a reflection of his own, was smeared with soot and grime. Scrapes and cuts had dried to a dull red and crumbles of plaster clung in her curls. She still held the vials of popeye in the hem of her T-shirt.

"What . . . what do we do now?" Her voice was tight and small.

"I don't know. Clean up. Have a drink. And I'm really hungry. Are you hungry?"

"We have to call the police."

"No. We have to call Pizza Hut."

"Connor, be serious! Something *exploded* in that house."

"I know." He went into the kitchen and opened the refrigerator door. There was only one jar of mustard and that held only a smear in the bottom. They would need a new hiding place.

"What caused it?" Zee pressed. He took the jars out of his pockets and set them on the countertop.

"I don't know."

"I thought you were supposed to be an investigator or something."

"I don't do explosions."

"Well, then, let's call someone who does!" She knew she was sounding hysterical, but couldn't help it; she was feeling that way, too. "We have to call the police, Connor."

He knew he should be more comforting, but he didn't know what to say. He hated that he had put her in danger, almost got her killed. He tried to keep his voice steady.

"Look. With a fire like that, the police are going to look for arson. If it was some kind of bomb, there will be evidence. If we go calling the police right now, they'll want to know what we were doing in Ulla's house. The carjacking definitely looks like a sham, but the police aren't pursuing it. I'm not eager to go telling anyone that we have what someone was willing to kill for, sitting on my kitchen counter right now."

"You really think Ulla was murdered?"

"I don't know if someone actually set out to kill her, or if things just went wrong, but I know it wasn't a simple random carjacking. Someone wants this serum."

Zee leaned against the doorframe. It was all so bizarre.

"How did you know where it was?"

"We looked everywhere else."

"No. It's more than that. How did you know how to break in so easily? And the way you went through that house, like you knew where everything was supposed to be?"

"Just lucky." Connor reached over and brushed some bits of plaster out of her hair.

"Stop." Zee pushed his hand away. "This is not some game or something. I don't know what's going on, and I don't feel very trusting right now."

Connor half wanted her not to trust him, to just go away now and be out of it. The explosion had changed things. She was right, it wasn't just a game anymore.

"Look, I'm sorry. I know some things because I work for a security company. And I know others because my father was a burglar. And I was, too, as a kid."

"A burglar."

"Yeah."

"Oh. Well, that's reassuring." She rocked back and forth a little and examined a burned place on her shirt.

"But now I work for the good guys," Connor said, with all the assurance he could muster. "And I want to take this to Chapmans first. We have connections in the police department. If we just go calling 911 right now, it all gets messy. If someone is really after this popeye stuff, they aren't average criminals." *Your average criminal isn't going to be breaking into a biotech lab at all. Anyone with the brains to know what they would want to steal from SeaGenesis would also be able to figure how to get it with some ease. The weak points are all human.*

"Why don't we get cleaned up and relax. Then I'll tell you anything you want to know about me. You can take a bath. There's a robe on the back of the door. Give me your clothes and I'll throw them in the washer. Or don't," he added quickly. "Keep them. Whatever you want."

"What are you going to do?"

"Think. Call my boss. And order a pizza. Do you like anchovies?"

Her head felt enormous. This was all too crazy.

"No . . ."

"Okay. No anchovies then."

"No, I mean we can't just . . ."

"We can't figure it out right now," Connor said firmly. He steered her toward the bathroom and pulled the robe off the door. Zee did feel pretty collapsible right now. She took the robe and let him push her gently into the bathroom without further protest.

Connor felt relieved. He needed time alone to figure this out. There was no doubt that the fire had been deliberate, the only questions were timing and targets. Did they just happen to arrive at the wrong time, or had they been targeted? These little vials of mystery serum. He picked one up and held it up to the light. What would make someone kill for this? A cure for AIDS maybe, but malaria? And according to Zee, popeye was not even close to being ready for human testing. Who would risk so much for an unknown?

How was Adam Fairchild involved? Lofton was angry over losing out on the EPA contract, but would he do something this drastic to get back at him?

Connor rubbed the sides of his head, which were starting to pound. He noticed for the first time the sickening stench of smoke on him. The basement bathroom was still unfinished, but the shower at least was hooked up. He got a towel and went downstairs. He was about to throw the clothes away, when he wondered if there might be some sort of evidence on them. Residue, or bomb dust or something? Explosives was an area he knew little about. He rolled the clothes up and stuck them in a trash bag. One of the uncles specialized in arson; maybe he would know. The hot water hurt his burns, but after examining them in the mirror, he decided none were too bad.

It was almost dark outside when he finished showering. The night was steamy. He opened the patio door and let Lucy in, who promptly began an excited sniffing of the house, intrigued by the confusion of smells that they had dragged in with them.

He opened a bottle of wine, poured two glasses, and carried one to the bathroom, where he was about to knock, when he considered she probably wasn't ready to have him traipsing into her bath. He could hear her moving around in the tub, the faint swishings through the door un-expectedly erotic.

He wrenched his thoughts back to the immediate and picked up the phone. On the fourth ring Mickey's answering machine clicked on and after a couple of seconds' pause Connor hung up. He didn't want to leave a message that might worry Lois and couldn't think what else to say. It could wait until morning. He pressed the disconnect, hit the first button on autodial, and ordered a pizza.

In the seemingly tranquil world of a coral reef, it is easy to forget there is a drama of survival going on. On the African plain, life is more visceral. Lions stalk, chase, leap, and bite. There is a thunder of panicked hooves, terrified squeals, and the roar of attack. The cheetah thrums with bloodlust. The falcon screams out of the sky. When the cloud of dust finally settles, the meal is a bloody feast of ripped haunches and raw flesh.

But in the sea, death is quiet and quick. One minute you are grazing your way from coral to sponge to sandy bottom, the next you are sucked into the void, the last flash of life a soft slide into oblivion. The predator remains impassive, there is no triumph in his cold fish eyes. It is a bloodless death, but no less a death. The Cambrian era, when the oceans first blossomed with life, was a far gentler time. Early creatures were soft and docile. Flagellates drifted unconcerned and pleosponges were one great soft underbelly. The coral polyp was just another free-drifting hobo in the great primordial stew.

But then came the fierce, toothy dawns. Primitive nibblers were re-placed by voracious devourers. God said let there be fish, and lo there were fish, and then lo there were bigger fish, and the big fish ate the little fish, and the drama began, the universal struggle to be something else in life besides food. Creatures of the sea developed defenses. Crabs hammered out suits of armor, clams built shells, crawled inside, and shut the doors. Starfish grew each new arm more crusty than the last. The soft-bodied corals put down roots and began to build little shells of calcium around their vital pulps, retreating during the day and emerging at night to graze upon floating creatures less clever than themselves. And so there is one goal for every creature, from the gazelle on the Serengeti to the anemone on the coral reef: *Do not be lunch.*

But among the disguises and tricks, the hard shells and spiny bodies of reef-dwellers, there remain a huge variety of soft, slow, seemingly unpro-tected creatures. Sea cucumbers and sponges flaunt their softness, sitting plump and appealing as cupcakes. Tunicates, aggressive as Jell-O, sway colorfully in the currents. Little tube worms blossom out of the coral, look-ing as frail as orchids on a battlement. But all these soft-bodied creatures carry within their flesh a chemical arsenal.

"So the theory behind grinding up every slimy little thing in the sea," Zee explained, "is what's poison to a predator is simply chemical activity to us and, potentially, medicine."

Connor had to wrench himself back to reality, having easily been lost in the sweep of eons and the drama of survival, forgetting that he had started out asking a pretty basic question. "Why are you looking for drugs in the sea?" Now his head was spinning with fish drama and he felt certain he would never look at a clam the same way again.

"Marine invertebrates have developed chemicals to protect themselves from predation. A lot of sponges are poisonous: worms, nematodes, anemones," Zee went on. She sat cross-legged on the couch facing Connor, who slouched with his feet up on the coffee table. It was two in the morning but neither could sleep. They were well into the second bottle of wine and only shards of a large pizza with everything remained in the box. Zee had fallen on the pizza like someone who had spent years on a desert island, which in fact she had. He had been pretty hungry himself. Evidently, explosions, once the shock had faded, gave one a grand appetite.

She leaned forward, her knee brushed against his leg, and she did not move back. Her eyes sparkled, her cheeks were flushed, and her voice was breathless with passion. Fish passion, Connor realized, and a bit of a buzz from the wine, but as long as he didn't have to actually regress entirely to the Cambrian era, he could start anywhere.

"It's the most exciting thing," Zee went on. "There is a really amazing invertebrate, the nudibranch. They're beautiful, all soft and ripply." She moved her hands in an undulating flutter. "The nudibranch eats poisonous anemones, but the nematocysts, the stinging cells, instead of killing the nudibranch, just pass harmlessly through and get stored in the nudibranch's own flesh. If a fish should eat the nudibranch, though, the nematocysts discharge and sting the fish."

It didn't actually sound like *the* most exciting thing to Connor. The phenomenon he was actually wondering about at that very moment was how she could use the same old soap he used every day, but have it smell so great on her.

"Of course, that particular nudibranch still winds up dead," Zee went on. "But the fish learns never to eat another, so the species as a whole has protection. That's another thing." She reached over to put her glass on the table and the robe loosened a little as she moved, showing nothing, but tantalizing with its accessibility. "Most species are willing to give up a few members in order to protect the group. The basic, singular goal of any organism is, after all, to pass on your genes. You know, perpetuate your species."

She had big brown eyes, Disney bunny eyes. Connor wondered when this dissertation on the origin of the species had started to sound like an erotic novel. He was beginning to think that a little passing on of genes wouldn't be a bad idea right now. But it would. It would be a terrible idea. The best idea would be to wrap her up and ship her out tonight.

"I'm sorry, I'm going on and on."

"No. It's fascinating. Is that it then? The meaning of life, the secrets of desire?"

She laughed. "In a way. Mr. Fish is attractive to Miss Fish when he demonstrates vigor, or strength, or speed, or whatever qualities she believes would give her offspring the best chance to survive."

"And us?" Connor lightly touched the hem of the thick bathrobe. "I mean, ah, people. In general."

Zee felt a blossom of sweat on her chest. Was she flirting? Was he? It had been a long couple of years on the island. A heady mix of desire and panic was taking hold as she realized she was growing aroused and tried to remember what to do about it. The dance of desire: squid flashing colors, groupers waltzing in a mirror display, crabs tenderly caressing the carapace of their mate; what did people do? She shouldn't do anything. Not with Mr. International Man of Mystery, burglar cum laude. She knew the type. Didn't need the type. Damn well couldn't resist it, either.

"It's the same, really," she went on. "All of the features we find attractive somehow give us information on the prospects of that person as a . . . potential breeder." *Damn! Why not just throw yourself at him?* What about all that free love on the commune where she grew up? Didn't her parents teach her anything? She blushed deeply and leaned back against the couch.

"Tell me some more," Connor urged. "What do beautiful eyes tell me about your, ah, breeding potential?"

Zee took a deep breath, but her heart was still pounding.

"Well, I can see predators on the horizon. That will help keep our herd safe."

"Hmmmmm." He rested one arm against the back of the couch, still not touching, but close enough to feel the heat from her body. "And nice skin?"

"Um . . . good health."

"I see." He reached slowly toward her and looped a finger through one of the short curls, pulled it up, and let it bounce back.

"Pretty hair?"

Zee felt a warm ache spreading throughout her body. "Health again. I am probably an able gatherer of nuts and berries."

"Yum." He smiled. A new flush, one blossoming not from the wine, crept into her cheeks. Connor's eyes slipped down her body, as if he could see anything through the bulky robe.

"What do curves and such tell me?" Their eyes locked now. This was a bad idea. Someone should stop it right now.

"Well, adequate pelvic girth," she said, "for one thing." Their arms touched. *Dear Ulla, what are you thinking, wherever you are? I pick up a guy at your funeral and get horny after your house burns down.*

"And for another?" Connor held her gaze.

"Do I need to explain it all?" Zee pulled back a little. Connor also eased off. A breeze rustled the trees outside and nudged at the window shades, bringing in a the damp honeysuckle cool of a summer night.

"So it's the same with you? With men I mean. With women and men," Connor asked.

"Well, yes," Zee replied slowly, trying not to focus on the effect, evolutionary or not, his body was having on hers. "The ideal male form is based upon atavistic indications of strength and health. A woman might notice strong legs, for example." She did not risk a look at his. "For chasing down wildebeests."

"Wildebeests," he said gravely, "have no chance with me."

"And strong arms." Her voice caught in her throat and she blushed. "Good for dragging prey back to our cave."

The wind blew stronger, with the edge of rain approaching. Zee looked up and their eyes met again, and she thought she heard laughter in the wind. This is kind of funny, she thought, and imagined Ulla sitting on a heavenly cloud, dressed in a pink satin sari, tearing pictures of cute boys out of teen magazines and throwing them down to her. Zee smiled and relaxed. OK, so he wasn't an axe murderer or anything. She had checked up on Chapmans; it was a legitimate company.

The robe had gone very loose by now and Connor could see the tops of her breasts, creamy white beneath the tan lines. He didn't need an explanation for why they were attractive. Zee examined his hand, where it rested inches away on the back of the couch. She paused over a scar on the back of his forearm and ran her fingers over scarred knuckles. She frowned.

"Hmmm. You're a fighter."

"I can fend off marauding tribes," he suggested hopefully.

"Or sow discord within our own. The alpha male thing has ruined a lot of cavemen."

"Naww, I went through that alpha thing long ago." Connor pulled her hand up to his lips and gently kissed her fingers. Zee shivered.

"I don't know anything about you, really."

"No, you don't."

How had their bodies come so close? Why-did it feel so comfortable? Zee wondered. The whir of the ceiling fan and the crickets of the night played rhythm to the seduction in the air. She could feel the heat of his chest and see the pulse beat in the hollow of his neck.

"Your heart is strong." She laid her palm against his chest. Connor searched her face, unsure if the touch was invitation or restraint.

"What does that tell you?"

"It tells me that the forces of nature are very powerful."

They kissed a long time. Her body melted into his. Zee felt like she was in the current again, being swept away, not caring this time if she drowned. Connor's hands moved over her body with unhurried pleasure, stroking her velvety skin. It could have been hours or days, the lush delight of touch was intoxicating. Finally they drew apart. Connor stroked her hair and looked into her eyes.

"This particular force of nature is getting hard to resist," he said softly.

Zee smiled. "Then don't."

11

July 1

Connor woke slowly, struggling toward consciousness through a thick confusion of memory and dream, his heart pounding in apprehension. Something was wrong. But what? Where was he? What town? What time? What danger? Police at the door? A wised-up mark come for revenge? A sore loser bringing friends? Or just another of Dad's pissed off girlfriends? His mind scrolled quickly through the possible situations. He lay motionless, eyes still shut, letting his other senses feel out what was wrong. Another person. A woman in bed with him. Wildebeests. Coral reefs, a lot of wine. A house exploding. Fire. He opened his eyes and let out his breath.

He saw that she was still asleep. Good. The rest of the pieces began to assemble. Malaria serum in mustard jars. He eased over closer to the edge of the bed. She didn't move. Good again. Slowly he swung his legs to the floor. A marching band of aches and pains started playing Sousa up and down his body. How the hell did they make love last night? And why the hell? It was a complication he didn't need right now. He reached for his pants, picking them up by the pockets to stifle the sound of any jingling change. Another of Dad's old tricks.

"Don't be creeping around on my account." Zee's voice sounded slightly amused and not at all sleepy. She turned around. The curly hair was a wild, loose tangle and in the soft light of dawn she looked like a kid. Then she rolled over on her back and the sheet outlined what was definitely a womanly body. A very attractive woman, he thought. So that explains the why. Now how soon could he get rid of her?

"Hey."

"What time is it?" Zee murmured.

"Just after seven. Go back to sleep."

"I have to get up. I have a meeting with Adam Fairchild this morning." Zee yawned, then sat up with concern. "Your burn." The burn was red and blistered, but not terrible. Angry purple bruising had started to bloom around it.

"It's fine."

Her face grew more serious and she looked away. A damp flowery breeze drifted in through the window and a big, slow bumblebee buzzed against the screen. Simplicity ended there.

"What do we do now?"

Connor grabbed a shirt off the chair. "When were you planning to leave? To go back to the island?" He dressed quickly, with a peculiar efficiency. It had been a while since Zee had awakened with a strange man. Was this abruptness due to circumstances or was he just an asshole?

"My ticket is for tomorrow," she said. "Back to Miami, anyway, then I'll have to make arrangements from there."

Connor paused, frowned. "Is there anyplace else you could go for a while?"

"Go, like where?"

"Go like hide."

"Why?"

"Ulla's house was searched and blown up. And she may very well have been murdered. The common denominator so far is the malaria serum."

"But I'm not involved with that."

"You are now. Anyone who knew you and Ulla were friends would suspect you knew everything. There's no point in you being the next target."

Zee got up. She looked around for her own clothes, then remembered they were still downstairs in the dryer. She pulled the robe on. Connor kept his distance. No little hug, no good morning kiss. Asshole.

"First of all, we don't know that her house was searched," she said.

"You saw some books out of place, that's all. And we don't know for sure that she was murdered. You said that yourself. The fire might really have been an accident. We don't know."

"And we don't know Santa Claus isn't coming down my chimney this year, but I'm still not wasting my milk and cookies." Connor jammed his feet into his sneakers and snapped the laces. "I just think it would be smart for you to stay out of the picture for a while. Let me get a handle on this."

"Fine. You play Sherlock Holmes, I'll go talk to the real police." She yanked the robe closed and brushed past him.

"Zee, wait—I'm sorry."

Zee went to the basement door and flung it open. Men. Maybe she hadn't been missing all that much stuck on her island after all. She went downstairs, pulled the wrinkled shorts and shirt out of the dryer and put them on.

When she came back upstairs, Connor was leaning against the back of the couch reading the paper.

"Would you mind dropping me off at the hotel on your way to work?" she asked coolly. Connor handed her the paper.

STEALING THE PENNIES OFF A DEAD MAN'S EYES

"Robbery attempt at home of recent carjacking victim results in explosion," the headline read.

> When Angela Morgan and her sister arrived at her late mother's house last March after the funeral, they discovered the family silver and their mother's charm bracelet, along with the television and everything else of value, missing. While they were at the cemetery, a burglar, knowing the house would be empty, had struck.
>
> Robbing the dead is a terrible crime. One that may be on the rise. The latest instance resulted in near catastrophe yesterday afternoon, when a burglar's cigarette apparently set off an explosion in the home of Ulla Raki, the scientist who was killed last week in a carjacking.

Connor felt an odd mixture of thrill and revulsion.

Investigators believe that a slow leak of natural gas, probably from a faulty water heater, built up over the days while the house was closed up. An intruder, thought to be the same person responsible in other burglaries of the recently deceased, somehow set off a spark. The house was completely destroyed. Two engine companies responded . . .

"Well, do you still think this is all just coincidence?"

"What does it mean?"

"It means someone is working awfully hard and awfully fast," Connor said grimly.

"Now we really have to talk to the police."

"No."

"Connor, this is getting crazy!"

"Look, whoever is behind this must have some pretty powerful connections to get a story this good planted this fast. Not to mention quite possibly pulling off a perfect murder."

"So we need the police."

"The cops have already accepted Ulla's death as a carjacking and if they're buying this crap, they're either too stupid to realize it or under pressure not to."

"OK then, the FBI."

Connor folded the paper up. "Let me talk to Mickey. He'll know how to get to the right people." He sat back and regarded her for the first time that morning with detachment. "Who would want popeye so badly? There has to be some value."

"No one. The drug hasn't even been tested in people yet, Connor," Zee pointed out.

"What about a black market?"

"Most of the people who live in malarial zones can't afford the existing medicines for the common types anyway, so why would they care if there were a new medicine for resistant strains? I don't know. I just don't know enough about it."

"So we need to find out more. You wanted to help. Help me understand what I don't know. Malaria, drug production, all that. What time is your meeting with Fairchild?"

"Ten-thirty."

"See what you can find out from him, without letting on that you know anything. Can you be a little cagey?"

"Well, shucks, Connor, I reckon I could maybe do that. Ph.D. don't actually stand for, like, Pretty Hip Dame."

"I'm sorry. I didn't mean . . ."

"It's OK," she stopped him. It was an awkward repair.

"Did Fairchild know you and Ulla were friends?"

"She was the one who told me about the position on Shadow Island, and wrote a letter of recommendation, but that wouldn't necessarily mean anything more than professional association to Fairchild. But we also sent letters to each other in the delivery parcels."

"Try to keep your friendship in a casual context, cover your own ass first. Then just try to draw him out. Don't put too much emphasis on popeye. Maybe ask about Cronzene twenty. It's mixed up in here some-place. And what about her lab assistant? You said he would be the most likely person to know the details of what she was doing here. Do you know his name?"

"Tom something . . . Su Thom! I remember she was impressed with him. I don't know his last name."

"I can find out. Chapmans has all the SeaGenesis personnel files." Connor looked at his watch. "But I need to hurry if I'm going to catch him before he leaves for work."

"You think he might know something?"

"He might, but I'm more afraid of what he might not know," Connor said grimly. "That working with this particular drug doesn't seem to be good for the health."

"He could be in danger?"

"Frankly, after yesterday, I'm kind of surprised he's made it this far."

Su Thom lived in a garden apartment complex just steps from a busy road on the older side of Silver Spring, Maryland. The place was well kept, but the sheer weight of years and old gloomy paint gave it an air of fusty sadness. It was the sort of place recent immigrants moved when they first broke away from the relatives, and the hallways were saturated with the smells of cooking oil, cumin, and diapers. Connor pulled up in front of the building just before eight.

Su Thom's apartment was in the basement. Connor knocked, but there was no answer. No use leaving a note. What would he say? Watch your back? As Connor went back down the hall, he heard the building door open, then hurried footsteps on the stairs. A young man brushed past him. Medium height, dark brown hair, Asian features. He carried his keys in hand, evidently just coming from his car. Connor watched until he got to the right door.

"Su Thom?" Su Thom looked up. Connor felt a shiver of recognition but did not place him yet. He saw that Su Thom also registered this, though neither knew what it meant.

"I need to talk to you," Connor said simply. "About Ulla Raki."

Su Thom stiffened, but his wariness ebbed. "I'm not talking to any reporters."

"I'm not a reporter. I want to talk about popeye."

Su Thom stiffened.

"I won't keep you long. If you don't want to talk in your apartment, I'll wait for you outside."

Su Thom hesitated for a few seconds, then slipped the key in the lock. Connor recognized a concentrated calm that belied the young man's wariness. Su Thom crossed the room and stood with his back against the wall.

"I work for a private security firm called Chapmans," Connor explained. "We handle all of SeaGenesis's security, and we're working with the police to try and help them find Ulla's killer."

"I talked to the police already. I didn't know anything."

Connor knew little about the young man, but recognized the scoured confidence of one who has lived too hard for too long.

"Did you know that Ulla took some samples of popeye home with her the day she was killed?"

Su Thom went pale. His eyes widened, then flickered briefly down to a place on his left arm just above the elbow. His right hand followed unconsciously, pressing against the skin. "No."

"Nothing is clear right now but it may be that someone is interested in obtaining those samples of popeye."

Su Thom tensed visibly and his fingers clutched his arm. "What do you mean?"

"Did you hear the news last night or this morning?"

Su Thom shook his head.

"There was a fire. Ulla's house was destroyed. I don't think it was an accident. And the carjacking. I'm not sure that was accidental, either."

"That's stupid. No one would kill for popeye. No one cares that it even exists." Connor's news hadn't appeared to shake him very much.

"You worked quite a bit with Ulla on popeye."

"Yes."

"But you didn't notice the samples were missing?"

"We had been directed to suspend work on it. To focus on other things." Su Thom walked over to the window. "Why does this concern you?"

Connor paused. *Because it's an interesting puzzle? Because it's a chance to prove I can do something? Because I'm showing off for the father whose approval I can never seem to win?* "I'm not sure," he said honestly.

"You were at the awards dinner for Dr. Fairchild," Su Thom said accusingly. "You're the one who jumped on the man with the gun."

Connor was surprised. "Yes."

"I heard about it when I went inside. Then I realized it must have been you. Why did you do it?"

"I didn't really think."

"You risked your life for an idiot."

"I just didn't think."

"And now you've come to warn me."

"To tell you to be careful. I'm not sure what's going on, but it involves popeye."

"And you are interested in this drug because you are so concerned for the millions of poor people in the world dying of malaria?" Su Thom asked coldly.

"Actually I never thought about malaria before this," Connor answered honestly. "I don't even know much about it."

Su Thom relaxed a little. He stayed by the window for a few long minutes.

"About those samples," Connor asked. "Was there anything different about them, anything special?"

"Those six vials were the last of a very consistent, very effective batch," Su Thom explained. "They were the best samples we had. Ulla was hoping to discover the key to synthetic production. Now she won't." He picked up his briefcase. "I have to go to work."

12

July 1

W hat the hell do you mean you were there!" Mickey stared at Connor with what the kids used to call his "death face." A deep purple flush and a thin whiteness around his mouth, a faint quiver in the corner of his left eye.

"I was there," Connor repeated. "In her house. There was no gas leak, no burglar, no spark. There was a bomb. Or something."

"A bomb *or something?*"

"Whatever it was, it wasn't this!" He slapped the newspaper with the back of his hand. "This is complete crap. It's a plant!"

"My god, Connor, you could have been killed! Are you all right?" Mickey got up and walked around the desk. "What's this?" He brushed back some of Connor's hair to examine a scrape. The big hand covered half his face, the gesture seemed almost tender.

"It's nothing. I'm fine." Connor suddenly felt awkward and a little off base. Why should it be so shocking that Mickey was worried about him?

"What were you doing in Ulla Raki's house in the first place?" Mickey's concern slipped quickly beneath chastisement.

"We went to see if there were some samples of a drug Ulla Raki was working on . . ."

"Wait a minute," Mickey interrupted. "Who's *we?*"

Connor stopped. It had all developed so fast. He quickly sketched

the events of the past two days. Meeting Zee at the funeral and examining Ulla Raki's car. He left out the part about receiving the FedEx with
the disks and Raki's letter. Mickey might feel more of an obligation to
report that to Dr. Fairchild. He had promised Zee he would try to keep
Ulla's reputation unsullied with charges of thievery. He kept the information within the context of what Ulla and Zee, two friends and colleagues, might have simply corresponded about. Mickey listened quietly,
his face inscrutable.

"Raki thought SeaGenesis was trying to suppress her work with popeye, possibly for financial reasons. According to Zee, Dr. Aspen, that's
plausible, since the market is primarily poor Third World countries. Anyway, her requests for primate testing were turned down, then she discovered that supplies of the raw material, this sponge that Dr. Aspen has
been collecting, were being diverted somewhere. We went to Ulla's house
to look for the samples."

"Why would you think she would have brought the samples home?"
Mickey was not going to let that just float by.

"She really cared about the project." He had constructed the story
and practiced it, but still wasn't too sure what Mickey would believe.
"Once a project gets shelved, according to Dr. Aspen, it's easy for samples to get lost or misplaced in a big lab. Ulla probably just wanted to
be sure this popeye stuff would still be around if they ever got funding
to continue."

"So you went to her house to look for it?"

"Then boom . . ." Connor waved his hands.

"But you did find this popeye stuff?"

"I think so. We found vials of something. Zee is going to test it.
According to Ulla's lab assistant, these samples might hold the key to
how the drug actually works."

"When did you talk to Ulla's lab assistant?"

"Just now. I thought he needed to be warned."

Mickey got up and went back to his chair, his movements slow.
"Warned about what?"

"I told him I had doubts about it being a simple random carjacking.
I told him to be careful."

"You've had a busy couple of days." Mickey pressed his fingertips together, stared at the ceiling, let out a big breath of displeasure. "So where is this mystery serum now?"

"At my house."

"Well, let's hope it isn't some deadly plague virus or something, shall we?" Mickey began to tap his huge fingers on the desk. "So what you're telling me is that Ulla Raki may have found a new cure for malaria, so someone killed her then blew up her house? All to get their hands on this drug. A drug that is, for all practical purposes, of very little value to anyone. Why?"

Put that way, Connor had to admit it sounded absurd.

"To destroy evidence, to warn off somebody else. Maybe a message to SeaGenesis. Blackmail. I don't know. It's all mixed up somehow, the malaria drug, this EPA contract, the sabotage on Shadow Island. And the carjacking is bogus. No question. You can't tell me all this is still co-incidence."

"No, but I can tell you that if something this drastic was going on with SeaGenesis, Adam Fairchild would tell me about it."

"What if Fairchild did something illegal in getting this contract for Cronzene twenty?"

Mickey frowned. "The accidents, or sabotage, were going on at SeaGenesis for some time before that contract was awarded. And if Dr. Raki was asking for monkeys to test on, she must have been working on her malaria drug for a while already. Years, I would guess. Why is all this happening just now?"

"I don't know. You're not telling me everything."

Mickey folded his arms across his solid chest and stared straight through him.

"I've never told you everything." There was teasing in his voice, but a strange disdain in his eyes. "Look. I'll talk to Fairchild. Meanwhile, let's lay off all this rabid sleuthing for the moment. Breaking and entering and stealing out of a dead woman's refrigerator is not the sort of thing Chapmans can be involved with. The police are already looking for the burglar who set off the blaze. It might as well be you."

"There was no burglar! There was no gas! Natural gas has a smell. We were in the house a good fifteen minutes. Neither of us smelled anything. Why are you having such a hard time believing this?"

"Why are you having such a hard time not believing it? A coincidental carjacking, an opportunistic burglar that heard about her death on TV and knew when the house would be empty." Mickey dropped the article aside. "Could it be you're just jealous because your old man never thought of this particular scam? It isn't a pleasant thought, but there *are* burglars who specialize in robbing the dead." Mickey went on. "They read the obituaries and know when a house is likely to be empty. Several burglaries of this sort have been reported over the past year."

"Then why . . ." Connor stopped, the question halted as the answer smacked him in the face. Mickey was lying. It wasn't just that Connor had never heard of this sort of burglary, or that his old man didn't do it. If the practice really was so common, Mickey should have a brochure ready to be mailed daily to everyone mentioned in the obituaries. "Chapmans Security offers our condolences for your loss. Protect the memories of your loved one from those who would take advantage of your grief. . . . You've suffered enough." Every funeral home in the region would be briefed on Chapmans services and offered a finder's fee for every client they brought in. There would be a Chapmans security guard house-sitting during funerals every day. But there wasn't.

"Look, Connor, it could be there is something going on with SeaGenesis. It could also be that you are letting it run away with you, making up conspiracies where there are none. Let me talk to Fairchild. If he's involved with something I'll give him a chance to come clean. Meanwhile, I don't like you having those samples in your house. For one thing, you really don't know what you have; it could be any kind of weird disease or something. For another, if it is this popeye stuff and if someone is trying to get it," Mickey looked at Connor with concern, "you could get hurt."

Connor nodded. "Sure," he said with no sign of the turmoil he felt. What was going on? Mickey was lying. The fact was strange and still oddly remote, like looking at a traffic accident from across eight lanes and a median strip. There in plain sight, but too far removed to be real. Mickey just did not lie. Not even the routine little social lies that smooth the everyday paths of life. It was the one thing above all he told the boys. *Say nothing if you have to, but don't ever tell me a lie.*

Connor left Chapmans and walked slowly to his car. Who could he go to? Mickey was head of the company, head of the family. For all immediate purposes, head of the whole damn world. Uncle Billy would be no good; he never questioned a thing his brother did. The police reported it as an accidental explosion. Why would it be anything else? How could it be anything else?

"Dr. Aspen, I'm glad to see you. Please sit down." Adam Fairchild waved Zee smoothly toward a chair and adjusted the blinds to cut the morning glare.

"I'm sorry I couldn't come yesterday, but you know, once I'm in civilization there are so many things to do. Shopping and all that . . ." Zee knew it would have to be a pretty violent blue-light sale at Kmart to explain the scratches and bruises on her face, but Fairchild didn't appear to notice.

"Oh, of course, I understand." He slid weightlessly into his chair. It was a modern design of chrome and black leather poised behind a desk of granite and frosted glass. "I spoke to the hospital this morning and they tell me Roddy Taylor is doing fine. I want to commend you on the way you handled the whole situation."

"Thank you. There were a few problems," Zee offered. "We probably need to keep certain antivenoms on hand in the future. Did the doctors say when he'll be able to come back?"

"Not for some time. No, I wouldn't think any time soon." Fairchild frowned and his forehead creased. "In fact, there are a few issues about the island that we need to discuss." Zee tensed. From third-grade scoldings to relationship breakups, *issues* and *discuss* were gloved euphemisms, warning for the slap to follow.

"I wish there was an easier way to break it to you. I certainly wish there were a better time." Fairchild rested gently folded hands on the desk, looking to Zee like the maître d' for the end of the world. "I'm afraid we are considering a suspension of operations on Shadow Island."

"Suspension?" She felt blindsided.

"We are of course very pleased with your work, and excited with your progress. Really. Very pleased." Fairchild paused for a brief, tight smile. "In fact, frankly, you've done a bit too good of a job. We have so many products in testing right now that we simply aren't able to handle much more. With two drugs going into clinical trials next month and field testing of Cronzene twenty coming up, I'm already stretching resources. I won't bore you with all the details, but the basic fact is the cost of operating in the Bahamas has simply turned out to be much higher than we anticipated. The board has been considering a suspension of operations for some time. To give us time to regroup. Now, since this accident is going to put Taylor out of commission for a while anyway, this seemed like the right time."

"But you can't. I mean . . . we're just getting things going. This was always anticipated as a five-year start-up at least." She stopped. Should she be more assertive? Deferential? Fairchild was impossible to read. He nodded gently with a placating smile.

"We are looking at moving the station to the Florida Keys. In fact, that's what I wanted to talk to you about. Since you and Mr. Taylor are both here now, you could check out potential sites personally. The doctor says he could travel in a few days if you take it easy. You could make it a sort of working vacation." Zee was dumbfounded and scrambled for reply.

"Dr. Fairchild, we can't move to the Keys. Shadow Island has unique conditions. That's why we chose it in the first place. The range of habitat, the purity of the water, the deep current upwellings, you're not going to get that in the Keys. The optimal conditions for some of these organisms are very narrow. You can change water temperature or salinity by two or three degrees and lose them completely."

"I'm sorry, Zee. The board feels it would be more prudent to focus all our resources on developing what we have, actually bringing some-thing to market." He slowly spread his palms outward across the desk as if smoothing out small wrinkles. "Now, of course, I should have men-tioned this right away, your future with SeaGenesis is completely secure. Don't worry about that. Until we get something else up and running in a better location, we'll make a place for you right here," Fairchild went on, his brow knitted in concerned understanding, his eyes sadly wise.

"Well . . . yes. But it will take some time to wrap things up on Shadow Island. I mean, I would like a few more days here first . . ."

"Oh, there's no need for you to go back. Arthur Padgette will be able to shut things down."

"But Dr. Fairchild, we just got a new group of grad students. We have dozens of projects underway."

"I'm afraid we had to bring the students back, Zee." Fairchild rubbed one hand briefly across the unwrinkled brow. "The insurance people have been hounding us about all the accidents. After Taylor's injury, well, they were worried about something happening with one of the students, lawsuits and all that. They wanted a halt to operations until all the insurance and liability issues could be re-examined. I hate to do this so suddenly, but there you have it. It doesn't make sense for SeaGenesis to pump a lot of money into Shadow Island right now when we were intending to suspend operations there anyway."

Zee had nothing more to say. It was all too sudden, too strange, and like a great snarl of fishing line, impossible to sort out.

"Don't worry about Shadow Island, Zee." Fairchild stood up, waving her graciously toward the door. "No one considers it anything less than a success."

Kerry Sullivan pulled her feet up on the bench of the Little Tykes picnic table and leaned her elbows on her knees, staring at Connor, trying to make sense of what he had just told her.

"I didn't know who else to talk to," Connor said apologetically. He looked across the yard. It was so quiet. He had never been here when the children weren't around. The girls were at the pool, Oliver was taking a nap. Toy-car roads were traced in the dirt among the roots of a tree and a one-legged Spiderman poked forlornly out from a knothole.

"Are you absolutely sure the fire couldn't have been an accident?" Kerry asked.

"It definitely wasn't like the paper said," Connor insisted. "Or like Mickey says. It wasn't a natural gas build-up."

"Why would anyone want to blow up the house in the first place?" Kerry asked. "What would be the point?"

Connor hesitated, unsure how much to tell her. "I think Ulla Raki may have stolen samples of a drug she was working on. Somebody wanted those samples, or at least didn't want anyone else to get their hands on them. I think the explosion was a last-minute thing. A drastic action, not well planned."

"Why?"

"Because causing an actual gas build-up would have been much easier and require no cover-up. This was a quick decision in response to something. And then, whoever did it had to have somehow pressured the fire investigators to go along."

Kerry's voice had an edge. "Mickey wouldn't be involved in anything like that."

"There's more going on with this case. He just won't tell me."

"Well, why should he, Connor? You've never been exactly reliable. Maybe he just thinks, whatever it is, you aren't ready to handle it. Or maybe, if there is something going on, he doesn't want to put you at risk." That was one possibility that hadn't occurred to him at all.

"But wouldn't he see that right now I'm at greater risk not knowing anything?"

"Now maybe, because you nearly got blown up. But not before. Did he expect you to go search the house? No. Did he expect you to go to the funeral and meet this marine biologist woman, or decide Ulla Raki was really murdered, or any of this? No, he probably expected you to just slack around as usual, getting by on charm and wit and as little effort as possible."

"At least he seemed genuinely worried that I was caught there."

Kerry didn't laugh. "Why do you talk like that?"

"Oh, you know what I mean."

"Mickey loves you, Connor. I don't know why you find that so hard to believe. And it isn't just because of Sean. I know you've always believed that, but it isn't true," Kerry persisted.

Connor stared down at Oliver's toys. "You really think Mickey would have kept me around, put up with me all these years if that hadn't happened?"

"If you hadn't saved his son's life? Connor, you are so weird. Why won't you even say it? You saved Sean's life. You jumped in the river and saved him from drowning. Of course that didn't hurt your cause with

Mickey. But it wasn't the only reason they kept you. Why can't you believe that?"

Why should I believe it? Kerry believed the best of people, but Connor would never be sure. He was a rotten, rebellious, street-wild brat when Lois and Mickey took him in, and he didn't get much better for a long time. Why would they want to disrupt their lives by keeping him? Then Sean fell in the river and Connor pulled him out. Connor's rescue gave the beloved son five more years before the car crash that finally took his life. And how could Mickey give him the boot after that? He had no choice but to keep Connor in the family.

A loud wail drifted from the house. Kerry got up off the little picnic table and squinted as she moved into the hot sun.

"Oliver's awake. Come on inside."

Connor followed her in, feeling even more confused. Oliver had climbed out of his bed and was sitting on the top of the steps, his face red and creased by the sheets, hiccuping small sobs. Kerry gathered him up with coos and pettings and offers of lemonade.

Connor waited downstairs. The door to Daniel's study was open. He saw two cardboard boxes, their flaps unsealed, old bits of junk poking up. There was a baseball trophy he recognized, a couple of old books, photos spilling out of an envelope. Lois was on a cleaning spree, he remembered, sorting out old closets and drawers. He heard little feet behind him and Oliver caught him around the knees. He turned and swung the child up.

"We're going swimming!"

"Well, it's a good day for that."

"Swimming!" Oliver declared, wiggling down.

Kerry nodded. "Go get your swimsuit on," she instructed. Oliver ran off. Kerry leaned against the door frame. She nodded toward the boxes.

"Go ahead and look through them if you want, if you think there's some deep dark secret. They're just junk. Old school stuff and things." She folded her arms and looked around the house. "If Mickey is not telling you something, he has a good reason."

"Kerry, if Mickey is in some kind of trouble, I want to help him. Has Daniel said anything?"

She sighed and looked away. "Not really. I don't know. A few odd things, but nothing significant." She hesitated. "You know he works for Chapmans?"

"I know he gets referrals for legal work."

"No. Daniel works for Mickey. Like the rest of you. Like everyone in this family. Daniel's law firm is part of Chapmans, a limited partnership and it's all under a corporation that came out of Mickey's shipping business."

"Mickey's business? I thought Mickey just worked for SST."

"He started out as chief of security, but went on to become a partner," Kerry explained. "Eventually he and some of the other partners managed a buyout and formed their own corporation. They split the shipping company up, sold off the pieces, and invested the money. Quite well, as it turns out. Now Daniel handles the investments."

"Why didn't I know?"

"Why?" Her voice tightened with exasperation. "Maybe because you disappeared the day you turned eighteen and only turned up over the past decade when you were in trouble, or worn out or . . . whatever. You don't think all Mickey's money comes from Chapmans, do you? Chapmans is a hobby, a charity for the cop relatives, something fun and challenging, a new empire to build. It makes a profit, but not that much. The house and the trust funds and the college tuition for every niece and nephew come from the corporation."

"How tightly are they linked?" Connor asked. "Chapmans and the corporation?"

"I don't know." Kerry stood stiffly, uncomfortable with the whole topic. "You would have to talk to Daniel. Mickey isn't doing anything wrong, Connor, whatever you're thinking. Without Mickey, this family would be nothing. All those uncles and cousins, they'd all still be on the force, or just now retiring, with a small pension and night jobs as factory guards. He's put seven kids through college so far. My girls swim at a country club."

"Well, you obviously married the right man." Connor wished immediately he could take that back. Kerry's eyes narrowed. "I'm sorry," he said. "I didn't mean that."

"I love Daniel."

"I know. I'm sorry."

"He's a good man, Connor. You could never see the way he really is. No, he's not as strong as you. He isn't as . . . as . . ." Kerry stalled out, her hands fluttering for words. She lowered her voice, glancing briefly at the stairway to see if Oliver was listening. "He is not a strong man but he is a good man, Connor. You don't know how it was for him. You want to know why Mickey kept you? Because you reminded him of himself. You were wild and defiant. Daniel was just an average boy. Sean was smart, athletic, charming, but you fit the Sullivan legacy better than either of them. All those damn Irish brawlers, union organizers, dockworkers, rabble rousers. It was hard enough on Daniel that Sean was already the golden boy, then you came into the family and pushed him totally aside. He could never be as good as Sean or as bad as you. I know what happened that day at the river. I know Daniel was scared to go in after Sean. It has haunted him all his life."

Kerry glared at Connor. She did love Daniel. *And what the hell else was I supposed to do? Wait around all my life for the times you might show up?* she thought to herself. Daniel was a good husband and a good father. If she had never felt the same passion, well, that didn't mean anything, really. That was all raging adolescent hormones.

"I'm sorry," Connor said gently. "I don't know what I'm doing here." Oliver rescued them, jumping down the stairs in his swimsuit, toys bouncing out of his sand pail.

"You were all being groomed, you know," Kerry said quietly as she tucked towels into a beach bag. "I think Mickey always envisioned a bit of a dynasty. But that ended. Sean died. You took off. So now Daniel manages the corporation, Mickey plays James Bond at Chapmans, everyone is happy." Kerry picked up the beach bag. "We have to go, the girls will be waiting."

Connor came home in a dark confusion, Kerry's revelations weighing heavily on him, both the emotional and the practical. He had never thought much about Mickey's business beside Chapmans. He was still working for Secure Shipping and Transport when Connor joined the family, but already freelancing as a security consultant. If there was a corporation with diverse investments, who knows what Mickey could be involved in? Did he have a financial stake in SeaGenesis? Was there some stock thing going on with popeye? Connor knew there was a lot of speculation in the biotech industry, and companies could soar or crumble based on the value of one drug. *I've never told you everything . . .* He would grapple with all that later. Right now there was the immediate problem of six vials of popeye to turn over.

He found Zee in the middle of the living room floor, surrounded by maps, graphs, and stern-looking scientific papers with tiny print and multilined titles. A pair of reading glasses gave her a slightly scholarly air but she looked so forlorn amidst the sea of paper that Connor's first impression was of one of Kerry's little girls cutting out paper dolls.

She looked up warily as he came in. They had parted that morning in a fragile detente. She wore a light cotton skirt and a T-shirt so old the fabric was thin at the shoulders. Lucy came tearing in. She slipped on the papers and plopped down between them, rolling indulgently for a belly scratch.

"Hey." Connor crouched down and obligingly rubbed the dog.

"Hey yourself."

The old air conditioner was chugging away, but the room was still warm and Zee's hair clung in damp curls to the sides of her neck. Connor picked up a handful of the mussed papers.

"What is all this?"

"Maps of malarial distribution, statistics on cases by year and region, research papers."

"Where did you get all this?"

"I just got back from the library at Walter Reed."

"The army hospital?"

"They've been at the center of malaria research for decades," Zee explained.

"Did anyone call since you've been here?" he asked as he checked the answering machine. The message light was not blinking.

"No. I've only been back half an hour. What's wrong?"

"Plenty." Connor strode to the kitchen where he yanked open the refrigerator. The samples were still there. "Can you make me something that looks like this stuff?" he asked urgently. "That might fool someone who knows what it's supposed to be?"

"Fool who?"

"Everyone." He slammed the door and smashed his hand against it in sudden rage.

"What happened?" Zee came to him with concern he couldn't bear. He turned away. "Connor, what's wrong?"

"It has to look convincing, maybe even hold up to some testing. Is that easy to do? Test something and know exactly what's in it? I mean, could they tell right away?"

"Connor, slow down. What happened?"

"Mickey is involved in this."

"What do you mean? How do you know?"

He hesitated, then finally told her.

"Mickey Sullivan is not just my boss. He's my foster father. He's never lied before. But he lied today. He's backing the news story about a gas leak." Connor paused. "I think he and Fairchild are both involved," he went on. "Blackmail, bribery, or something, I don't know. He wants me to bring him the samples of popeye for safekeeping. I can't waste any time here. Can you make some fake popeye that will fool him?"

"No. A basic run through a spectrometer will show up a fake."

"Shit. What about diluting it? Give up a little. Mix it with water or something? Would they know the concentration she was working with?"

"If they have her lab books they would."

"Well, think of something! Mickey knows I have the samples of popeye. I can't con him on this. There has to be something you can do. I told him I would get it to him right away. And I have to hide the real stuff somewhere." He began looking for a suitable container. It would have to be well hidden. Mickey might decide to come search the place himself.

"I guess I could cook it," Zee said tentatively. "We did bring it through a fire, and carry it home in all this heat. I don't know how stable it is, but it would be a plausible way to at least screw it up. Then they might not notice it was diluted."

"Good. Do it."

They worked quickly. Connor scrutinized the possible hiding places in the refrigerator for the real popeye. Mustard jars just wouldn't do for a second round. Finally he found a length of plastic tubing, funneled the popeye into it, then melted both ends, sealing it up. He wedged the tubing behind the vegetable bins in the fridge, running it underneath the rim. Zee heated the sacrificial ounce of serum and was glad to see it cloud up. That indicated some chemical change at least.

Suddenly Lucy ran to the front door and began to bark. Connor saw Mickey's car just turning into his driveway.

"Can you hurry?"

The malaria papers and maps were still scattered all over the floor. Connor swept them into a pile and stuffed them under the couch. He saw Mickey coming up the porch steps.

"C'mon, Lucy!" Connor whispered. "Get the squirrel! Go get the squirrel!" He opened the front door and the excited dog bolted out, her thrill at having a visitor overshadowed by the more delightful promise of squirrel. Lucy galloped off toward Mrs. Wickham's yard.

"Hey, get back here!" Connor called, as he shut the door behind him. "Damn dog!" he said apologetically to Mickey. "Hang on, let me go catch her before she gets out in the street and gets run over."

Zee hastily snatched up the vials and ducked around to the rear part of the kitchen where she could not be seen. Connor's running shoes lay by the door. She grabbed one, stuffed a dishcloth into it, and stuck the six vials around it so they were held in place. Pouring the adulterated serum seemed to take forever.

"Lucy, c'mere, girl!" she could hear Connor calling. Mickey paced slowly on the porch, peering in the window as he waited. All too soon Lucy realized there was no squirrel and came bounding back, happy with her second option of sniffing out a visitor. Connor dragged out a few more seconds with a proper scolding. Then he realized the door had locked behind him, and told Mickey to wait, he would go around through the back and let him in. Mickey said he could come around that way, and Connor couldn't come up with a reason for him not to, so he led him through the side gate, stalling as long as he could with a sticky latch, then into the backyard, holding his breath.

The kitchen was empty. The counter was clear. The pot was in the sink. Zee, he assumed, had disappeared down the basement stairs.

"Yeah, I just thought I would spare you the trip over," Mickey said nonchalantly.

"Sure. Yeah." They both stood there awkwardly. "You want a beer or something?"

"No. Thanks. I told Lois I would be home early."

"Right. OK."

"So where is this mystery serum?" Mickey pressed.

"Here. Right here." Connor held his breath as he opened the refrigerator door, unsure exactly what he would find. He found his sneaker. "I don't exactly keep a test-tube rack around the house," he joked. "Let me find you something to carry it in." He rummaged through a cabinet and found a Tupperware bowl. "I think this is one of Lois's anyway." He cushioned the vials in the plastic box with paper towels.

Mickey picked one up and looked at it against the light but his expression gave nothing away.

"So this might be some new cure for malaria?"

Connor shrugged. "Ulla Raki thought so. But she never got to test it. I hope it's OK. It was sitting out a long time yesterday before I remembered to stick it in the refrigerator." Mickey just nodded and closed up the box.

"What are you going to do with it now?"

"I'm not sure. It's the property of SeaGenesis." Mickey pressed the plastic lid down. It snugged into place with a soft whoof.

"Look, Connor, I'm sorry about this morning."

"It's OK."

"No, I mean it. It's just you threw me for a loop with all this. I'm hardly used to all of this, all this . . . investigating from you. Billy thinks maybe I've been keeping you in a box. Keeping you just in burglary and cons and such. And what I said about your father . . . you know, that was out of line."

"It's all right."

"You want to branch out. That's natural. I can go with that. I just need to see that you're really serious this time."

"Yeah." Connor was struggling. "Yeah, of course. That's fair." He pushed away from the counter. There didn't seem to be anything else to say and both men walked toward the front door.

"I'll let you know what happens." Mickey gave him a tight smile. "We'll see where we can work you in with some different kind of assignments, OK?"

"Yeah. Thanks." Connor walked outside with him. Mickey held the container with a forlorn acceptance, like a soup kitchen box lunch. He opened the car door, leaned in, and placed it on the seat.

"You know, Mickey," Connor said quietly. "There are a lot of people who would help you out of a jam."

Mickey gave him a peculiar smile.

"Thanks, Connor. I'll remember that."

Connor stood on the porch and watched him drive away. He went back inside and Zee came up from the basement.

"Do you think he was convinced?"

"For now." The afternoon was filled with bird song and the distant sound of a lawn mower, the world going on as usual.

"Connor, I've gone along with you on this so far. About not going to the police, but don't you think it's time to talk to someone? You said Mickey would help, would get us to the right people, but now you think he's involved. I don't know what to think, who to trust. Why didn't you tell me about you and Mickey? That he was your father?"

"Foster father. It just didn't come up."

Zee frowned. In a way he had a point; they had known each other only three days, and those days had not exactly left a lot of room for getting acquainted.

Connor pulled out a couple of beers. "Come on in here, I'll tell you whatever you want to know." The front room was starting to feel cooler. Connor sat on the floor and pulled the papers out from under the couch. He flipped through a couple as if seeking diversion, then dropped them.

"So what do you want to know?"

"I want to know I can trust you."

"What will convince you?"

"I don't know yet. Tell me about Mickey and you."

"The Sullivans took me in as a foster kid when I was ten. I grew up a thief. My real father and I traveled around, picking pockets, running small-time cons, ripping off houses, that sort of stuff. Mickey caught us breaking into his house. Dad went to jail. I was sent to a reform school." He briefly sketched over his escape and the circumstances of the eventual reunion with the Sullivans through the stolen sneakers with Sean's name in them. "Lois figured all I needed was some family values and moral guidance."

Zee finished her beer but held the bottle in her hands. She seemed to be receiving his story well, or at least with a thankful lack of pity.

"So did it work?" she asked. "Moral guidance?"

"I guess so. I haven't stolen anything since I was a teenager. And my adult arrests have all been misdemeanors."

"All?"

"Drunk and disorderly, disturbing the peace; that sort of thing, brawling in bars mostly. What they call it varies in different states. I had some stupid wild years. I'm over it." He couldn't tell if this was reassuring her or not.

"What's the worst thing you ever did?"

"Worst to me or worst to the law?"

"Both."

"Technically, I suppose grand theft auto, but that was on my juvy record. There was a felony assault charge once, but honestly, the other guy jumped me first, and I came out worse anyway. But the guy was a lawyer; the police weren't about to believe me over him."

"What were you doing fighting with a lawyer?"

"No, the question is, what was I doing *losing* to a lawyer." Connor laughed. "I beat him in pool. One of these yuppie pool halls in Bethesda. Took him for a hundred bucks. He thought I had hustled him."

"Had you?"

"Of course." Connor laughed and went to the kitchen for another couple of beers. "Some guys need hustling. And a hundred bucks, hell, that wasn't even an hour's pay for him."

"So what happened? Did you go to jail?"

"Just for the night. Mickey made a few calls, the paperwork got lost." The thought of Mickey's connections right now sobered him.

"So what was the worst thing to you?" Zee asked warily. Connor sat back down on the floor next to her with his back against the couch.

"I guess this time we broke into a house. When I was a kid with dad. It was a big house and looked really grand from the outside, but inside, everything was just old and shabby and poor. I think there were two old ladies living there. There was just nothing to take. They hardly had any food in the cabinets. The place had that old, awful, dying smell. They once must have had money, there were ratty old fur coats in the closet, but they had sold all their silver. They sold it one piece at a time. I found three butter knives in the box, along with a whole stack of little receipts. But I had to find something. Dad was pissed off. I finally found a coin purse, but there wasn't even two dollars there. But there was a brush and mirror set, tortoiseshell, really beautiful. It was the only nice thing there, and I took it. We got five dollars for it. I remember pulling these white hairs out of the brush as we drove to the pawn shop."

He looked up at her with a hard, almost accusatory look, resenting having to tell such a story. "I don't steal anymore. I might hustle a little pool now and then but I don't take a guy for much. Unless he's a real asshole."

"What about your mom?"

"I never knew her. She was seventeen when she met my dad. He was forty-three. They were both working in a carnival. She was doing a gypsy fortune-teller act. He loved her, but you know. She was young. She left. He raised me."

"I'm sorry."

"Nothing to be sorry about."

"So have you always worked for Mickey?"

"Off and on over the years, but I was never serious."

"Why are you serious now?"

Connor leaned back and stared at the ceiling.

"I guess I wanted to try real life," he offered lamely. "Now it's your turn."

"My life is pretty dull."

"Dull would be good right now."

"Anyway, you've probably read my personnel file."

"True. Did you really grow up on a commune?"

"It wasn't exactly a commune," she explained. "There were four families, and a few other people who came and went over the years, sharing these two huge old houses. Some of the men worked in town, carpentry, auto repair, stuff like that, but mostly we all grew vegetables and raised chickens for eggs and goats for cheese."

"Why did you ever leave?"

"It was a hard life. A lot of work. I realized much later, of course. Raising all these kids, for years there wasn't even real plumbing. We had a well and a hand pump in the kitchen sink. Mostly I think it was just the world changed. Land values went up, development came in, ideals were shattered. This was 1975. My dad was bored. We had men walking on the moon and he was tinkering with windmills. Then there was a measles epidemic. No one had been vaccinated and all the kids got sick, one died, my brother Redwood lost a lot of his hearing. Dad dusted off his old engineering degree and got a job in San Diego."

"That must have been a big change."

"God!" Zee laughed. "I had never been in a supermarket, never seen a bus. I had never walked on a sidewalk before! I mean, I must have, there was a town nearby, but not like suburban sidewalks, miles and miles of them. I had to wear shoes and my feet hurt. And all the people dressed so weird. So drab and all alike. I was used to tie-dyes and batik sarongs and ankle bracelets. That's how I met Ulla." Zee smiled at the memory.

"I was running away from home. I did it every day, I think, but only to the end of the block where I got scared and turned around. Ulla and her family were coming home from a cousin's wedding, and they were all dressed in Indian clothes. Turquoise and gold and sapphire blue, and her mother in all this jewelry! I thought, of course, that dressed like that, they had to come from my farm, and I ran up to them and asked them to take me home with them."

Zee's eyes were wet with tears. "I called them today. Ulla's mom is in the hospital. She couldn't eat or sleep. Lele says she just cries all the time." Zee wiped her eyes on the sleeve of her T-shirt and pulled the papers out from under the couch. "I want to know what happened to Ulla. I want to find out what's going on. Fairchild told me today he's shutting down Shadow Island."

Connor sat up, relieved to steer back toward the investigation. Factual labyrinths were easier than emotional ones.

"Why?"

"He said they were planning to shut us down for a while anyway because of operational costs, then Roddy's accident got the insurance people all nervous."

"Do you believe that?"

"I don't know what to believe anymore." Zee began to straighten the papers, sorting them back into relevant piles. "Was Mickey ever in the military? In Vietnam?"

"Yes."

"Do you know what he did?"

"He never talked much about it, just said it was dull. He worked as some kind of supply guy. Why?"

"Adam Fairchild did research on malaria during the Vietnam war. For the army, at Walter Reed."

"Fairchild?"

"He's a contributing author on some of those papers. He would have been in grad school, on a student deferment or something. If we're thinking about who would find popeye valuable, it makes sense to look at the military."

"I'm sure the military would be interested in new malaria drugs, but enough to kill for one? I thought you said the drug-resistant malaria was still pretty much isolated in certain areas."

"It is. And that's a little strange, too." Zee picked up one of the photocopied maps and pointed to a sprinkling of tiny blots scattered throughout Southeast Asia. "These are the primary locations where the deadly *P. falciparum* strain has emerged over the past twenty years. We need a better map, but what I see right now is that the movement of this malaria seems odd," Zee explained.

"How so?"

"Generally with a vector-borne disease, you would expect to see a transmission pattern following the vector's natural habitat, life cycle, or behavior."

"Vector-borne means carried by insects?"

"Carried by anything, mosquitos, fleas, rats. Malaria is carried by mosquitos, so we look at how mosquitos behave." She moved one finger over the map, spiraling outward from one of the shaded zones. "Mosquitos feed off an infected person then infect other people nearby. You would expect some jumps, of course." She moved her hand several inches away and began another spiral. "An infected person travels and brings the disease with him. Or an infected mosquito is moved beyond its normal range in a car or truck. That sort of thing is happening all over the world now with new roads and easier travel. Anyway, with a vector-borne disease you expect jumps, but then once jumped, we still ought to see it spread again in a gradual outward pattern."

"But this jumps all over the place," Connor said, squinting at the small map.

"Exactly, and then stays confined. Unless there is some obstacle, some significant change in terrain or habitat that would interfere with vector movement, we should see a more gradual spreading outward, and eventual interconnection of the zones. With our resistant *P. falciparum*, we have pockets of infection. The other odd thing is where we are *not* seeing this malaria. There are great gaps all over the place in regularly connected settlement areas. There could be a logical reason. The resistant *P. falciparum* might be less virulent than the types of malaria already established there. But it still raises questions. Starting in the mid-eighties, this malaria started jumping all over the place with no apparent natural pattern."

"There must be some pattern," Connor said gravely. "It just might not be natural."

13

Mickey's relief at finally having the vials of popeye only lasted about twenty minutes. As he turned down his own street, he saw a strikingly ordinary looking government sedan parked on the corner waiting for him. He slowed to a stop across from the car and was relieved to recognize Joe Simmons, an agent he had dealt with a few times when Chapmans needed, or could offer, assistance on certain cases. He had also employed the man's son for two summers during college. Mickey nodded in greeting and put his window down.

"Do you have a couple of minutes, Mickey?" Joe said benignly.

"There's a little shopping plaza up about a mile," Mickey replied. "Why don't you follow me there." Mickey drove slowly, desperate for time to think this through. *What was the FBI interested in? Nothing routine if Joe Simmons was making a personal call like this. This was a favor move, professional courtesy. Still, it couldn't be good.*

The two cars parked next to each other, and Mickey invited Joe over to his more comfortable and nicely chilled Lexus. The man slipped in with appreciative glances at the leather interior.

"Thanks for your time, Mickey. How have you been?" They dallied briefly on pleasantries: family, health, work, golf, how's so-and-so, then, as if both men knew that page was finished, they moved on to business. Simmons opened his briefcase and took out some Polaroid photos. "Do you recognize the clothes in this picture?"

"Only from seeing them on half the men on the street at any given time."

"Yeah, not much to go on there. The clothes came in this morning. That computer wiz, I think he's your nephew, Bongo or something, brought them in. He's doing a class on computer security with us. Things were slow for a change, and because it was from Chapmans, and hand-delivered and all, well, the guys took a look at it right away. Caused quite a bit of interest. I thought I should talk to you personally."

"I appreciate that, Joe, but I didn't know anything was even going there today. Who sent them in?"

"The lab request was made by a Connor Gale," Simmons went on in the same casual way. "Asking for analysis on explosives residue." Mickey nodded and stared at the photos. Simmons did not know that Connor was his foster son. The pictures of the singed and dirty jeans gave him a sick feeling. *Connor could have been killed.*

"Gale is fairly new and tends to charge ahead, if you know what I mean," Mickey said casually. "I'll have to have a little talk with him about procedure. What's this all about anyway? I take it you found something suspicious?"

Simmons made a noncommittal little sound as he took the photos back.

"You've helped us out in the past, Mickey. I just wanted you to be aware that after we get a better look at this, there will be a lot of questions. I thought you might like a chance to know that."

"Give me a hint here, Joe. My brain is addled with all this heat. What's going on? Is this some kind of weird new explosive or something?"

"Weird, but not new." Simmons tucked the photos back inside his suit jacket. "The lab found traces of residue from an early generation plastic explosive, twenty years old at least. The stuff never went on the market. It was too unmanageable. Very high explosive factor but unpredictable ignition patterns. It was temperature sensitive and degraded in certain conditions. It wasn't reliable. The thing is, this stuff is not exactly common. In fact, this stuff officially doesn't even exist. The whole lot of it was supposed to have been destroyed. So you see how we'd be curious, of course, to find it blowing something up now."

Throughout the neighborhood children had been summoned in to bed and the last bits of charcoal had long turned to ash in backyard grills. Another summer night fading into chirps and twitters. Connor paced the deck with a ferocious energy, pounding the railing with each point as if he could shake lose the answers.

"OK, this is what we know. Adam Fairchild once worked on malaria at Walter Reed. Thirty years later, Ulla Raki, working for Fairchild at SeaGenesis, comes up with a new cure for malaria. Fairchild discourages her, turns down her proposal for primate testing. At the same time, SeaGenesis is requesting more popeye from you, but shipments sent from Shadow Island never reach Raki's lab. Raki finds out about this and confronts Fairchild. Raki winds up dead. On Shadow Island, you guys suffer a series of accidents and then Fairchild tells you he's shutting down the research station entirely. We also have a suspicious government grant in the mix. Someone wants this new malaria cure. Let's call him . . . Mr. Stinger."

Connor swung a chair into the middle of the deck as if expecting Mr. Stinger to emerge from the shadows and occupy it. "Mr. Stinger is concerned with new strains of malaria which are resistant to all the available drugs. But resistant malaria isn't really a widespread problem. So why does he want it so badly?" He pulled another chair over and turned it to face Mr. Stinger's.

"Over here, we have Adam Fairchild. SeaGenesis is in financial trouble. Fairchild needs money. Either Fairchild knows the cure would be valuable to Stinger and approaches him, or Stinger learns independently about popeye and approaches Fairchild. Stinger is well connected, maybe government, maybe military. He pulls some strings. Stinger gets popeye, SeaGenesis gets a big government grant for Cronzene twenty, and Ulla gets dead." He stared at the chairs. There were still only two players, Fairchild and Mr. Stinger. Where did Mickey fit in?

Zee sat quietly, somewhat unnerved by Connor's manic energy. "If this Stinger guy is so well connected, why not just buy popeye from

SeaGenesis?" Zee asked. "Why subterfuge and murder? The defense budget is still high enough to put some money into a new malaria cure."

"Exactly. Why not just buy it? I think the value of popeye must depend on exclusivity. If my people have popeye and yours don't, my people can go places and do things your people can't. And if your people don't even know about popeye, I have even more advantage. Sole control over popeye allows me to go into these zones of infection." He had found a large *National Geographic* map of Asia which was now spread across the table, the corners weighted down with rocks. They had transferred the dots from Zee's smaller maps onto the big one. There was still no obvious pattern.

"Why does Mr. Stinger want to go to these areas so badly? What is there that's so valuable? Opium?"

"Connor, it still doesn't make sense," Zee insisted. "Ulla only started working on popeye two years ago. She's never done primate testing. We don't even know if it works in humans yet."

"Ahh, but someone else might." Connor saw returning skepticism on Zee's face. "Ulla made her first request for primate testing over a year ago. What if, while she was proceeding in the proper slow, scientific way, what if someone else just pulled out the throttle? Went ahead with the monkey tests and everything?"

"You still wouldn't be ready to even test in humans. No way."

"What if the stakes were high? What if you *had* to have this drug? I mean, how many monkeys do you have to try it on before you know it's safe for people?"

"That depends . . ."

"Let's say you had every indication it was safe," Connor interrupted, "and every motivation to rush ahead, how soon do you test in humans?"

"This is nuts, Connor!"

"Just play with me, Zee, just go along please? How soon?"

"No scientist in a million years is going to do something like this!"

"How soon?" Connor persisted. "A thousand people are going to die and this is the only possible cure. How many monkeys will convince you to try it in humans?"

"A dozen," she said with frustration. "I don't know."

Connor charged on, frustrated with the plod of science. "You got your monkeys. You shoot 'em up and they're still frisky the next day. All the blood comes up clean, no side effects and the malaria is cured. I'm ready to test in humans. What do I do?"

"Connor, this is stupid . . ."

"What do I do?"

"You inject a few people and look for allergic reactions. A rash, swelling, fever."

"OK, no reaction. What next?"

"Then you have to see how the drug is metabolized, if there is accumulation in tissues or organs, any chance of long-term damage."

"OK, no allergies, no nothing. Then what?"

"You wouldn't know that in a matter of weeks," Zee insisted, "or even months."

"I don't care about long-term damage. I have a fatal disease. If I don't use this drug I won't live long enough for that to matter."

She gave up trying to be logical and decided to play along. "OK, phase-two testing looks at efficacy," she explained. "Once you know your drug doesn't do any *harm*, you still have to see if it actually *works*. Does it cure malaria in the human body?"

"I have human volunteers," he declared. "Volunteers that already have this deadly malaria and know nothing else will cure them, and they really want to offer themselves as guinea pigs. How soon do I know that popeye really works?"

It seemed like Connor was enjoying all this, Zee thought with some disdain. It was just some big game for him. No one would do something like that! But of course they would. And it would be especially easy with malaria. In India, poor people would sell a kidney for a few hundred dollars. How little would it take to get them to try a new kind of medicine against a disease they all dreaded anyway?

"Connor, this is absolutely crazy! Even if your whole scenario were true, even if . . . if we really do have this band of evil mad scientists in secret labs somewhere testing in humans, there is still one serious flaw. Right now the only source for popeye is the living organism plucked off a coral reef. We haven't been able to synthesize it. Hell, we don't even know what the active compounds are to synthesize! Some of it works, some of it doesn't, and we don't even know why! Unless someone can produce the drug artificially, there's no hope of any large-scale production. And believe me, even if your secret mad scientist were Louis Pasteur himself, he's nowhere near synthesizing popeye yet."

"Well, what about just collecting it off the reef like you have been doing?"

"We don't even know how prevalent this sponge is. There is a lot of it at Shadow Island and we know it grows throughout the Caribbean, but not where or how much. We've been trying to grow it, but without much success. Besides, none of the farmed samples have had the mystery active ingredient."

"And you have no idea why?"

"No! I only saw Ulla's data two days ago!"

"Su Thom said this last batch, sample twenty-eight, was particularly effective and might hold the key to isolating the active compounds. Would you be able to find out where it came from?"

"We keep records of where and when a sample was collected, how deep, water temperature, surrounding organisms, all sorts of factors. But that's all at Shadow Island." Even as she protested, Zee realized she was offering another piece of the puzzle. What if there was something unique about Shadow Island? Some reason that popeye could only grow there, or only grow in the way to produce the bioactivity they needed? Damn! It made perfect sense and fit all too well. Fairchild wanted to shut down Shadow Island! Someone else could be way ahead of them with this research.

Was that part of her reluctance to accept all this? The fact that she might have to admit that someone else could have solved the puzzle she and Ulla had been unable to? Padgette? Could it be? She was ashamed that this thought sickened her almost as much as the theft of the drug itself.

"They don't want you back on Shadow Island." Connor spoke her very thoughts. "Someone knows that popeye actually does work and where the market is. Someone has already tested it," he went on eagerly. "Monkey tests. People tests . . ." He stopped abruptly. He stared at the two chairs facing each other. "A rash." He turned slowly back to Zee, patting his left arm just above the elbow.

"Su Thom had a rash right here, a red blotch. When I told him about Ulla taking the samples, he was disturbed. He tried to cover the mark."

Connor sat down, still clutching his own arm, trying to remember every detail from his talk with Su Thom that morning.

"That wouldn't be so unusual," Zee said quietly, "a researcher who really believes in something, trying it out on himself."

"Su Thom was as frustrated as Ulla, maybe more so. There was something about him. Something very determined, but also very dark." Connor frowned. "He talked about how the western world doesn't care about malaria. He was very bitter. Su Thom was testing on himself . . ." Connor stared out over the tangled yard. "He found out Ulla had taken the samples."

"Maybe Ulla discovered what he was doing," Zee suggested. "Maybe that's why she took the samples that night. And Su Thom . . ." She stared at him with growing horror, unwilling to follow the idea. Connor finished it for her.

"Su Thom wanted to get them back?"

The thick red drops fell slowly onto the table, each one a perfect crimson button. Su Thom tried to keep his hand steady. He slowly dipped the brush again. Carefully he touched the tiny brush to the box, taking care to stay in the lines. The paint was vivid and bright on the unfinished wood, a beautiful shade, arterial red. The box was a tiny coffin, crudely built of hobby store balsa wood strips. He painted with delicate strokes and finished off the picture. It was a picture of Uncle Sam. He was dead, arms folded, little Xs for eyes. Su Thom dipped the brush in the water and watched it swirl with the red paint. He opened a jar of black paint, and at the bottom of the coffin, he carefully painted his message: *RIP July 4.*

On the table, ready for the coffin, was a tiny plastic bag with one dead mosquito inside. The warning. One last chance. The only sound in the room was the low hum of his mosquitos in their cage. The lamp was bent low, focused on the immediate work. In the shadow just outside the pool of light, the microscope looked menacing and strange, hunched and black like some demon.

His own blood was clean. So far. He had checked it as soon as he got to the lab that morning. No sign of malaria yet. But then there wouldn't be. It was too soon. Su Thom was more annoyed than worried. If and when his blood smear showed the parasites, he would have to inject himself with popeye, and right now, he had no popeye. He had to find the samples and get them back. But even the possibility of his own painful death was not as disturbing as the thought of his experiment failing at this point. He felt the guilt churning up again. It was like a great black bird beating its wings in his face. If only he had been more careful. If only Ulla hadn't found out! His hand began to shake and he put the paintbrush down. *She could still be alive!* He rubbed his palms against his tired eyes. What else could he have done?

Connor knocked again but there was still no answer. There was no sound at all from inside. He had seen a light on in Su Thom's bedroom but the shade was drawn. Connor had watched for at least ten minutes and seen no shadow movement behind it. Su Thom could simply be reading in bed and not wishing to be disturbed. He may have fallen asleep. Or something might have happened to him. What was his role in all this? Villain or victim?

Connor tried the doorknob. It was locked, but it was a simple lock. He debated his options. Su Thom may have killed Ulla. Or someone else might have killed them both. He slipped his hand into his pocket and pulled out the little set of lockpicks. It was the same set he had learned with as a child. He hadn't used them in years and it took him a few long minutes to open the simple lock.

The room was hot and airless.

"Su Thom?" he called. "Su Thom, it's Connor Gale. Are you here?" There was no sound. The room was neat, no signs of a struggle. No murder weapon lying out on the desk.

Connor walked down the hall, checking the bathroom and bedroom. No sign of Su Thom. He went back to the living room where they had talked that morning. He stood still, looking, listening, trying to get the sense of the place and the man who lived here. Something was odd. The apartment was very clean. There was no garbage in the kitchen can, and no food in the refrigerator. Everything was spare and neat and very clean. Extraordinarily neat, even for a tidy person. He checked the bathroom, the medicine cabinet, the kitchen, letting the sense of the place tell its own story.

The story, he realized, was that Su Thom had not been staying here. This morning when he met Su Thom coming in the building, Connor had assumed he had returned because he had forgotten something. But now he suspected that he hadn't even stayed here the night before, or for many nights before. Was there a girlfriend somewhere? He opened the drawers of the desk, looking for an address book, old letters. Everything there was neat as well. Phone bills were clipped together. Student loan payments and credit card bills arranged in order. Most of these were simply blank monthly statements. Su Thom was not much of a consumer. There was only one restaurant in the past six months, a pair of shoes, and some car repairs. He paid on time, never kept a balance. The only statement with anything on it was the most recent one.

On May 23, Su Thom had obtained a credit card advance of five thousand dollars. The next day he took a three hundred and forty dollar trip through T. W. Perry's hardware store. Connor knew it well, since he had started doing work on old Mrs. Wickham's house. It was a great store where people actually knew things, and helped you. He also knew this old fashioned service was mixed with a modern computer inventory and billing system. It was almost nine o'clock, but they might still be open. He looked up the number and gave them a call.

"Hey, I'm sorry to bother you so late, but I was wondering, I bought a bunch of stuff there about a month ago, and I'm doing my books here, and realize I must have thrown away the receipt, which of course I need for tax deductions. But since I paid for it on my credit card, I'm wondering if there's still a record in your system, you know, a way I could get a duplicate receipt?" He heard the clerk sigh, but there was only a slight twinge of irritation in the man's voice.

"Do you remember the exact date?"

Connor told him the date of the purchase and gave him Su Thom's

credit card number. He heard a keyboard clicking busily in the background.

"Here you go, framing lumber, staple gun, hammer, nails, PVC pipe,
and . . . some kind of screening . . . maybe chicken wire, I'm not sure of
the code there. Looks like you're building a rabbit pen."

"Yeah. OK that's right, the rabbit, yeah."

"You want me to send you a copy of this?"

"No, that's OK. Thanks." Connor hung up the phone. Framing lumber, chicken wire? The items had been purchased a month ago. Just when
Ulla's request for monkeys had been turned down again. Was Su Thom
planning some sort of secret testing? A little monkey zoo to try out
popeye? Where would he build something like that?

Connor remembered the controlled young man he had talked to. He
had been passionate about his work and devoted to Ulla Raki. He might
have already started testing popeye on himself. What else might he do
for his cause? Did Su Thom have cages of monkeys hidden away somewhere? The cash advance had rented a space somewhere. A garage? A
storage locker? A house in the country where the chattering animals
wouldn't be discovered? What do you need to raise monkeys? How much
space did he need, and how much privacy? Su Thom's apartment yielded
no other information and Connor went home with more questions than
he had left with.

He found Zee asleep on the couch, a stack of the malaria papers still
half clutched in one hand, others scattered on the floor where they had
tumbled. She woke up with a start and a small gasp of alarm.

"It's me," Connor said softly. "It's okay."

Zee draped one arm over her eyes and let out a relieved breath.
Connor sat on the edge of the couch and her other hand crept into his.
She opened her eyes and they looked at each other for a long minute,
body heat building between them like a summer storm. Then they simply
fell into one another, hungry for touch, needing to connect. He kissed
her and the kiss was urgent and tasted of fear he would not otherwise
acknowledge. Zee pressed herself against him until she could no longer
tell where the edge of each of them began. Connor pulled her T-shirt off
and left her wrists tangled in the sleeves. He laid her down on the floor,
papers crumpling beneath her. He kissed her belly, salty and sweet. Their

lovemaking was fast and furious and bruising, exorcism as much as embrace. When they had finished, the demons were not gone, but pushed aside on the cloud of body heat that let them rest inside the puff of safety. It could not last, but it was a delicious bliss, to lie together on the bare floor for a few minutes, cool air spilling over their hot bodies. The bubble would seep, the pain and danger would snarl up around them again, but for a little while, things were peaceful.

Connor rolled off at last but kept one leg around her, as if she might tumble off the edge of the world. They lay together in silence until the papers started getting itchy and the air conditioning uncomfortably cold on their sweat-chilled skins. Connor peeled himself back and pulled her up so they were leaning against the couch, looking over the sea of papers that would now need drastic reordering. Reality was always there and needing to be faced. He felt Zee's heartbeat calming down against his arm. It was kind of nice not facing it alone.

"Do you want to stay?" he asked her, almost shyly.

"I don't know," Zee said. "The Holiday Inn has cable."

"The Holiday Inn is expensive."

"SeaGenesis is paying."

"Good. Then keep the room. But stay here tonight."

14

July 2

Z ee stayed, and in the morning Connor did not try to sneak out. They had no new solutions but at least a plan of action. Zee would go to SeaGenesis as Fairchild had requested for a tour of the lab, and to start the paperwork for her transfer.

"Talk to Su Thom if you can," Connor suggested. "But be careful. He doesn't know about the intercepted supplies of popeye. I'd rather not arouse any suspicions in his mind about you. And don't mention my monkey theory. He might not be happy about me searching his apartment."

"What are you going to do?"

"Try to find out more about Mickey's service in Vietnam." Connor knew there was an envelope of old photos in Mickey's study, faded snapshots showing a much younger and slimmer Mickey Sullivan in army uniform. He and Sean had found them once while searching Mickey's desk for cigarettes. Mickey had never told them much about his years in the war, insisting that it was all pretty boring. He never even fired his gun, just shipped crates of instant mashed potatoes around. Connor remembered in a couple of the pictures he was standing with a clipboard surrounded by cargo. In the background of one photo Connor also thought he remembered stacks of boxes with red crosses on them. Did he also handle supplies for army hospitals?

He drove to the house a little after ten when he was sure it would be empty. Lois was at one of her regular charity meetings. Breaking in would have been easy enough even if he hadn't helped install the security system himself, as she never turned it on during the day even when she went out, and usually left a basement door unlocked. She feared displaced relatives needing access. Cars broken down, or keys lost, or legs broken; frustrated teenagers or upset spouses running away from home then thinking better of it; dotty Great-aunt Dorothy lost on the way to lunch, all might someday wander by and need succor while she was out, and if wayward arctic explorers should show up, she wanted to be sure they could get in if they needed and feed the sled dogs, too. Everyone knew where the spare key was. It drove Mickey crazy, but it was one of those long-married compromises he had accepted.

Connor got the key from under the bird feeder and opened the front door. Still he felt guilty, burdened by his doubt and suspicion. He stood inside the foyer, chastised by the familiar smells: umbrellas and furniture polish, a trace of Lois's hand lotion which she always put on just before leaving. What was he doing here like this? He should just go to Chapmans and confront Mickey directly. What did he expect to find here?

He opened the basement door and went down the stairs to Mickey's study. He hadn't been in this room for years. It hadn't changed. There was another huge desk, but this one was old and scarred. It had belonged to Mickey's great-uncle, salvaged from a police precinct. The carpet in front of the desk was worn. The scolding spot, where each of the boys had literally been called on the carpet, to stand for assignment of punishment. No fidgeting allowed. Connor stood quietly in the center of the room, like any other break-in, trying to feel it out. It was weirder doing it with someone he knew. Or thought he knew. Connor circled the room once, getting a fix on everything so as to leave no sign. He glanced at his watch. Lois's comings and goings were not predictable.

The envelope of photos used to be on the closet shelf. Connor pulled open the door. There were two boxes on the floor, filled with Sean's old stuff. Connor squatted down and quickly looked through the boxes but found nothing of interest. There were school papers, a yearbook, photos, trophies. He missed Sean. If he were alive today he would have sorted all this out easily. He was the one to get things out of Mickey. What had caused him to go screaming out into the night with a quart of scotch and a black rage? He and Mickey had been fighting about something that night. Connor was upstairs in his room and heard them shouting down here. But Sean had always been so steady. And nothing else had been going on. No confrontation brewing. If anything, everyone was getting along happily at the time. Sean's baseball team was in the state finals and he had hit a triple that day to win the game.

Connor went back to the task at hand. He found the envelope of photos easily, but they were of no help. There were fewer than he remembered, and Adam Fairchild was not in any of them. He put them back. He walked over to the desk. Mickey's shape was pressed into the chair. Connor put his hand on the drawer. He couldn't open it. It wasn't locked, but he just couldn't. That was too much. It was time to talk to Mickey directly. Just ask him. Just offer to help. Trust him. *Let him trust me to help.* The sun creased the corner of the window and shone in on the far wall, dust dancing in the beam, scattering patterns on the old paneling and highlighting a crack that had begun to peel with age. Connor knew that crack, had caused it with the back of his own head.

The night his father died, Connor had come down here ready to kill Mickey. Connor was sixteen, tall by then, still skinny, but strong and in a blind fury. Mickey was standing by the TV changing the station and Connor jumped on him, fists flying. This was the man who had killed his father. Sent him away to jail where he could no more live than a wild horse in a carnival cage. Now he was dead and Connor wanted to kill the man who had caused it. Mickey sent him flying into the wall with one swing of his arm. He did not mean to be so forceful, but reacted out of surprise. Connor remembered the distinctive feel of the panel breaking under his skull. The crash did his head no damage, but knocked him senseless for a minute.

Then Lois and Daniel had come in, and everyone was shouting and screaming but all he felt was a soft gold-edged light and a foggy hush. That day had been a turning point. Sean had died just a few months earlier; now Connor had lost his father. Their lives were tangled with shock and hurt and blame, but in it there was also release and repair.

He went over to the wall and pressed his palm gently on the paneling. The crack had dried and widened over the years. Connor felt a wisp of warm air seeping through. The boards had a slight give. With a sudden flood of memory he remembered something else. The sound when his head hit the wall. It was a hollow sound. He stepped back and looked at the wall, picturing the layout of the house. The back steps were behind this wall. Under the steps was a closet for the water heater. But that closet was only about four feet deep. Connor spread his arms and measured the distance from the wall to the crack in the paneling. Just about six feet. There was no door from the garage side leading to this extra space under the stairs.

He searched out the edges of the panel. He ran his fingers along the molding at the top. There. The molding had the slightest bit of wiggle. The tiny finishing nails were loose. By slipping the blade of his pocketknife under it, it came free easily. Once the molding was down, the top edge of the panel was easy to grip. He pushed aside a bookcase and found all the little nails around the panel were loose. It was utterly low tech. Just a plain old piece of paneling loosened from the underlying studs. Not meant for frequent access, but easy enough to get into when necessary, and completely innocuous looking. He never would have even looked here except for the memory of the fight.

His heart pounded. Did he really want to know what was in here? There was no turning back now. He pulled the panel free. Inside was a space about three feet long by three wide, about five feet high where it met the back of the water heater closet, sloping to the ground at the bottom of the stairs. A roomy little storage place, full of neatly stacked boxes.

"As you see, the whole building was designed to bring in natural light, provide efficient space, and eliminate some of the harshness of the laboratory environment." Frank Teller, SeaGenesis's head of personnel, was giving Zee the full tour as if she were a visiting dignitary. She felt much more like a lab rat soon to be stuck in this maze. How could they even think of shutting down Shadow Island now?

"Subareas of the main labs are sectioned off to reduce noise, and soothing colors are used throughout." Teller smiled proudly as if he had designed the place himself. "Each principal investigator has a private space just off the lab floor."

"Where was Ulla's office?"

Teller's cheerfulness ebbed. "At the end of the hall."

"Could I see it?"

"There isn't much in there. I believe her father packed up all her personal effects." His footsteps slowed. "But you're welcome to see it if you like."

The blinds were drawn and the door was shut but not locked. The shades on the outside windows were drawn as well. The little room was dark except for a sad blue light cast by the computer monitor over the bare desk.

"That's odd, I didn't think anyone was using the room," Teller said as he reached for the light switch. The fluorescent light flickered and for the few seconds it took to come fully on, the scene was flashed as if under a strobe. The silver glint of the metal chair frame, the china blue of the carpet, the impossibly red pool of blood. A man lay motionless, crumpled on the floor behind the chair. Blood still oozed from deep gashes across each wrist.

"Oh my god." Teller stood in the doorway, motionless with shock. Zee squeezed past him. She squatted and felt for a pulse.

"He's still alive. Call 911!"

"Oh my god, it's Su Thom!"

Zee saw a scalpel poised on the edge of the desk, terribly clean except for the bright red on its point. She grabbed the scalpel, sliced through the hem of the man's shirt, then tore two strips of the cloth free. She reached up, yanked open the desk drawer and scooped out the pencil slot. Pencils and pens tumbled to the carpet like pick-up-sticks. Faces appeared in the doorway as news traveled throughout the lab. Zee heard someone in the office next door calling for an ambulance. A tall, thin man came in and helped Zee fashion tourniquets from the torn shirt and pencils. People were gathering outside the door.

"What happened? Who is it? Su Thom, Ulla's lab assistant. Cut his wrists!"

Su Thom? Ulla's assistant?

Zee's heart began to pound as she overheard the snatches of conversation. Su Thom was missing last night when Connor went to his apartment. Now here he was, barely alive. Did he really do this, or was it done to him? She looked around the office. What should she look for? There were no signs of a struggle, no other apparent sign of injury on his body. She felt carefully around the back of his head, but could find no lump or swelling. Maybe he had done it. Maybe he had killed Ulla, and the guilt just got to be too much. Outside, the speculation went on.

"Why would he do such a thing? . . . No, I didn't know him really. . . . He always kept to himself. . . . Is he going to make it?"

The rescue squad arrived. Then the police.

"Was Su Thom unhappy about anything? Depressed perhaps?"

Frank Teller stood by wringing his hands. "Unhappy? Oh dear. Yes, he was. Yes, of course. Ulla Raki. She was his mentor. Killed last week. That carjacking, you know. He worked with her. And I'm afraid . . . I do believe he was rather in love with her . . ."

Fairchild's secretary brought him the opened package, carrying it gingerly in front of her as if it were an offering on a platter.

"What should I do?" she asked nervously. "Should I call the police? I shouldn't even have opened the envelope, I suppose. It could have been a letter bomb. But the return address, you can see. It's from Kerr Biosystems, I thought it was some sort of promotional knickknack like we're always getting. A penlight or keychain or something." Her voice quavered. "Then this thing just tumbled out. It's horrible! The lid came off. Once I saw it, I handled it with a tissue, in case there were fingerprints or something."

She put the padded manila envelope down on the corner of Fairchild's desk. On top was a tiny coffin, crudely built of hobby store balsa wood strips. The little box was open, and there was a folded piece of paper tucked inside. Painted on the lid was a likeness of Uncle Sam, arms crossed, dead. At his feet in ghoulish black letters it said, *RIP July 4.*

"I'm sorry, Carol." Fairchild tried to reassure her. "I'm sure it's just another nutcase. I'll talk to security," he said calmly. Strange letters, threatening screeds, and occasional demonstrations were common enough in the business where some kooks always feared the evil fruits of bio-technology.

"It just didn't seem suspicious . . ."

"I'm sure it isn't anything to worry about."

He really wasn't worried as he took the letter out of the coffin. Then he unfolded it and the little plastic bag tumbled out. Fairchild held the bag up to the light and saw the mosquito. Even then it took a few seconds to register. He read the note: *"What if these were flying around your own backyard? Would you be more interested in a cure?"*

With a trembling hand he reached for the phone.

Zee was frightened by the look on Connor's face as he strode into the hospital.

"Where is he?" He glanced back over his shoulder then surveyed the waiting room and steered her over to a bank of telephones in a corner.

"In the recovery room."

"Who else is here?"

"Someone from SeaGenesis. Frank Teller, a personnel guy."

"No one else? No police?"

"The police left. Connor, tell me what is going on!"

"We have to get Su Thom out of here."

"Out of here? What are you talking about?"

Connor shook his head. "There's no way this was a suicide attempt."

"How do you know?" she whispered. "They say he was in love with Ulla."

"Su Thom spent a lifetime in hell before he was ten years old. He's not going to off himself over a broken heart."

"Well, what if he did kill her and couldn't stand the guilt?"

Connor looked around the waiting room once more, though he had no idea who or what he expected to see. "It's possible. But I'd like to give him a chance to tell us. Let's find the cafeteria."

"The cafeteria?"

"We need badges if we're going to get anywhere in the hospital."

Connor easily lifted a couple of hospital ID badges in the cafeteria and plucked a stethoscope out of an intern's lab coat pocket. For good measure, he pinched a clipboard from a nurses' station. A clipboard could always get you places.

Zee shuddered as she watched his cool thievery. It was all too bizarre. She tried to wipe the image of Su Thom from her mind, the glossy black hair, the fresh white shirt, the red blood.

They found out Su Thom had been stitched up and transfused and was being held in the recovery room until he was stable enough to be transferred to the psychiatric ward. The recovery room was one long, brightly lit room. A large sign on the double door forbade visitors. Connor and Zee peered through the windows. Six patients were in the room now, lined up on gurneys. A row of monitors reported their vital signs. Everything seemed quiet and serene. A plump, grandmotherly nurse sat at the center control station. A short, red-haired nurse in a pink smock was at the far end of the row, checking blood pressure. Su Thom was four gurneys down from her, easy to spot because of his black hair and bandaged wrists. A doctor was bent over him, consulting a clipboard.

Connor turned away. The elevators were just around the corner, and there was a stairway at the end of the hall. Suddenly Zee gasped and grabbed his arm, yanked him back to the window.

"Connor, that man is not a doctor! He was at SeaGenesis. I saw him in the lab! He was in the crowd of people watching. He was dressed like a workman. He's sticking something in Su Thom's IV!"

"Shit!" Connor burst through the door. The man in the white jacket looked up, then turned and ran, his hard-soled shoes skidding on the smooth floor. A hypodermic needle fell and spun under Su Thom's gurney. The red-haired nurse shouted and dropped her stethoscope. The desk nurse reached for the phone. Zee ran to Su Thom's side and pulled out the IV. The man got to the end of the ward, then, realizing there was only one way out, spun around and ran back. Connor tackled him, hurling him backward against an EKG machine. The man was a few inches shorter but broad and stocky. He came back with a roundabout that sent Connor flying. Connor leapt to his feet, grabbed the machine, and slammed it into him. The nurses fluttered on the periphery, commanding them to stop, shouting for security, and moving patients out of the way.

The man lunged at Connor across the machine, grabbed hold of his shirt and twisted him off balance, slamming him against the floor, tipping the EKG cart. Tubes of cream flew out and a roll of paper bounced and unwound across the floor. Plugs and wires tangled across both men. Then the man jumped to his feet. He looked at Connor with murderous rage, but realizing the likelihood of reinforcements any second, turned and sprinted for the door.

Connor jumped up and grabbed Su Thom's gurney. "Come on!" Zee picked up the fallen hypodermic, snapped the needle off, and shoved it in her pocket. The older nurse grabbed the gurney and tried to stop them. Zee shoved her off. A hospital security guard appeared at the door as they hustled their way through.

"We're the police!" Connor declared, whipping his wallet out of his pocket and flashing his Chapmans ID quickly at them all. "Secure this room!" He shoved Su Thom's gurney past the guard and out the door. A little confidence in the middle of chaos goes a long way. Not too long, but long enough.

"In there," Connor pointed toward the stairway. They pushed the gurney inside the doors, then Connor pulled Su Thom's unconscious body onto his shoulder in a fireman's carry. They hurried down two flights to the basement. Zee peeked her head out the door. The corridor was quiet. Laundry and cleaning carts were lined up against one wall. The linen carts were five feet tall, with tubular steel frames, broad, deep shelves, and heavy vinyl side flaps to close it all in. Perfect. Zee found one that was mostly empty, held back one of the flaps, and Connor slid Su Thom on the middle shelf, then crouched on the bottom shelf.

"Find the loading dock," he whispered. Zee dropped the flap and began to push the cart down the hall. Her heart was pounding. She saw two men in maintenance coveralls coming toward her. She was dressed in a nice skirt and blouse, appropriate for a job interview, not for pushing laundry carts around. She leaned as far as she could to the opposite side, letting the bulky cart shield her.

Zee saw daylight coming from the left. The cart had a bad wheel and was hard to turn. It skidded into the wall, and she heard a muffled grunt from inside. She pushed the cart out on the loading dock. Now what? They could hardly just walk off down the street carrying Su Thom.

There was a man unloading crates of produce from a refrigerated truck and another man in heavy white coveralls and gloves piling red biohazard buckets into the back of a van.

"What now?" she whispered.

"Is anyone looking?"

"Not yet, but there are people around." The flap slowly lifted and Connor slipped out.

"Hey!" he called to the man in the coveralls. "God, I'm glad I caught you. You need to . . . ah . . . go to two south." The man frowned.

"I never pick up there."

"Not a pickup," Connor replied, grasping to concoct a story. "A . . . leak." He gestured vaguely at the biohazard buckets and gave Zee a desperate look for help.

"It's nothing to worry about," Zee said, adjusting her hospital badge with feigned authority. "Just a formality. Some radioactive waste may have been mixed with biohazard. They'll just check your exposure badge and we'll do a quick sweep of the van."

The man grumbled some more but slammed his door shut and went off to have himself checked. The produce men were sitting on crates, having a smoke, not paying attention. Connor carried Su Thom down the steps and loaded him into the back of the van. Zee grabbed a stack of towels for cushioning and jumped in beside him. *Great, now they were escaping in a truck full of toxic waste.* Connor started the van and they drove uneventfully down the street.

"Come up here and get my keys," he instructed tersely. Zee climbed between the buckets to the front of the van and took the keys. "I'll drop you off at my car." He gripped the steering wheel and checked the mirrors. "Ten minutes, maybe fifteen if we're lucky, and the cops will know about this van." He slowed down as he approached his parked car. "There's a shopping mall not far from here, Lakeforest, I think. Meet me there." She nodded and jumped out.

The little coffin was dwarfed in Mickey Sullivan's big hand. Fairchild shifted nervously at his desk, the letter spread open between them.

"You're sure the mosquito is infected?" Mickey asked calmly.

"Yes goddamnit! I examined it myself. It's full of malaria! Brain-exploding, no-cure, dead-in-a-week *P. falciparum* malaria."

"That's impossible."

"I know what it looks like, damn it!" Fairchild's tanned face had developed a tic, a circular spasm that arced from eye to lip on the left side. "He could have hundreds, thousands of them!"

"Where would Su Thom get hundreds of *Anopheles* mosquitos? And if he did, how would he infect them all with a rare strain of malaria that is only found in a few isolated regions of Southeast Asia?"

"He's a brilliant fucking scientist, that's how! And Ulla Raki had samples of the Asher strain in the lab!"

"You can't be sure it's that."

"I can't be sure it's not."

"Could anyone else tell? Another doctor, looking at this strain of malaria, would he be able to tell it was . . . different?"

"No." Fairchild rubbed the side of his head. "They would know it's *P. falciparum* and eventually they would know it was incurable, but you would have to do DNA testing to determine the exact strain."

"So we're covered." Mickey put the little coffin down on the desk. Fairchild recoiled. "Su Thom probably just got a few infected mosquitos from a lab somewhere and sent one to you as a threat."

"Well, why don't you just go *ask* him!" Fairchild glared at him, his face white. The ambulance had left an hour ago but there was no word yet from the hospital. "Christ, you better hope he lives. What the hell were you thinking!"

"Whatever do you mean?"

"You never said anything about killing people and blowing up houses and . . . and all this!"

"I don't know anything about killing people and blowing up houses," Mickey replied with icy menace. "Su Thom cut his wrists in his grief over Ulla."

"Oh, right. Another accident."

Mickey turned away. Fairchild was the worst sort. A whiner. A pansy. A greedy, manipulative bastard who hadn't the balls to stand up to the trouble he had so coolly courted.

"Su Thom could have a plague ready to drop in our lap." Fairchild's voice trembled. "If he dies, we have no idea where the mosquitos are."

"Don't get ahead of yourself, Adam."

"Ahead of myself! This has got completely out of hand! I told you, we should have just cut Ulla out of it months ago. But no, you had to let her go on."

"It was a calculated risk," Mickey said tersely. "We needed her research. She was so close."

"So then when you do decide to intervene, you go off on your own and try to double-cross me!" Fairchild was almost whining now. "Steal my keys! And why the hell didn't you just use the security set? That's where you screwed up, getting Connor involved."

"Opening the lockbox where the security keys are kept triggers its own alarm," Mickey explained as if Fairchild were a dim-witted child. "It records the time and date of entry. I was only looking out for your best interests, Adam. I thought it was best for you simply not to know."

It had been a good plan, sneak into the lab and exchange Ulla's good samples of popeye for bad ones, then let the experiment simply fail. It would have worked. But then Lofton went nuts and Connor got interested. Mickey rubbed the back of his neck where a headache was starting. He had allowed for unexpected circumstance. He had considered a dozen things that might go wrong. What he hadn't accounted for, he realized now, was passion. Ulla Raki had been too passionate about her work; now Connor was passionate about unraveling a mystery. *What was he trying to prove?*

Fairchild had regained some composure and sat back down at his desk. "I want you to know that I've kept records documenting all of our . . . business."

"And what business was that?"

"I went to you in good faith with a drug that I thought my government might find valuable. That's all. I never asked you to manipulate the EPA contract. I had no knowledge of what you were doing with popeye."

"You know, Adam," Mickey said, "popeye is very important to our clients. You understand that, don't you?"

"Shut up!" Fairchild turned away. "I'm not listening to this."

"You don't know who you're dealing with."

"I don't want to know. I told you that from the beginning."

"Yes," Mickey said sarcastically. "You just assumed I was selling popeye to the Little Sisters of the Poor."

"I have no part of that. I promised you exclusive rights to popeye. Whatever you've been doing with it I don't want to know. I only care about what we're going to do now! What is Su Thom going to say when he wakes up? If he wakes up."

"I'll take care of it."

"You know what happens if any of this comes out, don't you? You know what people will call this?"

Mickey knew. The sheer bad luck would not count, the mistakes, the misplaced faith in science. The worst it was, really, was hubris, wasn't it? Hubris and greed, the old standby sins from Oedipus to Lear. But no one would see it that way. He knew what they would call it. *Genocide. Biological warfare.*

Fairchild's phone chirped and he picked it up. He listened for a minute then put it down again. He looked as if he might faint.

"Su Thom is gone. I don't understand it. Frank Teller said someone kidnapped him from the hospital."

Connor parked the van far at the far end of the shopping mall parking lot. Zee pulled up just a few minutes later. Su Thom was starting to come around and protested vaguely as they lifted him out of the van and into the backseat. Connor found a pair of shorts and a T-shirt in his trunk. The bandages would still be a problem. He dug further and found a flannel shirt. Hard to explain in ninety-degree weather, but it would have to do.

"Put these on him. Tell him he had an accident, don't get him upset. I'll be right back." He pulled out the pocketknife, unfolded the screwdriver blade, took the license plates off his own car and walked up the row until he found an older model station wagon filled with car seats and a litter of toys. Most people would probably not notice their license plate had been switched, but a mother steering a brood back to a station wagon most certainly would not. If they were lucky, it might go unnoticed for days.

When he returned to the car, Zee had Su Thom changed and laid out in the backseat, unconscious again.

"What now?" she asked. Her eyes were big with fear and her mouth was set in a tight line. Connor squeezed her shoulder, unable to offer more solace right now.

"Escape." He got behind the wheel and started the car. *Escape to where, though?* He turned back onto Route 270 and headed north. He saw a sign for Route 340. With sudden inspiration, he decided to go to Harper's Ferry. It was only an hour's drive from D.C. It was thick with tourists on weekends, but a sleepy village during the week. Su Thom drifted in and out of consciousness as they drove. The suburbs gradually paled out behind them and soon they saw the haze of mountains ahead. Six lanes eased into two and pavements yielded to rolling hills and farms. For all its importance in the world, the nation's capital yielded physical territory quickly. They spoke little, both too overwhelmed.

It was amazing how the feeling of escape came back, Connor thought as he drove. He remembered that sense of clean promise he always felt with his dad as they hit the open road and whatever town they were fleeing finally disappeared behind them. *Let's shake this dust off our feet!* his father would laugh. And they would shake their feet and get in the car. Whichever car it was at the time, they all blended together in Connor's memory, long and old and low, smelling of gin and cigarettes and sun-soft vinyl. Radio stations would fade in and out as they drove along and Dad would tell him about the next town, about how all the people there were so rich they just left their diamonds out on the dinner table and wouldn't things be easy then. No matter how good or bad things had gone, no matter if they were leaving behind a good, sweet woman or a pack of angry deputies, they were always happy on that first turn out of town. But today there just wasn't road enough in the world.

They checked into a motel on the outskirts of Harper's Ferry. Zee listened with amazement as Connor smoothly concocted their story for the desk clerk. They were high school teachers from Cleveland, touring Civil War sites with their Japanese exchange student. He chatted on as he filled out the register with fake names. *Would you have a map of the town? And how would we get to Antietam battlefield? What about a place to eat? Well, maybe they would just get something light. Sanyun is pretty tired. Jet lag, you know, and a little stomach trouble. Not used to American food yet.*

Zee tried not to look as stupefied as she felt. She smiled and nodded and listened incredulously to Connor's easy charm. The woman was practically flirting with him. She was in her sixties, with badly dyed hair and great rolls of white arm fat cascading out of a green polyester blouse. When Connor complimented the crocheted doll skirt decorative toilet paper roll covers on display on the counter, thus inviting a few minutes more discussion on the local craft shops, Zee felt a sudden uncontrollable fit of the giggles approaching. Her nerves were shot.

They drove around to the door of their room. Su Thom was still groggy, but Connor propped him up enough so he got to the room more or less standing, in case anyone was watching. Once inside, Connor gently eased him down on one bed. Zee checked the bandages and felt his pulse. He was pale and beginning to twitch as he came around.

"Is he okay?" Zee asked wearily.

"I guess so. His pulse is steady. He isn't bleeding. He's almost conscious."

"Can you stay with him a little while?"

"Where are you going?"

"To get some food, juice for him. And I have to call Mrs. Wickham, ask her to go over and feed Lucy." He had a sudden stampede of thoughts. Would Mickey do something to his dog? No, how could anyone be that rotten? That rotten? Shit, how would he ever look at the world after this?

By one in the morning, Su Thom was fairly alert and beginning to make sense of all they had told him. The idea that someone had tried to kill him did not really seem to bother him. He related what he remembered in an impassive way. He was in Ulla's office working on the computer. He heard someone come in and started to turn around. Something hit him on the back of his head. Not very hard, just enough to daze him, but then there was a needle stick in his arm. That was the last thing he remembered.

Su Thom had not seen the man, but felt his hands and described them as large and strong. The man at the hospital had broad hands and was powerfully built. The late news on TV had no mention of any mayhem at the hospital. Once again, someone was exercising considerable pull to keep things quiet. Connor straddled a chair next to Su Thom's bed.

"You have no idea who would want to kill you or Ulla?"

Su Thom shook his head.

"Who would want popeye so bad?"

"Nobody wants it. That's the whole problem," he said bitterly.

"Did you kill Ulla, Su Thom?" Connor threw the question in unexpectedly, in the same casual tone. Su Thom did not even flinch.

"No," he said simply. "Why would I?"

"Because you thought she had given up on a drug that you cared very deeply about. Because she found out you were testing it on yourself."

Su Thom tensed and turned his face away.

"She did find out?" Connor pressed. When Su Thom finally spoke, he was fighting back tears.

"Yes. She saw me injecting myself. That's why she took the samples with her that night. That's why she was killed. Someone knew she had taken the samples and wanted to get them back. I am responsible for her death. But I didn't kill her."

"You're not responsible, Su Thom." Zee touched his hand but he jerked it away and seemed to draw himself even more closed.

"What about your other experiment?" Connor asked. Su Thom stiffened. "Did Ulla know what you were doing?"

"What are you talking about?" Su Thom's voice was tense.

"The primate studies, Su Thom," Zee said gently. "We know SeaGenesis kept turning down your requests. You bought materials from a hardware store. Stuff to build cages." Su Thom looked away. Zee touched his shoulder. "It's OK. But we need to know. If you have monkeys somewhere, we need to get them."

"There are no monkeys," he said. "I couldn't get any. It's impossible

to get monkeys." Su Thom sank back against the pillows and closed his
eyes. Zee looked at Connor and nodded, accepting his answer. It would
be difficult to set up any sort of backyard primate center, even with a
couple of monkeys.

"Let him rest, Connor," she said quietly.

"Just a little more. Can you do a little more, Su Thom? Just look at
these maps?" Su Thom nodded and opened his eyes. Connor picked up
the maps of malaria distribution. "Whoever is after popeye wants to be
able to go into areas where this deadly *P. falciparum* is a problem.
What's there? Opium?"

"It could be anything," Su Thom said. "Opium for sure. It could be
political. There are still a lot of factions vying for control of land. There
is also a lot of old forest around here and here." He pointed to some
places. "Logging is very profitable. And this is a big mining region:
gems, precious stones, emeralds."

Gems. Connor's heart sank. He thought of the emerald necklace
Mickey had given Lois for her birthday. *It couldn't be that.* If Mickey
were involved, Connor at least hoped it would be for something grander
than simple greed.

"Would a mine owner want something like popeye to protect his
workers from malaria?" Connor asked.

Su Thom shook his head. "Peasants go to work in the mines knowing
there is bad malaria there," he explained. "They have been dying for
years. It would be easier and cheaper to replace your workers than to
give them popeye."

"Okay, what if popeye was cheap and readily available?" Connor
pressed. "What if all the peasants had access to it?"

Su Thom considered this. "There are many areas where people don't
live because the malaria is so bad. If there was no threat of disease,
peasants would want to move in, and the big landowners would not be
happy. That happened in the Amazon."

"But that isn't a remote consideration for ten or fifteen years," Zee
reminded them.

"There has to be a reason!" Connor walked over to the other bed
where they had spread out the larger map. *What was the pattern? Where
was the value?*

"Connor, it's late. Su Thom has to get some rest." But Su Thom was not sleepy. He was, in fact, rapidly growing more alert. He picked up the maps of malarial distribution, arranged them in chronological order and flipped through them like a cartoon flip book. Connor saw what he was doing and went back over to the bed. Going forward, the shaded zones enlarged then splintered and jumped all over the region. Flipping backwards, however, they shrank again until they coalesced into one central area.

Su Thom tapped the earliest map. "You know what this is?" Connor and Zee bent over the map. Su Thom traced out the pattern of malarial dots. It was a long, winding stripe, following the mountainous Laotian panhandle from Vietnam to Cambodia.

"Shit." Connor finally saw the pattern.

"What is it?" Zee said. "Do you see something new?"

"Yeah. Ground zero. This is where the deadly malaria originated." His palm rested lightly on the Indian Ocean while his finger pressed hard on Vietnam. "The Ho Chi Minh Trail."

15

July 3

Zee finally fell asleep around three, but Connor stayed up with the maps and notes, and his own private demons. Su Thom could hear him from the next room and see the light under the door. He lay quietly, keeping himself awake with the control he had mastered so long ago. His body wanted desperately to sleep, and his arms throbbed from the injury, but he would wait for his chance. To keep alert, he thought about his silver dragons. He imagined them taking flight in a great cloud against the sunset. Soon enough. *Be ready for your chance,* his mother had taught him, during those endless years in the camp. *You are small and poor and weak, but fortune comes along like a little frog, and if your eyes are open and your hand is quick, we will have the little frog for our dinner.* It had been a long time since he had had to eat frogs or snails or snakes or rats, but not so long since his mother's sweet voice was silenced. Would Connor never go to sleep?

Finally, as the sky was beginning to lighten, Su Thom heard Connor open his outside door. Su Thom peered out the window, saw him walk through the motel parking lot, then start down the road at a slow run. He waited until he saw him appear and disappear again around a bend in the road below, then he got out of bed. He was already dressed, still in the same shorts and T-shirt Connor had found for him in his trunk. He crept into Connor and Zee's room. Zee was sleeping soundly. The car keys were on the dresser.

They had come to no plan last night. No real answers, either. Connor and Zee meant well, but they didn't know how the world really worked. Let them talk to whoever they wanted and find out whatever they could. He was the only one who could really end this. Someone was trying to control access to popeye. Someone was always trying to control the poor. But this time it was different. This time they were using disease as a weapon and the hands of the American government were all over it. This changed everything. They had the power then, but now it was his. He had to get back to his nursery. His little silver dragons would be hungry.

It was difficult to drive at first with his injured hands. The fingers on his left hand would not close properly. The sun rose red before him as he drove out of the mountains. Tomorrow the sun would rise over millions of happy Americans celebrating the Fourth of July. It would be their last real day of independence. From now on, they would be connected to the rest of the world in a way they never imagined. There would be no more warnings, no examples, no chance for Fairchild to relent.

As he watched the morning shift slowly to blue, Su Thom felt the last soft places of his heart harden. The mosquitos were ready. Hundreds of silver dragons sparkled in his basement hatchery, each one fat and hungry and swarming with malaria. Tomorrow. Tomorrow was the perfect day.

"Wake up, Zee. We have to go. Su Thom's gone. He took the car." Zee woke to a shake on the shoulder and Connor's abrupt bulletin. Su Thom was gone. She forced herself quickly out of sleep and they were out the door in five minutes. If the nosy desk clerk had suspicions she would just have to stand in line.

The Harper's Ferry train station looked like something Norman Rockwell would have painted, but fortunately the MARC trains that came through were modern. They could get to Union Station in downtown Washington in ninety minutes.

Connor sent Zee in to buy tickets, then called Mickey at home. It was six-fifty. The train was due in seven minutes.

"Connor? Where are you?" Mickey's voice started out groggy with sleep, eased into relief, then shifted to anger, all in a few seconds. "What in god's name is going on?"

"It's a long story."

"I'm sure it's a goddamn epic. Where are you? Where's Su Thom?"

"Listen to me. We have to talk. I don't trust your phone."

"No one has tapped my phone. Connor, we have to talk."

"Exactly. So meet me at eleven, on the mall in front of the Smith- sonian Castle." The train was coming around the bend and slowing. "I have to go." Connor hung up the phone before the whistle sounded. Zee came out of the station with their tickets. The commuter train was almost empty. Connor wasn't sure how full it usually was, but there was defi- nitely an air of lassitude among the few passengers. Tomorrow was the Fourth of July and a Friday; maybe everyone was starting the holiday early. Fourth of July. Fireworks and picnics and sparklers and water- melon and beer. And on the other side of the world, jungles full of deadly malaria and over it all some unseen hand, manipulating it all.

"Where do you think Su Thom went?" Zee asked.

"I don't know. He was scared."

"But he was safe with us."

"He couldn't be sure. We couldn't be sure."

"Maybe he went to stay with family or friends."

"I don't think he has many friends, and his family is in Boston," Connor explained. "There isn't enough gas in the car to get there, and he doesn't have any money, credit cards, or even ID with him."

"He wouldn't just go home, would he? Whoever tried to hurt him might be watching for him there."

"I think he would anticipate that. But then again, he might be one of these guys who's a genius in science but has no common sense."

"What are we going to do now, Connor?"

"I arranged to meet with Mickey. I'll just find out what's really going on." The emerald necklace sparkled in the back of his mind. He remem- bered how shocked Lois was to receive it. How she touched it like it burned. He looked away, silencing any more talk. He did not know what to expect from Su Thom. He had researched the man's personnel file from SeaGenesis, but the details there only gave a hint of the life the young man had lived.

Connor's own difficult childhood and brief taste of orphanhood was nowhere close to what Su Thom must have experienced, but he remembered his own sense of fear and isolation after his father was sent to jail. After only a couple of weeks on the street, he had begun to feel like something not quite human. How had it been for the young Su Thom?

Even after the Sullivans took him in, Connor remained shut off. For years he had not risked any emotion at all. It was as if all people had stopped being real, and he was the most unreal among them. He had been brought back by love and time and probably by the genetic stew that shaped his disposition. But what if there had been no steady Lois pulling him along, no playful Kerry tempting him into adolescence? No Sean and Daniel teaching him the rules of boys that he had never learned? Even Mickey, stern and distant as he had been, at least nurtured his mind and talents.

Su Thom had loving and supportive adoptive parents, but what if the damage had already been done? The train picked up a few more passengers at each stop. By the time they pulled into the Rockville, Maryland, station, the train was still only a quarter full. A few more reluctant commuters trudged toward the train. There were tourists as well, dropped off by relatives to venture into museum land on their own. They stood out like pelicans in a peach tree, with their fanny packs and terrible shorts and relentless pointing.

And there were cops. Connor noticed them at once, and it jarred him out of contemplation. Not just cops, feds. Two of them got out of a plain white sedan and headed toward the train. To Connor, who had learned to spot cops like most kids learn to spot old ladies with candy, everything about them screamed their identity. The suits might have worked on a regular day but on this pre-holiday heat wave day, the office-bound had gone decidedly casual. But it was posture and the way they got out of the car that clued him in more than anything. Cops get out of a car like they're eight feet tall and been cramped in there for days. They pause, do a little rolling thing with their shoulders, hitch at their pants, then look up and down the street, first one way, then the other. Even when they're in a hurry, like these two, it was automatic. They stretched, they rolled, they hitched, they looked, they walked toward the train.

Connor grabbed Zee's arm and pushed her up out of the seat.

"We have to get off the train. Out the back." He was hustling her down the aisle. "Those two men are cops."

"What two men?"

"Getting on the train. Red Hair and Bad Tie. Move."

"Wait, maybe we should talk to them."

"Cops *you* find might be friends, cops that find *you* aren't." Connor pulled Zee into the space between cars. "Walk toward the Metro station," he whispered. "Don't look back. If we get separated, don't go to my house. You can access my answering machine from a pay phone for messages. The code is seven-six. You know how to do that?"

Zee nodded. "But they can't be after us." She was trying not to be frightened, but not having much choice. "How could they know we were even here?"

"Mickey has caller ID," Connor said grimly. "It would have been easy enough to trace the number to the train station at Harper's Ferry." *So the tip-off had to come from Mickey!* "They wouldn't have known where we were going to get off, so they sent people to get on here. Rockville is the first station the MARC train connects with the D.C. subway."

Connor glanced back and saw one of the men walking down the aisle toward them. He turned his face and shifted so his body obscured Zee's. The other guy must be searching up front. The train gave its departing whistle.

"Now!" They jumped down on the platform just before the train doors closed. Zee started to run but Connor caught her arm.

"Just walk fast." Connor's thoughts were racing. *Someone got two agents mobilized and in place within forty-five minutes. Who had that kind of power? Were the men legitimate federal agents or goons for hire?* They were only halfway to the Metro entrance when they heard the screech of brakes. The train stopped. Hard footsteps pounded behind them.

"Run!" Connor urged. Zee jumped onto the escalator and began to run down. Connor whirled around, braced himself on the handrails and swung his feet into the chest of Bad Tie. The man fell backward but he kicked at Connor's ankles as he fell. The second guy, the one with red hair, reached over his partner and grabbed Connor's arm. Connor wrenched away, grabbed the handrail and vaulted out of the escalator chute.

"Get the girl! Get the girl!" Red shouted. Bad Tie took off down the escalator after Zee. The two escalators were separated by a broad metal slope like a giant sliding board. Small raised studs thwarted any childish intentions of using it for such, but a thin film of oil and grit made it impossible to do anything but slide. Connor scrambled for balance, slipped, tumbled, and rolled down yards of studded metal. Red, his body reacting just a split second faster than his brain, had jumped up right after him and was also sliding. Connor groped for a hold on one of the studs. As soon as he did, Red's shoe came sliding into his fingers. Connor decided to surrender to gravity. He pulled in his arms, squeezed his legs together, and let himself roll.

He tumbled all the way to the bottom and shot off like a sack of laundry. He landed with a thud on the tiled floor. People were shouting and running to get away. Connor sucked in a breath and got to his feet, staggering across the still-spinning floor. Red had managed to stop somewhere up the slide and was momentarily frozen, considering his options, not particularly liking the one Connor had just chosen. Connor reached for the steadiness of a wall. He saw Bad Tie sprinting back up from the subway platform toward him. That meant Zee had escaped. He pushed himself off the wall and raced for the escalator, grateful for the narrowness that now at least kept his feet more or less under him. He sprinted up, elbowing past startled commuters.

Red had made his way back and was trying to run up the down escalator. Bad Tie was somewhere behind him. Connor reached the top and dodged through the commuters. A couple of Metro police, alerted from below, yelled for him to stop, but it was only a feint. They were there for fare jumpers and subway snackers, happy to leave the real criminals to the real police. Connor glanced behind him and didn't see either agent. He dodged between cars and ran across the street, through a parking lot and down an alley. He ran until he couldn't run any more. He ducked around the back of a furniture store and leaned against the wall trying to catch his breath. He sat down on a crate and leaned into a thin triangle of shade. He was soaked with sweat, covered with oil and grease, and stranded in Rockville.

Had Mickey set this trap for him? God, life was much simpler when you just didn't trust anyone. Dad was a thief, a con man, and a falling down drunk, but at least you knew what to expect. Back then the rest of the world was divided easily into marks and other crooks. There was no supposing, no wondering. You might hook up with someone for a job or a hustle, or a road trip, but you sure as hell didn't trust him. *You trust yourself, and you trust me. You get in trouble, that's all you got. You and me and the wits the good lord saw fit to give us.* It had taken Connor twenty years to develop that trust with Mickey Sullivan. So here he was, trusting. And screwed.

Zee slipped into the subway car just as the doors were about to close. Her heart didn't stop pounding for another dozen stops. She rode as far as Union Station. She wasn't sure where else to go, but as far as a place to hang out for a while it seemed as good as any. There would be lots of people around, easier to get lost in a crowd. She searched in her purse but came up with only a pair of sunglasses for disguise. *Disguise.* This was getting way too crazy. *Go to the authorities,* she thought. *But which authorities?* Two of them had just tried to chase them down.

She got off the subway and flowed with the crowd up the escalator into the cool marble of the station. What to do first? What had happened to Connor? And how much should she rely on him anyway? Her instincts were still to go to the police. Bring it all out in the open, and let people who knew what they were doing do it. Yes, Connor was smart. And good in a pinch. Quite probably he had saved Su Thom's life yesterday. But did he actually know what he was doing? She hardly knew him, really, and what she did know was all swarmed up in that primal urge thing. Damn passion. The chemicals of attraction. There was nothing romantic about it. Evolution again, just another rabbit from the gene pool's hat of tricks.

The theories that had made such horrible sense in the middle of the night were looking less sound in the cold light of morning. She walked the long halls, feeling very alone despite the crowds. The historic station had been beautifully restored, and was now a mixture of working train station and shopping center. There were a multiplex cinema and food court on the ground floor, and elegant restaurants above. Tiny specialty shops flanked the great hall, one of which had very cool and comfortable looking sundresses in the front window.

Zee desperately wanted to change clothes. Two days in a skirt and blouse were getting to be torture. Plus they weren't exactly too fresh by now. Zee went into the store, tried on the sundress, handed over a credit card, and had the clerk snip off the tags. Walking out, she felt foolishly relieved. There was one easy decision, anyway. Now just about ninety-nine more, and this thing would be set right. She should be on her way back to Shadow Island by now. What was going on out there? Could Padgette really be involved in all this? All this *what*? She desperately wanted to talk to someone with a level head and clear perspective. She didn't know anyone else in Washington. She considered calling her mother, but then she would just worry. Roddy. Of course. Zee searched out a restaurant with a quiet telephone nook in the back. After considerable button pushing, she finally got the number for the hospital and connected to his room.

"Hey sweetie! What're you doing up there? Must be some swell life you can't give a poor suffering mate a call for two days!"

"Oh, Roddy. Are you okay?"

"Sure. I had to fight my way off their bloody chopping block, but it looks like the leg stays on. Still ugly, but it'll mend. You'll have to muck on without me on the island for a while though. Speaking of which, shouldn't you be on your way back by now?"

"I wish. God, everything is so crazy."

"Zee, what's wrong?" Roddy heard the panic in her voice.

"I don't know where to start. But that's part of it. Fairchild is shutting down Shadow Island."

"What? Can't be. I just talked to him an hour ago. He said nothing of the sort."

"You talked to Fairchild?"

"Yeah, he called me. Wanted to know if I had heard from you, actually. What are you still doing up there anyway?"

"Fairchild called you this morning?"

"Hello? Earth to Zephyr. What's going on? Have you even talked to our boss lately?"

"No, actually. I've been ah . . . kind of busy."

"What's wrong, honey? You sound strange."

"I met with Fairchild the day before yesterday and he said he's shutting us down and moving the station to the Florida Keys."

"Zee, maybe you misunderstood him."

"No."

"He told me you were supposed to fly back down here today," Roddy explained. "I'm getting released and he said you would be here to pick me up."

"He said I was flying to Miami today? Oh, Roddy, all this crazy stuff is going on . . ."

"What kind of stuff?"

Zee pictured him lying there helplessly in bed, his arm and leg bandaged, weak and helpless. Knowledge of the popeye problem was not turning out to be healthy.

"I . . . I can't explain it all now. I'll talk to Fairchild. Listen." She hesitated. What should she tell him? "Just be careful. I'll see you soon."

Zee hung up and leaned against the phone, watching the crowds of people. A man on stilts dressed like Uncle Sam was handing out leaflets, and signs in in store windows advertised huge Independence Day sales. She'd had about enough fireworks already. Shadow Island sounded like the most perfect place right now. Silence and sky and the soft water washing over her feet. Flying to Miami today. That would be perfect. Except for the minor little problem of someone trying to kill her along the way. Zee rummaged in her purse and found more change. She dropped it in and punched in Fairchild's number. The phone rang once before she realized what she was doing. They had already been trapped once today with simple caller ID. She hung up. She would not tip them off again so easily. Her palm left little beads of sweat on the receiver.

"She's at Union Station. Go." Mickey clipped orders into the phone then set the receiver down gently. Fairchild glared at him.

"We got a hit off her credit card and her phone card," Mickey explained somewhat smugly. "And the hospital confirms that a call came in five minutes ago for Roddy Taylor."

"I meant what I said. No more accidents. I will go to the police. I'll tell everything." Fairchild's smooth, handsome face had suffered in the past week. The eyes were sunken and the skin seemed translucent over the cheekbones, as in a man suffering fever. "I've left papers, you know. To be opened in the event of my own untimely death."

"That's very foresighted of you." Mickey checked his watch. Zee wasn't the best one to find but she would be the easiest. His men should be there in ten minutes.

"Killing people was never supposed to be part of this," Fairchild pressed. "I never expected anything like this would happen."

"Oh, don't rehearse your defense with me, Adam. Now just stay here and shut up. Don't talk to anybody about Su Thom. Especially the media. Nobody."

Killing people really was never supposed to be a part of it, Mickey thought as he left. It made things too complicated. Raki couldn't be helped, though. They couldn't very well use popeye as long as she was around; she would eventually hear about it, suspect something, make noise. No, she had to go. He felt bad about it, but it was necessary. Killing was always necessary, wasn't it, one way or another, to someone or another. He did it in the war and got a medal for it. And he hadn't pulled the trigger himself, hadn't committed that mortal sin. Anyway, it wasn't a sin to kill in self-defense, or to defend one's family. *Oh, Connor*, he prayed as he drove downtown. *Let's just hope you understand.*

The national mall is a broad green stretch of grass, bordered by pebble paths and surrounded by stately trees. Anchored on one end by the Lincoln Memorial and the other by the U.S. Capitol, centered by the Washington Monument and flanked on all sides by the Smithsonian museums, it is tourist central. All day long they crisscross, from the Air and Space Museum to Natural History and back, forging earnest paths from dinosaur bones, to Eskimos, to the rise of the steam engine. But eventually even the most stalwart need a respite, and the grassy mall welcomes them. Giant trees provide picnic shade. Shoes are loosened and babies finally doze in their strollers. Moms mediate childish arguments and dads look at maps. It is a peaceful place, a wide open, very public place.

Connor got off the Metro at the Archives stop. The Smithsonian stop was closer to the castle, where he had told Mickey he would meet him, but this way he entered the mall from the north side and could see from afar if there was anyone hanging around. He saw no one suspicious. But who would look suspicious right now? Farther down toward the Washington Monument, flatbed trucks full of Portajohns were being unloaded for tomorrow's Fourth of July festivities. Lights were being hung and sound systems checked at the Sylvan Theater. The crowd would start arriving early, to stake out the best spots like settlers in a land grab.

He walked toward the castle. He saw Mickey sitting on a park bench. Connor glanced around. If anyone had come with him, they weren't obvious. Even if they were here, what could they do to him out here? Mickey saw him coming and got up. He was casually dressed, in khaki pants and a polo shirt, but there would still be no mistaking him for a tourist. There was nothing carefree in his face or posture.

"Connor. You're all right then."

Connor halted some distance away, still wary.

"Why wouldn't I be?"

"You sounded strange on the phone. What the hell is going on?"

"You tell me. Why did you send those goons after me on the train?" Connor saw denial flare in Mickey's face, then quickly ebb.

"I had to find you," Mickey said simply. "You were in danger. Look, Connor, there is a lot going on here, a lot you don't understand . . ."

"No, you're wrong," Connor said, stepping closer. "There is a lot I *do* understand. I found your little hiding place under the back stairs."

Mickey was blindsided. His face reddened and he inhaled sharply. He blinked hard and stared at Connor.

"I see." He pulled out a handkerchief and wiped the back of his neck. "You found . . . how did you . . ." His voice was strangled and he coughed to clear his throat. Connor said nothing, just stood there, perfectly still, with that dark gaze of his; the posture for cops, probation officers, juvenile court judges, and a hundred of Mickey's own lectures. Daniel and Sean used to squirm, shift, slouch. Connor just stood like one of those Easter Island statues, grim and stony and gazing right through you.

"When did you . . . find it?"

"Yesterday."

Mickey looked away, staring out over the dome of the Capitol. "I see." His voice was steadier now. "I'm sorry you had to find out like that." He reached to touch Connor's arm. Connor recoiled. Mickey's eyes narrowed. Connor was angry to have betrayed his skittishness so easily.

"Come sit down, Connor. There is a lot we have to talk about." He turned his back and walked toward a bench. Connor followed. They sat silently a few minutes. Mickey looked across at the glistening dome of the Museum of Natural History, trying to assemble his thoughts. He hadn't expected this at all. How the hell did Connor find the boxes? The problem of Su Thom was still burning like a flare in the back of his mind, but now Connor had come along to spill a pool of gasoline around it. He had to find Su Thom and for that he needed Connor. This would have to be handled carefully.

"It isn't like it seems," Mickey began, only too aware how lame that sounded. "We never dreamed things would turn out so crazy. You have to understand how it was back then. The world was different." Connor said nothing, letting the weight of silence press on Mickey. "It sounds worse in those documents. So . . . calculating. But it wasn't like that," Mickey went on. "It isn't like everyone thinks, you know, the CIA as some kind of evil empire. We weren't over there just trying to kill innocent people and screw things up."

The CIA. Evil empire? Connor felt a shudder of horror but kept his voice neutral.

"Tell me how it all started in the first place. How did you get involved?"

Mickey sighed. "I was just a kid," he explained. "A wiseass kid, not
so different from yourself. I wanted to get somewhere in life. I was
eighteen, working on the docks in Baltimore, no hope of much better.
You know where I came from, Connor."

"Yeah, I know."

"Vietnam was just starting. This was years before any protests or
any of that. The military was always the way out for kids like me, so I
enlisted. I'd been working on the docks since I was fifteen, so the army
put me in supply. I was kind of pissed off at first. I had ideas of glory.
But you meet a lot of people in supply. People who need to get things
done, or get around some stupid army regs. Whatever. I knew how to
play all the games. It wasn't that different from the Baltimore docks;
adjusted manifests, overlooked cargo, that sort of thing. I got to know
all the players. I was good at it. I was offered opportunities. It's seduc-
tive." Mickey went on, relaxing a little. "They get you thinking how
you're important. How someone has to get things done, and you're the
only one for the job."

"So was it your idea? Your own plan?"

"It wasn't any sort of plan at all. Not in the beginning. We were
trying to control traffic along the Ho Chi Minh Trail, to cut off the supply
routes for the Viet Cong. We were working with the Laotian hill tribes.
We needed to keep them on our side. We'd give them food, weapons,
money, medicine. Had a lot of malaria around there. So we gave them
medicine, and they helped us disrupt traffic along the trail. It was the
kind of thing we've always done, are still doing, all over the world. Give
away goodies to keep people in our camp. No big deal. The Laotians
and the Cambodians were just as interested in keeping the Viet Cong
suppressed as we were. They'd felt threatened by Vietnam for centuries."
Mickey looked at his watch. They were wasting valuable time.

"Go on."

"People started coming down with a new strain of malaria. Two
of our guys got sick with it, even though they were taking the pills.
We all took malaria pills, it was standard. But this new strain was really nasty. It didn't respond to any of the medications we had, and it

killed you pretty quick. Most kinds of malaria just make you sick. This *P. falciparum* causes cerebral hemorrhaging, basically blows up your brain.

"We eventually found out that the Laotians had been hoarding the medication, giving it to friends and family. They weren't taking the full doses. The weaker strains were killed off, but the stronger ones began to grow resistant. We didn't know that would happen," Mickey went on. "Who would have thought? We weren't doctors, we were *spooks*. Who ever heard of incurable malaria? We sent samples back to the States, to Walter Reed. They were working on all sorts of new drugs and vaccines. They isolated the new strain and came up with a drug that would kill it. So we were OK again."

"But that wasn't the end of it," Connor pressed.

"No. There were long-term issues in the region to consider. There were all sorts of factions vying for power. We needed a way to exert influence in the long run."

Mickey paused and looked over at Connor but could not gauge his response. "The disease was already there. We were just going to take advantage of it."

Connor stared steadily away, not trusting himself to meet Mickey's eyes. *"Long-term issues? A way to exert influence?"* He felt like he was crossing a minefield; any question might be the wrong one.

"You had already seen it get out of hand once." Connor strained to keep his tone even. "Why didn't you suppose that would happen again?" Mickey looked at him with a puzzled frown and Connor knew he was on shaky ground.

"Who ever suspects their big ideas are going to fail?" Mickey went on resignedly. "We had antibiotics for everything. Smallpox was almost wiped out. We expected a cure for cancer any day. And then, frankly, by that point, we didn't care. We hated them. They had beat us. Dragged us down. The whole lousy war. You don't understand, Connor. Your generation . . . oh, what the hell. It made sense at the time. But in the end, it was a little over the top even for the CIA. The project was shut down and the records destroyed. All but the ones I kept for myself. You learn early on to cover your ass."

The project shut down . . . ? His mind was swarming with questions but he knew he had to be cautious. In the distance, calliope music from the merry-go-round grated endlessly through the heavy air.

"How did Fairchild know to come to you when he wanted help with the EPA grant? Did he know you were with . . . you worked for the government?"

"He knew I knew people and how to get things done," Mickey explained almost boastfully.

"Through Chapmans?"

"Chapmans is not connected," Mickey said. "When I started Chapmans I retired. That was the early eighties, a pretty low point in our history. The CIA was accused of everything but poisoning Tylenol. SST wasn't needed any more, and there wasn't really anyplace I could go inside the agency. Operations had changed, the world had changed. And I was ready to move on. I took a buyout." Mickey shrugged. "But you never lose all your connections, or your leverage. SeaGenesis needed the EPA grant to stay afloat. Fairchild knew about Raki's malaria research, and popeye, and thought the government might be interested."

"So you arranged the EPA grant in return for exclusive access to popeye."

Mickey nodded.

But why was exclusive access so important? Connor kept working his way around the direct question.

"Fairchild had worked on malaria at Walter Reed. Did he know all the details? About the whole project?"

"No. He had some suspicions, that's all."

"How did you know popeye was really effective?"

"We tested it, of course. In Somalia."

"On our soldiers?"

"God no. Of course not. Just natives."

Just natives. This man who had harangued his sons about cheating on school tests was now talking about subverting government grants and *manipulating* a deadly disease.

"Look, Connor," Mickey went on, a twinge of impatience now working its way back through the initial shock. "I'll be happy to tell you all the details you want, but right now there is something more urgent we have to deal with . . ."

"No." Connor knew he couldn't keep this up much longer; maybe if he went right to the heart of the man. "Were you ever going to tell me this?" Connor asked quietly. "Or did you figure it would be too much for me like it was too much for Sean?"

Mickey's face flushed a deep red. His *death face*.

"Is that what happened that night?" Connor pressed. "He found the closet, too?"

Mickey was rigid now and Connor wondered if he was about to have a heart attack.

"I heard you fighting that night. I was upstairs in my room. I heard Sean shouting. I thought it was just a fight. He was saying how he couldn't believe you would do something like that. Is this what he was talking about?"

"He found the closet." Mickey's voice shook. "Your mother had over-flowed the bathtub upstairs and sent him down to see if the water had come through. The top of the panel had come loose. He pulled it open, found everything. He wouldn't let me explain. He just flipped out. And there wasn't anything so bad. Just those few documents and things. Just those few things, enough to cover my own ass if I ever needed to. I don't know why it upset him so much. It was nothing. You saw it."

"No." Connor said quietly.

"What?"

"No, I didn't see anything."

"You found the closet." Mickey stared at him.

"I found the closet. I got the panel off. I got one box open and saw it was full of papers. I saw a title: *The Mosquito War*. Then Lois came home. I didn't see shit." Connor got up off the bench. He did not feel triumphant, only drained. "I didn't read any files. I didn't know shit. Until now."

Mickey stared at him, shock turning to fury. "Damn you!" he hissed. "You goddamn bastard!" He lunged at Connor, slamming a hand across his face. Connor fell hard, in a burst of dust, surprised more than hurt. There was a startled shriek and a few tourists scampered away on the pebbled path. Mickey towered over him, a shadow against the sun.

"Bastard!" The shadow bent, the sun slammed Connor's face. The huge hand raked at his shirt. Mickey pulled him to his feet. Connor was surprised to be hit, glad in a way. It changed things. Made it easier. On the periphery, startled tourists watched, but no one interfered. Mickey swung at him again, Connor dodged, threw up a hand to block the blow. Mickey grabbed the arm and slammed a fist into his stomach. Connor doubled over.

"You *conned* me!" Mickey's loss of control and the rage on his face was more disturbing to Connor right now than the actual revelation. That was all still too vague, needing time to become real. *Mickey working for the CIA. Engineering the spread of disease. The great moral guide of his life.* There was blood in his mouth. He tried to spit.

Two men were running toward them. So they *had* been watching. It was the same two from the train this morning. One of them grabbed Mickey and pulled him back. The other caught Connor and twisted his arm behind him. Mickey shrugged free and composed himself.

"You know, I had hopes for you," he said bitterly. "That was the only reason I took your lousy ass in. I thought you had potential. But you know what? You're still just a piss-ass little second-rate con man." Mickey spit in the dust. "You think you know everything now? You know *shit*! Bring him," he instructed the men. He turned and walked off without a backward glance.

Connor leaned over and began to vomit in the grass. The Washington Monument daggered up and down in the corner of his eye as he heaved. He stumbled a little, turned his head and vomited squarely on the arm-gripping man's loafers. The man recoiled and as soon as Connor felt the grip loosen he kicked at the other man's knee, wrenched himself free, and took off running.

16

If the fundamentalists are right, mankind is saved only by the blood of Jesus; but for *Anopheles*, mere mortal blood will do. She bears no particular malice toward humankind, does not in fact really seek him out. To the *Anopheles*, a man is as good as a mouse. She is only seeking a blood meal, and that only for the urgency of motherhood. What could be more simple, more pure? The itch and welt is an accident, a reaction to the anticoagulant she injects while sipping her nectar. She does not try to carry plagues; the fevers are spread as innocently as the pollen that clings to a bee. It could be argued, from the mosquito's point of view, that human troubles with her are simply a deficiency of our nature. It should be such a simple matter. Her nourishment requires no death of prey. Who should grudge a fellow creature a few drops of blood? What feeble organisms we are to crumble so easily.

So, too, the malaria plasmodium is only answering God's most universal directive: *Go forth and multiply.* To the parasite, the red blood cell is simply a womb, and the damage done in the end is of no more importance that the cracked eggshell after hatching a chick. It is the circle of life. The pure and simple lust of the gene pool.

Su Thom reached into the cage with his gloved hand and pulled out the saucer. Only a few drops remained. It seemed to him that the humming had changed pitch. It was less urgent now after the meal.

"But still not satisfied, I know," he whispered reassuringly. It was only sugar water. Just enough to keep them going, without ruining their appetite. "Tomorrow," he said. "There will be blood. Tomorrow you can drink your fill."

He felt lightheaded as he walked up the steps. The wounds on his arms throbbed. The afternoon sun beamed in the window, reflecting starkly off the bare white walls and floor.

Zee had to call Connor's answering machine twice to understand his message. The second time she took careful notes then spent another five minutes deciphering it. Obviously fearing that someone else would listen to the messages, he had concocted a simple but effective code relating to personal things they had talked about. *The first two letters of your favorite sea creature*—M and A for Manta Ray. *The third letter of that invertebrate that eats the stingers*—that would be D for nudibranch. She was surprised at what he had remembered about her; the name of her childhood pet goat, the color of the skirt she had been wearing the other night. Even so, she wasn't sure she got the name right. Madam's Organ? What the hell kind of a name was that? *Meet me there as soon as you can.* There was tension in his voice and he told her twice not to go to his house or her hotel. Madam's Organ turned out to be a bar in Adams Morgan, a funky neighborhood of bars and ethnic restaurants in D.C. It was an old, flaky-paint building with purple trim and a neon sign flashing SORRY WE'RE OPEN.

Inside she was greeted by a stuffed seagull and an old man with a frenzy of white hair and a mad sheen in his ice-blue eyes. He lit up at the sight of her, slid off his stool, and wavered toward her with embracing arms and vigorous endearments in drunken Russian. It was just after four and the bartender, only recently out of bed, jail, or recovery, by the looks of him, was wiping dazed circles on the scarred wooden bar. She fended off the Russian with a smile and a stiff arm. She went up a lopsided staircase and found Connor upstairs shooting a solitary game of pool.

He looked unwashed and worse for wear. She could see why he would choose this place. His left eye was bruised and there was a small fresh cut on his lip above a stubbled chin. He would have looked sexy,

Zee thought, in a battered desperado way, if the whole world were not crumbling around them. He straightened up and looked at her, leaning on his cue stick like it was a staff.

"Connor? Are you all right? What happened?" For a moment he almost didn't recognize her in the sundress.

"I'm fine," he said. "You look nice."

"It's a disguise." She sat down on a creaky wooden bench which may once have been a church pew and leaned her head against the wall. She didn't know where to start. It was good just to sit down and feel safe. Connor walked over and handed her his beer.

"I'll get you a drink. What do you want?" he asked.

"One of these." She raised the bottle. "And about four of those." She nodded at the empty shot glass sitting on the edge of the pool table. Connor went downstairs, returning in a few minutes with two fresh beers and two shots of Jameson. Zee tossed hers back without a flinch and washed it down with the beer. She savored the immediate burn and felt the day's terror begin to loosen its grip. She pulled at the skirt of her dress, fanning air on her legs. The gesture was careless and mildly erotic. Connor had felt such absolute flatness of emotion since the talk with Mickey that this twinge of arousal brought him inordinate relief. Perhaps he wasn't dead and in a dream after all.

"You look like shit," she said. "What happened? Did you talk to Mickey?"

"Yes." He got up and went back to the pool table.

"And?"

He racked the balls and broke them with a hard, straight shot. "Mickey has been in on this since the beginning. He used to work for the CIA." As he shot ball after ball, he told her what he had learned. It was a dry recitation of facts punctuated only by the solid crack and muffled drop of each shot. When the basics were finished, the table was clear. He leaned against the far wall, absently twirling the cue between his fingers. Without the focus of smacking balls he seemed to stall out. Zee stared at him, overwhelmed for the moment, both with the facts of the revelation and compassion for how he must be feeling.

"How did you get him to tell you all this?"

"He thought I already knew. Yesterday I found a secret closet under the stairs in his house. It was full of papers. I didn't have time to read any because Lois came home, but I let him think I had." He no longer felt smug about conning the story out of Mickey. The truth was too ugly.

"Anyway, I didn't really find out shit. I know there is more to it, but I couldn't hold up the con much longer. I didn't know what I was supposed to know. I mean, if I actually *had* read his papers." He stopped and tossed back the rest of his whiskey. "I don't know how many people are involved or why they felt they had to kill Ulla and blow up her house. At the time, there was just so much." He trailed off and sat down, his hands still clutching the pool cue as if it were the only connection to reality. Zee came over and sat beside him.

"I never dreamed . . ." His voice caught, and he struggled to control it. "Mickey worked for the CIA for twenty years. The shipping company he worked for, Secure Shipping and Transport, it was a CIA front company. Who knows what the hell that was really doing! His whole life is a lie. And I don't even know all of it yet."

Car doors slammed outside and they both tensed. Connor went over to the big window at the end of the room and looked down on the street, but it was only someone stopping into the carry-out next door.

Zee folded her arms and leaned against the wall beside the window. "Look, I know all this has come out of nowhere, and it's really very weird, but there must be someone we can go to for help. Even if Mickey still has CIA connections, I just don't believe the entire agency can be behind something like this. They can't just go around killing people and staging explosions and . . . stealing malaria drugs. This is too big! They can't possibly expect to get away with something like this."

"They *have* to get away with it!" They have to keep this buried. What do you think would happen if this became known? This is the CIA and the United States government sanctioning a plan of biological warfare!"

"No." She stopped him. "It isn't that bad. Look, long ago, in a screwed-up war, some people were shortsighted and stupid. They limited supplies of malaria medications and that accidentally resulted in the emergence of new strains. There!" She threw up her hands. "I'm sure they have plenty of PR guys who can shape it up even better. Of course it will be damaging, but it isn't like they were actually spreading disease or infecting people, or intentionally *breeding* these deadly new strains.

It was biology running wild. It was idiot assumptions that they could control a disease that has been around for millions of years. It was an accident." She stopped. There was a long, dreadful silence.

"Was it?" Connor said softly. An awful realization was dawning. *Breeding the strains . . .*

"No." Zee backed away, shaking her head. "No." She sat back down on the bench, pulling her knees up to her chest.

"You said it yourself," Connor pressed. "Why would they be putting so much into this cover-up? They've been acting like the risk of exposure outweighs everything else. But you're right. Manipulating the supply of malaria drugs was bad, but not fatal. *Breeding* deadly new strains? *That's* fatal. That's biological warfare." *I've never told you everything.* He could hear the mocking in Mickey's voice.

Connor took a deep breath and looked at his empty glass. "I don't think this stuff is working."

"It is for me," Zee said. She had never been much of a drinker but had gained a sudden new appreciation for the lush peacefulness the liquor imparted. She knew it was illusion, but at this point illusion felt pretty damn good. It couldn't be true. They were just tired and stressed and letting paranoia run rampant. Who could do such a thing?

"If it's true then we really have to go to someone."

"We can't. Not yet."

"Connor . . ."

"Wait!" He grabbed her arm and sat them both down. There was a noise at the bottom of the stairs and they stiffened, but it was just the old Russian clattering his way toward the door.

"Look," Connor went on, whispering now. "We don't know who to trust. We have no proof of anything, and if Mickey is spooked, there will be no proof. It might be that those papers in his closet are the only documents around."

Proof. Zee suddenly felt a rush of excitement despite the dreadful reality at hand. They were ready to kill for popeye.

"They know it works?"

"Yes. They tested it in Somalia." Connor rubbed the side of his head.

Zee stared out the window, thinking about Ulla. Could she have known? In those horrible minutes of terror when she was yanked from her car, did she realize they were after popeye? Did she realize that meant it *really did work*? In those few seconds, did she feel a thrill beyond the immediate fear? It was a small comfort, but all Zee had, to think that in those last awful minutes of her life, Ulla had the satisfaction of knowing her work was good.

Su Thom sat on the sleeping bag, his back propped against the wall. The empty house was dark except for the gentle pool of light from the desk lamp on the floor beside him. He felt good. He felt as if there was something glowing inside him. If he had thought about it objectively, he would have realized the physical signs of stress, the deceptive calm of emotional collapse, and the toil of trauma. But he just accepted it as a benediction of the righteous. Tomorrow it would be over. His duty would be satisfied, his revenge assured. Whatever happened to his own life was irrelevant.

Open on the floor beside him was the duffle bag that contained the few clothes and personal items he had brought over here. He took out the small tin box. Inside were the tattered memories and pathetic boyhood treasures he had saved. There was a shoelace from his baby brother's shoe. A barrette, long rusted, that his mother used to wear, and a little brush that she used to scrub clothes. There were some red sequins from the beautiful dress of one of the whores in Bangkok. He couldn't remember her name, but she was always kind to him, and gave him little plastic packets of jelly that she got from one of her regular clients at a fancy hotel.

There were bits from his American life, too, grade school medals and a little bottle of his new mother's perfume, the contents long evaporated, all scent gone. But he was after a more bitter token. He had to scrape along the bottom to find it. He had saved it since the day he was a little boy diving for the pills that would save his mother's life. A paper clip. He closed his eyes and pictured the memory that had never faded. The fat American man on the dock, digging deep in his pocket, his hand arching back against the blue sky, the shower of sparkles through the air, the sweet plonk as they hit the water, the fury and desperation of finding it was nothing but pennies and paper clips.

Su Thom took out the paper clip and his brother's shoelace. He slid the paper clip onto the shoelace and knotted it around his neck. He pressed his hand against it hard as if imprinting the shape into his flesh.

As Connor and Zee pulled into his driveway they heard Lucy barking and yelping with joy, crazed from being left alone all night and day. Connor did not correct her for jumping up when they walked in. He gave her a dog biscuit. The house was stuffy and he slid open the patio door. A figure moved in the dark. Connor froze. A large shape rose from one of the chairs on the deck.

"It's just me." Mickey stepped back, holding up his hands. "I'm not here to hurt you." Lucy nosed at Mickey then trotted back to Connor, oblivious to the tension among the humans.

"What are you doing here?"

"We weren't through with our discussion." He looked at Zee and nodded, as if waiting for a proper introduction. Mickey seemed smaller. Perhaps it was just the squeeze of shadows. The kitchen light fell in an angular slab, slicing him diagonally across one shoulder.

"What do you want?" Connor repeated.

"I need you to find Su Thom." Mickey reached for his briefcase. Connor pushed Zee behind him. "I'm not going to hurt you, Connor," he said as if the suggestion wounded his feelings. "Despite what you must think of me right now, I really don't want to hurt anyone. I'm sorry about everything today. I want a chance to explain it all. I know this isn't the time, but there isn't any more time right now." He opened the case and took out a manila envelope. Mickey opened the envelope and shook the little box out into his broad palm.

"Su Thom sent this to Fairchild. It arrived yesterday afternoon." He set it on the table and walked over to the edge of the deck, giving Connor distance. Connor switched on the outside light and walked over to the table. He saw a tiny wooden coffin, with a caricature of Uncle Sam, dead, arms folded across his chest. At his feet, in black lettering: *RIP July 4*.

"There was a mosquito inside," Mickey explained somberly. "It's infected with *P. falciparum* malaria. He claims he has hundreds more."

"Your private vintage?" Connor asked sarcastically.

Mickey ignored the barb.

"He may just have obtained a few dead mosquitos from a lab some-where. There is also a chance he has someone sending him live mosquitos from overseas. Su Thom took out a large credit card advance about a month ago. Enough to send someone to Asia to collect mosquitos for him."

Or enough to rent a place and raise his own mosquitos, Connor thought with rising alarm. Two-by-fours, heat lamps, screening . . . The man at the hardware store hadn't been sure of the price code. Thought it was chicken wire. That had made sense to Connor at the time. He was thinking about monkey testing. What if it wasn't chicken wire, but window screening? Su Thom was not building monkey cages, but mosquito cages!

"Logistically, I can't see him smuggling back very many mosquitos," Mickey went on. "But we can't take that risk."

RIP July 4. Connor closed up the little coffin as if this could shut away the terrible truth.

"Even if he has just a dozen mosquitos, with a routine kind of ma-laria, people could get hurt. He's obviously planning something for to-morrow. You have to find him."

"Why?"

"He trusts you."

"No, I mean why stop him? What's the big deal? You have a cure."

Mickey shut the coffin lid and took a deep breath. "We don't know that."

"You tested it."

"It was one small test. And the drug is still inconsistent."

Connor stared at the little box in his hand. He rubbed his fingers over the sides as if massaging a genie's lamp, but there was no redemp-tive spirit on hand tonight. How many mosquitos could Su Thom actually have raised and infected? Would he really release them? At stake could be hundreds, possibly thousands of lives. If Mickey found Su Thom, he would probably kill him. If Su Thom wasn't found at all, he might kill innocent people.

"I don't know where he is. I don't know where to even begin look-ing," Connor said truthfully. "But I would guess that if you went to one of your government connections, got all the CIA and the FBI and, hell, the army or whoever, involved, someone would find him pretty quick.

Especially if they knew the whole story. Go to the TV news." Connor looked at his watch. "It's just after nine, you could certainly make the eleven o'clock, maybe even the ten. Get his picture up there. Someone must have seen him somewhere."

"Connor, I'm sorry. This can't come out now. Not yet. It's more complicated." Mickey stepped closer, into the light. His face looked old and gray. There were heavy circles under his eyes and a gaunt pallor to his skin. He looked tired, defeated. "Our family could be in danger."

"What do you mean?"

"I've been supplying popeye to certain interests in Asia," Mickey explained with a creepy matter-of-factness. "One of these is a very powerful Cambodian called Son Loc. We promised him an exclusive, and confidential, supply of popeye. He has people over here. They were the ones who killed Ulla Raki. They blew up her house . . ."

"Oh, for god's sake, Mickey, don't try to con *me!*" Connor threw the little coffin at him and turned away in disgust. Mickey, startled, caught it as if it were nitroglycerin.

"It's the truth!" Mickey barked. "Listen to me. Look at me here, I'm practically grovelling. I need your help. Son," he said in a gentler voice. "This man has a very long reach."

"What does it matter if anyone else knows about popeye?" Connor interrupted. "Why does this guy, if there is even this guy, have to keep it a secret?"

"Son Loc is an extremely important political figure in Cambodia. Our government is interested in his cooperation. He also owns one of the largest gem mining operations in Southeast Asia, as well as several other interests. Everyone knows the area is full of deadly malaria and he controls the land only because he controls the disease. He can get workers all right, but he needs loyal managers, supervisors, engineers, distributors, guards. He needs popeye to keep them safe. If popeye was available to everyone, Son Loc loses his advantage. I know you must hate me right now." Mickey sighed. "If I could take back everything I ever did with this whole project, believe me, I would. I never meant to hurt anyone. But don't think about how much you despise me. Think about Kerry and the children. Think about Lois. Our family is in danger. Son Loc has threatened us. You saw what he did to Ulla's house. It was a warning."

"Why should I believe you? Why would he bother to go to all that trouble? You're already deep in his pocket, why threaten the family now?"

"I tried to pull out. Told him I didn't want to be involved any more. But it isn't that easy. I can prove it to you, Connor," Mickey said evenly. "You can talk to the FBI. They tested the residue on the clothing you were wearing when Ulla's house exploded. It came from an old plastic explosive that hasn't been in use for twenty years. The FBI had no idea where it came from, but I knew because I sold crates of this shit to Son Loc fifteen years ago. That was the sort of thing we did in SST. Move guns, explosives, supply militia groups overseas. I sold him tons of this shit. You can't get it anywhere else. He uses it for his mines. He used it to blow up Raki's house. To send us a message. Now he has threatened our family."

Our family. Connor felt overwhelmed with confusion. Why did that sound so strange? *Our* family. He saw a brief kaleidoscope of picnics and birthdays and little girls in summer dresses and Oliver playing with his Hot Wheels cars in the dirt by the old tree.

I need your help." Mickey looked imploringly from Connor to Zee but she just stood silently inside the kitchen.

"I'm sorry for a lot of things, Connor. I wanted to be a good father to you. I know I failed. But Lois is a good mother. Don't think about how I let you down; think about her." Mickey put the coffin back into the briefcase, snapped it closed, and walked down the steps toward the back gate. He left without another word or a backward glance.

Connor stood like his feet were chained to the center of the earth.

"Do you believe him?" Zee asked quietly.

"I don't know."

Lucy nuzzled under his arm and he sunk his fingers into her thick, warm fur.

"How hard would it be to raise mosquitos and infect them with malaria?"

Zee frowned. "I don't know. Labs must do it all the time but I don't know what's involved. Why?"

"The stuff Su Thom bought, the framing lumber and window screening that I thought was for monkey cages . . ."

"Oh god." Zee sat down. "Connor, Su Thom wouldn't do that. He, of all people, knows what malaria can do."

"He also believes there is a cure out there. And thanks to us, after last night, he also knows that what he thought was just a natural disease was in fact manipulated by the U.S. government. He started out angry because Western nations were ignoring tropical disease, now he finds out we weren't ignoring it at all, we were actively making it worse. I'd do it. If I were him. Sure." He got up and looked around the kitchen as if he had misplaced something essential but didn't know quite what it was. "We have to find him."

"You need to sleep. You haven't slept since the night before last. And it's late. Where would you even begin tonight?"

"I have to do something. I have to find him. I started all this. I screwed it up from the start." He paced through the small house.

"You did not. Connor, stop."

"Shut up!" He threw up his hands and turned away. "I'm sorry," he added immediately. "I thought SeaGenesis was being blackmailed or something. I thought I would solve this big case and impress Mickey. He was trying to keep me out of it from the beginning. I wouldn't listen. I just kept blundering along . . ."

"Connor—Ulla would still be dead. Su Thom would still be breeding his mosquitos. That was all in motion before you even got suspicious. Ulla took the serum because Su Thom was testing it on himself. If you want to do something now, let's find Su Thom. If he's really raising these infected mosquitos he needed a place. Someplace out of the way."

Connor nodded. She was right. It was nothing but self-pity to fall apart over guilt. If they found Su Thom, they could stop him. And save him from Mickey. Su Thom needed a place, but not too far from either his apartment or SeaGenesis. He was smart; he would have paid in cash. But there were other ways to find him. They could look up new electric accounts, call rental agencies. Su Thom still had Connor's car, he could work his Chapmans connections with the police to find it . . . only it was eleven at night and tomorrow was a long holiday weekend. And Mickey would be doing all those same things, only with all the resources of Chapmans and possibly the CIA to help him.

17

July 4

When Connor finally tumbled into sleep, sometime just before dawn, it was a tar pit of sleep that kept him sunken and immobile until sunlight woke him. He was lying on the couch, books of county maps spread all around him. He was disoriented for about twenty seconds, then everything jumped into focus. Mrs. Wickham had a giant American flag hanging from her front porch. Fourth of July. *RIP July 4*. Soon everyone would be busy frying chicken and packing up the beer. And Su Thom would be hidden away somewhere, opening the latch on a cage full of deadly mosquitos.

He got up and saw Zee, barely awake herself, coming out of the bedroom, carrying pages fresh from the printer. She had spent most of the night on the Internet, chatting with nocturnal entomologists.

"Did you find out anything?" Connor rubbed his eyes.

"Some." She frowned. "The life cycle of the *Anopheles* mosquito is only fourteen days from egg to adult. And eggs could be obtained from a number of sources fairly easily, including just going out to some neighborhood marshlands. They're indigenous. Not common, but they're around. The CDC still has a malaria monitoring program. There are actually a hundred or so cases a year originating in the U.S."

"And how about infecting the mosquitos once you have them?"

"It isn't that hard." She turned and looked at him gravely. "And Ulla did have a sample of the Asher malaria in her lab."

"The guy that died in New York a few months ago?"

"Yes. Samples of his blood and tissue were sent to Walter Reed and CDC and a few other labs. They culture the malaria from the tissue."

"How much did she have?"

"It doesn't matter. Once you have a strain going, it isn't hard to culture more. You keep it alive in hamsters."

"OK." Connor nodded.

"It doesn't mean he *did*," Zee insisted. "Or even that he used the Asher strain. Mickey could be lying. We don't know."

"No, we don't." Back in the living room he turned the television on, half expecting to see Su Thom's picture as the latest homicide victim. Instead there was just a lot of fluff about the festivities down on the mall. People were already gathering, ready to camp out all day to secure prime viewing spots. There would be bands all day, and the National Symphony playing on the west lawn of the Capitol at night. Connor hated crowds and had not gone down there for the fireworks since high school, when Kerry used to orchestrate a big group. She loved to sit directly under the fireworks. He remembered watching her face, with an expression of pure, childlike delight as the explosions bathed her in colored light. Was she packing up her own children right now in preparation for the big night?

Connor felt a slow creep of dread. *RIP July 4 . . .*

The television cameras panned the mall from a helicopter. He stared at thousands of colorful dots sprinkled in the green grass. Thousands of bare arms and legs, half a million targets. If Su Thom really was planning to release his mosquitos . . . no, he would never do something like that!

"Su Thom sent the mosquito to Fairchild as a warning," Zee said. "If we can convince Fairchild to just go public with information about popeye, that should stop him. Or I could go public myself. I work for SeaGenesis, I helped develop popeye. I can call up some media people right now."

"That might have worked a few days ago," Connor said somberly as he stared at the TV. Happy people were flying kites and throwing Frisbees. A puzzled baby in a floppy sun bonnet toddled off into the wide green distance.

"Right now I don't think Su Thom is going to depend on an example. I think he may be depending on a catastrophe."

The battle itself is what history remembers. The clash of men on the field, the plan of attack, the maneuvers and shots and casualties. The more mundane facts of war are largely lost to esoterica. Ten thousand troops moved here and there on this battlefield, but how did they get there in the first place? How were they fed and sheltered? Where did they go to the toilet?

How does one get five hundred mosquitos into a jar? Of all the technical challenges Su Thom had conquered so far, this was actually the most difficult. He had two gallon-sized jars with wide mouths, but had overlooked the actual mechanics of transfer. He tried scooping the mosquitos out with a little fishnet, but that was slow and he had to take the lid off the jar to shake the net, and half just flew back out again. He considered unstapling the screening and rolling them up, but that would require unrolling and shaking them out again. They had to be in the jars. A jar could be broken in a hurry. Jars full of these dragons were as good as bombs.

Finally he decided to coax them in with what they wanted the most. Blood. He opened the hamster cage. He had, despite himself, grown rather fond of the little creatures, but it was the best way. He gently lifted one out of the cage. It was a fat golden hamster, with a white chevron on his chest and one white paw. Su Thom cupped him in the palm of his hand, stroked him lightly on the silky fur, thanked him for his service, then with a quick, practiced twist, snapped his neck. He did not want the little creature to suffer.

He put the limp, furry body in the bottom of one of the jars, then fashioned a little dome of screening to cover it. This way, he hoped, the mosquitos would be lured into the jar by the body, but unable to actually reach it and fill themselves up on hamster blood. He needed them hungry. They had a far richer meal awaiting. Su Thom put the jar into the first cage, and watched. It took ten minutes or so, but gradually the scent of flesh drew them in, and the first jar began to fill.

By noon, the grassy mall around the Washington Monument already seemed full. But by nightfall, twice as many people would crowd in, until blankets were edge to edge with no stripe of green anywhere.

"Hey, we got plenty of room over here!" Jason raised an unsteady beer toward a group of girls, a nubile little caravan of bare legs and blowing hair, sundresses swishing as they maneuvered their cooler and blankets and knapsacks through the crowd. There were six of them, long and lean and dark and lovely, or fair and lovely, and one a little fat and not even all that lovely, but what the hell. It was the Fourth of July and everything was fine in America. They wore shorts and tank tops and flimsy little frocks.

"Wake up, man. Check it out!" Jason poked at Tony but got no response. They had been out since morning and a Stonehenge of empty beer cans circled their blanket.

"C'mon over," he invited again. "We got a bottle of Jack . . ." One of the girls looked at him, looked at her girlfriend, rolled hers eyes and went on. Jason rolled over on the tattered blanket, and nudged his other housemate.

"Peter. Check out those swirly little dresses, man. Is this a great country or what!" Jason grinned. "Didja ever think, like, what if we were in, like, Iran right now, you know? We *could be*, you know that? Just luck we got born in this great country. Just our luck. We could be in fucking Iran or someplace where all the chicks have to wear those long black dresses and hoods and shit. And there's no fireworks."

Peter leaned up on his elbows and laughed. "I didn't know you were so patriotic."

"Damn right I am. I love this country. Hand me another beer, would'ja?" Peter shoved the cooler toward him with his foot. He wasn't much of a drinker, and between the heat and the hours of Frisbee, the couple of beers he did have had felled him. He missed Susan. They had planned to spend the day together, then her father had suddenly decided to take the whole family to their vacation house in Maine. She could have stayed; they had a fight about it. But Dad was insistent.

"Yeah, it's a good thing we had George Washington and all those guys fightin' for us," Jason went on. " 'Cause back then the chicks had to wear almost as much clothes as in Iran. No swirly little dresses, man."

The huge crowd suddenly became a little swirly itself, and Jason flopped down on his back. The ground was moving, too, he noticed. But nothing he couldn't hang on to. He was twenty-two. Plenty of experience with this. He looked up at the clear blue sky, creased only by the sharp white point of the monument. Fireworks. That was later. Cool.

"Here, take this creature!" Georgia Strong thrust the screaming infant toward her husband as he walked in the door.

"I've got to get out of here. He's been crying all day." She pulled off her baby-stained clothes as she talked, pitching them onto the omnipresent laundry pile in the kitchen. How could one little baby generate so much laundry! Her husband took the baby in his big hands and examined him as if he was checking a roaster for quality.

"Is he sick?"

"The doctor says he's just teething, but he's got to be busting out with ivory tusks for all this squalling." She yanked a clean pair of shorts out of the dryer and wiggled into a jogging bra. Martin, tired as he was from work, admired the sight of his wife as she changed so nonchalantly in the middle of the kitchen. She had recovered her figure quickly.

"Poor little guy," he cooed. "What shall we do with you?" He reached under the baby's T-shirt and rubbed the plump tummy. The baby giggled, gurgled, and cooed, then resumed his howling. Martin put him into the swing and wound it up.

Martin opened the freezer and took out a veal knucklebone, boiled white from the stockpot. "Here you go, Fido." The baby squeaked and reached eagerly for the bone, then finally quieted down and settled back for a contented and drooly gnaw.

"I thought you were only going in for an hour." Georgia immediately hated the nagging tone in her voice, but she couldn't help it. She felt so stuck here. He had his new job, he had his photo in *Gourmet* magazine.

"One of Atlanta's hottest young African American chefs to take over one of Washington's premier power restaurants. . . ."

"It's a big deal tonight, baby. I have to make sure it's all perfect. I have fifty pounds of crabcakes to make, and four hundred chocolate twigs to weave into baskets."

"What in heaven's name are you doing with crabcakes and chocolate twig baskets on the Fourth of July anyway? Whatever happened to hot dogs and fruit salad in one of those zigzagged watermelon baskets?"

"Sounds perfect to me." He kissed the side of her neck. "But this law firm is paying a hundred and twenty five bucks a head; they can have chop suey if they want." The party was a big event, and Martin was eager to get back to the kitchen. Fourth of July was a big party night, when most of the available pool of catering staff would rather party themselves. Caterers were recruiting anyone with two arms and two legs. He was relying on the restaurant's cleaning crew to help fry crabcakes and serve the champagne. Inexperienced help had to be supervised closely.

Still, he felt bad. It was tough on her. A new city, leaving friends behind, being alone with the baby all day.

"What do you say to a nice romantic dinner later? We'll open that bottle of Chateau Margaux, I'll grill some fillet, make some of that morel sauce you like," he murmured into the side of her neck, roving his hands lasciviously over her body. Georgia giggled.

"Silly. We can't have morels and French wine on Fourth of July!" Georgia laughed and pushed his hands away. "Fourth of July is for my mamma's fried chicken and coleslaw."

"Okay, how about I cook us some hot dogs, get a six-pack of lousy American beer, and who knows, maybe we'll even have a few fireworks of our own." He grabbed her around the waist, kissed her hard, and dipped her until they tumbled onto the laundry pile.

"They found my car." Connor put down the phone. "It's in a new housing development in Gaithersburg called Magnolia Grove. Residents remember it being there since yesterday morning, but no one saw who left it."

"It's there right now?" Zee looked up apprehensively. It was four-fifteen. They had spent the whole day futilely chasing after every possible scant lead they could think of and coming up against one brick wall after another.

"Yeah." He got the rental car keys and looked around as if there were something else he should take with him, but had no clue what it might be.

"Do you think Mickey knows, too?" Zee asked.

"Probably."

Connor looked out the front window. There was no one obviously watching the house, but then they weren't supposed to be obvious. Mickey was probably already on his way, if not there already. It was time for speed over finesse.

"Then let's go." Zee grabbed her sneakers.

Magnolia Grove was a new development on the bleak edge of suburban sprawl. The streets were smooth with new paving and named after flowers and birds. Chrysanthemum Way and Hummingbird Place, Hyacinth Street and Woodpecker Drive. The landscaping was sparse so the barren hills and long, winding roads made it easy for Connor and Zee to see the cars slowly creeping up and down the bucolic lanes. Magnolia Grove was crawling with feds. They weren't even trying to be discreet, no delivery trucks or plumber's vans, just four government sedans with government heads swiveling side to side. Connor saw Mickey's unmistakable white hair inside a distant white sedan cruising through the heart of the development.

Connor stopped the car at the top of Aster Road. He saw his own car parked in a cul de sac two streets over. There was one sedan halfway down that road, obviously watching it. Connor opened the car door.

"What are you doing?"

"Taking a look around."

"And if they see us?"

"It might rattle their cages a little. And it might stop them from shooting Su Thom on sight." He stepped out feeling a little less confident than he sounded, feeling like a target. The air seemed even hotter out here, cooked by the vast bulldozed hills. Most of the houses showed signs of habitation. Late-model cars, mostly minivans and Tauruses, declared families. There were borders of pansies and reedy little trees staked out in front yards, withering in the heat. Air-conditioner units thrummed steadily. At the edge of the development a scraggly row of trees had been left. Past them, Connor could see a slope, a ditch full of tall grass, and just beyond that, the fresh-turned dirt and yellow bulldozers of yet another development under construction. A huge sign begged for visits to the model sample home and promised low, low financing. Only two rows of townhouses appeared finished, and there were only four cars on that street. Another few months and it would be just like this place. But right now it looked desolate, the turned-up earth baked into hard yellow ridges. Very desolate. And very close. Connor got back in the car.

"Slide over and drive," he ordered. "Go back the way we came in."

"Why, what did you see?"

"I'm guessing there's a road on the far side of that next development. Let me out when I say, then drive around and wait there. If anyone gives you trouble, just get lost."

"What . . ."

"Just do it," Connor interrupted. "Don't get out of the car. If we're lucky, I'll meet you there with Su Thom." He grabbed her hand and gave it a quick squeeze.

"OK, slow down." He jumped out of the car, ducked into the little grove of trees and ran down the grassy bank.

Su Thom had not emptied the cages, but both jars were dark with mosquitos, a couple of hundred in each. The rest he would leave behind. Later, if they didn't believe him, they could come and see for themselves. He put the gloves on again, reached into the cage and fastened a bit of netting over the top of each jar with a rubber band. He pulled the jars out and put them side by side into the wicker suitcase, slipping a bit of cardboard between them for cushioning. He closed the lid and snapped the buckles shut.

He felt clear. There was no doubt, no second thoughts. His body ached and he felt hot and shivery. A crushing headache had begun that morning. The symptoms did not worry him; rather, they were a triumph, the final confirmation of his success. He was infected. His body was weak, but his spirit was strong. He walked up the stairs, switched off the light and shut the basement door behind him. He picked up the suitcase and opened the front door.

"Hello, Su Thom." Connor was waiting at the bottom of the steps. Su Thom clutched the case to his chest but otherwise did not start or flinch.

"You have the mosquitos in there?" Connor asked.

"In glass jars. If I drop it, they break."

"There are better ways."

"It's too late."

"No. I'll take you to the FBI right now, and you can tell them everything. Or whoever you want, a TV station, a hospital, wherever you want to go. You can tell them all about popeye. You can show them the mosquitos. You don't even have to be identified. We could just drop the mosquitos off at a TV station. Zee and I will speak for you. We'll get some expert to examine them, and the whole country will know."

"They *know* already!" Su Thom said with steely calm. "They know but they don't care. They will not care about malaria until it affects them."

"Ulla would not want you to do this, Su Thom."

"Ulla lived in a different world."

"This will not honor her."

Connor took a step closer. Su Thom stiffened.

"I can let them go here just as well."

"Your mosquitos are carrying an incurable strain!"

"I don't believe you."

"You used the Asher culture."

Su Thom looked down, and Connor thought he saw a real struggle going on.

"I can't help that now," Su Thom finally said.

"Look, Su Thom, I know why you did this, and I know you never meant to release the mosquitos. You just wanted to show them how easy it would be. We can still do that."

"No!" Su Thom backed away. "It is too late."

"They're watching my car. You'll never get to it." Su Thom looked around again, a flicker of doubt on his face. "Come with me. This isn't the way. Zee is waiting to pick us up. Ulla was her friend, too. She wants to help you."

Su Thom was wavering. He looked once more over to the neighboring development where his escape vehicle was trapped. He unlatched one of the clasps on the wicker case. "If you try anything, I will break the jars. I swear it."

"Okay." Connor turned and started walking toward where he hoped Zee would be. The ground was chunky with dry clods of dirt. They came to the road and stood on opposite sides. Connor for once didn't know what to say, couldn't think of a useful con. He looked down the road. It wouldn't be that hard just to walk away right now. Leave them all here to sort out their own damn mess. He needed no part of this. He thought of all the people down on the mall waiting for fireworks. They should have been smart enough to put on some mosquito repellent in the first place. He could slip away, get to the highway, and catch a ride. Another town, a few games of pool, a little hustle or two, a room by the week in a cheap motel, get back out west, Canada maybe, someplace far and cool, get lost and to hell with Mickey and the CIA and all of them. *All of them.* Lois, Kerry and the children. What if it was true? What if there was a vengeful Cambodian with a truckload of old explosives? It was too crazy. But that made it just crazy enough to be possible.

They both tensed at the noise of a car. A rooster tail of dust obscured it until it was almost upon them. Then the car slowed and they saw Zee behind the wheel. She stopped between them.

"Hi, Su Thom. You OK?" She got out of the car.

"You drive," Su Thom commanded Connor. "You stay here." He showed Zee the wicker case. "If anyone tries to stop us I will smash this on the road."

"Where are you going?" Zee asked gently. "Why don't you let me come with you?"

"You tell them," Su Thom repeated, wiping the sweat from his eyes. "In the house over there, in the basement, are more mosquitos if they doubt me. Some have escaped the cages, so be careful."

"Popeye doesn't work!" Zee said desperately. "It *doesn't work*. It won't cure malaria." It was the one good lie Connor hadn't thought of. "They tested it," Zee went on. "It doesn't work. It's no good."

"I don't believe you. They killed Ulla. They know it works." Zee saw the gaze of a man committed to his mission and not afraid to die.

"Get out of here, Zee," Connor instructed her quickly. "Go to one of those houses and call . . . I don't know, the FBI . . ." Zee nodded. Suddenly they all turned at the sound of a car roaring down the dirt road.

"Go!" Su Thom shouted. "Now!"

"What about this St. John?" Amanda Mountclair fussed in the mirror, scrutinizing her dress. "Genene said the party is casual but I think she tries to sabotage me. Last June? At that book party? For that ex-senator? She says 'oh, it's just a casual little backyard get-together,' so I show up barelegged in sandals and a cotton skirt!" She daubed on perfume. "I was so embarrassed!"

Frank Mountclair smiled to himself. If Amanda did indeed own a cotton skirt, it would no doubt be hand-spun from some rare handpicked cotton, designed by Donna Karan, and sold for a small fortune by one of her regular retinue of adoring salesladies at Neiman Marcus.

"You look splendid, dear," he offered with a peck on the cheek. He was not put off by her frippery. It was rather understood, in fact, in their circles, that adornment was the woman's job, as serious as the national debt. She was thirty-four, twenty years his junior. A trophy wife, his second, and starting to worry. Frank had been featured in *Washingtonian* magazine last month as one of the twenty most powerful men in Washington.

"Did you show Claire where the sparklers are?"

"Yes, yes," Frank replied.

"How about money for the pizza?"

"I left it on the hall table." Frank sighed. He envied the au pair who would get to spend the evening eating pizza and waving sparklers. His daughter's slumber party sounded like much more fun. He was not enthusiastic about going out tonight. The Fourth of July traffic was always terrible because of the crowds, but his firm had reserved the entire rooftop of the Hotel Washington and brought in the city's hottest new chef to cater the event.

Amanda slipped a lipstick into her purse. "Rosa? Rosa!" She called overly loudly for the maid. Rosa Jiminez snapped the last ruffled Laura Ashley pillowcase on the fluffy down pillow and stepped out of the fairytale decorated child's bedroom.

"Oh there you are." Amanda smiled. "You put fresh sheets on both beds and made up the trundle?"

"Yes, ma'am."

"Is the Dixie cup dispenser full in Caitlin's bath?"

Rosa just smiled and nodded. It was ten after six and she should have left a half hour ago. She usually only cleaned once a week, on the live-in's day off, but Mrs. Mountclair simply couldn't face the preparations for her daughter's slumber party alone, and had begged her to come.

Rosa was eager to leave, but she wanted to please Mrs. Mountclair. The Georgetown/Foxhall Road set almost exclusively used Filipinos for servants and maids. If she did well here, recommendations would come. Although her husband insisted the money was in office cleaning, Rosa still preferred private homes. Especially these beautiful old homes with their dark oil paintings and thick oriental rugs. If she pleased the Mountclairs, maybe next would be Foxhall Road with real mansions, maybe a place for her brother Turino when he finally came. He would make a good houseman, a good job for him, since he wasn't so strong. She had never seen a Hispanic houseman, but he was educated and handsome. He had manners and those elegant musical hands.

"One more thing, Rosa." Amanda brushed by her for a quick peek in the child's room. "Could you get out five of the crystal parfait glasses? Not the Steuben, just the Waterford, those are the cut glass ones? In the smaller cabinet? I promised the girls they could use them for sundaes. They may need to be washed."

Rosa suppressed a groan. Her sister Carmen needed the van to take some of the others downtown for a catering job.

"Yes, ma'am," she said. "And the silver spoons, too?"

Su Thom held the suitcase outside the window. Connor winced as the car jostled over a small bump. They were downtown approaching Constitution Avenue. It was almost six o'clock. Mickey was following in his car, with two others trailing behind him. No one was making a move yet. What had Mickey told them?

"This is a good time to stop, Su Thom," Connor suggested. "No one is going to do anything stupid with so many people around." Traffic was beginning to slow dramatically, and there were police at every intersection, guiding huge volumes of fireworks-bound pedestrians across Constitution Avenue. Connor glanced to each side as they went through an intersection and saw two police cars ease out toward them. A helicopter droned overhead. Were they in on the chase now, too? He hoped to god they all knew what they were dealing with.

"It's not too late."

There were fewer cars around them now. Squad cars were parked at every intersection. A large van maneuvered to block most of the road ahead. Su Thom stiffened and tightened his grip on the case. A man in black climbed on the roof of the van. A SWAT team, Connor realized. A bomb squad and a SWAT team. Mickey was ready for anything. What had he told them?

Some people were beginning to notice, but for most of the thousands still streaming toward the mall, the only thought was to find a little space to lay out the blanket. For the quarter million already assembled, the world beyond their picnics had ceased to exist. No one could even see Constitution Avenue, let alone wonder about the blocked-off streets, the slowing car, and the delicacy of glass jars.

Even if Su Thom did drop the case, there was still a chance, Connor thought. The jars might not break. Or if they did, it would take a while for the mosquitos to find their way out through the wicker. He could grab a blanket and throw it over the case. Some of these people must be carrying mosquito repellent. If they acted quickly they could contain most of it, couldn't they?

"Let me stop, Su Thom. Talk to them."

"Talk does nothing."

The people close to the street, having decided whatever was going on had to be bad, were gathering up children and hurrying away. There was a minor panic erupting on the edge of the crowd. They were probably thinking guns or bombs. How simple that would be. Connor slowed down even more. The roadblock was only a few hundred yards away now.

"There are kids here, Su Thom. Look around. Families and children."

"There are families and children in Vietnam," he replied dispassionately. "The human race is a family. Sometimes the branches must be trimmed so the whole tree may flower."

"Oh, cut the crap!" Connor clenched the wheel in frustration. "None of this guru haiku Zen crap, OK? No more silver dragons and trimming branches. You're doing this because you're angry, and you probably have every damn right to be, your mother died of malaria, and your people are dying, and the West doesn't give a damn and you want some kind of revenge, and maybe you've actually worked yourself up into some kind of psychosis by now and really are just nuts, but there is nothing *noble* about this. If you let those bugs out, you're just a common murderer. No better than some guy with a gun shooting into a crowd." Su Thom looked startled, and a few inches closer to reality.

"These people don't have to die."

"What would it take?" Connor grasped at the hint of offer. "What do you want? I can get Fairchild out here to confess. I'll get him to dance a jig in the middle of the road if you want. Look, there's a TV news truck up ahead. You can tell the world yourself."

"No one has to die."

"Right. You just *show* them the mosquitos. Show them what could happen. Like you intended in the first place."

Su Thom was shaking his head. "They don't have to die because there is a *cure*. Ulla found the cure." A look of peace came over Su Thom's face. He looked straight at Connor and his eyes shone with an almost beatific calm. He smiled. "All right. Tell them we will talk." Su

Thom pulled the case back in the window and held it on his lap. Connor breathed a sigh of relief. He stuck his arm out the window and waved to Mickey to stop.

Suddenly he heard the door click. Connor turned but Su Thom was already halfway out of the car. Connor grabbed the back of his shirt. It was damp with sweat. It stretched. It was oddly cold. Everything moved so slowly. Connor kept pulling on Su Thom's shirt with his right hand and reached around with his left to shift the car to park. Su Thom had one foot out. He held the suitcase out in front of him, already over the pavement. In the weird slow-motion of disaster, Connor let go of the steering wheel and lunged across the seat. Su Thom struggled. Connor grabbed for the case and felt his fingertips on the rattan. Then Su Thom twisted sharply and broke free. Connor jumped across the seat and went out after him. Police were running everywhere, guns drawn. People screamed and ran and fell in panic. Su Thom stumbled. The case bumped against the curb but there was no sound of glass breaking. The white car stopped. Mickey jumped out, a radio in his hand.

"Don't shoot! Don't anyone shoot!" Connor shouted. Su Thom scrambled up. He looked confused. Two more cars screeched to a halt. People were running and screaming and diving to the ground on top of children, expecting bullets. Uniformed officers froze in place, guns drawn. Su Thom stood still for a minute, the case held out in front of him, his thumb on one of the latches. *Keep him on the grass*, Connor thought as he walked toward him.

"There isn't enough popeye, Su Thom," Connor said calmly. "There are too many people here." Su Thom looked at him, clutching the case to his chest. Connor felt a flicker of hope. He saw fear and doubt in the young man's eyes.

"Don't do this. Not this way." Suddenly a shot cracked out. Su Thom darted back and ran toward the road.

"Don't shoot!" Connor screamed. "He has a *bomb*! Do *not* shoot!" Could they even hear him? Guns were leveled at him, everyone was shouting.

Su Thom stood amidst a litter of scattered lawn chairs and hampers in the road. He seemed frozen. He gazed at the puzzled and terrified faces of people watching him. They crouched among the trees, sheltering their children, beseeching Jesus. Su Thom unclasped the second latch.

"No!" Connor shouted. More shots rang out, a staccato burst that seemed to go on forever. Su Thom leaped, uncoiling his body with the fluid grace of a dancer. He threw the case into the air. The lid flew open, the jars soared slowly out, making a beautiful arc against the blue sky. Connor thought he could even hear a little whoosh of air.

Then the graceful form jerked with the impact of bullets. Su Thom crumpled to the sidewalk, bones breaking with an audible crack. Or was it the jars? Connor reached him, caught him as he fell. The body had no weight. Su Thom's blood was hot on his hands. In the edges of his sight Connor saw people darting in terror, blurs of color behind a little wooden fence like a cage of panicked finches.

"Hold it right there!" Rough hands flattened him on the sidewalk, twisting his arms painfully, a knee on the back of his neck, handcuffs. More shouting, sirens, radios squawking, the helicopter thumping over-head, so close he could feel the vibrations in his chest. Finally they hauled him to his feet. Mickey was there with a badge out, in charge. A whole swarm of men surrounded Su Thom, guns pointed despite the motionless body and the spreading pool of blood. Mickey's two men grabbed Connor by the arms, almost lifting him off his feet.

"Don't say a word," Mickey hissed in his ear. "Get in the car," Mickey directed. Connor saw bloody footprints all over the sidewalk. An officer was calling for a bomb squad. Connor looked up, his thoughts still horribly slow. "It's the mosquitos," he mumbled. "You have to tell them . . ."

"Shut the hell up!" Mickey grabbed him by the handcuffs, opened the car door, put one hand on top of Connor's head and pushed. Connor got one knee up on the seat when he felt a vicious upward yank on the cuffs and Mickey's fingers curling like a claw at the back of his neck. His balance gone, he felt himself being shoved forward. As hard as he could, Mickey rammed Connor's head into the opposite door.

18

Connor woke up slowly, struggling through a dense confusion. His head pounded. Finally, consciousness lumbered closer and he cautiously opened his eyes to test it. He was lying on the floor in the back of a van. There was blood all over his shirt. Reality came rushing back. It was Su Thom's blood. Out the back window he could see by the light that it was early evening. He could tell by the speed that they were on a highway. He sat up slowly. There was a man in the back with him. Buzz cut. Square jaw. Tight lips. Sunglasses. Big, strong, white as a soup bone. Almost funny the way he looked the complete stereotype of the CIA goon. It was one of the men who had been with Mickey on the mall yesterday.

The soup bone saw that Connor was awake and gave a little grunting nod toward the front of the van. Mickey came back and the soup bone moved to the front seat. Connor pulled himself up into a sitting position, leaning against the side of the van. Mickey looked at him, his eyes narrow, shaking his head slowly.

"What am I going to do with you, Connor?" he said.

"Su Thom. Is he dead?"

"I suppose so," Mickey answered coldly. "We didn't stick around to find out." Connor saw the whole thing again: the slow graceful toss, the crack of bullets, Su Thom's weightless body crumpling on the sidewalk.

"What about the mosquitos?"

Mickey glanced at his watch. "It's under control."

"Where's Zee?"

"She's all right."

"Where is she?"

"Someplace safe."

"What happens now?" Connor said. His head pounded and his words seemed too thick.

"I haven't decided yet. Any suggestions?"

"Give up popeye. Leave the country. Let us go."

Mickey smiled. "I wouldn't count too much on that particular scenario." He looked at the man in the front seat.

"Jack, hand me that bottle of water, will you?" The man passed back a bottle of water, glaring down at Connor like a pit bull. Connor sat up straighter and tried to look out the front window but from this angle saw only sky. Mickey pulled a pill bottle out of his pocket, shook out a white tablet.

"Here, take this."

"No thanks, my headache isn't that bad."

"It's to make you sleep." Connor let Mickey put the pill on his tongue. He raised the water bottle to his mouth. Connor took a sip then spit the tablet back into the bottle. Mickey was not fooled. He held the bottle up to the light and saw the pill swirling around the bottom.

"Let's not make this difficult, Connor, okay?" Mickey said tersely. "This has been a long day." He poured out all but an ounce of water and swirled this around until the pill dissolved. Then he took Connor's chin in his massive hand, shoved the spout into his mouth and squeezed. Connor choked on the bitter medicine but could not keep from swallowing.

"What are you going to do with us, Mickey?" Connor asked again. Mickey just looked out the front window. *Would he really kill me?* Connor wondered with weird objectivity. *Could he do that?*

"I'm just going to take you someplace out of the way for now. You've been working hard. You could use a little vacation."

"You know Zee has been going over all Raki's data and she knows a lot about popeye. You'll need her to produce the amount you're going to need."

Mickey said nothing, just rubbed his hand over his forehead and sighed.

"Is there really any Cambodian threatening the family?"

"The threats are real, yes."

"It's just I'm having a hard time believing a couple of Cambodian henchmen could pull off a fake carjacking quite so flawlessly. And covering up the fire. I see a guiding hand at work here."

"That doesn't mean they won't do something on their own. I know how these people operate."

"I bet you do. Did you know we were in there? When you decided to blow it all to hell?"

"I didn't know it was you," Mickey answered evasively. "I had people watching the place. They only knew someone had gone in."

"And the accidents on Shadow Island?"

"We needed a plausible reason for SeaGenesis to pull out. They were losing money, and we offered to take it over."

"Why Shadow Island? Why not just go get your own damn island?"

"It's the only place the sponge grows well. It needs the cold updrafts from the deep water trench and exceptionally pure water. Most of the developed islands have too much run-off and silting."

"Gee, maybe you could just contribute to Greenpeace or something, you know, clean up the reefs, ecology and all that."

"I'm glad to see you are keeping a sense of humor."

"So whose idea was it to breed the new strains of malaria?" Mickey gave him a dagger glance but Connor saw fear behind it. *So it was true. It wasn't all just a simple accident.* "I'm just curious, that's all," Connor went on. "It can't have been simple. Zee didn't think it was even possible. Who did the actual breeding?"

"The Japanese had a big biological warfare operation during World War Two," Mickey said grudgingly. "There were still a few old guys around in the sixties, back when the project was still official."

Still official. Connor's head began to throb. The CIA hiring Japanese doctors to engineer a biological warfare project for the U.S. government. He struggled for composure. "So they bred the new strain, resistant to all cures but your own. Then what?"

"Like I said. It was too over the top. The company got scared, and canceled the program."

"Leaving a nice stockpile of both the disease and the only cure," Connor realized. "So then what? You just released all your deadly mosquitos, then offered up the cure for sale to the highest bidder?"

"Nothing so crude. We knew who to approach. We worked out some deals. Everyone got a little something." Mickey's nonchalance was chilling. "They were crawling with disease over there anyway. It's not like it was some kind of clean country." Mickey's tone, part confessional, part boasting, frightened Connor as much as the facts of the story. It was the tone of a man resigned and weary, dangerously unworried about any further consequences.

"After the war there was a lot of political shifting. Son Loc seemed the most promising to the U.S. But peasants were trying to spread out and grab his land. The threat of malaria had always kept them out, but by then there were enough medications available to make them bolder. Our *P. falciparum* just brought back the balance."

"Until your only cure started to fail. What were you planning to do about it? If Dr. Raki hadn't come up with popeye?"

"We had people working on it."

Connor turned to look out the window again. How to handle this now? All the threads were unraveling too fast. "You're going to need gallons of popeye now."

Mickey looked away.

"Hundreds of people were just bitten. You have to treat them," Connor said.

"With a drug that doesn't exist?"

"You're willing to risk a malaria epidemic in Washington?"

"There's not going to be an epidemic."

"Su Thom released hundreds of mosquitos!" Connor felt overwhelmed. Everything up until now he could almost explain, even as it repulsed him. It was a plan out of control. There were others involved. Government approval. But to withhold the only cure now, with hundreds of lives on the line? Connor could accept pride and greed and stupidity, but this would be evil. Cold, pure evil. Mickey could be faulty. He could be thoughtless and imperious, but he could not be evil.

"Look, I'm not sure you've thought this thing through." Connor groped for some way to change Mickey's mind. "Look at it practically for a minute. If people start dying, you'll never be able to keep a lid on this. You will have doctors and scientists examining this malaria and someone is going to figure out it was an engineered strain!"

"They won't find out anything of the sort. New diseases spring up all the time. They come into the country from someplace else. Trust me, Connor. It's not a big deal."

"You can't do this!"

"I have to do this! I will not risk my family!"

"You can give people the drug without revealing its origins," Connor suggested. "No one has to know where it came from. Say it's just a new drug that is still in the experimental stage." Connor felt like he was bargaining for an extended curfew or use of the car, not for hundreds of lives. He felt nauseated and dizzy, and realized the drug was probably starting to take effect. He had only a few more minutes to try and bargain this out.

"Saying the disease is from Haiti or somewhere isn't going to work, not after a few good epidemiologists start unraveling it. If you get the serum to Washington now, we can make it all come off as a terrorist attack by a deranged young man. I'll back you."

"When were you suddenly so concerned with the fate of the world?"

"Mickey, be realistic. Once this city starts getting involved with an epidemic, there is no way you can hush this up. Su Thom leads to SeaGenesis. Plenty of people at SeaGenesis knew Ulla Raki was working on malaria. Someone is going to start connecting the dots." Connor scratched at the wobbly foundations of a scheme that might convince Mickey. He was going to have to come up with the best con of his life right now.

"Look, okay. I can't say I'm all that wrapped up with a bunch of strangers dying. You're right. What I want here is just to get the hell out of all of this and go on with my life. You need popeye to take care of your clients in Asia, right? Fine. But there is no chance in hell of long-term supply. Not until you synthesize it. If you ever can. They're going to find out about Shadow Island. You won't have your secret production lab any more. The sponge can't be farmed." Connor sorted quickly through all Zee had told him, trying to gauge how much Mickey would know, and how much he could bluff.

"Plus, you know how the samples have been inconsistent? Zee has been working on this. She thinks the active compounds only come after a certain age—it's some kind of reproductive enzyme that kicks in at sexual maturity." *Damn, did sponges even have sex?* The night of their first lovemaking came back in disorienting swirls of memory. "That's why only some of the samples show bioactivity." He must be doing okay; Mickey looked interested. Now was the time to play him carefully.

"The sponge doesn't mature very fast. It takes six years, maybe more. So the chances of a steady supply are pretty small. Right now you're in a bind. You need enough popeye to satisfy your people in Asia, but face it, any way this turns out, you're going to run out again." Mickey was looking at him suspiciously but with interest. Connor raced on, feeling the drug start to deaden his limbs.

"Take us to Shadow Island. Tell Zee we have to make the serum for those infected in Washington. Scour the reef now. Pick up every sponge you can get your hands on in the next few days. Let Zee and Padgette cook up all the popeye they can. You take it to your people. When the troops arrive on Shadow Island in a few days, and you know they will, you and the world supply of popeye will be gone. Unless you find some other place in the world with the same reef conditions and clean enough water, Shadow Island is your only hope, and you've only got a few days to milk it."

"And what do you get out of this?"

"My ass alive. And Zee's. You don't kill us. We'll dive for you, help you collect, make the serum. It's a win-win kind of thing." His words were slurring.

"How do I know you won't talk?"

"I've seen what you guys can do. And there's Lois. If I expose you it would hurt her. She was good to me. I won't do that to her. I can just walk away. I've done it lots of times."

"What about Zee Aspen? She seems the zealous type."

"She has family. She wants to live. We can convince her to stay quiet."

Mickey leaned back with his arms crossed, considering the proposal.

"I can't trust you."

"Look. I don't really give a shit if everyone dies of malaria, OK? Here, there, or anywhere. I just want to go on with my life." He felt his words going fat in his mouth and felt he was babbling, but kept on. "You know me, Mickey. I don't give a crap for the world. I'm not some global . . . global village kind of guy. I'm . . . I'm . . ." Connor struggled but could not force off the soporific any longer. He couldn't finish. He didn't know what he was.

19

The crowd roared with delight as the fireworks exploded overhead. Rosa Jiminez looked at the children, their faces turned up in awe, small hands clasped in delight, feet stamping in the grass. They were so excited to see the fireworks. She felt for her husband's hand and clutched it. In El Salvador, when the night sky was filled with explosions, they had huddled in fear. But that was so long ago and far away. Now they were here, in beautiful America where nothing bad could ever really be so bad. It was an extravagance to be here. They had turned down the chance to work for the caterer at the big fancy law office party. The two of them, forty dollars an hour, four hour minimum, but big parties were usually six hours or more, it was a lot of money. But they had promised the children. And the cleaning business was going so well. It was worth it, to turn down a job for this beautiful night. *Oohs* and *ahs* rippled through the crowd as blue streaks melted into gold, and the gold twirled slowly to earth. Next year they would have enough money to bring Turino. The cleaning business was thriving now. Houses by day, offices by night. Fernando and Jose were talking about buying another van.

Poor Turino, how he would love to see these colors! But he was sickly and could not work much. It was important that those who came first could earn money for the others. The fireworks came faster now, explosions of light filling the whole sky. Louisa, her youngest, got scared and began to cry. Alba gathered her little sister in her lap and whispered for her not to be afraid. Alba was a good girl, Rosa thought proudly. She was almost fifteen. Next week they would go shopping for her dress for the Quinceañera. Alba would have a beautiful dress. And they wouldn't serve those cheap store-brand sodas—no, real Cokes and Fanta Orange. And some nice wine, too. She would buy some fireworks, too. Why not! Fireworks made you feel so good, like your heart was full.

Her heart was full. Rosa squeezed Fernando's hand. He pulled his wife close and kissed her. He kissed her a long time and the children began to giggle. Rosa did not even notice the sharp sting on her ankle.

"There is still a lot of confusion over exactly what happened here tonight," the reporter intoned, trying to ignore the crowds that peered from the dark behind her. Live broadcasts were hell most of the time, but with a boisterous Fourth of July crowd goggling over her shoulder, it was impossible. They were lured to the TV lights like moths.

"There are reports that the FBI has become involved, but they have not yet released a statement. This is what we do know . . ." She looked down at her notes and privately wished immediate death to a nearby group of obnoxious college boys.

"The suspect, who is at this point identified only as an Asian male, in his late twenties or early thirties, led police on a low-speed chase from Maryland to the mall, where he was finally halted by roadblocks. Police thought he had a bomb. There was another man in the car with him, either a hostage or an accomplice. The police are not clear on that. But the important thing is that the alleged bomb was not an explosive device at all. Although this has not yet been confirmed, some witnesses claim the man actually had a jar filled with insects, apparently mosquitos."

Jason stared into the bright TV lights and leaned heavily on Peter. "What's going on? All that light. It's like a spaceship landing or something."

"Come on, you guys. It's a news camera." Peter, as always the most sober and responsible, tried to drag his friends away.

"Wow. They're like filming the alien landing? And they landed on Fourth of July. Like in the movie!"

"No, asshole, it's just a TV camera. She's talking about mosquitos."

"What mosquitos?"

"Police believe that the act was some sort of protest," the reporter went on. "As I said, we don't have all the details yet. The perpetrator has not yet been identified and we only have speculation and rumors at this point." She cupped her hand around her earpiece to hear the studio anchorman's question.

"Look, man!" Jason punched Tony and Peter, who nearly toppled over. "The alien chick. She's talking to her planet man."

Peter saw two policemen coming over and coaxed his housemates out of camera range.

". . . That's right, Tom." The reporter smiled at the camera. "One of the rumors is that this was some sort of AIDS protest or statement, but we want to stress that mosquitos absolutely do not carry or transmit HIV, the virus that causes AIDS. The authorities right now have not confirmed that it was in fact mosquitos in the jar. But let me stress, it is impossible for mosquitos to transmit HIV, the virus that causes AIDS . . . As far as the West Nile virus, or any other mosquito-borne diseases, officials will certainly be looking for that as well. As I said, everything is still very uncertain right now . . ."

"OK, man, we're going." The police were shooing the crowd away from the TV reporter. "It's OK, we're cool." Peter dragged his friends away. "Come on, guys."

"What about the spaceship?"

"It isn't a spaceship, Jason. It's a TV camera."

"Oh right. Alien mosquitos. I got bit by a lot of them."

"Well, let's go home," Peter suggested, "and we won't get any more bites."

"Yeah? Good idea. 'Cause these alien mosquitos are, like, really hungry."

"Oh, my god." Amanda Mountclair gasped as she walked into the disaster area that had once been the newly renovated living room of their Georgetown home. All the sofa cushions were stacked at one end of the room, with an assortment of mops and brooms poking over them. Four little girls and a very startled nanny, all in newspaper hats, looked up from their fortress.

"Daddy!" Marissa vaulted over the battlement and ran into his arms.

"My goodness, what's all this?" he said cheerfully.

"We're playing Fourth of July!" Marissa shouted excitedly. "We killed all the redcoats and now we're having a snack in the fort."

"From one terrorist attack to another." Amanda sighed.

"I'm sorry, Meester Mountclair." Claire, the French au pair, began picking up cushions. "I did not expect you so soon. After the fireworks, they are a little excited to sleep right away."

"This is the Potomac River." Marissa dragged her toe across the carpet runner. "And Caitlin was George Washington. To cross the river? Like in the picture? But now I am. And we killed all the British." She swept a hand proudly toward the field of dead stuffed animals.

"It was the Delaware, dear, not the Potomac," Amanda corrected. She was not about to let twelve thousand dollars a year in private school tuition be corrupted.

"I'm sorry." Claire blushed. "I don't have straight all your history."

"It's fine, Claire. I'm glad they're having such fun." Frank ruffled his daughter's curly hair. Amanda eyed the seventy-dollar-a-yard raw silk slipcovers for any signs of war damage.

"We've just had a very difficult night." Amanda sighed. "Some AIDS protest shut down the entire street for hours! We had to walk miles for a cab!"

"Come on, girls, all zee revolutionaries upstairs now to bed! And take zee redcoats wiz you!" The little girls began picking up the stuffed animals, still giggling with excitement.

"Thank you very much for having us over tonight, Aunt Amanda." Caitlin was ten and much more aware of social protocol. "We had a very lovely time. You look really pretty, too." She fingered the little red, white, and blue beaded evening purse. Marissa saw her cousin admiring the purse and, with the proprietary rights so clearly established in little girls, took it out of her hand.

"Amanda lets me take this to school sometimes," she bragged.

"She does not."

"Uh huh. Well she *said* I could *sometime*." The other girls came scampering over, lured by the guaranteed exotica of an evening purse. "Look, there's a secret compartment." Marissa opened the jeweled clasp on the evening purse. They bent over the purse, stroking the creamy silk lining, exploring the gold lipstick case, the abalone shell compact, the precious tiny perfume bottle, the delicate silver comb. The little purse was rich with the musty scent of perfume and cosmetics. Lured by that scent, one small mosquito had also come to explore the purse a few hours previously while it sat open on the table. Lost in the satiny folds, it had become trapped. Now it felt the fresh air and the luscious aroma of the mingled breaths of four little girls. It stirred its tiny wings.

"Let me see." Caitlin snatched the bag away.

"Hey!" Marissa grabbed it back.

"Girls, come on now. Izz time for bed." Claire extricated the evening bag and began to shepherd the girls away. The mosquito, newly freed from its prison and attracted to the sugary smell of the children, landed on the nanny's blouse where it rode upstairs into the slumber party bedroom.

Georgia was nearly hysterical when she finally heard Martin's car pull into the driveway. He had called to tell her he would be late, traffic was horrendous, don't wait up. The "mosquito bomber" was the lead story on the eleven o'clock news, though no one really knew anything. There was a lot of footage of police milling around and the bomb squad in their heavy spacesuits.

The reporter kept saying that no one was believed to have been hurt and that it wasn't a real bomb, that police believed it to be just a protest, but what if it had been a real bomb? It happened just outside the office building where Martin was catering the party. What about Oklahoma

City and the World Trade Center? She knew it was stupid to think this way. It was stupid to get upset; what was wrong with her?

The baby finally fell asleep in her arms, and Georgia put him down on the couch. She could not take him to his crib. The nursery, with its duckling wallpaper and Winnie the Pooh sheets seemed too far away. The whole world was dangerous now. Where was Martin? What had happened?

He came home tired and annoyed and was surprised to find his wife sobbing.

"Honey, it's all right. Nothing happened. It was just some kid pretending to have a bomb. It's okay." He held her and petted her hair and looked at their sleeping son and felt a strong, terrible love. He had had the same thoughts, as the rumors swirled around the buffet tables. "I was parked in for hours. The street was jammed with police and then news trucks and all the people walking back from the mall. I couldn't even get out to the street."

Georgia just cried. Martin said he understood and did, a little, but mostly he was just tired. He opened the wine that had been meant for their special dinner and they sat cuddled together on the couch, the sleeping baby tucked securely between them. Georgia finally fell asleep in his arms. She looked so peaceful, he did not want to move, even when the mosquito bites on the back of his hand began to itch.

20

July 5

In the bright tropical morning on Shadow Island, with palm trees waving in the breeze and gentle waves massaging the sand, everything seemed even more absurd. In the lush tranquility and the absolute calm, it seemed to Connor that there could not logically be a crisis anywhere, certainly not an engineered disease and thousands of people soon to die a horrible death. Perhaps he had dreamed it all. He shuddered. What he had really dreamed was huge clouds of mosquitos darkening the sky, gigantic mosquitos thrumming overhead like helicopters, eyes whirling, stingers jabbing at his body, fountains of blood spurting from victims. He saw Su Thom's body twisting with the impact of the bullets, his bones shattering on the pavement, his eyes wild and triumphant.

It had been dark when they landed last night, and Connor was still groggy with the sleeping pill when Jack and Mack or whoever he was dragged him to a room and handcuffed him to the bed. He heard the plane take off again this morning, then they came and unchained him, fed him some coffee and stale cereal, and took him to the dock.

He did not know what they had told Zee, and her face did not tell him anything. She was pulling scuba equipment out of a shed. She looked up, met his eyes, did not smile, but did not look afraid. In addition to Jack and Mack there were two Bahamians, and a tall, bony, red-bearded man that Connor assumed was Arthur Padgette. What was his role in all this now? He was fidgeting with a collection of small nets and bags and would not meet Connor's eye. He knew something was very wrong, but he also sensed he was better off not knowing too much more. A *cover your ass* kind of guy, Connor thought.

"Get him some gear," Jack directed Zee.

"But he's not a diver."

"The useful live longer."

Connor smiled. "I catch on pretty quick." What had they told her? Did she think they were diving for popeye to bring back to Washington? Zee hesitated only a second, then opened the wooden door and pulled out another regulator. He pulled a tank out of the rack and Zee showed him how to set it up.

"Never hold your breath. Stick with me. This button puts air into your vest to control your buoyancy. Don't touch it. I'll do it for you. Can you clear a mask?"

"Sure. If you tell me how."

"Shit. Kevin, this isn't safe." Kevin was the thug Connor had been calling Mack. It seemed a particularly wrong name, a boyish, apple-juice kind of name. Kevin just shrugged.

"OK. I'll cuff him back up."

"No." Connor took the mask. "We need as many divers as we can get." Zee adjusted the strap on his mask and showed him how to push on the top of it, tilt his head back and blow through his nose to clear out any water.

"The sponge is green," Zee briefed them. "I'll find one and show it to you. It looks like a little blob of spinach. Once you all know what you're looking for, we'll do a slow sweep along the wall. The top of the wall is about ten feet below the surface. The sponge doesn't grow much below eighty feet, so let's stay above sixty for this first dive so we can have more bottom time. We'll arrange ourselves one on top of another, about five to ten feet apart."

She considered where to put Connor. Generally one kept a novice diver above thirty feet, but buoyancy control was more difficult at that shallow a depth. A diver could float up ten or fifteen feet without even noticing, and if he did hold his breath, he could incur some serious lung damage. It was easier to stay level in deeper water, but there was more inherent danger if the diver panicked or freaked out. Connor, she figured, was more likely to be awkward than terrified, so she opted to keep him around forty, and put herself just above him.

"Paggie, how about you start at sixty feet, then Jack, then Kevin. Connor, you stay just above Kevin, then Gordon and Pete." The two Bahamians looked bored, not thrilled with having a woman in charge. "I'll move around, help everyone learn to identify the sponge."

They all got in the whaler. Padgette started the outboard and steered them away from the dock. In less than three minutes Connor saw the pale green water change abruptly to dark blue. They were over the edge of the wall. They anchored and Zee helped Connor put on his gear. The backroll off the boat was easy enough, except he flooded his mask. The equipment felt much less awkward in the water.

"You have to clear your ears as you descend," Zee said. "Hold your nose and blow gently. Ready?" Connor nodded. Zee took his inflator hose and let the air out of his BC and he began to sink. They went down slowly, feet first. Ten feet, twenty, thirty. *Thirty feet down. Thirty feet was the length of a bus. Thirty feet was a first down.* Zee gave his inflator button one quick squeeze. Connor was startled by the noise, but glad to feel his descent slowing. He looked up. The surface seemed a million miles away. Zee was right beside him, her eyes round with worry. Connor smiled and gave her an OK sign. Zee pointed a direction and they began to swim. His body wanted to sink or float, his fins kept crashing against the reef, but finally he began to have some control, and finally, to actually look around.

Connor had seen his share of underwater nature shows on TV, but nothing could capture how it really was. There were fish everywhere. Schools and swarms and pairs of fish, of every imaginable shape and color. On the reef itself, everything seemed alive. Furry, hairy, smooth things, things with many arms, things like little trees, things like nothing on earth. Connor looked for the sponge but he felt like a space alien, who, having crash landed in an earthly jungle, was ordered to wade into the bizarre foliage and pluck a clover. Then he felt a hand on his arm, and Zee pointed to a bumpy little green blob. It did look like a clump of spinach. So that was it. The cause of all the trouble, the hope for half the world. A cure, a curse, the holy grail, the anvil around his neck.

Mickey adjusted his tie and tried not to squirm on the hard wooden seat. The conference room was filled to overflowing, and he and Fairchild were crowded against the far wall. They had been questioned last night by D.C. police, and this morning by the FBI, but there was still so much confusion over jurisdiction that intense scrutiny had not yet been a problem. There was no way to avoid involvement. He had, after all, been present during the chase and Su Thom had of course been identified as an employee of SeaGenesis, which brought Adam Fairchild into the picture. Mickey had produced someone to stand in for Connor, who in the confusion had not been closely observed. Mickey explained that Connor was one of his employees who had helped them find Su Thom and that he had rushed him into the car because he thought he had been injured. But why had he disappeared from the scene? Su Thom's house was another contamination zone, he explained. He had organized the Sea-Genesis biohazard response team to go in and fumigate, to kill any escaped mosquitos. He didn't mention those extra couple of hours he needed after this to sort out the evidence, leaving mosquito cages and malaria factory intact, destroying notebooks and an incriminating journal. It was exhausting, all this improvising.

So far the focus was on Su Thom's unstable behavior after the death of Ulla Raki. So far, the story was holding up okay but Mickey knew that as more was discovered and tension mounted, scrutiny of SeaGenesis would also increase.

It was now July fifth, four in the afternoon, and this was the first coordinated meeting. There were representatives from a dozen government agencies as well as local officials packed in the conference room. At least thirty reporters were camped outside waiting for an official explanation for their five o'clock broadcasts.

Dr. Quentin Beggley from the Centers for Disease Control and Prevention was introduced. He was a small man, bent and homely, almost gnomelike, but dynamic. He surged toward the podium, an armload of papers cresting before him, his body pitched forward with a habitual tilt of indeterminate urgency. He started without preamble.

"Yesterday evening an undetermined number of mosquitos were released outdoors on the grounds of the Washington Monument. Examinations of several mosquitos captured at the scene show that they were all of the species *Anopheles*, and all were infected with malaria. All of the ones examined were in an active transmission state." Mickey felt like he had swallowed a stone. Now it would start. This was the final challenge. If he could get through this, he could still come out okay.

Dr. Beggley recited the facts with no trace of the anger and frustration he felt. He had not even been called until this morning. In the confusion of the moment, the situation had been muddled for eighteen vital hours. They wouldn't even have any mosquitos to examine if not for one quick-thinking cop who had thrown a blanket over one of the shattered jars, trapping a few of the slower escapees. Still, they had not been taken to a lab until this morning, then not diagnosed properly until noon.

"The mall and surrounding area were sprayed with insecticide this morning, and I have requested a more extensive spraying of the city and surrounding regions. Nevertheless, as it now stands, each mosquito may have bitten several people," Beggley said gravely. "We don't know how many were released, but we must expect that in five to ten days, several hundred, perhaps more than a thousand people, will become ill with malaria."

Murmurs erupted throughout the room and hands shot up with questions.

"Now hold on a minute." The mayor got up. "You're telling me we have to test everyone who went to the fireworks last night for *malaria*? There were half a million people out there!"

"Mr. Mayor, sir, don't worry about the expense . . ." George Summerall, the president's chief of staff, got up from his seat in the front row. "The federal government will provide the funding for testing . . ."

"There is no test," Beggley interrupted.

"No test?" Summerall frowned. "What do you mean no test?"

"We can't diagnose malaria until the parasites multiply to the extent that they are visible in a blood sample. That often doesn't happen until after symptoms are present, which can be five to fourteen days."

"Are you saying there is no way to know who is infected until they start getting sick?"

"Basically, yes," Beggley said tersely, displeased with the interruptions.

"So every man, woman, and child who was outside last night is a potential victim?"

"Actually, the potential for infection is not limited to those on the mall. There was a breeze last night. And mosquitos fly," Beggley said with a twinge of sarcasm. There was a stunned silence as the information began to sink in. Now he had their attention.

"The fact is, ladies and gentlemen, over twelve hours elapsed between the time of release and the time of first aerial spraying. During those hours, the infected mosquitos had a chance to disperse over the entire city. In addition, any number of mosquitos may have been inadvertently closed up in coolers, wrapped up in picnic blankets, and shut inside cars. They may have been lost in the folds of a shirt of a visiting relative, packed away in a suitcase on an airplane, and at this moment, they may be having their next blood meal and transmitting their parasite load in Texas, Florida, California, or New York." The room had grown deathly still and Mickey felt vessels in his neck throbbing.

"We consider the entire Washington metropolitan region as a primary infection zone," Beggley continued. "But we cannot rule out infections in the rest of the country."

"So what you're saying is, we have to treat everyone as if they were exposed." Summerall prided himself on calm in a crisis. "Give absolutely everyone in the area who incurred a mosquito bite last night antimalarial drugs, right? What does that entail?" He turned to the director of health and human services. "Logistics, supply, availability—what are we looking at here?"

The director of HHS just looked at Beggley, unwilling to break the news himself.

"What?" Summerall pressed. "The president is considering this an act of terrorism and will authorize whatever funds are necessary. You need the army, field hospitals for shots, whatever you need."

"There are no shots," Beggley said gravely. "There are no drugs."

"What do you mean there are no *drugs*?" Summerall pressed. "Of course there are drugs for malaria. Malaria's been around forever. You don't die of malaria these days. That's like, like dying of the bubonic *plague*."

Beggley sighed, but decided not to mention the fact that about a hundred people actually did contract bubonic plague in the U.S. every year and some did, in fact, die.

"Although tests are still preliminary, this type of malaria appears resistant to all known treatments." A few faces still looked puzzled. Beggley made it clearer. "There is no prevention. There is no cure."

"So people could die?" Summerall asked quietly.

"People *will* die," Beggley said, looking slowly around the table. "This type of malaria is called *P. falciparum*. It is unusually virulent. I am in touch with researchers in Bangkok, Singapore, and Kuala Lumpur for more information on this particular strain, but if it is as aggressive and resistant as I suspect, we can expect a ninety percent mortality rate."

There was a prolonged silence. Summerall took a deep breath. "OK." He carefully repositioned the notepad he had brought. "Okay then." He smoothed the blank yellow page. "Right . . ." He looked at his watch. He looked around at the others. No one said anything. "So what do we tell people?"

Beggley frowned. "What do you mean? We have to tell them the truth."

"Are you out of your mind?" Summerall's cool crumbled. "You want me to go out there and tell those reporters that sometime in the next week people are going to start dropping dead all over the region and there is not a damn thing we can do about it?"

Beggley gritted his teeth and began passing around papers. "We will have a more detailed strategy session later with FEMA, the army, and the Red Cross. In the meantime, I'm requesting a quarantine."

"Quarantine!" The mayor stood up. "Are you out of your mind? You cannot quarantine the city!"

"Not just the city, Mr. Mayor, surrounding counties as well."

"It's impossible." Summerall frowned. "That will shut down transportation on the entire East Coast!"

"Hopefully," Beggley replied.

"You'll have riots."

"Then we'll have to call out the National Guard."

"This is the *capital of the United States.*"

"And it is ground zero for what could become a national epidemic
of an incurable disease!" Beggley leaned over the podium, his voice hard
and clear. "Let me make this plain. Malaria is transmitted by mosquitos.
Aside from the mosquitos released last night, there are plenty of indigenous *Anopheles* mosquitos in this area. With the wet summer we've
had there's a bumper crop. Now there could be as many as a thousand
people infected yesterday. There might not be anything we can do to
save them, though I promise you we will try. Our primary goal right
now, however, is to prevent malaria from establishing a permanent foothold in the United States!"

"I'm sorry." One woman with a FEMA badge raised her hand. "I
don't understand. I mean, this isn't the tropics. We've never had a problem with malaria in this country before, why would this be cause for
such alarm?"

"Actually the United States has had a tremendous problem with malaria before," Beggley explained. "This disease used to be endemic from
Canada to Mexico. It felled George Washington's troops. Half the soldiers in the Civil War were infected each year. We managed to eradicate
malaria through a very intensive public health campaign starting in the
nineteen forties, mostly through mosquito control. DDT wasn't invented
just to kill birds and pollute the water, you know, it was the main weapon
in the U.S. antimalarial war."

"So why haven't we had a resurgence before this?" the woman persisted. "Infected people must be coming into the country fairly often,
and you say we still have the kind of mosquito that transmits it. Why is
this situation different?"

It was a good question. Beggley knew he had to make them understand the gravity of the situation.

"Malaria is spread from person to person, but only after a lag time.
The parasite needs time to develop inside the mosquito's gut from one
to three weeks before it can infect someone else. After the antimalaria
campaigns of the forties and fifties, the *Anopheles* mosquito population
was reduced, but most importantly, the pool of infected people declined
rapidly. The chance that the right mosquito would bite an infected person,

then live long enough to transmit the disease a week or more later dropped, essentially, to zero.

"Urban populations spread out to the suburbs. Fewer people sat around outdoors in the evenings when the *Anopheles* likes to feed. People moved to houses with window screens and air-conditioning, and stayed inside watching TV. The pool of infection was reduced, and this has helped maintain a malaria-free country.

"The *Anopheles* mosquito, however, still thrives throughout most of the country. Eradication programs have been eliminated. We also have, particularly in cities like Washington, a resurgence of conditions that promote malaria. You have a large, concentrated population of urban poor. Many don't have air-conditioning. They sit out on the porches and stoops in the evening. The children play outside on the sidewalk." Beggley could see that he was finally getting his point across. "Abandoned houses and empty lots offer lots of standing water, perfect breeding grounds for mosquitos."

"What if we distribute mosquito repellent?" the mayor suggested hopefully. "Tell everybody to wear it all the time they're outside?"

Beggley gritted his teeth. "Mosquito repellent is certainly part of our strategy. But the hard fact is, we might not be able to save those already infected. It is possible, however, that with a quarantine we *might* be able to avoid a national catastrophe."

The crowded room was now silent and the temperature seemed to have gone up twenty degrees. Outside, the clatter of television equipment could be heard as the press grew impatient. Mickey glanced at Fairchild and saw that his face was white. He hoped to god the man didn't faint. Beggley knew he had their attention now and like a good performer worked to hold it.

"Let me tell you about *P. falciparum* malaria," he said gravely. "The parasite bores into the red blood cells, where it begins to reproduce. It starves the tissues and organs until they turn to jelly. Then it invades the brain and causes cerebral hemorrhage. Basically, it blows your brain apart. I have worked with tropical diseases for thirty-one years. I was on the treatment team for Randall Asher, the man who appears to have brought this strain from Bangkok several months ago. This is the fastest progression, and most deadly form of malaria I have ever seen. If we act now, we might only lose a couple of thousand people. If we do nothing, this is going to be a huge new chapter in the plague history of the world."

The silence was ghastly.

"So, Mr. Summerall, will you explain the situation to the president? And Mr. Mayor, can I count on your support for a quarantine?"

"Not just D.C.? Suburbs, too?"

"I'm requesting a twenty-mile radius around the release zone."

Summerall nodded. "OK. But we can't . . . we can't say it's *incurable*. Not yet at least. Not just . . . like that. Besides, you don't know there isn't something that will work, do you? Not for sure? It's possible something can be found."

"Of course it's *possible*. New drugs are being discovered all the time." Mickey felt Fairchild squirm and put a hand on his arm. "But in the meantime," Beggley went on, "we have to prepare for a plague."

"There will be no plague!" Summerall got up and grabbed his notepad to his chest like a shield. "It is a situation. A . . . a . . . *disease*. This is the United States of America! We *do not* have plagues!"

"So Jason, what did they actually *say*?" Peter leaned over the sandwich his housemate was making and put his palm down on top of the bread to get his attention. "The guy on the news tonight. About this malaria thing?" Peter had just come home from work and only knew what he had overhead on the Metro.

"Okay, it's like this dude was some kind of Vietnamese orphan, who gets, like, adopted over here and becomes this science guy, only then he goes wacko and raises a bunch of mosquitos with malaria, because he doesn't think we're paying enough attention to malaria, 'cause like, his mother died of it or something."

"But what's going to happen now?" Peter pressed. Jason dragged the bread across the counter and went on swirling the peanut butter. He shrugged.

"Well what did they say we were supposed to do? Get a shot? What?"

"They said that, like, if you got any mosquito bites on the Fourth of July you should call some number. Some kind of mosquito hotline or something."

"Because we might get *malaria*? Christ, I'm going to Maine in two days to see Susan. I can't get malaria."

"Oh and you can't go, 'cuz there's a quarantine."

"A quarantine! They can't do that! How can they do that?"

"Sure, they just park big trucks or tanks or something on all the roads and you can't get out." He rolled the bread up so the peanut butter squeezed out the end, and took a huge bite. "Cool, huh? Like a war or something. Only no one gets shot at."

"So what are we supposed to do?"

"Nothing. Just chill. Those guys always get all—oh this is an epidemic—and all that. They probably just want us to buy their medicine, you know? And like pay for a doctor visit. It's summer, right, no one gets sick or anything for real, so they're like, drumming up business. Anyway, people get malaria all the time. It's no big deal. You take what is it, that stuff in gin and tonics."

"Quinine," Peter said resignedly.

"Yeah. Right. Hey, you know what we should do. Man, we should have a malaria party!"

"A malaria party?"

"Yeah! Party scene has been dead this summer. Everyone will come. We can drink gin and tonic and shit!"

"Oh, right. And everyone can dress like natives from a malarial country."

"Cool! Yeah! That's like jungles, right? Chicks can wear like grass skirts and coconuts!" He held his cupped hands out where the coconuts would obviously be worn and Peter could not help laughing. Life with Jason was never dull.

21

The perpetrator was identified as a lone radical who was upset that Western medicine was not adequately addressing the health problems of the Third World . . . the CDC urges people not to panic. They have set up a special toll-free hotline to answer questions. Those infected are not expected to show symptoms until July ninth at the very earliest. We expect most to become ill between the eleventh and the sixteenth . . ."

Georgia Strong heard only bits of the report between the baby's squeals and splashing. She knew more about malaria now than measles. Martin brushed aside her worries. They had searched every inch of the baby's skin and found no mosquito bites. Yes, Martin had been downtown, but he was inside most of the night. And besides, what were the chances—a thousand in half a million.

But that came out to one in five hundred. And that didn't sound like such high odds really, Georgia thought. And what if, like the one doctor on CNN said, each mosquito bit three people? What if the spraying hadn't actually killed them all? She hadn't even taken the baby out of the house for the first two days. Even now, his wading pool was set up inside a screen house she had bought yesterday at Sears. She had a can of insect spray beside her like a six-shooter ready to draw.

Damn, she hated this city. And of all the fears she had when they moved! She worried about the crime in Washington, about Martin's new job, about where to live; black or white neighborhood? Never anything like this. Never a plague. She missed her family. In Atlanta there would be people she could talk to. In Atlanta there were no stupid lobbying firms having catered parties for the Fourth of July. Or if they did, they had barbecue and hot dogs; normal food that didn't need a chef.

So far, the investigation had not tightened up enough to threaten them, but Mickey could feel it coming. So far it was still playing out as the desperate act of a deranged young man pushed over the edge by the tragic death of his mentor and lover. They showed them the little coffin and the note. The FBI questioned Fairchild, but Mickey secured a good lawyer, ostensibly to protect his client in the inevitable lawsuits, but really there to shut Fairchild up the moment anything got too close to the subject. Still, Fairchild was crumbling. Mickey wasn't sure how much more he could take.

Mickey was more confident in his own strength. David Marsh, the CIA deputy director of operations, had called him in for a chat, but it had seemed cordial and superficial. Of course the CIA was investigating. To have an ex-officer involved, even tangentially, with an act of terrorism, was cause for examination.

Mickey told the same story he had been telling the police. Sea-Genesis was a client of Chapmans. Fairchild had turned to Mickey when he was worried about Su Thom after Ulla Raki's death. No, they had never anticipated anything like this. They had no idea. There was no way to know what Marsh actually knew about his work during the war, or the operations of Secure Shipping Transport. Marsh had been appointed when the agency was being rocked by scandal and tales of gross ineptitude. He was heralded as the white knight who could lead all to righteousness. Mickey assumed Marsh had ordered a search of classified files, but he was confident that everything incriminating on the "Mosquito War" had long since been destroyed. Even if he did dig something up, reformist as Marsh might be, Mickey was sure even he wouldn't expose something like the Mosquito War.

July 8

How does it work? Zee stared at the graphs. The answer was there somewhere, it had to be. Why did some samples of popeye work and not others? They had recorded information on every sponge they had collected in the past—depth, temperature, estimated sunlight, cohabiting organisms, size, and so on—but so far, there was no real pattern. There were good sponges from thirty feet and from eighty, from the biggest and the smallest. But there had to be something the good ones had in common. She just had to find it. She took another sip of coffee. It was late, but evenings were the only time she had in the lab. They began diving each day by eight, as soon as the sun was high enough for good light on the reef, and continued until around six. There were breaks between dives, of course. No matter how urgent the collection was, the rules of safe diving could not be violated.

She and Padgette had spent most of the past two nights in the lab painstakingly testing each individual sponge and extracting the ones that showed a high percentage of the active compounds. If only they had Ulla's last batch! That sample, which hopefully was still securely hidden inside Connor's refrigerator, might hold the key.

She went back to the lab bench and checked the printout on the spectrograph. This was a good batch. That was some relief anyway. She noted the results and transferred the collection data to the graph. Connor had collected these sponges just yesterday, thirty feet down on Reef Area 46 A. Connor actually seemed to have some kind of magic touch. All the sponges he collected showed a high level of bioactivity. Why? For the first two days, while he was still learning to dive, he barely picked up any at all, and what he did was usually ripped carelessly off the reef as he struggled with buoyancy.

She stepped back and rubbed her eyes. How long did they have? Randall Asher, victim one, had symptoms only six days after he was bitten. That meant people in Washington could start getting sick in another two days.

Would this cure them? She wondered as she looked at the green fluid in the flask. More importantly, would it even get to them? Mickey had promised it would. That was the deal. He would provide the cure and they would keep silent forever. It was a bitter deal, but the only one they had. She hated that he would get away with everything he had done, but at least lives would be saved. In this epidemic, anyway.

She heard the door open and Padgette came in. He too looked haggard. He went right to the table and looked at the printout and his eyebrows went up in appreciation.

"Do you have another sample ready to run?" he asked.

"No. Sorry. I've been looking at past data. I know there is a pattern here somewhere."

"I've been looking for months. It seems completely random."

"It can't be random."

"I *know* it can't be random," Padgette said with an air of pique. "I said it *seems* random."

There was still tension between them. Zee was not entirely convinced of the ignorance Padgette claimed, and he was not convinced, or not wanting to be convinced, that the situation was as diabolical as she described. He thought the whole story of the CIA engineering a strain of malaria absurd. He believed simply that popeye was a valuable new drug that had to be kept close to home for the time being.

"There are huge patent issues at stake," he explained defensively. "Until we synthesize popeye, or at least isolate the active compounds, it's just a sponge. Anyone can go pick it up and do whatever the hell they want with it. Look at Brazil! They're trying to claim royalties on anything pharmaceutical companies develop from their natural plants. As if ten years of research ranks the same as some witch doctor brewing up his jungle leaves."

He admitted to having engineered what he believed was mild sabotage in order to help Fairchild shut down Shadow Island. He swore he had never intended for Zee to be in real danger in the current. He never suspected it was so strong, and didn't know about the downdraft. He had noticed it one day and thought it was just a tidal surge. It was just meant to scare her and rattle the insurance people. The scorpion fish he did feel guilty about. He had transferred three of them to the nursery area, but most people just had a painful sting, not a deadly reaction. He claimed to have had nothing to do with the bee's nest in the scuba shed.

"It's financial," he insisted blindly. "Fairchild doesn't want to be saddled with a drug like popeye on the open market, but he isn't ready to abandon it altogether. He has people overseas willing to fund more research. The collection permits here are all through SeaGenesis. When we shut down the station, we lose collection rights. It gets messy, red tape and all that."

He thought the story of Su Thom and a malaria epidemic a complete exaggeration.

"Even if there are a few cases, there are plenty of malaria drugs available," he pointed out. "And they couldn't use popeye anyway. It hasn't even been tested in humans."

Zee finally gave up trying to convince him. They went about their work silently. Zee prepped sponge after sponge for extraction. Padgette tested sponge after sponge for the active chemicals. It took three hours to get through all the sponges collected that day. A disappointing forty percent were worthless. Padgette cleaned up the equipment and went off to bed with the calm fatigue of the dispassionate observer. Zee sat at the lab bench staring at numbers on pages. *It could not be random.*

Zee got up and stretched. She went outside for some fresh air. She felt exhausted, frustrated, and enormously lonely. She and Connor were never allowed near each other except on the dives, and then still not allowed to talk. Even now, Kevin was sitting on the porch keeping an eye on her.

"You pack'n it in?" he said hopefully.

"Not yet." Zee tried to stifle a yawn. Gordon, one of the Bahamians, was sitting on the steps, carving a figure out of a piece of driftwood. The guardian goons had warned her not to get friendly with them, either, but she went over and sat beside him anyway.

"That's lovely." Gordon blew some chips from a crease and handed her the little figure. It was a man in a cloak with a lamb in his arms.

"For the nativity." Gordon smiled. "I make da whole set, Mary, Joseph, baby Jesus, sell up the shop in Nassau."

The carving was detailed, with a delicacy she would not have expected from such big hands. *Delicacy.* Zee almost dropped the little shepherd. It was like the cartoon lightbulb flashing on in her head. Gordon had a light touch in more than carving. She remembered how, from the very first dive, he had the knack of prying the sponges off the reef without damaging them at all. And all of his samples were worthless.

Excitedly, she ran back in the lab. There was one bit of information they had not put into the equation, she realized. Who had *collected* each sponge? There wasn't a column for it, but the information was there since everyone was given a set of numbered bags. Zee looked over that day's page. Most of the useless sponges brought in that day had been collected either by Gordon or herself. The best samples had been collected by everyone on the first day of diving, and by Connor on the second day. Zee went to the shelf and pulled out old lab books.

This was it! The best samples of popeye had always come from sponges collected soon after a new group of grad students arrived. Early on, when they were still getting used to technique, they tended to mutilate the sponges. After a few days, they were better at getting it off intact. That was it. This sponge was releasing chemicals in response to damage. It was one of the most basic elements of invertebrate zoology—chemical defense! A fish starts nibbling on this sponge and the sponge churns out some kind of repellent. The fish gets a mouthful of nasty and leaves it alone. And accidentally, as unaccountably as tree bark yielding aspirin or flowers curing cancer, these chemicals also happened to cure malaria. She had discovered the key to popeye!

"There must be something you can do! Someone you can talk to! You know how this town works!" Amanda Mountclair was getting more hysterical with each passing day. At first it had been simply a sizzle of drama throughout her circle. The idle rich craved scandal the way a drowning man craves air. *"Did you hear about poor Amanda! . . . They were out there in the middle of all those mosquitos! . . . They walked right by where it happened! . . . Oh my goodness, I heard she was bitten all over . . ."*

Her proximity to the event increased with each phone call, automatically awarding her an exalted status.

"No, Frank wasn't stung at all, just Amanda."

"Malaria? But isn't that a foreign disease?"

Malaria had the allure of the exotic, the romance of fevers. Malaria, her friends imagined, involved suffering beautifully on a rattan couch beneath a gauzy drape of mosquito netting while a handsome, dark-eyed lover wept. And anyway, what were the chances she was actually bitten by one of the infected mosquitos anyway? But by day four, the novelty had worn thin. The news was starting to report grisly details of what to expect from cerebral malaria.

"They say your brain just explodes!"

"I don't believe there isn't a cure," Amanda insisted. "They probably just don't have enough of it to give to everybody. You must find out! I absolutely cannot take any more of this pressure."

"Dear, I have been talking to people. No one knows anything different."

"Then you're talking to the wrong people. This is supposed to be your job, Frank! Knowing the right people. You seem to do it very well for all those . . . those politicians and corporations you lobby for. Are you telling me you can't do anything for your own wife!" She held out her slender, tan wrist, where one tiny red welt marred the skin.

"Look at this! I got it that night! Walking all that way to get a cab."

"Amanda, dear, I *am* talking to people. But you have to understand, people are not exactly available for lunch these days. They are trying to prepare for an epidemic."

"That your wife is very much a part of!"

"I've called everyone I know who can find out anything. People at Harvard, Johns Hopkins, World Health." He kissed her forehead. "If you need it and it exists, I'll get it." The assurance placated her somewhat. He would send flowers. It wasn't that he didn't care, it was just such a small chance that she would be affected. They had walked through the area five hours after the mosquitos had been released. She had one bite. Washington was full of mosquitos in the summer. What were the chances that this one bite came from an infected mosquito?

"Daddy?" Marissa came in and leaned on his lap. Her face was flushed and warm.

"Hi there, bunny." He stroked the golden hair. "Have you been playing upstairs with Claire?" He had not let her outside since the Fourth.

"No. I don't feel good Daddy."

July 9

"Bruise the sponge," Zee instructed everyone the next morning as she handed out collection bags. "I think injury causes the sponge to release the chemicals that make popeye work." She looked excited but exhausted, and Connor was sure she hadn't slept at all.

He rarely saw Zee except when they were diving. She and Padgette spent every available minute in the lab. Connor was never left alone. Either Jack or Mack, as Kevin would always be to him, dogged him constantly. Each night he was handcuffed to the bed. They had been at it for four days. Connor had no idea how much popeye they had produced so far. Did Zee really believe Mickey intended to send it to Washington?

As he lay on the beach between dives, Connor tried to work out some sort of plan. Physically overpowering Mack and Jack seemed unlikely. They had never eased their diligence with him. When he wasn't diving, he was handcuffed to something. He couldn't be sure of Padgette's allegiance one way or the other. The Bahamians kept to themselves, hired hands content with good pay, knowing enough not to want to know more.

If there were some way to do it underwater, sabotage their air tanks or something, it still wouldn't do much good as either Mack or Jack or Padgette always waited in the boat. With each passing day, Connor knew they were getting closer to the time when the investigation in Washington would get too hot and the plane would return to carry off what they had produced. Then there would be no chance.

Even if he could subdue Mack and Jack, there was still no way off the island. They took the spark plugs from both the whaler and the Zodiac's outboard out each night.

Connor stretched his arms out and ran his fingers through the sand. The sun pounded on his chest. What was going on back in Washington? Su Thom's identity should have led someone to SeaGenesis, then eventually to Ulla Raki and to the fact that she was working on a malaria cure. Could Mickey and Fairchild still be keeping quiet? What about the other layers of people? *We had the necessary approvals* ... How high up had the Mosquito War actually been approved? Could they all still keep it quiet with thousands of people in danger?

"Let's go." Mack kicked his foot and Connor opened his eyes, squinting into the sun. He heard the whine of the outboard and saw Jack returning with ten freshly filled tanks. They had covered almost a mile of reef by now. Connor peeled himself up off the sand and waded into the water. A chill stabbed him, like an icicle run straight through from head to toe. He shivered. Zee looked exhausted, with deep circles under her eyes. She seemed to droop a little as she picked up the damp wetsuit.

They fell easily into the routine by now, descending quickly to begin another hunt. This was the fourth dive of the day and the water felt colder. Connor saw a couple of sponges and stopped to pry them off. How many did they need to save each person? How many to satisfy Mickey? He had skipped over as many as he could on his sweeps, hoping, perhaps futilely, that after Mickey took off with his supply, there might still be a few people alive who could benefit. He stopped to put the sample in his collection bag, taking care to crush it. When he looked up again, he realized he had drifted. They were swimming into a slight current. He tucked his bag in and kicked to catch up. A current. Like a shock of cold water, the beginning of an idea began to form.

He managed to talk to Zee at the end of the day while they were filling the tanks. He told her his plan, such as it was.

"You're crazy!" Zee whispered. She lifted an empty tank into the water tank and hooked it up to the compressor.

"It's our only chance." Connor lifted a newly filled tank in each hand and carried them over to the rack. Jack was on the end of the dock, so they had to talk in quick whispered snatches.

"For one thing, they'll never let us dive alone."

"Tell them it's dangerous."

"Are you kidding? If I tell those guys something is dangerous they'll be pushing each other out of the way to go. Besides, it *is* dangerous."

"In a few more days, people start getting sick. You don't really believe Mickey is going to take this stuff to Washington, do you?"

"Even Mickey couldn't just let hundreds of people die!"

"Then why aren't there a hundred Navy divers out here?" Connor whispered.

"He said we had to keep the whole thing quiet."

"That's bullshit and you know it."

Jack heard them talking and barked from the end of the dock.

"It's the only chance," Connor whispered. "I'm ready to take it. I just need you to help me set it up."

Zee twisted the valve onto another tank, opened the line, and watched the gauge start to creep up. *It was nuts. It was no kind of plan. It wasn't even half a plan.* But she was already starting to work it out in her mind, considering the terrible possibility of it.

Quarantine. A notice nailed to the door, a ribbon barring disease from the streets. From the Black Death to scarlet fever, the stigma of quarantine had always been sharp, but the logistics never so unwieldy. The nation's capital and parts of two states were now the red zone. No one could leave the red zone. There were National Guard trucks at every road. The airports were ghostly quiet. Amtrak trains flew through without stopping. Truck drivers fumed in line waiting for the special transit passes that would allow them to pass. There was no concern about people stopping once inside. Stories of this new plague had grown exponentially with every mile as facts faded beneath blossoming horror. Dead in an hour. Brains exploding like dropped watermelons. Agony so fierce people clawed their own eyeballs out.

Inside the red zone, panic bubbled just below the surface. People with no mosquito bites demanded the right to flee, some stripping off all their clothes at the roadblocks to demonstrate unmarred skin. There were riots. It was a racial thing, people declared angrily. A mostly black population was being held in a concentration camp to prevent them from contaminating the white suburbs.

There were fights in store aisles over cans of mosquito repellent. When the planes passed overhead spraying out bellyfuls of insecticide, instead of cowering at the thought of cancerous chemicals, people ran outside and lifted their arms, as if a dusting post facto could still work some magic.

Herbalists sold potions. Energy balancers pumped up their auras and visualized away the parasites. Faith healers, realizing pretty damn good odds, pronounced cures left and right. In the midst of it all there were the cold, hard details to arrange. Testing stations, hospital beds, needles and syringes and IVs and faxes, hundreds of faxes. Protocols and procedures, diagnostic techniques, prognosis, treatments. Few local doctors had ever seen malarial blood smears outside a textbook, so the CDC sent photos and set up a website. There were insurance negotiations and inventories of body bags.

And in the background, like the steady buzz of a mosquito, there were rumors of a mystery cure.

Su Thom's deed had flooded SeaGenesis with attention. Damage control was still in progress. On July 6, Fairchild, carefully prepped and genuinely earnest, appeared on *Nightline*. With appropriate remorse, he expressed his horror at the terrorist act of this disturbed individual, all the while carefully distancing SeaGenesis from any blame or responsibility. In hindsight, yes, they might have seen that Su Thom had a severe personality disorder, but he never gave any hint he was so unstable. *He was quiet, kept to himself, never gave anyone trouble.*

They had issued daily press releases since then, stamping out every little fire before it could rage out of control. Fortunately, the few SeaGenesis employees who knew that Ulla was even working on malaria didn't know anything specific. It was easier for them to understand the complexities of research anyway. The general public had no idea what went into drug development. Ulla's drug had not even been tested in monkeys yet.

Still, some of the stories were starting to play up the poor orphan angle, the misguided deeds of a troubled young man helpless in the face of a drug company's stubborn greed. One tabloid had even christened him a martyr. "SeaGenesis cancels promising malaria research—lack of funding drives zealot to desperate act."

July 10

"You killed Queen Elizabeth! You stupid pigs!" Zee wailed. Connor looked up in alarm. Mack and Jack stopped in surprise as she came running down the little bluff to the dock. "Queenie!" she sobbed. "You shot her!" Her face was red with anger. Connor had never seen her cry before and had not expected that when he did, it would be over a great, ugly fish, lying in soggy repose on the wooden scaling table.

"Why did you kill her?"

"Why?" Jack looked startled and even a little scared and guiltily tried to hide the spear gun behind him like a kid. "Well, for dinner." He shrugged. "I mean . . . it's a *fish*." They had taken to spearing something every day on the last dive, blatantly ignoring the law, and the sense of fair play, that fish were only to be speared while snorkeling.

"She's not just a fish!" Zee stroked the slimy mottled back as if it were a cat, then gently spread its fins and straightened its limp tail. The fish was an enormous, ugly, black grouper with cold gray eyes and a mouth you could park a truck in. "Oh, Queenie . . ." she murmured. Padgette came out of the lab.

"Zee?" Padgette approached and stood looking at her across the fish. "What's wrong?"

"Oh Paggie. They killed Queen Elizabeth."

"Queen Elizabeth?"

"You know. The grouper that lived in that little cave just down by those two big barrel sponges." Zee waved vaguely toward the reef. "She's been there for years." Zee wiped her eyes with the unslimed back of her arm. "Roddy showed her to me. I used to visit her all the time." She all but spit at Jack with anger. "How could you!"

The five men all stood awkwardly by the scaling table. Connor almost laughed at Jack, who had, for the first time ever, lost all his bruiser facade and looked like he had just broken his mom's favorite ornament.

"I'm sorry. I didn't know." He sounded almost genuinely sorry. "I mean, I didn't know it was like your pet or something."

"Besides that, a grouper that size is ten, twenty years old. She ought to be left to reproduce." Zee turned toward Connor with a dagger look but a quickly mouthed warning. *"Don't eat it!"* Then she spun away in disgust and marched back up to the lab.

Damage to the future of the world grouper population or not, the guilt over spearing her pet fish didn't last long, though out of deference to her feelings, they at least didn't ask her to cook it. The Bahamians grilled Queen Elizabeth down on the beach while Zee sat alone up in the dining room with her canned soup and crackers. Connor, pleading consideration for her feelings, also refused the fish, enduring their ridicule and satisfying his hunger with a peanut butter sandwich and a can of beans.

What the hell was going on? Maybe it was just the strain getting to her. Or maybe, he realized later that night as he heard the unmistakable sounds of Mack or Jack retching in the bathroom, maybe this was all part of her plan!

Dr. Beggley did not believe in the secret cure but he wanted any chance he could get. The reports coming in from Asia were bad. The Asher strain had only been identified three years ago, but it was the scariest type of malaria anyone had ever seen. The prognosis for Washington was grim. Beggley picked up his phone and hit the newest number on the speed dial.

"SeaGenesis, how may I help you?" a beleaguered voice answered.

"Adam Fairchild, please. This is Dr. Beggley."

"I'm sorry, Dr. Beggley, Dr. Fairchild is still out of the office. Would you like to leave a message?" Beggley pressed his fingers to his forehead in frustration.

"I've left messages for the past two days."

He tugged on the bushy eyebrow, gazed through the door into the adjacent situation room, where dozens of people bustled over plans and papers. Logistics, supply, public relations, field hospitals. Getting ready. As if they could.

"Tell him this," Beggley said sharply. "Tell him I have a court order to search SeaGenesis files for information on experimental malaria drugs." He paused, giving her time to write it all down. "Tell him it would be better for the company, much less public, if he just cooperates."

"Dr. Beggley, SeaGenesis is not involved in malaria research." Her voice sounded weary. The calls had started coming in. Frank Teller had given her an official company statement to read. Still, they called back, not satisfied. She didn't know what else to say. She was just a secretary. This shouldn't be her job.

"Tell him this is a national emergency and the president is considering martial law." It was a stretch, but Beggley figured she wouldn't be up on the requirements for invoking martial law. He wasn't all that sure about it himself, but if they didn't come up with something in the next day or so, there could easily be riots. Already people were swarming the hospitals and screening centers.

"If there is even a remote possibility that SeaGenesis has any promising treatment, even as an adjunct therapy, I have to know about it, do you understand?"

"You have to speak with Mr. Teller . . ."

"Teller is a bag of rot with a tired script! Tell him I'll be there in one hour with a court order." Beggley hung up before she had a chance to object. Immediately his phone lit up again, calls backing up, calls flooding the system. "I want the man in charge . . . You can't tell me there is nothing you can do . . . We have six hundred seventy-one cots coming from supply, but no pillows anywhere . . . Your two P.M. meeting with the infection control team has to be moved . . ."

"You have to talk to Beggley." Fairchild sounded hysterical. Mickey rubbed his temples where an omnipresent headache had settled. "He won't let this alone! You have to do something!"

"OK, Adam, relax." Mickey's voice was calm as usual. He had sequestered Fairchild away at the Greenbriar resort with a couple of minders. "You can call Beggley. Go ahead and tell him about Raki's research. She was working on a cure but it turned out to be useless. The rats died or something. We have the doctored data for him, and I'll have the lab book ready soon. You know the science, make it work for us."

"I must say I strenuously object," Fairchild offered, less strenuously than he claimed. "Perhaps we should consider making popeye available for treatment after all."

"Adam," Mickey continued solicitously, "I know you think of me as a downright ruthless son of a bitch. And you're right. I am. But there is no way in hell I would let thousands of Americans die of this. There just isn't enough popeye to be had! You know where we are with this! I could come up with maybe fifty doses. You want to see medical ethics in a flat-out brawl, you tell me which fifty out of a thousand get to live!"

Fairchild fell silent. He looked around the plush suite, through the window to the peaceful green golf course. It was just plain difficult, being a leader, a pioneer. As if Mickey could read his thoughts, he went on.

"Why don't you just stay out there a few more days, Adam. But first call Beggley and put his mind at rest. Let him know that popeye simply doesn't work. Tell him you'll give him Raki's research. He's grasping at straws, that's all. Just call him and put his mind at ease. We're taking care of all this. We can take care of you, too." There may have been a threat there but Fairchild didn't want to hear it.

July 11

"Looks like ciguatera," Zee said with only a hint of triumph in her voice. "It serves you right for eating old Queenie." Mack and Jack had retched themselves silly all night and were still doubled over with cramps the next morning. Padgette was shaking as he pored over a textbook, vainly searching for a counterpotion even when he knew there was nothing to be done.

"It's a natural marine toxin," Padgette explained weakly. "Fish get it from eating certain plankton."

"It builds up in their flesh." Zee took over when he obviously found the strain of talking too taxing. "So your greatest risk is in *big old fish* like Queen Elizabeth!" She hauled out the first aid box and found some

Pepto-Bismol. "You won't die anyway, it takes a while to build up sen-
sitivity. But maybe you'll learn something!" She snapped the first aid
case shut.

"So I guess it's just Connor and me diving today. We should get
started."

Jack shook his head. "No way."

"We can't lose a whole day!" Zee protested. "It's been a week since
the mosquitos were released. The plane is due tomorrow and I'm not
wasting a whole day of collecting. We need every ounce. Anyway," Zee
continued firmly, "I know where to find the mother lode of popeye."

Jack glared at her with suspicion.

"We haven't gone before because it's a dangerous dive," she pre-
empted his question. "It's deep, it's tricky, and there are lots of sharks."
Padgette looked up, alarmed, suddenly realizing her intention.

"The cut? You want to dive the cut? But what about the . . ." Zee
stared at him hard. He could sink the plan right now.

"What about the sharks?" he finished. Zee let out her breath.

"I'll take that chance. There is a cut in the reef at the end of the
island," Zee explained. "Something about the place makes it great for
popeye, only it's deep and the honeycombs make it easy to get lost, or
trapped. Plus the sharks. That's why we haven't gone there before, but
if Connor's willing, I am."

Connor did not have to feign apprehension. "Sure," he said. "I've
got nothing to lose."

"No." Jack growled.

"Look. I have two liters of popeye in there," Zee said. "That's only
about half of what we need. I made a deal with Mickey. We're only
putting ourselves at risk. Just Connor and me. It might be our last chance.
You know someone in Washington is going to find out about this place
and come looking pretty soon. Just let us do the one dive," Zee pleaded
sweetly now. "Who knows, you might get lucky and we'll be eaten by
the sharks and off your hands for good!"

Zee turned and walked toward the dock, not giving them a chance
to refuse. "I'll take the pony bottles for backup air," she informed Padgette as she pulled two smaller tanks out of the scuba shed. The pony
bottles were the size of a home fire extinguisher, with their own little

regulators already attached. Zee fastened them in brackets alongside the primary tanks. She tucked a smaller cylinder of "spare air" into the pocket of her BC. It was only about the size of a can of hairspray.

Padgette watched the preparations from the narrow shade of the scuba shed, sweating heavily. His head pounded and his lips were still numb. Goddamn fish.

"We'll take this for the sharks." She pulled out a lightweight three-pronged sling spear, not the monster pneumatic weapon Jack had used on the grouper. It didn't look like it would kill much more than a goldfish. "It's just for poking them away if they get too curious." The Bahamian divers listened from the shade, starting to feel more fortunate about their poisoning. "So who's going to stay with the boat?" she asked cheerfully. "Padgie?"

"I'll go." Jack spoke up, still not trusting them entirely.

She and Connor hauled the gear to the whaler and loaded it aboard. Zee wished she could have thought of a reason to take the Zodiac, since it was slower.

"Well, I guess that's it. Let's go."

There was a slight southerly wind, rare for this side of the island, and it stirred the water into a small chop. Jack clutched the gunwales as they bounced along. Zee took land sightings and guided him to the cut.

"I'm ready if you are." She smiled at Connor but he saw apprehension in her eyes. There had been no chance to discuss the plan. It would be his own improv from here on. They geared up and rolled into the choppy sea. Connor felt a slight current almost immediately. Zee pulled a length of nylon rope out of her BC pocket and quickly clipped them together. Their eyes met. No turning back now. Together, they let the air out of their BCs and dropped below the surface. Zee felt tense and fought against the fearful memories. According to the tide tables, they should just be catching the turn of the tide and with it the strongest wave of the current as it surged out to sea. By the time they were twenty feet down it was already hard to kick against it, but they managed to struggle to the reef and catch hold. Zee led him into the first crevice she could manage, giving some shelter from the current. Connor pointed to the pony bottle on Zee's tank. He pulled a mesh bag out of his BC pocket. Zee held up one palm, signaling him to wait.

She pulled off one of her fins and handed it to Connor while she wiggled her foot out of the neoprene booty. She replaced her fin, took the spear gun and slashed the booty. Then she took out the can of spare air and wedged it securely under some coral. Next she produced an already tattered and bloody diving glove from her BC pocket. She looked at Connor and shrugged, as if to say, *this is the best I could come up with*. She pressed the valve on the spare air and rigged it to stay open. A stream of bubbles began to rise up through the cracks in the reef. Zee let go of the torn booty, the snorkel, and the bloody glove and they began to drift up. Then she pointed away from the reef. *Let's go.* Connor frowned and shook his head. He grabbed her arm and unclipped the line that connected them. Zee pulled it back. Connor pointed to her, then to the surface. *You go up. I'm going alone.* Zee shook her head. She made the sign for *stay with your buddy*. Connor shook his head adamantly. Zee gave him the finger. Before he could object again, she reclipped the line and launched herself out into the current. The tether yanked at Connor and he could not pull her back. Whatever they were in for, they were in it together.

The current seized them, dragging them along with biblical force. Connor held his breath. It was a dangerous thing to do underwater, but it was essential that Jack not see their bubbles moving out to sea. The bubbles from the spare air would hopefully be enough decoy to delay him until they were too far to be noticed. The reef rushed by in a blur of color, then fell away entirely. The blue water began to suck them into its cold heart. Connor felt his head spinning and lost all sense of direction or depth. Even though Zee knew what to expect this time, she was still terrified. She knew they would not really be sucked into some bottomless vortex, but it still felt like oblivion.

The water grew darker and felt vastly empty. No reef, no fish, no sunlight. Connor began to feel drunk. He felt like laughing and thought he heard music. He had never imagined so many shades of blue. Suddenly, he felt a tug on the line. Zee was pulling him up. The current had loosened a little. They were swimming up. Up and up, seemed like a hundred miles. The peaceful haze began to vanish. Finally his head cleared. He groped for his gauge and saw they were at eighty feet. They had swum *up* to eighty feet! They hovered there a minute. The current continued, but it was lighter now. They drifted gently; a rocking chair instead of a roller coaster. Connor looked around and still saw nothing but blue. The sun was directly overhead, so there were not even shadows to orient on. He felt completely lost.

Zee looked at their gauges. She had about 1,700 pounds, Connor only 1,000, still pretty good. She led Connor up to sixty feet, then forty. At this shallower depth they could swim for maybe another twenty minutes. She turned the console over and consulted the compass, aimed them west and began to swim. They had not gone as deep as her first misadventure, but she guided them both through the decompression levels anyway, moving up to shallower depths as they swam, so when they finally ran out of air it was safe to surface. Shadow Island was just a faint strip on the horizon. The sun was deliciously hot, the sky full of air. For a while they floated together in silence, unable to speak, too exhausted by the swim and drained by the fear, the only connection between them the tug of the line.

Zee finally spoke, her voice choked, stalling on the first few words. "We need to get set up here. Drop your weight belt." Connor groped for his buckle and pulled the weights free, letting them plummet. Zee, more adept with the gear, unbuckled hers but held on to it, slipping the weights off but keeping the belt itself. "Now put some more air in your BC, you'll float better. Here, you can inflate it orally." She showed him how to blow into the valve.

"Turn around," she instructed. She unfastened the pony bottle from his tank and dropped it in the mesh bag, then had him release the one from her tank. The two canisters clinked together. She pulled both their empty scuba tanks free and tied them together with the weight belt. She had chosen the brightest yellow tanks, hoping to increase their visibility from the air. There were lots of small planes in the Bahamas. Lots of boats, lots of chance to be picked up; lots and lots. She tied the mesh bag with the canisters of popeye securely to Connor's BC, then clipped them both together again.

"How much do you think we have?"

"I have no idea. Fifty doses, a thousand. I don't know what a dose is. I left them some dummy serum."

"Will they know it's fake?"

"If Padgette tests it he will, but I also messed up the spectrometer. And he might not want to know. I think he's starting to believe me about the whole thing. I'm hoping he will want to help us. If he can get to the radio alone, he could call for help."

Connor didn't say anything. He had been counting on Zee remaining on the island to somehow send help. No point in arguing now. They floated silently for a long while, letting the sun warm their faces and listening for the sound of a motor. Would Jack and the others really be fooled? Or were they speeding out here right now to hunt for them?

"At the very least, Padgie will send help," Zee said. "Tomorrow, once they're off the island. I don't think he's really keen on them killing us. But there are boats around all the time; fishing boats, sailboats . . ." She didn't sound too convincing.

"Someone will find us." Connor pushed away the other possibilities. They were off the island. They had the serum. There was no turning back now. "That was good. The booty and the glove. That was smart."

"Thanks."

"How did you know they would spear your pet fish?"

"Anything they speared would have been my pet fish," she said. "Though I did like that old grouper. Roddy had been doing some ciguatera studies and there was some of the toxin in the fridge. I put some on my hands and rubbed it all over poor Queenie."

Connor laughed. "And if they didn't catch anything at all?" he pressed.

"I don't know. I could have tried to pass if off as botulism from a bad can of beans. It would have been harder to explain."

"Nice con. You could have quite a future with the CIA. Maybe Mickey will put in a good word for you when we get back." The joke didn't seem quite funny enough. The wind was still blowing gently and a faint current continued to carry them away from the island. The very best outcome was still not going to be comfortable. It was very likely they would float all night, maybe longer.

"So how are we fixed for lunch?" Connor asked. "I brought two pints of water and a bag of raisins," he said, patting the pockets of his BC.

"One pint of water, a tube of chapstick, and two rolls of Lifesavers."

Lifesavers—this threatened to give her a fit of the giggles. God, she hated nervous giggles.

"Hell, we're a castaway Club Med!" Connor laughed. As far as drifting in the open sea was concerned, they were relatively well off. They had wetsuits and flotation vests. They had calm, relatively warm water. People had survived amazing amounts of time floating in open seas. Days even, in cold, rough conditions with no life jackets. Alone and crazed with thirst. This wouldn't be so bad.

Zee looked out over the endless blue ocean, pictured the bottom, some thousands of feet below, the deep trench that made Shadow Island unique. The deep trench that was like a highway for pelagic fish and for the sharks that fed on them. Sharks for miles around would already be picking up their signals. The electrical twitching of muscle, the peculiar scent of human. They would cruise in to investigate, and they would find Zee and Connor dangling there like Peking ducks in a Chinatown window.

Frank Teller met Dr. Beggley at the door and escorted him right to Ulla's lab. Of course SeaGenesis was happy to comply. They just didn't have anything to offer. But come along and see for yourself. Beggley did. Teller took him to the lab and handed him a printout of Raki's computer files.

"What about her lab book?" Beggley tossed the pages aside scornfully. He knew the only reliable information would be there, in her own handwriting, in her own lab books; the notes, drawings, and graphs that documented daily experiments.

"I'm afraid that may have been given to her father by mistake along with her personal things. He lives in California. We've put in a call."

"Mr. Teller, do you realize that if evidence ever comes out that SeaGenesis was holding back any information that might be helpful in this crisis . . ."

"Oh no." Teller stopped him. "Of course not. Why, we couldn't. I couldn't. Personally. I would not do that. Nor would Dr. Fairchild. Of course. But we have nothing. Ulla Raki was simply nowhere near anything that could be called a cure. She hadn't even done primate testing. That's what Su Thom was upset about. They had submitted a proposal for primate testing months ago. SeaGenesis wasn't in a position to approve it yet. Su Thom just wouldn't accept that."

Beggley's heart sank. It had seemed too good to be true.

"Su Thom built it all up in his head," Teller went on in a sorrowful tone. "He wanted popeye to be a miracle drug, but it wasn't. I wish we could help you. All those poor people."

"Excuse me, do one of you know anything around here?" Beggley and Teller looked up and saw a man standing at the door. He was tall and blond and despite the came he was leaning on, he looked like he could have stepped out of the pages of a surfer magazine.

Teller frowned nervously over the top of his glasses. "Who are you? How did you get in here?"

The man reached in the pocket of his jeans and pulled out a Sea-Genesis ID card. "I'm Roddy Taylor. I work for SeaGenesis."

Teller scrutinized the ID doubtfully.

"Roddy Taylor? I'm sorry, I don't know you."

"I'm the station engineer on Shadow Island," Roddy explained. "I'm trying to find Zee Aspen."

Teller looked blank. "Zee Aspen?"

"Shadow Island? Head of the research station?" Roddy pressed, turning to Beggley. "Hello? She came up here for Ulla Raki's funeral, now she's gone missing."

"Missing?" Teller blinked. "Why . . . no. Of course not. Look, I'm busy at the moment, why don't you wait outside and I'll be right with you."

"No." Roddy limped closer. He was a good head taller than both men and used it to intimidating advantage on Teller. Beggley, however, was unruffled. "You know anything?" Roddy turned to him.

"Less than you. I don't work here," Beggley replied. "But could this person have anything to do with a drug called popeye?"

Roddy frowned.

"I'm Dr. Beggley, of the Centers for Disease Control and Prevention." Beggley pulled out his own ID and showed it to Roddy. "I'm in charge of the response team. How did you get through the quarantine?"

"Getting *into* a plague city isn't much of a problem, mate, it's getting out can be tricky. But I'm not planning to leave anyway until I find out what happened to my friend. No one in this bloody place wants to tell me what the 'ell is going on. Zee called me a week ago, she was all messed up in something. She's been missing since then. I've been trying to talk to Fairchild, or anyone who might know what's up, but all's I get is the smooth-over. I've been in Florida with a crook leg, and now you got this bloody malaria epidemic going on and Zee Aspen is missing. I want to know what is going on."

"Well, that makes two of us." A small, tight smile flickered across Beggley's tired face. "Why don't we go have a talk, Mr. Taylor."

"Hello, is this Mrs. Strong?"

"Yes." Georgia shifted the baby to her other hip and cradled the phone on her shoulder.

"Hi, Mrs. Strong, how are you doing this evening?" The voice was pleasant and warm with the smooth friendliness of a phone solicitor. Georgia glanced at the clock. She hadn't noticed the time. Six o'clock, the witching hour for telemarketers.

"I'm not interested."

"This call concerns an important health issue, Mrs. Strong." The voice took on a solicitous urgency. "I'm calling from the CDC. The Corporation for Disaster Control. Mrs. Strong, have you heard or read anything about the recent terrorist attack in Washington, D.C., on the Fourth of July?"

"Yes. Of course," she said guardedly.

"Now the purpose of this call is not to alarm you, but to provide you with some information. The CDC is concerned with your family's well being and we want to offer you an opportunity to help protect your family." Georgia dragged the phone over to a chair and set the baby on her lap. The woman went on.

"Now Mrs. Strong, have you heard anything on television or radio, or perhaps read it in a newspaper, about this disease?"

"Yes." Georgia's voice wobbled.

"After extensive testing and research, medical officials have discovered that this particular strain of malaria has no cure. While they continue to test combinations of drugs, there is a high possibility that no cure will be found. Are you aware that the only way to determine if someone is infected with malaria is to wait until they exhibit symptoms?"

"Yes."

"Are you aware of those symptoms, Mrs. Strong?"

"Umm, headache; fever, maybe a flulike feeling."

"That's right, Mrs. Strong. Very good. The symptoms usually appear between seven and ten days after infection, but they can occur earlier than that." Georgia heard the faint rustle of a page being turned at the end of the line. She pictured rows and rows of student nurses, or Red Cross volunteers, manning the phones at the CDC. It was reassuring.

"Now Mrs. Strong, has anyone in your family complained of a headache in the past two days?" Georgia felt her palms go clammy. Martin had come home from the restaurant last night with a throbbing headache. He had gone off this afternoon still feeling, as he put it, "a little crummy."

"My husband. But he has been working quite a lot. He's a chef."

"Your husband." Georgia heard the scratch of a pencil. *Someone was checking on them. Someone cared, it would all come out all right.*

"And do you have a family doctor?"

"Yes. Well, we have a health plan. We've just moved here, we haven't needed a doctor."

"Well, as you said, your husband's headache might just be routine, but it would be a good idea to see your physician as soon as possible."

"Yes. Of course."

"How many children do you have, Mrs. Strong?"

"One. Just the baby."

"And do you work outside the home?"

"No. Not now."

"So your husband is currently the sole source of income?"

"Yes."

"Mrs. Strong, have you thought about what might happen to your baby should either you or your husband fall victim to this fatal malaria?" The smooth voice went on quickly now. "Many young families are not

prepared for the financial burdens resulting from the sudden death of a
spouse. Even if you have traditional life insurance, your policy may not
provide adequate coverage. Here at the CDC, we are concerned for your
family's welfare in this time of uncertainty and impending tragedy. We
would like to offer you an opportunity to participate in a special policy
offer."

Georgia felt her brain moving slowly, as if through syrup. *Symptoms,
headaches, Martin dying . . . life insurance!*

"We are offering twenty-five thousand dollars of coverage for only
two hundred dollars. Now this opportunity is available for the next two
days only. There is no physical exam or blood test required . . ."

Life insurance. Georgia began to laugh, then the laughter turned to
tears, and the receiver grew too heavy to hold. She dropped it on the
table. The voice continued, stringy and remote. The baby reached for
the receiver, gurgling with pleasure. He clutched it with stubbly fingers
and began to chew on the mouthpiece as the sales pitch continued to
spill on.

". . . We take VISA, MasterCard, and American Express . . ."

In the Bahamas, the evening is usually a golden time. The sun eases,
the breeze ruffles up, and long palm shadows stripe the tranquil beaches.
On the reef, day fishes are nooking in for the night and night fishes
emerging to feed, feeling the currents with cautious fins. People sip pink
drinks and settle in porch chairs for the sunset. The sun sinks, leaving a
shimmering path to the horizon. It is easy to imagine walking along the
golden lane, right over the calm water to the edge of the earth.

Or just any bit of land, Connor thought as he watched the sun road
sparkle in front of them. They had been drifting for eight hours. The day
had passed easily enough. They talked, told jokes, passed long, silent
stretches, sipped the tepid water from the tiny bottles. There was even a
strange peaceful feeling, not surrender exactly, but something like that.
They had taken an action, made a decision, and taken the first frightening
step. Now there was nothing to do but wait and float. Nothing to struggle

against, nothing to work for. It was all in the hands of fate now and in that realization was a terrible sweet release.

As the sunlight waned, Zee shivered. Connor held her close but the wetsuits didn't allow any body to body warmth. He made up a game, *this isn't as bad as* . . . this isn't as bad as having your eyeballs scratched out by emus. But he couldn't keep it straight. He kept losing track of what wasn't so bad. So he mined Zee's life for stories, begging her family, her games, her first boyfriend, favorite book, tales of distraction, tales of a different reality. It was like an endless first date, but she didn't mind; distraction was all they had. For hours she transported them back to the hills of northern California where her hippie parents had pursued their Xanadu. She remembered the smell of the soil and how blessedly solid the earth felt when you were kneeling in it, pulling carrots. That was all she wanted now, land.

She told him about her older brothers, Redwood, Phoenix, and Sky (now Randy, Pete, and Steve), her tormentors and champions, who built multistory treehouses with rope bridges and trap doors. To Connor it all sounded as foreign as Mars.

But now her voice was starting to go. Connor wanted to squeeze more memories out of her; he was greedy for her stories. The sky grew dark. A thin silver of moon appeared but clouds obscured most of the stars. His head throbbed steadily and his limbs ached. About what you would expect after floating for twelve hours. It didn't have to be anything else.

Zee talked about the future, about research she wanted to do, places she wanted to dive. Connor could not imagine much future beyond dry land and a cold beer. He had no future. Any chance of "real life" seemed gone now. Whatever urge had compelled him to turn around and start driving home a year ago had been totally destroyed. After this he would have no job, no family, no nothing. A dog maybe. If Mrs. Wickham was taking care of Lucy. There was nothing out there for him but emptiness. They drifted, even half-dozed for minutes at a time, the tether line keeping them together with gentle tugs. Once Zee woke with a start and a strangled cry. Connor wrapped his arms around her and could feel her heart beating.

"How you doing?" he asked.

"Okay, I guess. My skin is starting to crawl in this wetsuit. If I ever get it off, I'm going to dive naked the rest of my life."

"I knew I was going to like this sport." He turned her around and began to massage the back of her neck. The two canisters of popeye clanked softly together as he moved. He could feel her muscles relaxing, then suddenly they tightened again.

"What's wrong?" he said. "Too hard?"

"No. Nothing's wrong," she said unconvincingly. "Something just bumped my leg."

The house was shaking. It was one A.M. The music was on full volume and a hundred people were dancing. Word had gone out that Jason and the boys were having a party. A malaria party. *Carpe diem.* Summer was dragging and the quarantine was a big pain in the ass and everyone needed a party. The old ramshackle row house shared by six guys was known for blow-outs. Not much furniture to move, plenty of room to dance, not much to damage. There was a downstairs porch for the keg, and an upstairs porch for cooling off and smoking.

Jason had built a huge papier-mâché mosquito piñata, long since bashed to pieces, spilling a cache of candy and condoms. Besides gin and tonic (the quinine factor had to be explained to most people) there was a thick and potent "blood punch" concocted of Hawaiian Punch, lemon pudding mix (for lifelike viscosity), and grain alcohol. Jason had turned out to be a sort of slacker Martha Stewart. Despite the last-minute arrangements, the party was indeed a roaring success, except for the fact that not a single girl showed up in a grass skirt or coconut shell bra.

"Bummer, man, guess they didn't get the concept," Jason said as he pumped the keg.

"You guys are so crude." A short girl with twisty blond hair and a Barbie nose chastised them. "This is really a serious thing." She wasn't wearing a grass skirt either. "Malaria is really a bad disease. We just don't realize it because it doesn't affect us much here." Jason looked at her uncomprehendingly. There was one in every crowd. Sober as god and wanting to talk ideas.

"I mean it. People are going to start dying in a couple of days and you're laughing about it."

"Well hey, you got to die of something," Jason said blissfully. His head was whirling and he went out to the back porch for some air. He leaned against the house. It was a good party. A great party. He could feel the steady thump of feet through the boards. People were dancing on the upstairs porch. He looked up. The boards were visibly shaking. The overhead light was twirling frantically on one remaining wire. Grit got in his eye and stung. He bent over and wiped his eye. More grit and dust fell off his head. Jason looked up and saw a thin, steady trickle of dirt spilling down from where the top porch joined the house. It struck him as vaguely wrong, but he couldn't decide why. He looked around the rest of the roof. A large crack ran all the way along the back of the house, between the brick wall and the wooden porch.

"Hey!" Jason grabbed Peter's sleeve. "Hey, look up there." He pointed to the corner where the dirt was now a steady stream, to the now gaping crack. "Is something wrong with the house?"

"Holy shit!" Peter shouted. "Get off the porch! Everybody get off!" The group around the keg looked at him uncomprehendingly. "Get off now!" He ran in the house. "Tell them to quit dancing up there!" The music was too loud. No one heard him. The stairway was crowded. He pushed his way up, shouting. "Everybody off the porch! Off the porch!" He ran into Tony's room and hit the stereo power. The music stopped abruptly. Just in time to hear the terrible crash.

Two hours later, after a dozen ambulances had taken the most seriously injured to four hospitals, and the cuts, bruises, and simple fractures were now waiting treatment, the cruel irony of a malaria party became even sharper.

"There is no blood," the nurse repeated.

"What do you mean there is no blood?" Peter pressed frantically. "We'll give blood. How much do you need?" Peter, always steady and almost sober, had assumed leadership in the middle of chaos. The collapsing porch had fallen on at least twenty people and the thirty or so

who had been dancing there were flung in a heap, some as far as the
rear alley. Six people needed immediate surgery. Jason had a ruptured
spleen. A tall, skinny girl from his organic chemistry class had a crushed
chest. There were other major injuries, internal bleeding, fractured skulls,
a possible broken back.

"We got a hundred people who will give blood right now. Just tell
me where to send them."

The nurse shook her head. "No, no, honey."

"They will . . ."

". . . of course they will. Just hush and listen for a minute here, let
me tell you what is going on." She was a middlo-aged black woman
with graying temples, soft brown eyes, and a storybook voice. Peter
wondered if they brought her in specifically for bad news. "You know
about that mosquito business, right? About the malaria?"

"Yes." Peter ran desperate hands through his hair. He couldn't believe
this was happening. "That's what the party was for." Tears suddenly
flooded his eyes. "God . . . this stupid malaria party."

"You had a malaria party?" She looked surprised, but not chastising,
maybe even a little amused.

"Yes." Peter broke down and began to sob. "Like, anyone could die,
so we might as well have a good party first. I . . . I mentioned that . . .
quinine was for malaria . . . Jason said we should have gin and tonics . . .
oh god."

She smiled. A real good smile and patted his shoulder. "It's OK,
honey. I see." She gave him a minute to recover. "Well, here's the problem," she went on in the same soothing voice. "Since malaria is a blood-
borne disease, the Red Cross has not been able to accept blood donations
from anyone in this area since the Fourth of July. That's why none of
y'all can be donors either; we can't be sure you aren't infected. Now
blood banks go real low in the summer anyway, especially around hol-
idays. People are away on vacation, busy with other things, don't get
around to it. Also more accidents on the highways and we use up more.
So right now, we have no blood for your friends to have surgery." Peter
nodded and wiped the tears on the back of his hand, too wrecked and
exhausted to be embarrassed.

"Now we are calling all over the East Coast to round up some blood.

But you got to understand, it's going to take a little while. This is a major disaster here. Some of these boys and girls need a whole lot of blood and we can't start surgery until we know we have enough. And all the other blood banks are experiencing the same holiday shortage, though it won't be as bad as around here, of course."

Peter looked out through the glass door to the anxious faces in the waiting room. When had everything changed? It seemed like the whole world was different. Everything he had always accepted as normal, simple and normal, not like the space shuttle normal, but like *plumbing* normal, had changed. Diseases came out of nowhere, houses fell apart, and the very life blood of his friend was vanishing before his eyes.

The first bump was barely a touch. More like a little push of water, the idea of mass, more than mass itself. Connor tried to believe that it was Zee bumping into him, but of course it wasn't. She was in front of him, half cradled in his arms. The bump was at the back of his knee. He tried to hope it away, but the second bump could not be denied.

"I'm getting bumped," she said simply. He felt her stiffen. They had both thought about this, but never mentioned it, as if naming the specter would make it real. It wasn't bad in the daylight. The ability to see a shark gave them confidence, delusionary as it probably was.

"I'm going to get the spear," he said calmly. He unlooped the handle of the spear gun from where they had secured it to her tank valve.

"We should stay very still," she whispered. "Don't panic."

"OK, I won't panic."

His deadpan made her giggle. God, she hated that about herself! Nervous giggles—Zee pictured the tremors of laughter traveling through her body into the water, exciting the shark. They both stopped talking for a minute, letting nerves settle.

"We do have some advantages here," she said, finally recovered. "Sharks are cautious. They explore something carefully before they attack. We are a big, strange-looking thing to him, especially close together. We look bigger. And the wetsuits will help. He might bump us some more, but try not to . . ." She let out a small yelp and jerked away.

She turned immediately and clutched his arm. Connor clenched his teeth as the shark bumped him again. Harder. Head first, then side, then tail, feeling him out with its whole body, the edge of the dorsal fin crashing into his thigh. He stabbed the spear downward but felt only water.

The sliver moon drifted through the clouds, giving a stingy light. Connor held on to her with one hand, while the other continued to sweep the water nearby with the small spear. Long minutes passed. The water was calm.

"Maybe he's gone."

"Yeah."

Suddenly Zee was jerked from his arms. In the faint moonlight, Connor saw her eyes white and round, the swirl of her hair rushing up around her face. He felt the clutch of her fingers and then she was gone. He grabbed for her but the small hand was already out of reach. Zee was dragged under. The tether went taut and Connor was pulled with her. Salt water rushed up his nose, into his mouth. Connor stabbed frantically with the spear but did not strike the shark. Then suddenly the line snapped. His inflated BC popped him back to the surface.

"Zee!" he shouted, swiveling desperately, scanning the water for sign of her. There was nothing. Not a ripple or swirl, no splash, no bubbles. The surface was smooth and undisturbed as a lake.

"No!" He unclipped the buckles on the vest and slid out of it. He took a breath and dove down. He felt nothing. Salt stung his eyes. He swept his arms out but touched nothing. Lungs burning, he finally surfaced. She was gone. Completely gone. Then she was there again, popping back up to the surface with a huge gasp for air. Connor swam toward her and she screamed and grabbed at him. The shark hit again. Connor felt the rough body brush against him in a long, taunting arc. He thrust the spear down, and felt something this time; a hard, solid force. The tiny spear could not pierce the tough hide. The shark swam away. Connor felt the swirl of its tail against his ankle.

"Come on, you fucker!" he shouted. He had never felt such fury. It was as if all the rage he had ever had was boiling over. He tucked and dove again, kicking hard in a meaningless direction, thrashing with the spear. The shark was down here somewhere, a torpedo of sleek power. And here he was, ungainly earthling, arms and legs flailing. No match, hardly more than a snack. The gingerbread man. *Well, damn you!* He cursed. *Swallow me whole and I'll kill you from inside!* Connor felt the pressure, the bow wave coming at him. He struck out and felt the spear points rake down the shark's body. He felt a fin or tail, something narrow and hard under his hand. Sandpaper skin, curiously warm. Or was it just friction? He needed air and grabbed at the surface.

"Connor!" Zee was screaming. His heart pounded. He dove again, stabbing the empty water like a madman. Barely seconds of breath this time. Back to the surface.

"Connor, stop it! He's gone. Stop!" But he could not stop. He stabbed a circle all around them, but felt nothing. Zee made a small spasmodic crying sound and reached for him.

"Connor, please . . ." she cried.

"Are you bitten?" Connor grabbed at her arms. Hands, fingers, smooth black wetsuit, unscathed. He ran his hands down her body. "Did he get you?" She couldn't talk, she just trembled all over in a soundless terror. Connor took a breath and dove under again, feeling the rest of her. One leg was fine, no rips, no gashes in the wetsuit. The other leg the same. He felt her foot; her bare foot. One fin was gone. He reached for the other and felt a jagged edge halfway down the blade. The shark had bitten off the end of her fin. Connor swam back up.

"It's okay. He just got your fins." He held her face in his hands. "He's gone. It's okay." Zee nodded and clutched at him. Connor saw his BC slowly drifting away. His flotation. Tied to it was the bag with the two bottles of popeye. "Stay right here," he gasped.

Zee grabbed him. "No!" Connor just pointed at the drifting BC, lacking the breath to explain. He began to swim toward it. There was no real wind, it couldn't be drifting that fast, but he couldn't reach it. It was a million miles away. He kicked harder. He felt his limbs seize up, his chest tighten, his whole body turn to lead. He could not move. The popeye drifted slowly away. He was alone, in the middle of the sea, over miles of deep black water. He had to swim now, just this little way, but he could not move. It was only a few yards, but his body had no power. The shark was down there. Dark master of a black sea. He would never escape this ocean, never escape Mickey or the black life that had engulfed him.

He looked toward the sky, but there were no stars, no moon, no light at all. It was an indifferent sky, empty and dark as the sea. There was nothing left anywhere in the world but a cold black void and all was evil and evil would win. He didn't need to swim. He didn't need the two canisters. Let them drift away. It didn't matter anymore. He needed nothing. Not a home, not a family, not a father or anyone else. Here he was, alone and lost and dissolving in the sea, and it was fine. The BC floated on. Those clanking bottles. Why did he want them? He couldn't remember. Oh yes, people would die. But people always died. People had to die. It was natural. The dark sea was swirling him into her bosom. Here was a place for him, in the black heart of the sea. He closed his eyes and felt for the vibration of the shark. Willed it to come, prayed for the slam of its jaws on his body. *Why put it hard on yourself, son?* He could hear his father's voice, soft and slow. *Why put it hard on yourself?* He stopped swimming. It seemed he floated a long time. Then there was a sound, like distant music, or maybe just the wind. He opened his eyes. There was light all around him. Bright sparkles dancing in the clear water, like the sky had spilled its stars. He moved one hand and sparkles trailed through his fingers.

He moved his hand again and the sparkles whirled over his fingers. It was real, not delusion or trick of night. The water was full of light, a brilliant galaxy of silver swirling all around him. The sparkles gave off some kind of energy, too. Strength returned to his bones and made them solid again. He did not understand this light, and because he did not understand, he began to feel something like hope.

Connor closed his eyes. He saw the sea with its millions of strange new creatures, the African plains thundering with wildebeests and a flock of little girls in summer dresses. He did not understand any of it and that was somehow good. If he did not understand all this, how much more was there? Maybe, eventually, something would make sense, some parts of the world would fit together for him. In the enormity of his ignorance, there was joy. In the kaleidoscope of his own stupidity there was strength. Smacked with the vastness of his ignorance, Connor knew there was hope.

He suddenly came back to reality. A clear, steady reality. He saw the bottles drifting away. He began to swim again and the luminescence swirled with every slow stroke. He reached out and touched the vest and held on to it. It had not drifted so far. What was he worried about? There was a sound behind him and Zee was there. Had she been there all the time? So close? She guided his arms through the straps, snapping the buckles.

"We're safe," Connor whispered.

"I know."

"He's not coming back."

"No." She held them together. In the east, just above the horizon, Connor thought he could make out the slightest shifting of blue.

22

July 12

Icalled the pediatrician," Amanda Mountclair reassured her husband. "He wasn't in, but he will call as soon as he gets back. Caitlin's mom called and said she's come down with something, too, so I suppose it's another one of those childhood things."

The girls had been indoors all evening on the Fourth, and day and night since then. No reason to worry.

"And how are you feeling?" he asked dutifully.

"Oh, just fine. Fine so far," she said brightly. "How is everything downtown? What is the buzz?" It was day seven. D-Day, D for disease. The minimum incubation period was over, symptoms would begin, and parasite levels would start getting high enough to see on blood tests.

"There's some tension," Frank said. "No one really knows what to expect."

"Are there really enough beds? Genene said they would have to put up an army camp on the mall!"

"No, no. Hospitals quit taking elective surgeries days ago and they can overflow to Baltimore or Richmond if they have to. There are med-evac helicopters on standby."

"And have you found out anything else?" she asked pointedly. Her husband hesitated and Amanda felt a little thrill.

"There are a few malaria drugs that are used outside the United

States but not approved here yet. There is some talk that the FDA will allow their use." Amanda frowned. That was entirely undramatic. The rumors were much more interesting. She heard a noise and turned to see Marissa coming downstairs. She looked sleepy and flushed and about to cry, probably just woke up from a nap. Whatever was she doing down here?

"Just a minute, sweetheart. I'm on the phone," she called to the girl. Marissa came over, squinting at the bright sunlight. "She just woke up from a nap," Amanda said brightly. "No, she looks fine." She smiled and brushed the tangled blond hair back from the little girl's face. "She's a little warm. I'll call the doctor again."

"Mommy!"

"Marissa, I've told you about interrupting when I'm on the telephone, haven't I, honey?" She was not too chastising; the child wasn't feeling well after all.

"Yes, but Mom, Claire won't wake up."

"What do you mean she won't wake up, dear?"

"We took a nap. She read me a story and we both took a nap and now she won't wake up."

Amanda found the au pair curled on her bed, burning with fever. She opened her eyes when Amanda shook her, but her gaze was vague. She mumbled in French. Marissa began to cry. Amanda called 911.

Two hours later, the epidemic had officially begun.

"But that's impossible. Our nanny has *malaria*?" Beyond her sheer surprise, Amanda sounded almost indignant. "But how *could* she? She was nowhere near the mall. We live in Georgetown. The wind was blowing the other direction, they said, and the spraying should have killed all the mosquitos."

"I don't know where she got it, Mrs. Mountclair," the ER doctor explained. "But her blood test is positive and we're admitting her to intensive care."

"Intensive care?"

"I'm sorry, but she's in a coma."

"But, but she was all right this morning."

The doctor looked down at Marissa and saw the girl was shaking her head.

"She wasn't OK this morning?" Marissa shook her head again. "Do you know when your nanny started feeling sick, honey?" she asked gently.

"Yesterday. She took Tylenol."

The doctor made a note on her clipboard. Then she squatted down by the child and touched the back of her hand to her cheek.

"And you're feeling a little hot, too, aren't you?"

"The pediatrician saw her yesterday," Amanda explained. "She and her cousin both have a little touch of something."

"Do you know if your daughter has had any mosquito bites in the last week, Mrs. Mountclair?"

"Mosquito bites? Oh my god, no." Amanda yanked Marissa to her side in a protective clutch. "She can't! I didn't even let her play outside this week."

"Please don't get upset, Mrs. Mountclair. It's probably nothing to worry about. How about it, Marissa? Do you have any nasty old itchy bites?"

"On my foot."

"Only on your foot? That's not much for a girl as sweet as you. Do you remember how long you've been scratching your foot?"

Marissa shrugged.

"Since yesterday? Day before?"

"There was a mosquito in our room, at the sleepover. Caitlin squashed it on the wall with my *Beauty and the Beast* slipper. It made a big squash. It was blood from its belly, Caitlin said."

"A mosquito in your room?" Amanda looked shocked. "How could it get in there?"

"It came out of your dress-up purse," Marissa said. "I saw it there."

"Oh my god." Amanda realized what she was saying. The Fourth of July sleepover, the evening purse. She remembered leaving it sitting open on their table, outside on the terrace at the Hotel Washington. "Oh god. I've got to call my husband."

"Why don't you come in here with me." The doctor held open the door to the emergency room. "Have a seat there and I'll take a sample of Marissa's blood. We'll take a look right now. It won't take long."

The droning woke Zee. There was no transition, just a sudden complete alertness, followed by a sense of marveling over the fact that she had slept at all. The sun was already hot. She remembered watching it rise, grateful for the warmth on her face, for the reassurance of light after such a black night. She did not remember growing drowsy, just shutting her eyes to feel the warmth. But the nap had done her good. Or maybe it was just the simple joy of waking up alive. She wiggled her foot. Yes, the fin was really gone.

But the sound, what was the sound? A faint, steady droning. A plane! She felt a rush of elation, followed by a stab of fear. She spun around, scanning the sky for the glint of metal and finally saw a speck, high up, coming from the east with the rising sun. Mickey returning to pick up the popeye? If he left at first light, this could be him. But what if it wasn't? It could also be a search plane looking for them.

"Connor?" He was drifting nearby, also asleep. She pulled on the tether line and he stirred slightly. Maybe she shouldn't wake him. Sleep used up a few terrible hours. The plane was too high anyway. How far had they drifted by now? She pulled at the legs of her wetsuit, trying to shift the seams where they were starting to chafe. Her lips were sore and cracked and stung in the salt water. She blew more air into her BC and floated a little more easily. When she looked at Connor again, his eyes were open.

"Connor?" He stared down at the water as if surprised to find himself here. "Connor, are you okay?"

"The lights," he mumbled. "There were lights in the water."

"Bioluminescence." She smiled. "Nice, huh? Tiny plankton producing chemical light." He moved his hand through the water as if looking for them. Zee gave him a puzzled stare.

"You can't see them in daylight. Are you sure you're all right?"

He did not look all right. He had a glazed expression. "Yeah, I'm fine."

In epidemics as in war, nothing is real until the first bodies start to fall. For six days the impending epidemic had been cause for debate, argument, speculation, reflections on mortality. But now it was about death. D-day. The incubation period was over. Throughout the city, the microscopic sporozoites injected so innocently by the mosquitos began erupting from their red cell wombs like crocuses in the spring.

By evening of that first day, there had been a hundred and seventy-four confirmed cases of *P. falciparum* malaria and over six hundred thousand hysterical calls to doctors, clinics, and the special hot lines. TV news reporters did live interviews outside hospitals with grieving relatives, fomenting even more panic. The careful plans, the meticulous orchestration began to crumble almost immediately. Officials begged repeatedly that only those with active symptoms needed to be tested, but still everyone demanded their blood scrutinized. Plans were in place to hospitalize up to three thousand people and to test maybe twenty thousand. But on that first day alone, over fifty thousand nervous citizens stormed the medical gates.

There was a riot in a TV station, when an infomercial offered a Chinese herbal medicine, known for centuries to cure malaria, for only $19.95. The toll-free number was jammed immediately and then people stampeded down to the studio, desperate for the jars on the table.

Hospitals were out of syringes. Churches were out of holy water. There was still no blood. Jason died. Susan escaped from her family in Maine and flew back to be with Peter. He took her to a lake in Virginia, just inside the quarantine line, but empty nonetheless. He swam out to the middle of the cold water, dove to the bottom, and sank his hands in the mud. He brought some up and gave her a handful and asked her to marry him. She cried and said it wasn't like the *plague*. Wasn't like the Black Death. It was going to be over soon and life would be normal again.

It was only day one.

Alba Jiminez sat in her mother's kitchen surrounded by her mother's Spanish-speaking friends. When she finally got through to the hotline, she translated all their questions and all the answers. Where should they go if they didn't have a doctor? Who would pay the bill? And what do you mean there isn't any medicine? It took a long time, all the questions, all the answers, and the medical words that she didn't know in Spanish. The women weren't worried at first, because malaria was something they knew. But then Alba had to explain some more, how this kind was different. It made your brain swell up and there was no medicine for it. Most had not heard about this. Few had time for the news. Finally, there were no more questions. A malaria epidemic. No cure. Ah well. It was just one more thing. Husbands lost jobs and drank themselves to death. *Hail Mary, full of grace.* Sons joined gangs and got shot. *The Lord is with you.* This new thing. One more thing. Nothing to do but go on cleaning, scrubbing, mopping, and hope their employers didn't die without signing the paychecks. *Blessed art thou among women and blessed is the fruit of thy womb . . .*

Martin Strong knew something was wrong. There was no more blaming it on overwork or muscle strain. His head ached, his joints ached, and he felt so tired he could barely get out of bed. He did not want to tell Georgia. She had been so skittish lately, so worried and nervous. It wasn't like her at all. He had known her since high school when she was on the cross-country team and he was clumsy and slightly overweight. Too embarrassed to try out for a team, he used to run by himself in a park on the other side of town. But sometimes he would see her there, having run all the way from school. She would smile and wave. One day, she stopped and asked him why he didn't go out for the boys' track team. She said he had a nice stride. And the way she said "stride" caught him up and melted his heart.

But it was normal, his mom said, after a baby, for a woman's hormones to be a little crazy. And all the changes, the move, his new job. Now this. He could feel the blood pumping through his head as if it was full of golf balls. He had been so cavalier about it. Of course he wouldn't get sick. One out of five hundred. He never won anything. Now his legs felt like stockpots full of stew. He could hear her in the kitchen, talking to the baby and putting away the dishes. He sat up and forced his legs off the bed, reached for the glass of water on the nightstand. His hand shook and he dropped it.

"Martin?" Georgia's voice floated down the hall. He tried to sit up and look healthy. It didn't work. She saw right away. But where there had been fear and uncertainty all week, he now saw calm and courage in her eyes. She knelt by his side and felt his head and told him it would be OK. She reached for the phone.

The sun climbed, peaked, and began to arc down again, gaining painful intensity with every beaming hour. The second plane passed around noon. A commercial jet, nothing but white streaks in the sky. Neither of them said anything. It was too hard to talk now, their throats parched, their minds numbed. Connor had dozed fitfully all morning and never seemed to be completely alert even when he was awake. Zee grew increasingly worried. His body had no fat, nothing to draw upon, a faster metabolism, too. She remembered lying next to him in bed, his body radiating heat. Would they ever enjoy the simple pleasure of sleeping together on clean sheets?

The sun was stupefying. Connor thought he heard another plane once, faintly, from the direction of Shadow Island, but saw nothing and so dismissed it. It was late afternoon, and they were beginning to feel the combined despair and relief of the dropping sun when another plane appeared on the horizon.

It was a small twin-engine prop plane, but too far away for signaling. It crossed the distant sky and vanished from sight. But then they saw it again. Flying in the other direction. Flying low. Flying a grid. Searching. Still they didn't say anything, as if saying might make it vanish. The plane came closer with each pass until finally they began to believe in it.

Connor used his mask to catch the sun and signal like a mirror. Zee took off her remaining half fin, which was bright yellow, and waved it. The plane came closer, dipped lower, banked away sharply, and they could clearly see a person's face in the passenger window waving at them. Then it leveled out and took off in the direction of Shadow Island.

"Oh god. Do you think that was Mickey?" Zee said.

"No."

"Then why did he leave us?"

"He can't land here." Connor laughed. "He can't *land* here. There isn't any *land*." He sounded a little nuts.

It was the longest time in the world. Floating, waiting, straining for sound, hearing mirages. Who would it be? Rescue or execution? Had Padgette discovered the serum was switched? Would he tell? Was it someone else? The FBI? The Coast Guard? The CIA? And if that, were they coming to save them or destroy the evidence? They didn't really see the boat coming. First it wasn't there, then it was. A beautiful white hull trimmed in blue. The whaler from Shadow Island. The roar of the engine filled the universe, then suddenly it dropped to a low throb and they could hear the sound of the hull against the water. A face leaned over the side. Rough blond hair, wide crazy grin.

"Roddy?" Zee gasped. "Roddy, is that you?"

The dock felt strange underfoot. Fresh water like liquid silver poured on their heads from the shower, cold and clean and sweet. Skin in the air again, the softness of a towel; it was like being born again, literally. They had come from the salty womb into the air, as wrinkled and red as newborns. Zee stood under the shower and drank out of the water bottle at the same time. She could actually feel her body coming back to life, the parched cells uncurling like ferns on a dewy morning.

"Easy there, mate." Roddy steadied Connor as he tried to walk up the dock. "Where you going, anyway? Sit here a minute and get yourself unscrambled." He steered him toward the bench. Connor couldn't remember where he was going, just that it was all urgent. His brain felt cold and small. He bent over and dropped his head between his knees. Zee lay on the dock, a towel over her scorched face, letting the sun warm her body.

"Just catch up here a few minutes, then we'll take you up to the house, have some proper hot showers, something to eat and get on our way."

"Where did you come from? How did you know what happened, where to find us?" Zee asked.

"I kept calling SeaGenesis from Miami," Roddy explained. "Trying to find you. Your last phone call was so strange. Then when no one would give me a straight story, I just came up to see for myself what was going on. Some guy at SeaGenesis tried to stonewall me. But there was a Dr. Beggley there, too. He's the guy in charge of the epidemic."

"Does he know about popeye?" Zee asked eagerly. "Did you tell him about it?"

"I didn't know anything to tell. But there were rumors about SeaGenesis having something. Ulla Raki was working on a malaria drug. I got a radio call through to Padgette and he got me in the right direction."

"He told you we escaped?"

"No. There must have been people around he didn't want to know. He was cagey. Just said that you had tried to dive the cut and either drowned or were attacked by sharks. Said he found a torn-up glove. I knew you wouldn't have drowned, and any shark that bit you would have spit you out." He laughed. "So I decided to come look for you. Beggley got me through the quarantine, I flew to Nassau last night, then chartered a plane this morning. I knew roughly where you had to be, with prevailing wind and currents. If you really were alive, that is. So here we are."

"There wasn't anyone on the island when you arrived?" Connor asked.

"Not a soul. But I didn't exactly search. I was in a hurry to get the boat."

"So what is going on?" Roddy asked. "What is all this about? And who are you?" He looked at Connor.

"This is Connor. Connor Gale. He started investigating Ulla's death and . . . it's complicated," Zee said. "But this," she held up the mesh bag with the two pony bottles, "this is popeye. This is Ulla's malaria drug."

"True?" Roddy beamed with excitement. "And it works? How do you know?"

"The CIA tested it," Connor said.

"The CIA?" Roddy stared from one to the other, finally beginning to realize the extent of things. "Whoa." He turned and looked back up toward the compound where the plane was waiting on the little airstrip.

"Well then." He waved a hand toward the plane. "Let's go save the world. Think your legs'll stand?" Zee held out her hand and he pulled her up off the dock. Connor stood and found muscle memory returning. They started walking toward the buildings. Roddy whispered in Zee's ear, "Awful lot of trouble to go through just to meet a bloke, dearie, but does he have a brother?"

Zee laughed and hugged his arm. The world was beginning to feel like it hadn't felt in a long time. They caught up to Connor. Zee loosed herself from Roddy's support and, almost shyly, took his hand.

"You guys get dressed, and I'll see what's left in the pantry in the way of food," Roddy said. "I'll also radio ahead to Nassau about a flight home. Suppose Uncle Sam will hire us a private jet or something?"

"No. Don't radio anyone," Connor said sharply. Zee looked at him with alarm. "It's just better we don't attract any more attention," he explained. Roddy looked at their sunburned faces, the ravaged look of fear and exhaustion still raw, and nodded.

"OK then, let's get back to Nassau and we'll figure it out from there. I've got some clothes in my bungalow should fit you," he offered Connor. Zee went to her own bungalow to pack a few things. Despite the tropical afternoon, she felt chilled. She pulled on a pair of pants and a sweatshirt, socks, sneakers, as if by covering all her skin she could ward off any more danger. She grabbed a duffel bag and stuffed in the books and personal things she could find. There was no way to know when, or if, she would ever return to Shadow Island. What about all her work? What about the nurseries, the collection records, all the data? She sank on the bed, suddenly crying. Whatever came of all this, SeaGenesis was bound to sink, and it was unlikely there would ever be another project like this. It was all over. She blinked back tears as she went outside. Roddy and Connor were just coming out of his bungalow. Roddy's clothes were slightly baggy on Connor, who also wore a sweatshirt despite the warm day.

"I need to get Ulla's lab books," Zee said. "And there's a copy of the data from the Somalia testing here. We'll need that for dosage." Zee started walking toward the lab.

"Wait." Connor frowned and rubbed his head. She shouldn't go in the lab, but he couldn't think why. He looked around at the quiet bungalows and lab. Roddy was following her. It was nearly four by now and the sun cast his shadow long across the sand and bent it up on the stucco wall.

"Stop!" Connor shouted. Roddy turned, puzzled.

"Don't go in there." His head ached so it was hard to think. *What was wrong?* The sun glinted off the windows.

"Connor? What is it?" Zee walked back to him.

"The windows . . ." He groped for the right way to say what he meant.

"Windows? What do you mean?"

"All the glass . . . is still there." *Glass breaking, an explosion, the walls collapsing. Memories of Ulla's house exploding.*

"Connor, you're not making sense. Come on." Zee tried to pull him along, but he shook her off. Mickey was a scorched earth operator. He blew up Raki's house. Why would he leave the lab intact? There was too much evidence there. An explosion here would be very simple to arrange and explain. Roddy was on the porch.

"Tell him to stop." Connor squeezed her arm.

"Roddy, stop!" Zee shouted, puzzled. "Wait."

"What's wrong?" Roddy turned and bounded down the steps. His foot caught on something and he tumbled forward into the sand. The lab exploded.

"She's gone, Mr. Mountclair." The young doctor switched off the monitor. "I'm very sorry. There was nothing more we could do." Frank

Mountclair closed his eyes, took a deep breath, and stood up straight. His shoulders were tight and his hands stiff from gripping the metal bed rail so tightly. He looked at the clock. It was just past eleven. The rain poured steadily in the night. The doctor drew the sheet up over the beautiful young face.

"Yes. I understand. I was just hoping . . . her parents are flying in from Paris. Where will you take her now? It might be easier if they didn't have to see her someplace, someplace grim." He couldn't bring himself to say the word. *Morgue.*

The doctor shoved her hands deep in the pockets of her lab coat. The bed was urgently needed. The ER was beginning to back up with malaria victims waiting for admission and there were three patients in the wards turning critical as they spoke, needing to move upstairs.

"I'll see what I can do," she promised. It was a promise she was making a lot these days, but rarely keeping.

"Thank you. I have to get back to my daughter now." As he hurried up the stairs to the pediatric intensive care unit, he wondered how to break the news to Marissa. Claire had been her nanny for almost three years. The child would be devastated, if she lived to know. As he entered the ward and automatically looked toward Marissa's bed, his heart lurched. There was a convergence of activity around her bed. Too many shoulders bending over her, too many quiet commands, urgent responses, arms reaching out of the pack and snatching things off trays, lights flashing and buzzers beeping.

Amanda floated toward him, crying, reaching for his hands. "Oh Frank, her fever just suddenly went up. It was awful. They're trying to cool her down." She brushed a finger expertly up under her bottom lashes to catch the tears without smearing. Another doctor came rushing over, and a nurse gently steered them back to the waiting room, out of the way.

"How is Claire? Is she any better?"

Frank shook his head and sank into the plastic couch. "She's dead."

Roddy came to with a groan. He was being dragged across the sand. He heard a loud roar. He blinked his eyes and saw spinning propellers.

His back was hot, as if sitting too close to a fireplace. He shuffled his feet in the sand and tried to get his legs under him.

"Come on, Roddy!" Zee shouted. "Run." The Bahamian pilot's face stared at him from the little cockpit, his eyes wide with fear. He waved frantically for them to hurry. Roddy glanced over his shoulder and saw flames roaring from the lab. The landing strip was too close to the building. He understood. He stumbled to a run, leaning heavily on Connor and Zee. They climbed aboard the little plane. It began to move even before they got the door shut.

They tumbled into seats as the plane took off. The flames were roaring below them. Nearby trees had caught fire and the smoke rolled up around the tiny plane, casting them into sudden twilight. Then the sky was blue again. They were out over the water, climbing higher. Zee watched her world grow smaller and smaller. She could make out the shapes of the nursery cages still in the shallows and watched the water turn from green over the sand to the deep azure where the reef fell away. The wind had picked up and little whitecaps were forming. The plane banked and started north, leaving Shadow Island behind.

A slight headwind snatched precious minutes from their flight time, and when they arrived in Nassau the flight to D.C. was already boarding. They bought tickets on Roddy's credit card, after a few more minutes convincing security that despite being ragged and absent any luggage, they were not escaping felons. They staggered to the back of the plane and fell into seats. Zee felt giddy with relief. Connor was quiet. The need to act, the need to think and keep it all tight, had displaced the fog and pain in his head, but now, as the adrenalin began to ebb, he felt suddenly like the bottom had dropped out. The jet's engine roared and the plane thundered down the runway. Connor felt like a thousand G's were pressing him into the seat. A queer heavy darkness crept around from the back of his head, pushing a crinkling brightness before it, like glitter on the crest of a big black wave. His body seemed disconnected. He could hear Zee's voice, but it was so far away. Then he thought he felt her hand against his skin, but it felt like she was touching him through layers of paper.

"Roddy, something is wrong!"

Connor's jaw hurt and his teeth clattered and he wondered why the plane was shaking so much. Finally it stopped. The light came back on and he felt fresh air blowing on his face. The only odd thing was that he was slumped uncomfortably and Zee was kneeling on the seat beside him and Roddy was leaning over from the next seat holding his shoulders down. He felt tired and still a little foggy, but oddly relaxed.

"Connor? Connor, say something."

He pulled himself up a little. "What's wrong?" he asked, blinking.

"You had a seizure or something." She felt his pulse. It was racing. "You were shaking. How do you feel now?"

"Fine. Cold." It was a peaceful feeling, actually. The headache was still there, but not so bad. He was just tremendously tired. A flight attendant, seeing the commotion, came down the aisle.

"Is everything all right? Are you ill, sir?"

"Could we have a blanket, please? And maybe some water?" Roddy asked calmly.

"I'm OK." Connor pulled himself up in the seat.

"And some juice, please," Roddy said practically. "Or food maybe; they were shipwrecked, you see. Terrible ordeal."

The attendant looked doubtful, thinking more likely burned-out drunken tourists, but returned quickly with juice and packets of pretzels.

"It's just the adrenalin," Connor said weakly.

"It's not just that, Connor," Zee said with realization. "You got bit that night, didn't you?" she said quietly. "You've got malaria."

23

Zee spotted them first this time. Suits and ties and hard shoes and badges at the ready. Feds. Four of them. They were waiting at the gate as they got off the plane.

"Shit." Connor tensed and looked up and down the corridor. There were few other people around to notice or care. Even though Dulles Airport was outside the red zone, flights into a quarantine city were not exactly popular. One of the officers stepped forward.

"Zee Aspen, Connor Gale, and Roderick Taylor?" Zee had the knapsack slung over one shoulder and tightened her grip. She could feel the two bottles of popeye clink against her side.

"What do you want?" Roddy bristled.

"Would you come with us, please?" The man made a gesture not unlike a concierge. The four men kept their distance but fell into position around them.

"Are we under arrest?" Connor asked calmly.

"No, sir. We're just asking you to accompany us. There are some people who need to talk to you."

"We can't go," Zee said firmly.

"Dr. Beggley is one of the parties waiting for your arrival."

"Beggley?"

"He's the guy running this epidemic," Roddy told them, still looking skeptically at the officers. "He's the one I told you about. Got me out of the city yesterday when I wanted to go look for you."

Zee looked at Connor, and he gave a slight nod. There was no breaking away and making a dash for it anyway. She could barely stand up and Connor looked as steady as meringue.

The men shifted like herd dogs subtly nudging their quarry along. They walked silently through the terminal. Zee saw the headlines on a newspaper in a gift shop. EPIDEMIC BEGINS! EIGHT HUNDRED DIAGNOSED SO FAR. In smaller type below: *Seventeen dead, hundreds more critical, hospitals overwhelmed.*

Eight *hundred*? That couldn't be right. And people would continue to be diagnosed for the next week! The two liters of popeye seemed pathetically small. She heard Connor cough and turned. He was reeling and looked about to faint.

"Connor!" He staggered and reached for her, grabbing her shoulder for support. He stumbled against a bank of lockers. Roddy and one of the officers tried to catch him, but his knees buckled. Zee felt his hand clutch hard on her shoulder but she couldn't keep him up. Connor clattered against the lockers as he tried to get to his feet.

"Come on, mate, relax, just hold still a minute," Roddy urged. The other officers stood awkwardly by, unsure what to do. The head man quietly instructed one of the others to go fetch a wheelchair. Connor grabbed hold of an open locker and pulled himself unsteadily to his feet, then began to fall again, hitting against the metal doors so it sounded like a garbage truck crash. Finally he just gave up and slid down. The whole thing happened in less than a minute but to Zee it seemed forever. "Connor, just lie still, we're taking you to the hospital."

"No," he whispered as he reached for her hand. "I'm fine." He pressed a locker key into her palm. It was then that Zee noticed her knapsack, with the containers of popeye, was gone. The wheelchair arrived and Connor got into it without protest. Zee slipped the locker key into her pocket. They proceeded through the rest of the airport without incident and went outside to the waiting cars.

It was raining, a steady, ordinary rain that promised to last the night but not refresh. The officers put Zee and Connor in one car, Roddy in another. They turned off at an exit for McLean. No one talked. Finally the cars stopped and they got out. They were at an ordinary-looking ranch house set comfortably back from the road among the trees in the rich and leafy suburb.

Inside, the house was cool and bright. Connor squinted. The headache had settled into a steady background throb and while he still felt weak and achy, the confusion had lifted. It didn't have to be malaria at all, he thought. There were plenty of reasons to feel like shit right now.

There were three men in the room, all strangers to Connor and Zee. The men stood as they entered and one came forward, clearly in charge. He looked to be in his early sixties with a fair amount of steely gray hair combed smoothly back from his forehead. Dark eyes, military carriage, aristocratic bones, but a small, inelegant mouth. He wore glasses with modern frames a shade too expensive looking, his only apparent vanity.

"Thank you for coming. I'm sorry for the nature of this meeting. I understand you've had quite an ordeal. I'm David Marsh, deputy director of operations for the CIA. This is George Summerall, the president's chief of staff, and Dr. Beggley of the Centers for Disease Control. You are here as private citizens, you are not under arrest, you are free to leave whenever you like." He clasped his hands behind his back. It was a posture of subtle contradiction, exposed, like a dog baring its belly in submission, but with the squared shoulders and erect head of authority. When nobody made a move for the door he accepted that they would stay.

"Mr. Taylor, I'm going to ask you to accompany this agent to another part of the house for the time being." The head officer stepped up close behind Roddy.

"Like hell." Roddy threw off the man's hand and moved protectively toward Zee. Almost immediately the door opened and the other three men stepped inside. No one drew a weapon or moved to restrain him. It was all very civilized.

"It's all right, Roddy," Zee said.

"They've just 'ad a whacking bad round of things and that one might have your damn malaria." He nodded at Connor. "They need a doctor."

"Yes. I'm sorry I must be abrupt with you right now, Mr. Taylor, and simply ask you to leave," Marsh said firmly. "It is necessary to conduct separate debriefings and we're rather pressed for time. Everything will be explained to you shortly."

"We're OK, Roddy," Zee assured him. "Go ahead." Roddy left scowling.

"If you wish to go to the hospital, we will take you immediately," Marsh offered. "Or if you prefer, Dr. Beggley can attend you right here. The house is equipped for a variety of purposes and any medical supplies we may lack can be quickly obtained."

"We're fine," Connor said. "We don't need a doctor."

Beggley looked them both up and down with a quick but experienced assessment. "You are both obviously suffering dehydration, and my professional advice would be to go to a hospital."

"We're basically OK," Zee assured him. "Except . . ."

"Except really hungry," Connor broke in. Beggley looked at him doubtfully.

"While you might be feeling relatively well right now, there are a number of serious complications that can develop from dehydration and this sort of exposure."

"What sort of exposure?" Connor said evenly.

"What do you mean?" Beggley frowned. "They said you were picked up at sea after floating for over twenty-four hours."

"And how did *they* know that?" Connor glared past him at Marsh. Zee realized what he was saying.

"You *knew* we were out there?" Zee asked angrily. "You knew and you didn't send anyone to rescue us?"

"No." Marsh's reply was firm. "Believe me. I have come into this game very late. We did not know you even existed, Dr. Aspen, or that you were on Shadow Island, until Dr. Beggley ran into your friend Taylor at SeaGenesis late yesterday afternoon." This was the same account Roddy had given them and Zee began to halfway believe the man.

"Roddy placed a radio call from SeaGenesis to Shadow Island and spoke to Arthur Padgette. We had wiretaps on the phones and overheard the call, but Padgette was rather cryptic. He said you had drowned in a current or been eaten by sharks. We didn't know what was going on at the time. I am sorry." Marsh took off his glasses and rubbed his forehead and Zee noticed now that there were dark circles under his eyes. "I had no idea you were in danger."

"It is true," Beggley assured them. "Roddy knew Padgette was trying to tell him something. He told us about this cut in the reef, and figured you had tried to escape that way. We thought, naturally, you were in a boat. Anyway, Roddy was insistent that he go immediately to Nassau to look for you. He said we couldn't risk a delay of trying to explain everything to the authorities. I agreed. I got him on a flight. All we really knew at that point was that Raki had been working on a malaria drug and that it came from a sponge you were collecting on Shadow Island." Beggley sighed. He was still unclear himself on the subsequent details and more immediately concerned with getting to the core of all this. *Was there really a drug? Did it work and how much could they get?*

"I first talked to Dr. Beggley soon after Roddy left," Marsh took up the story, "I then sent officers to Nassau to follow him. My men missed Roddy in Nassau, but found out he had chartered a plane. We assumed he went to Shadow Island, so they also chartered a plane and flew directly there." Marsh frowned. "We haven't heard from them since. The plane landed on Shadow Island but has not returned to Nassau and there's been no radio contact. Did you see another plane on the island?"

"They stole the plane to escape!" Zee said. "Jack, one of Mickey's men, is a pilot. When we got back to the island with Roddy, everyone had vanished. And they rigged the lab to blow up if anyone went in. They must have stolen the plane and escaped with what they thought was the serum."

"Serum?" Beggley's eyebrows bristled up. Zee looked at Connor, suddenly unsure what to say.

"Please sit down." Marsh waved them toward the couches. They all moved into the seating area like wary guests at a dreaded party. Beggley took a seat opposite Marsh, praying for a quick end to the talk. *Then it was true. The rumors of a secret cure. Three hundred forty-six people had been diagnosed positive today. Half of them could be dead by morning.*

"I understand that you will be skeptical of everything I tell you," Marsh said. "You have unfortunately experienced some gross abuses on the part of this agency. I offer my apologies and my personal assurances that it is over with," he said seriously. "Over the past few days I have learned a little about this agency's involvement with malaria during and after the Vietnam War, in a project known as the Mosquito War. I know Mickey Sullivan was involved with that operation, and I believe he has something to do with all this now." He looked for a reaction from Connor, but saw only a steady, dark gaze.

"Mickey has *killed* people over this drug," Zee said angrily. "He's selling it to drug lords or somebody in Asia. He killed Ulla and he tried to kill Su Thom!" Marsh looked to Connor but he remained silent. He seemed totally disengaged.

"Do you have any evidence to implicate Sullivan in the murder of Ulla Raki?"

"No." Connor shook his head.

"He's been selling popeye? People have been using it?" George Summerall grew intensely alert. "That means he knows it works!"

"He wouldn't go to those extremes unless he knew it worked, would he?" Zee said. She felt even more frustrated and confused.

"Apparently, Mickey Sullivan has never had a problem with extremes," Marsh said evenly, gauging Connor for reaction. "In the old days, when this agency was . . . *less accountable*, Secure Shipping Transport handled a lot of unpleasant business."

Connor looked away. Summerall looked about ready to jump out of his chair.

"I suspect the two of you know far more than I do about all this, and I hope we have a chance to discuss it very soon," Marsh went on. "Right now, however, our top priority is this epidemic. Last night we learned that Ulla Raki had indeed been working on a malaria drug at SeaGenesis. We located Adam Fairchild." The name came out of his mouth like a forkful of bad meat. "We convinced him to cooperate with us. We also found the vials of popeye hidden in your refrigerator." He nodded toward Connor with a slight apologetic gesture.

"Did you feed my dog?"

"Your neighbor has been taking care of the dog."

Connor nodded and looked around the room as if bored.

"Can we use it?" Zee said, growing excited but still dazed with the sudden turn of events. "Mickey tested it on humans. In Somalia. I saw

the study results in the lab at Shadow Island. It was a fairly good protocol; twenty participants, double blind testing."

"Will that help?" Summerall broke in.

"No. As is, it's just paper," Beggley explained. "If we could talk to
the doctor who conducted the studies, if we found some of the participants, if we had blood smears, if we had six months instead of six
hours . . ." He rubbed his hand down the side of his face and glared at
Marsh. "God knows I want this drug to work," he said gravely. "But we
have very little reliable data to go on here. I'm not sure I would be ready
to let people try it even with informed consent."

"There is another possibility," Marsh said tentatively. "When popeye
first began to show promise, and Dr. Raki requested primate testing,
Fairchild knew the only immediate value might be in keeping it secret.
Although he denied Raki's request, he sent samples of the compound to
a lab in Texas for primate testing. Popeye was tested as a proprietary
compound. No one at the lab knew what it was, or what it was intended
to do. This morning we sent a courier with a sample of the serum from
Connor's refrigerator, and the lab was able to confirm that it was indeed
the agent they tested a year ago."

"All that tells us is that popeye doesn't kill monkeys," Beggley reminded them. "It doesn't mean it cures malaria in humans."

"But the primate testing would qualify moving to phase one clinical
trials in humans anyway, wouldn't it?" Zee pointed out. "I know phase-
one testing in humans is technically looking at safety, not efficacy, but I
don't really think people are going to *object* if it works. The primate
testing proves it's safe."

"In *monkeys*," Beggley reminded.

"We have been talking to the head of the FDA and other authorities,"
George Summerall broke in. "There are, of course, extenuating circumstances in this case, namely, this disease is fatal. We might be able to
let people volunteer and accept the risks with, of course, informed consent. There is precedent in the case of AIDS drugs, as you may know.
Accelerated testing protocols due to the demonstrated fatality factor.
Should this drug be administered to anyone, you, of course, will be
completely exempt from any personal liability, or subsequent legal ac-
tions resulting from negative outcomes."

Zee stared at him. "Oh. Good."

"God knows I'm willing to look at it." Beggley leaned forward, his spidery brows crumpled up in concentration, staring at Zee and Connor. "There's just one more thing. Do we actually *have* any?"

"Yes." Zee hesitated. "It's . . . not here. We didn't know who to trust."

"Of course." Marsh gave a tense nod. "How much is there?"

"About two liters. I don't know how many doses that is, though. The Somalia tests were done when the potency of popeye was still a variable. Since then, I figured out how the sponge was producing the essential compounds and we have a stronger concentration."

"We need more than that." Summerall got up and pulled out his cell phone. Marsh turned back to Connor and Zee.

"I don't suppose an expression of my gratitude on behalf of the United States is going to mean a whole hell of a lot to you right now," Marsh said dryly. "But I'm offering it anyway."

"The president will want to thank you personally," Summerall added hastily, like a child reminded of his manners and eager to get them over with. "At a more appropriate time, of course. Right now we have a team of navy divers on standby to fly to Shadow Island and collect more of the sponges. We'll have Taylor accompany the navy divers and show them the sponge."

"You can't do that," Zee interrupted.

"I understand there is still an untapped area where the sponge grows abundantly, this cut in the reef?"

"Yes, but . . . but you can't collect there! The current is six or eight knots and the place is full of sharks."

Marsh allowed a slight smile. "If the Navy Seals can't handle current and a few sharks, we can stand to lose the lot of them and save the taxpayers some money."

"But you don't understand. A mass harvest could wipe out the species completely!" Zee felt like she was caught in a whirlpool. "This sponge requires unique conditions. We just don't know enough about it to go collecting it heavily. A mass harvest could exterminate it! I want to stop this epidemic as much as you do, but what about the future? And anyway, we don't own that reef. The sponge belongs to the Bahamas, not us."

Summerall beeped his phone off and looked impatiently at Marsh.

"It is easier to ask forgiveness than permission," Marsh said in a somber but matter-of-fact tone. Zee thought of Su Thom, his dark eyes brooding with anger. She saw him as a child, holding the body of his dead mother, saw the faces of a million children throughout the world suffering from malaria.

"Why do we have any more right to popeye than anyone else in the world?"

"Because we can get it and they can't," Marsh said bluntly. "Because in the next presidential election, no one in Bangkok is going to vote. I'm sorry." He was respectful but unyielding. "It's a harsh reality, but a reality nonetheless. We discovered it, we can get it, they can't, so it's ours. We should be better, but we are not." Marsh got up, as if physically repulsed by his own sentiments, and walked to the edge of the light circle.

"There are almost a thousand confirmed cases already. We need this drug. May we count on your assistance to help Dr. Beggley with the preparation?"

"Yes . . . but no," Zee stammered. "I mean, you can't do this . . ."

"Dr. Aspen," Beggley said sadly. "We have a critical mass of infection."

Summerall cringed, as if he really didn't want to hear this part again.

"If we don't eliminate this epidemic now, there is a good chance malaria can become entrenched in the United States again," Beggley explained. Zee rubbed her eyes and leaned back in her chair, trying to think what to do. It was as if they had built some vast rickety Tinkertoy roller coaster and were now all crowded in the front car careening down. Wiping out the epidemic might mean wiping out the only cure.

"Where is Mickey now?" Connor spoke at last.

"At home," Marsh said. "We don't have enough evidence to arrest him at this time."

Connor nodded. All the voices had faded to an eerie drone over the faint hidden hum of air-conditioning. He pushed himself out of the chair and walked out of the pooled lamplight, over to a dark corner. He watched the rain through the patio door and saw their reflections in the glass. He wiped the sweat off his forehead with the sleeve of his T-shirt and shivered. The rain was heavy now, and the steady hum sounded like a jar full of mosquitos. Maybe it would just keep raining forever and wash the world clean. Raindrops clung to the glass, caught the light, sparkled like stars.

It had been raining the night they robbed the Sullivan house, twenty years ago. He remembered his father admonishing him, as he boosted him up to the roof of the garage, to wipe his feet once he got inside. Connor did better. The window he climbed through was in Sean's room. Connor saw the new sneakers lying by the bed. Took his own wet, muddy ones off and put the new ones on.

Where did it really start? With overzealous young soldiers in a twisted war? With the greed of a shanty Irishman who saw the chance to make his fortune and pull his laboring family into respectable circles? With the orphaned Su Thom vowing revenge over the body of his mother? With his own pathetic decision, sometime during these years, to go ahead and trust this man, to examine his life and credit it worthy and want, he felt disgusted with himself to admit it now, but to want Mickey's love? He could trace back blame a long, long time. Pull at threads and wonder which might have spun it differently. All it came down to was this. People everywhere, aching and dying in the dark.

"Connor?" Zee came up beside him and stood a few feet away. A grateful distance. "Come with us to the hospital. I think you're sick."

"I know I'm sick," he said sarcastically.

"I mean really, Connor. You have a fever." She reached to touch him. He tensed and turned away.

"I'm fine." He slipped his hand up and found the latch on the patio door. He should say something to her. But there were no right words. He shoved the door open and ran out into the rainy night.

"Connor!" Zee screamed and caught his arm but he pulled away. The others jumped up in surprise. The front door opened and one of the officers stepped into the room. Marsh restrained him with a glance. Zee ran out in the rain, but Connor had already vanished. The neighborhood had thickly landscaped yards and plenty of big trees. The only noise was the steady slap of rain on the flagstone patio.

Rosa heard her daughter and her friends laughing and talking in the hallway, then the door burst open and Alba came in, shaking the rain from her jacket and filling the apartment with the smell of clean, wet hair and bubblegum.

"Mama, you should go see the kittens, they're so funny. They're so soft and little. They jump at my ribbon . . ." She stopped. He mother was sitting at the table, her rosary looped around her fingers, a row of candles burning before the virgin, her face wet with tears. "Mama, what's wrong?"

"Nothing is wrong, sweetheart." Rosa smiled and held out a hand toward her daughter. "Nothing is wrong." Alba came over and slipped onto her mother's lap. The candles were pretty against the dark windows, flickering shadows on the glass. Rosa stroked her daughter's hand. Alba counted the candles, one for everyone in the family and one extra.

"One for your uncle Turino," Rosa explained. Every night, since they heard about the malaria, she had gone into the children's bedroom and examined each arm and leg. She brushed her fingertips through the soft, dark hair and turned the sleep-heavy bodies over one by one, searching for mosquito bites. They had been a long way from where the mosquitos were released. There was no reason they would have flown all that way when there were miles of skin right there nearby to feast upon. But still every night she lit the candles. One for each of them, whispering each name in blessing and beseeching the saints for favor.

"Your father and uncle bought the new van today, did you know that? So now we are a cleaning empire! Maybe a few more months and we bring your Uncle Turino up, yes?"

Alba nodded. She barely remembered Uncle Turino except for the way he played guitar. Silly songs he made up for the children and beautiful melodies that made the adults dance or cry. But he was her mother's favorite brother, and Alba vowed she would start working faster when she helped her mother clean houses.

"Now you go take off those wet clothes before you get a cold. How did you get so wet just running over to next door?"

"It's finally cool, Mama. I like the rain. It feels good."

Rosa tucked her daughter into bed. She put on her nightgown and robe and turned off the lights. The little votive candles cast enough glow to illuminate the little apartment. Such a big family. One candle for each and the room was bright.

Hidden by darkness and rain Connor disappeared quickly into the connecting tangles of yards. Once it seemed far enough and he simply could not run any more, he began to slip up to houses and peek in the kitchen windows. The rain was a great help. At the third house he saw what he was looking for. Keys on the kitchen counter just inside the garage door. He had no idea how to hot-wire a modern car and besides, *why put it hard on yourself*? Crime was so damn simple. He found an unlocked garage door. Slipped into the kitchen, took the keys and drove away, the rain masking all noise.

Now he stood outside the Sullivan house. Watching, summoning strength. There were lights on in the kitchen and the living room. The bedrooms were all dark. It was nearly 2 A.M. Mickey was still up, a shadow in the living room, a small lump of head above his favorite chair, bathed in the blue light of the television.

Connor stared at the back of that head and took a deep, steadying breath. He could just walk up to the window and blow the top of Mickey's head right off. Easiest thing in the world. Once again, he looked up and down the street. The rain had thinned, but runoff was rushing down the gutter. He had left the car several blocks away and snuck here through backyards.

He walked cautiously through a gap in the hedge and started across the lawn. All around in the shadowy dark, the memories of this house were like boulders in his path. The boundary lines of every backyard game tracked like trip wires across his intentions. The night air echoed with the noise and laughter of family parties and the thunder-run of little cousins racing after birthday cake. He ducked into the shelter of the old tree. The wet branches smelled lush and the leaves trembled. He stepped on something and felt it crunch, squatted down and saw it was one of Oliver's Hot Wheels, lost among the tree-root highway. He put it in his pocket and leaned against the tree trunk.

Connor knew where the motion detectors were and how to avoid them. He knew exactly where he should stand for the best shot. From the front lawn, just to the left of the peonies. One true shot to the back of the head. The impact would knock Mickey forward, out of the chair. Connor pushed himself off the tree trunk. He had never in his life even held a gun, let alone fired one. His father would never consider it. A gun was a dishonorable weapon to him. *If you can't survive on your wits and charm, boy, and a good quick getaway now and then, well, you probably have no business in the business.* He had no gun now. He walked up the path and rang the front doorbell. Mickey looked out the side window then quickly opened the door.

"Connor, thank god! You're all right!"

"Don't." He walked in, brushing past Mickey. The bright light stabbed at his eyes, down his neck, all the way to the base of his spine. The smell of the foyer, that furniture polish and umbrella smell, was overpowering.

"They said you were lost in a current, or killed by sharks or something. I had people looking for you . . ."

"I said don't!" Connor shouted. "Don't you fucking lie to me now!"

"Be quiet," Mickey admonished. "You'll wake Lois."

"Lois isn't here." Connor leaned on the stair rail. "You sent her away. She's in Maine with Kerry and the kids."

Mickey tensed and Connor saw he had a pistol in his hand. Connor laughed.

"We both know you aren't going to shoot me, so why don't you put that thing down. You might feel tempted. And you don't handle temptation very well, do you?"

Mickey's eyes narrowed and his lip trembled with anger.

"Believe me. If I need to, I will shoot you right here."

Connor sat down on the steps. "And explain it how? You thought I was a burglar? You didn't *recognize* me?" he said mockingly. "Your own son?"

"What are you doing here?"

"I guess I could ask you the same thing. Shouldn't you be, I don't know, fleeing the country or something?"

"What do you want, Connor?"

"I'm not sure. It's funny, I had a lot of time to think about it. All those days on Shadow Island, then two days just drifting at sea. Lots of time to think, but I don't know what I want. What do you think? Give me some fatherly advice."

"Connor . . . I never meant for you to get hurt. You have to believe me. I thought we had a deal. I would have let you go, just like we agreed."

"We brought back the serum."

Mickey's eyes brightened and he lowered the gun.

"Where is it?"

"Somewhere safe."

"What do you want?" Mickey's voice trembled with tension. His skin was gray, his eyes dark and sunken. "What do you want? You want money?"

Connor felt the room getting wavy and leaned against the step, focusing on the hard edge pressing against his spine.

"I want an emerald," he said. "I want an emerald for every poor bastard who died of your malaria."

"Oh what, you've got a big conscience all of a sudden?" Mickey scoffed. "What, did you have some kind of orphan bonding thing with that gook? Now you feel responsible or something?"

"Yes, I feel responsible. I should never have believed you. I should . . ." He stopped. It wasn't like he thought it would be. The anger wasn't holding him up. Here inside this house, there was too much between them, too many memories; Christmas trees and bicycles and Mickey kissing Lois in the kitchen. This was his only real home, his only real family. This was where he learned to be a man. There were days it was horrible, and there were days, lots of days really, when for no reason, everyone was just happy.

"Look, Connor, this was all a big, stupid, tragic accident," Mickey said, more gently. "Things got out of control."

Connor felt the room spinning and clutched the banister. "You left me to die out there."

"No . . ."

Connor pulled himself up and cursed the room for continuing to spin. "And for me, you know, I can understand. I was just some grubby kid off the street. But Sean was your own son. Your real son. He found out, and he went and drove into a tree! And then, you just went *on with it*. For all these years? That's the part I just don't get. You saw what it did to Sean and you kept on with it."

"Shut up! Sean ran out of here just as upset a dozen times before that! All you boys did! He just had a wreck that night. It had nothing to do with any of this!"

"He found the boxes. He read the papers. He realized his own father, the all-wise and all-powerful, was . . . was . . . I don't know, what exactly do you call this anyway? Mass murder?"

"It was nothing like that . . ."

"Right," Connor said bitterly. "Most despots don't pretend everything was just an accident."

"It was an accident . . ."

"You *bought* yourself a deadly disease! You hired people to concoct it. You let it loose and you sold the cure for blood money."

Mickey raised the gun and aimed it at Connor's head.

"Oh, don't," Connor said tiredly. "You'll ruin the carpet." He sank back down, angry at his feeble state.

"Then get up!" Mickey shouted. "I'll kill you someplace else." Connor felt the black wave thundering up around him and struggled for consciousness.

"Get up! I swear to you. New carpet is not a problem. Lois would be happy to come home to new carpet."

"And me dead? You know, she does kind of like me." Mickey's face was deep red and his hand shook. Connor watched him with a strange remoteness, impassively almost. *Would he really shoot me?* He couldn't know the answer.

"Relax. You don't have to kill me," Connor said quietly, as he felt himself slipping into the blackness. "Your damn scientists took care of that years ago." He slumped against the rail in a dead faint. Mickey stared at him, the gun slowly dropping as he realized what he was saying.

"You have it?" he asked. Connor did not respond. Mickey slowly backed toward the closet, keeping his eye on him, keeping the gun ready. It looked convincing. Connor did in fact seem very sick. But he was equally capable of a con, too. Just the sort of thing he would think of.

Mickey opened the hall closet, felt around on the shelf and took down his briefcase. He thumbed the combination and took out a pair of hand-cuffs. Crouching warily, the pistol trained on Connor, he crept close and clapped a cuff on one wrist. Connor gave a small twitch, opened his eyes, then slid limply against the stairs, his head hitting with a gentle thud. Mickey, expecting a fight, was genuinely surprised. So it wasn't a con. He felt a flicker of remorse but, over that, a wave of relief. Could he really have shot Connor? The boy who had saved his son's life? The boy had grown up and had turned out to be everything Mickey always claimed to have hoped for. But not at all what he had expected. Or counted on. He did love Connor. He did. But he wasn't his real son. He couldn't lose his family. That was all there was.

"Sorry it had to come to this, son." He pulled Connor up by the wrist and draped his arm around his neck. "Come on, stand up." Connor stirred slightly, but his feet weren't holding much of him up. Mickey dragged him through the kitchen to the garage. He pushed Connor into the backseat of the car and clipped the other end of the handcuff to the front seat headrest. He went to open the garage door but found he was shaking severely now. *Take your time. Think this through. Don't screw it up now.* He took a deep breath. He got out of the car, went back into the kitchen, and poured a good shot of scotch, tossed it down, poured another. He leaned on the counter and drank it slowly. He felt calm now. Steady. *Connor has malaria. All I have to do is put him somewhere for a couple of days. It wouldn't be like actually killing him, wouldn't be murder, would it?*

He took the bottle with him and went back to the car. Where should he take him? Connor looked pretty sick. People were dying within twenty-four hours of the first symptoms. How long did he have? There was no treatment, not without popeye. Mickey started the car and pushed the garage door button. He turned as he backed out of the driveway. Connor's eyelids fluttered as if trying to wake up.

"You won't suffer," Mickey said quietly. "I'll make sure you don't suffer." The words filtered through to Connor with a sad finality. Was that odd? To feel only sad?

24

To local TV newscasters, the epidemic was the promised land. After years of nothing but plane wrecks and floods and the occasional edge of a hurricane to gorge upon, they were in heaven. Like flies too long trapped in a house with nothing but the measly poop of a thin old cat to feast upon, they found the malaria story was like being set free in a stockyard.

Georgia Strong looked down on the mass of reporters with disgust from the window of her husband's hospital room. They had swarmed when they arrived, her husband on a stretcher and the baby wailing. His minor celebrity status, ATLANTA'S HOTTEST AFRICAN AMERICAN CHEF TO HEAD UP D.C.'S PREMIER POWER RESTAURANT, didn't help. There had been cameras and microphones and faces bobbing all around, flashes blasting like some kind of Hollywood opening. They loved the baby. They were hungry for orphans. She would be damned if she was going to provide them with one.

Right now something was happening. People were running around with clipboards. Cell phones were raised to every ear. Trucks were coiling down antennas and packing up their lights. She could not hear anything from here and assumed they were setting off to a more grisly scene. Martin had been sent to Sibley Hospital, where the less acute were being treated. There was nothing here so far but worry and weeping. Not enough blood and guts.

"Honey, what's going on?" Martin asked. He was stable, so far.

"Oh, those reporters are finally leaving," she said. "Going back to their coffins before sunrise, I suppose." She watched the cars and trucks rush away, then came to sit on the edge of the bed. "How you doing, baby?"

She had never thought of something like this. A car accident, cancer maybe, when they were old. When they were old *together*. Two years ago in her bridal pledge, those words *till death do us part* had seemed a promise years to come. Now it was a close and cruel reality.

Down on the street the gossip was flying; the excitement was electric. Dr. Beggley had just showed up at Walter Reed, in a hurry, with a strange woman, at one in the morning, carrying a mysterious knapsack. All over the city, phones and pagers were bleeping. The camera team that was already camped out at Walter Reed got footage of them arriving, and the videos of Zee were zipped off to a dozen stations where research staff dragged her identity out of cyberspace within fifteen minutes. Running her name through the on-line services quickly led to the old articles and the interviews. "She's smart, she's sexy, under the sea or behind the microscope. In the race to cure cancer, Zee Aspen hunts for new drugs in the sea . . ."

Zee Aspen! So there was a SeaGenesis connection! Hurrying to the lab with Dr. Beggley in the middle of the night! It couldn't get much better than this!

Fortunately for Dr. Beggley, Walter Reed was a military compound, with fences, gates, and guards. Even if one of the reporters made it over the fence and past the MPs, the chances of finding the right lab amidst the labyrinth of old redbrick buildings were slim. People worked here for years and still got lost.

Once inside, they got right to work. All of the serum had to be tested and refined. They couldn't be too optimistic. It was still such a longshot. Popeye might not really work. And even if it did, this particular batch of popeye might not. It had suffered a difficult journey. They could not be too hopeful. All the other dramas of the night were pushed aside.

Almost all. Zee could not forget that Connor was out there somewhere in the dark, wet night. Marsh assured her they would find him, take care of him.

Beggley poured the popeye out of the first pony bottle into a beaker. The color looked off, but Zee attributed that to the harsh fluorescent light. But when they ran the first sample through the spectrometer, they both stared in horror at the results.

"It isn't right." Zee stared incredulously. Beggley examined the reading. "This isn't popeye!"

"Could Padgette have suspected and made a switch?"

Zee stared at the pony bottles. "I don't know. I was careful. I was sure he didn't see me. But I don't know."

"He could have suspected something the next morning when you insisted on diving the cut."

"He did suspect! That's just it. He might not have known when I planned the dive, but afterward he had to have suspected because he tipped Roddy off."

"Which would be all the more plausible if he knew you didn't have the real popeye with you," Beggley said gently.

"Shit." All those hours in the sea, holding on to the thread of hope even as it frayed in her hands, how could it snap now?

"So either Padgette has it, or someone switched it since you were rescued."

"That's impossible. The only time the serum was out of my sight was when it was in the locker at the airport." Zee ran back through everything Marsh had told them at the safe house. He had sent officers to Nassau after Roddy; why not have a couple of others waiting for them? Following them on to the plane? But the knapsack was never out of her sight.

Beggley swirled the mystery serum around and sniffed it.

"This smells like lemonade." He tasted it. "It *is* lemonade. You had the only key to the locker?"

Zee nodded.

"And it wasn't broken into. You saw it yourself."

"Well, the CIA could probably manage to break into an airport locker without being too obvious, couldn't they?" Beggley suggested dourly.

All of a sudden Zee felt like her heart had skidded to a stop. She buried her face in her hands, unwilling to consider the other possibility.

"What?" Beggley pressed. "What is it?"

"The CIA wouldn't need a key to get in the locker, but neither would Connor."

"You think he switched the serum?"

"He must have."

"Why?"

"He might not have trusted Marsh. Maybe he thought he could use it against Mickey. I don't know. I just don't know."

The steady vibration of the car coaxed Connor back to his senses. He opened his eyes, rolled his head slowly back into place, and felt the cold band of steel around his wrist. The sky was faintly brighter with the first hint of sunrise. They were on the beltway. Must have been driving awhile. The rain was just a drizzle now. He looked up and saw Mickey in shadowy profile. He was hunched over the steering wheel, his hands opening and closing in a nervous rhythm. He looked old. Mickey glanced in the rearview mirror and saw he was awake.

"We're going to the hospital, Connor. It will be OK."

"Sure," Connor said quietly.

"I can get you the medicine. I know where to get some." Mickey sounded like he was pleading. Connor was too tired to care.

"Marsh knows everything. Fairchild told him everything."

"Fairchild doesn't know shit." Mickey turned and glared at him, the motion sending them swerving. "You still think you can con your way out of everything, don't you?"

"Yeah. Even if it weren't the truth I'd probably try that one," Connor acknowledged. Mickey kept his eyes on the road.

"It doesn't matter what he tells them." He did not sound so confident anymore. "They won't expose this. They can't. The Mosquito War was an official operation. The CIA hired those doctors, not me."

"A lot of high-up guys are pretty nervous. They need a scapegoat."

"It won't be me."

"You're nothing to them."

"Shut up, Connor. You don't know shit."

"You're nothing but a part-time mick laborer to them. You moved their guns around, you handled some dirty work, but you were an errand boy. They're closing ranks. And you're on the outside." He felt some energy returning, a strange, clear focus of thought, as if his body was dredging up every last resource for a final effort.

"I can expose the whole thing," Mickey insisted. "They know that. They won't risk it."

"A well-oiled shredder and a few bottles of Wite-Out and the cheese stands alone."

"Shut up!"

"The Mosquito War never happened," Connor went on. "They called it off. Then it was your own baby."

"The *agency* hired the Japs! They started this . . ."

"And *they* stopped it! But then *you* went on with it! The worst the CIA is guilty of is messing with the distribution of malaria medicines thirty years ago in Laos. And not foreseeing that one of their officers could go quite so wrong for quite so long. The rest is all your own deal. Manipulating a disease for your own profit."

Mickey stared at the road. Connor's voice was low and hypnotizing.

"We brought back a lot of popeye," Connor went on, in the same quiet, conversational tone. "So there might only be a few hundred deaths. Not thousands. I guess that will help. But maybe not. How many got killed in the Oklahoma bombing? It was just a hundred and some, was it?" He could see Mickey's shoulders trembling. The dawn was breaking, soft and gray and drizzly. The road glistened with rain. A terrible idea was creeping up in Connor's mind. He pushed it back. But it rustled up again in soft solution. He knew where they were now, in Cabin John, his own neighborhood, just a couple of miles from the American Legion bridge. They were doing construction work on the bridge, resurfacing and new guardrails.

"Maybe you should slow down a little, Mickey. You're going kind of fast here. The road is slippery." Connor stared out the window. Traffic was still light, but soon it would pick up. "You could have a bad accident." He couldn't do this! But Mickey wanted to kill him. Mickey would let everyone die of malaria.

Connor felt nothing. Strangely nothing. No fear, no grief, no remorse, nothing but quiet focus. Even the pain in his head was background, the fever burning in some other person.

"That would be hard on Lois, you dying in a car wreck. She would be devastated. The whole family would. They love you. And respect you, too. That's the thing, isn't it, respect. Honor."

"Shut up, Connor. We're going to a hospital. Nothing's going to happen."

"Good. You don't want to have an accident. But of course, you must have some good life insurance. Right? You're the kind of man to think of things like that. Lois would be OK. The family would take care of her. She would miss you, but she's the kind to keep your memory alive. Telling the grandkids stories about you and all that. What you made of your life. How you brought the whole family up. Respect. That's the thing, right?"

"Stop it!" Mickey shouted. Connor's voice, low and hypnotizing, was eating at him. "I know what you're trying to do!"

"Then do it," Connor said. *Eight miles to the bridge. Five or six minutes.* "They're doing work on the bridge," Connor went on softly. "They have those cement barriers up. There's a gap at this end . . ." Mickey stared at the lines in the road, stared at the fragments of his life.

"I never meant it to go this far. You have to believe me."

"I do believe you."

"It was just an opportunity. I needed the money. The kind of place I was in back then . . . I didn't know what would happen. The agency threw people like me out all the time, after we did their dirty work."

Mickey's protestations sickened him but Connor spoke gently. "I know. You had the family to take care of. All your brothers, all the kids . . . you made us all what we are." *And what am I? What have I become?* "Now your son is deathly ill and you're taking him to the hospital. The road is wet. You're upset and driving too fast." Connor was sickly thrilled at his own finesse. "You skid. You hit the end of the barrier. At the very end of the bridge. It's the only place a hit would really send you over. You didn't see it in the rain. I'm thrown clear. It was just a terrible accident. Lois will never know the truth," Connor said softly.

The truth. Mickey grabbed the bottle of scotch, stuck it between his knees, unscrewed the cap, and took a big drink. The discovery had killed Sean already, what would it do to the rest of the family? How could he live with that? The bridge was just up ahead somewhere, obscured in rising fog.

"I only wanted the best for my family. . . ."

"I know, Mickey. I believe you." Slowly Mickey shifted a trembling hand to his pocket, fumbling for what seemed like minutes. He pulled out the key to the handcuffs, turned and reached the huge arm across the seat.

Mickey's broad fingers clutched clawlike against the back of the seat. There were no pure emotions anymore. Pathos and revulsion tugged at Connor. Anger, betrayal, pity, and something like love.

"Son, I'm sorry." It was almost a sob. Mickey turned. Their eyes met. Where Connor expected to see bitterness and anger, there was only weariness and maybe sad relief.

"I know," Connor said gently. "I know." He reached out and touched the giant's arm. Mickey clutched at Connor's hand. The grip was not so mighty now. An old man's grip; an old man who was desperate, lost, and scared to die. Mickey squeezed hard, then let go.

Connor's hand trembled as he unlocked the cuff from his wrist. He had trouble seeing the tiny lock. He put the cuffs and the keys in his pocket. The fog parted and they could see the bridge straight ahead. It was an eighty-foot drop to the gorge of the Potomac.

"Give me the bottle," Connor said. "I'll get rid of it, too."

"Oh, damn it, Connor!" Mickey wept. "You better not be shitting me now! You take care of Lois, or I swear to you, I'll crawl out of hell and haunt you for the rest of your life."

"I swear, Mickey, no one will ever know."

"Connor." There was no restraint of tears now. "I'm dying with a mortal sin."

Connor felt a new wave of guilt. A man's life was one thing, his immortal soul, even if you weren't sure you believed in all that, another.

"You've confessed to me. I'll tell Father Paul." Did that count? Confession by proxy? He wasn't sure of the mechanics of absolution.

"And I'll get a priest here," he promised, resolve fading. Connor wasn't sure he could go through with this. But he had no chance to change his mind. Mickey hit the brake hard. They skidded. The car slowed.

"Go! Goddammit go!" There was no time to think now. It was happening. Connor yanked the door open and jumped out. He hit hard, slid and rolled. The car swerved, fishtailed onto the shoulder, spraying him with gravel. Connor felt the sharp grass stinging his bare arms as he rolled down the embankment. He heard the screech of tires as they caught the road again, the engine gunning. Three seconds, maybe five. He pulled himself up on hands and knees. He could not look, but he could not shut his eyes. The car hit the end of the barrier, the impact like a thunder crack, spun around through the construction debris, then sailed over the side of the bridge, flipping in the air, tumbling over and over, in and out of the fog, down to the rocky river bed.

Marsh stared down into the gorge where only the rear of Mickey's car protruded from the river.

"What do you mean, he isn't anywhere?" he snapped. "Look harder. He might be unconscious." Marsh did not raise his voice, but the force of his anger had the officers cowering. He looked over to the collection of police cars and rescue vehicles that had already assembled at the bridge. If he could avoid getting the police further involved it would be good. A team was gearing up to rappel down the gorge. A police boat, unable to navigate the low water, idled a few hundred yards upstream, its divers unneeded. If the impact hadn't killed Sullivan, he had soon enough drowned.

"You're sure you saw Connor jumping out of the car at the bridge? He couldn't have gotten out anywhere before?"

"We never lost the tail from the time they left the house," the officer assured him nervously. "Sullivan didn't seem to know where he was

going. He drove around for almost two hours. We didn't anticipate anything like this. Then it all happened so fast."

"How long until someone went back to look for Connor?"

"Two or three minutes. We only stopped long enough to call you, to
see how you wanted it handled before the police showed up."

Marsh cringed as he saw a news van pull up. At least the epidemic
might keep the coverage here light. He walked toward his car. Few people outside of senior government would be likely to recognize him, but
in Washington you could never be too careful. He wasn't eager to have
speculation as to why the CIA's DDO had showed up at a car crash.

"Send someone to Connor Gale's house. It isn't that far from here.
He might have caught a ride. Call in everyone else you can. If he didn't
get a ride somewhere, he's either on foot or hurt. He may also have
malaria. I want every inch of ground searched."

The police rescue team had reached the bottom of the gorge and
were rigging safety lines to let them wade and swim out to the car to
recover the body. Marsh's phone beeped.

"Yes."

"It's Beggley. We have a problem."

"Your phone is not secure."

Beggley understood. "We have two bottles of lemonade here."

"Lemonade?"

"There has been a switch."

Marsh sucked in a breath. "You're sure?"

"Positive."

"Do you know who?"

"Any of your boys?"

"It wasn't us."

"Okay then, either Padgette or Connor."

"I see."

The world was hot and he was inside the heat. A dense jungle heat,
heavy and smelling of stones. He had no idea of time or place. It would
have been pleasant except that something had gotten into his head and

was cranking it apart from the inside. He could not move. He opened his eyes and saw bright sparkles of light. Sun dappling through the trees. He watched the sparkles for a long time. The sun was high overhead. That meant something. Then he heard sticks crunching, noises getting louder, then oddly enough, he dreamed Lucy was there, licking his face, barking and yelping her squirrel yelp.

It was so real, he reached up. His hand curled into warm fur. His fingers met a damp, eager nose. Happy dog breath spilled over him as Lucy panted with excitement.

"Connor? Connor, are you there?" He heard Mrs. Wickham's voice. Then there were Mrs. Wickham's sturdy old walking shoes and her old red gardening pants coming through the underbrush toward him. Connor struggled to sit up, but everything hurt.

"Don't move, dear. Oh, my goodness."

"What time is it?" His throat was dry and hot and he could only whisper.

"A little after ten, I should think." She knelt beside him and tried to push Lucy out of the way. "Can you drink some water, dear?" She slipped a surprisingly strong arm under his shoulders and helped him sit up. She put a canteen to his lips, an ancient metal Boy Scout canteen in a patched green canvas holster. The water was cool. Connor groped for a tree and propped himself against it. Lucy chased herself in silly circles and licked his face so hard he almost fell over.

"Get back, girl. Back." It was hard to summon the authority of command. Mrs. Wickham grabbed the dog's collar and pushed her to a reluctant sit.

"Where are we?"

"About a mile from home. In the woods near the canal."

"What . . . how did you find me? What happened?"

"Some men came looking for you. When they told me about the wreck on the bridge and that you had disappeared, I thought you might have started home along the towpath or through the woods. Maybe you had a concussion and were delirious. I decided to let Lucy try to find you. I hope you don't mind but I went in your hamper and got a pair of your socks for her to sniff. I wasn't sure if she knew what she was supposed to do otherwise. I mean, she wasn't trained for that, after all, but I thought it was worth a try. She's missed you terribly. Are you badly hurt?"

"No. What men . . . ?"

"They didn't say. They looked like some kind of federal agent types. The regular ones, you know. I'm sure their undercover boys are better at blending in," she added kindly. Connor wasn't sure he wanted to know why his elderly neighbor was apparently so familiar with federal agent types.

"So what would you like me to do now, dear?" She screwed the lid back on the canteen and looked through the woods toward the towpath. "Shall I call the park rangers to come get you?"

"No." Connor scrambled for a plan. He had to move fast. "I can make it home." It seemed less a possibility once he actually stood up, but Mrs. Wickham gave him her walking stick and they started toward the towpath. It was only a hundred yards or so, but the short walk had Connor drenched in sweat and considering a change in this plan. Then he discovered the change in plan was just driving up.

Marsh got out of the car and leaned on the door. Zee got out and ran over to Connor.

"Connor, what happened? Oh god, you're a mess!"

There was a park police car stopped about twenty yards back, but the officers didn't get out. Mrs. Wickham took it all in silently, brushed some dirt off her red trousers and straightened her blouse in a way that let you know that if she had been expecting such a commotion she would have put on something a little nicer.

"Well, I think it's time for me to go on home, dear. It's almost time for *The Frugal Gourmet*. I'm overrun with zucchini and he promised to help." She smiled at Zee.

"Nice to see you again, dear. Maybe the two of you will stop by later and have some zucchini bread." She nodded to Marsh as she passed. Connor almost laughed. They waited silently until she was out of hearing distance, then Zee asked directly.

"Connor, did you switch the serum?"

Connor said nothing, but looked at Marsh.

"A clerk in a snack shop at the airport remembered you buying three bottles of lemonade around midnight last night," Marsh said. "That's what Beggley identified in the switched serum."

"Connor, please, whatever you were thinking, it's okay. No one is going to steal it now. We need it."

He still said nothing and Zee felt frustration mounting.

"Why? Why are you doing this? You have no right. Connor, say something!"

"Where is it, Connor?" Marsh pressed.

"I sent it to Vietnam." He sat down on the edge of the path and stared over the flat green water in the canal.

"What? You didn't," Zee said warily. "What do you mean?"

"It seemed the thing to do."

"You wouldn't."

"He couldn't," Marsh interrupted. He walked over and stood beside Connor. "What do you want?" he asked softly.

"Control the drug, control the region. Isn't that how it works?"

"Yeah, that's how it works." Marsh raised his hand and waved off the second police car. Unable to turn around on the narrow towpath, the car began to back up in a little cloud of dust. "You've got the serum, it's your game now. What do you want?" Connor was grateful there was no appeal to save the dying victims or any more of that crap.

"What do we want, Zee?"

"I don't want anything! Connor, stop this! People are dying!"

"Oh, come on. Just because we're in the middle of a plague doesn't mean we can't have a little fun," he said sarcastically. "This is your big chance. What do you want? You want them to call off the Navy and leave you plenty of popeye on the reef? You want a new job? A big research grant?"

"I can't believe you're making this into . . . extortion!"

"Why not?" He watched a pair of dragonflies hovering over the water, the sunlight glinting off their wings. "Anyway, Marsh, while she thinks about it, this is what I want. First, Mickey Sullivan is out of it. The Mosquito War never happened. One mention of his name in association with any of this crap and I'll expose everything. One hint in the press that his death was anything but an accident and I make sure the Mosquito War is front page news. I have documents showing CIA official involvement."

Marsh said nothing, but couldn't disguise a look of surprise and relief.

"Make it work. You can do it. Second, Su Thom. He did not know the mosquitos carried a drug-resistant deadly strain. He chose the sample at random. He, in fact, never intended to release the mosquitos at all. He was just going to show everyone what he could do. It was supposed to be a dramatic point. That is the story. Most of that is true anyway. You can play up the whole war orphan heart-jerker thing."

"All right."

"And third . . ." Connor felt the black wave creeping up on him again and fought it off. The insect buzz was getting too loud to hear himself think. He wiped the sweat from his forehead. "And third, whatever she says," he waved a hand at Zee, "about the serum. Using it. Who gets it, all that. I don't know, but she's smart. Whatever she says." Zee knelt beside him in the grass, reaching for his hand and understanding. Lucy butted in happily and Zee fended her off.

"OK, this is what I want," Zee said, her voice quavering. "Dr. Beggley has complete control over who gets the drug if there isn't enough. No favoritism, no highest bidders, no political favors."

"I think I can promise that."

Emboldened now by the power, Zee shook her head. "I want a letter from the president by the time we get back to the lab, stating that. That Dr. Beggley has the complete and sole authority to establish treatment protocol, based exclusively on medical factors."

"A letter from the president."

"I guess he could fax it."

Marsh smiled and nodded. "Anything else?"

"We hold back enough popeye to continue testing. We have to have some samples to try and synthesize it."

"Agreed."

"And . . . I don't know. I think that's all. Connor?"

"Sure." He squeezed her hand, but her face was waving back into the dim distance. "Where did you put the serum?"

"It's in the hollow tree," he told them quickly as consciousness ebbed. "In Mickey's front yard."

25

Most lived, some died.
Does it really matter who?
Were some more worthy?

The questions swirled through Connor's delirium like bits of old newspaper in a gritty wind, tattered, irrelevant, but inescapable. For two days he hung suspended between the living and the dead. News of the epidemic sifted in through his fever dreams, overheard or fantasized, he couldn't tell. People dying, children's bodies shriveled up, the serum useless, chaos, riots, vats of popeye closed up in a bank vault, sparkling in the cold light like vats of melted emeralds. A huge sepulchral room where seven judges sat behind an iron wall, dispensing droplets of the precious cure to those who could prove merit. A line of supplicants stretched to the horizon, single file, silently inching forward, as every few seconds someone died and fell from the line like pickets from a rotting fence. Sharks came, wiggling furiously over the dry land, their sleek bodies distorted by gravity, their teeth falling out from the air, and fed on the bodies.

Zee slept in a chair by his bed that first horrible night, when they didn't know if popeye would work or not. Then it did begin to work and there was nothing more for her to do. That was almost worse. Dr. Beggley gave her tranquilizers and succor with his family and she slept for twenty hours straight. She woke from a dream where she was with Connor in a garden where everything was cool and green and fantastic birds soared all around and a huge flock of emus walked peaceably by.

There was almost enough popeye for Washington. Su Thom's mosquitos had infected one thousand three hundred and sixty-three persons. Two hundred fourteen died before the drug was available. Of the rest, some victims were already too far gone, some feared an experimental treatment, but most accepted the drug, and most of them lived. Debates fluttered around on the Sunday chat shows—*What is our duty to the diseases of the Third World*—and were put to rest in the bed of sharp words and good intentions. By the time the crisis was past, the topic had vanished. No one wanted to think about it anymore. It had been too real. And bubbling along beneath the surface was always the idea, never spoken, that maybe, just maybe, we are spared because we *deserve* it. Maybe the plagues have been driven from our shores, not through luck of climate and wealth of resources, not because of air-conditioning and window screens, but because of virtue. Maybe we are a little smarter, a little better, a little more deserving.

By July 30, when there had been no new cases in ten days, the epidemic was declared over. Those that lived went on with life. Some were better for it. Some were not. A whirl with death can be ennobling, but just as often it is merely a nuisance. Those who died were made heroes, a tradition peculiar to American disasters. For the plague orphans of America there were scholarship funds and trips to Disney World. For the plague orphans of the Third World, there was simply another notch of despair.

For the United States, it was over. On Shadow Island, deep in the fierce, clean current, half a dozen little patches of popeye had been left untouched by the navy divers. Perhaps it would be enough. To the Bahamian government, the president sent diplomats and largesse and declarations of undying gratitude. There would be a state dinner, too, in the winter perhaps, when the memories were not so acute.

Lois and Kerry came to the hospital every day to see Connor. For the first few days, he feigned sleep, unable to face them. He knew Lois craved something from him. He had been in the car. He was the last one to see Mickey alive. She wanted last words, reassurance, memories, another ending. But he was empty. Connor was trapped now in the greatest con of his life. Could he pull it off? Could he look in her eyes and hide the truth well enough? When he pictured the future, he felt waves of panic. How could he be in this family now? No one would ever know the truth, but everyone would know something. There would be looks, whispers, and relief when he was gone. He was pretty sure Lois knew nothing and Kerry had guessed a lot but neither would ever speak of it. He missed Mickey's funeral, but Kerry came afterwards, bringing foil-wrapped bundles of food from the aunts and Oliver, who climbed astride Connor's legs and waged a plastic action figure war up and down his chest. The little boy would start kindergarten next year, and join the endless progression of family events, first communions, confirmations, graduations, marriages, babies. Connor would send cards. He would con-coct reasons for his absence, and then over the years, they would stop expecting him. It couldn't be any other way now, but he felt sick at the thought, as if he had eaten great gobs of sweet sugar icing.

Daniel came once, alone. He was pale and gaunt and reeked of cig-arettes. He stood stiffly by the bed and stumbled through the usual hos-pital overtures, then tried for thanks and apologies, but none of the usual words really worked. Connor gave him a plastic dinosaur that Oliver had left behind. Then he told Connor there was money for him.

"Mickey had a will."

Connor felt his blood go cold.

When he left the hospital, the world felt strange. Everything seemed extra bright, intense, exaggerated. Infirmity was strange to Connor, and sometimes enraged him. He wanted Zee always near, then felt suffocated by her presence. He craved her love and despised her pity but could not distill one from the other, and so sometimes hated her. They made love, and slept entwined then woke across a breach. When Zee left in the morning, Connor felt relieved. He walked through the small rooms and sat outside with the sun on his face, and tried to read the paper, but none of it really made sense; then he walked back in and looked at the clock and it wasn't even an hour and he wanted her back. Her blouse draped across a chair, bright and flimsy as a tropical flower, the bathroom still smelling of her shampoo, her coffee mug dripping in the dishrack: her tokens left him insane with longing, then inexplicably angry. Anger seemed, in fact, his only sure emotion, but even that was vague. There was nothing pure anymore, nothing simple.

Zee spent her days at SeaGenesis with Dr. Beggley, analyzing blood samples, charting all the patients who had been treated with popeye, trying to concoct a testing protocol in retrospect. It was absorbing work and she was grateful for that. There was comfort in the exactitude of science. But outside of the lab, she felt lost. The frigid air-conditioned buildings, the vast concrete world outside was bleak and oppressive. She missed the sea. She missed Connor the way he used to be. It would just take time. Sometimes she thought maybe they were in love, but how could they be, really? Sometimes they talked about the whole thing and sometimes there would be nightmares, but it was over. Most lived, some died. Life went on.

They drove to the beach and camped on Assateague Island, where they could hear the waves from their tent, and that was good. They even laughed about the mosquito bites. On the last night, they built a fire on the beach and counted seven shooting stars. Then Zee told him she was leaving.

"For eight weeks at first," she explained. She had been offered a position as a naturalist aboard an exploration cruise ship in the South Pacific, something her mother had heard about. It was a small ship and stopped at isolated atolls as well as the usual ports, Tahiti, Samoa, the Cook Islands. Zee would give talks and slide shows and take the passengers snorkeling. It would be perfect. The Real Career could wait a while longer.

"You could come," she offered tentatively. "They need some other staff besides naturalists; staff assistants, Zodiac drivers, you could do that easily enough."

But they both knew he wasn't coming. Whatever they were doing, whatever they had become for each other was too tangled right now. The time apart would be good.

Billy Sullivan kept asking Connor when he was coming back to Chapmans and Connor said soon, then he wasn't really sure, then maybe not for a while. Then Billy quit asking.

August was easier. August is always easier, a month of torpor and surrender, a tranceable month when expectations are there but still blissfully out of reach. Connor worked on the house, grateful for the physical labor that left him stronger and pleasantly exhausted at the end of each day. The tension and oddness began to fade and sometimes it was like they were two regular people, a regular couple having regular dates and fun.

Dr. Beggley went back to Atlanta and Zee organized all the data from Shadow Island, backed it up, and stored it away in a closet. Maybe someday there would be another chance, but not with SeaGenesis, Epidemics, it seemed, were not good for one's stock. Fairchild had filed bankruptcy.

On the first of September Zee left for the South Pacific. The air was crisp and cool and Connor drove back from the airport with all the windows open and the radio on full blast. He went straight to the canal and ran himself to exhaustion. When he got back to the little wooden bridge where he crossed to go home, he saw a figure out of place. A man in a suit, waiting for him.

"Hello, Connor," David Marsh said. "You look much better."

Connor wiped his forehead on the sleeve of his T-shirt. "What do you want?"

Marsh smiled. "Well, I don't suppose conversational overtures are going to make it any less surprising, so here it is." He leaned against the wooden railing and looked around as if simply taking in the scenery. "I want you to come work for me."

Connor stared at him. "Do I still *look* delirious?"

"You need a job. I need someone like you."

"Like hell."

"You've seen some very black aspects of this agency," Marsh went on, unperturbed. "Everything from stupid blunders and venal greed to pure evil. There are other sides."

"I'll bet."

"You don't need to give me an answer right now."

Connor clipped Lucy's leash on. "Look, Marsh. I have nothing to offer. And if I did, I sure as hell would offer it someplace else."

"You just saved the United States from its first terrorist attack with biological weapons. I'd say you have plenty to offer."

"Oh, doesn't that sound grand." He walked back a few steps. "Did it occur to you, Marsh, that I *caused* the whole damn thing in the first place? I screwed up every step of the way! I never suspected Mickey until it was too late, and if Su Thom hadn't found out about the Mosquito War, he never would have released his mosquitos in the first place! Hasn't that occurred to you?"

"Yes."

"Well, there you go."

"So have you learned anything?"

"Learned? Yeah, plenty."

"That's all I'm looking for." Marsh pulled out a card. "These are my private numbers. Call me when you are ready."

Epilogue

ee looked out the window as the plane took off, watching the monuments fall away into a postcard view. Such grand and orderly beauty; emerald green and gleaming white, the colors of money and purity. She looked away from the window and the woman next to her turned her face away, but not before Zee noticed she was crying.

She was a Hispanic woman, her age disguised by a life of hardship. She could be forty or sixty.

"Are you all right?" Zee asked.

"I'm sorry," Rosa Jiminez murmured. She pulled a tissue out of a big mound in her purse. She smiled and wiped her eyes. She nodded toward the window. "Is just so beautiful, you know? To see all the city like that. All the monuments. We are lucky to be here." She took a deep breath and smiled. "Ah! I just cry!" She pressed trembling lips together. Her brown eyes filled with fresh tears.

"My whole family is here, but I had one brother left still in El Salvador. My little brother, his name is Turino. We were going to bring him up maybe this winter, but now." She shook her head. "I get a call instead that he has died."

"I'm sorry," Zee said.

"He was a musician. He had this fever." Rosa nodded toward the plane window as if the disease hung just out there. Her voice dropped to a whisper. "This malaria? It was just a big problem here? This is what my Turino die from. Not this terrible kind, just the regular kind. The kind we always have in my country. Now I go home to bury him."